The Angel of Forgetfulness

The ANGEL of

FORGETFULNESS

Steve Stern

VIKING

VIKING
Published by the Penguin Group
Penguin Group (USA) Inc., 375 Hudson Street,
New York, New York 10014, U.S.A.
Penguin Group (Canada), 10 Alcorn Avenue,
Toronto, Ontario, Canada M4V 3B2 (a division of Pearson Penguin Canada Inc.)
Penguin Books Ltd, 80 Strand, London WC2R 0RL, England
Penguin Ireland, 25 St. Stephen's Green, Dublin 2, Ireland
(a division of Penguin Books Ltd)
Penguin Books Australia Ltd, 250 Camberwell Road, Camberwell,
Victoria 3124, Australia (a division of Pearson Australia Group Pty Ltd)
Penguin Books India Pvt Ltd, 11 Community Centre, Panchsheel Park,
New Delhi – 110 017, India
Penguin Group (NZ), Cnr Airborne and Rosedale Roads, Albany,
Auckland 1310, New Zealand (a division of Pearson New Zealand Ltd)
Penguin Books (South Africa) (Pty) Ltd, 24 Sturdee Avenue,
Rosebank, Johannesburg 2196, South Africa

Penguin Books Ltd, Registered Offices: 80 Strand, London WC2R 0RL, England

First published in 2005 by Viking Penguin, a member of Penguin Group (USA) Inc.

1   3   5   7   9   10   8   6   4   2

Publisher's Note
This is a work of fiction. Names, characters, places, and incidents either are the product
of the author's imagination or are used fictitiously, and any resemblance to actual persons,
living or dead, business establishments, events, or locales is entirely coincidental.

LIBRARY OF CONGRESS CATALOGING IN PUBLICATION DATA
Stern, Steve, 1947–
  The angel of forgetfulness / Steve Stern.
    p.   cm.
  ISBN 0-670-03387-1
    1. Lower East Side (New York, N.Y.)—Fiction.   2. Time travel—Fiction.
  3. Heaven—Fiction.   4. Angels—Fiction.   I. Title.
  PS3569.T414A84 2005
  813'.54—dc22   2004057155

This book is printed on acid-free paper.

Printed in the United States of America

Set in Minion and Optima   Designed by Francesca Belanger

for Sabrina,
like it or not
and to the memory of my mother,
Rose L. Stern

The Angel of Forgetfulness

The end of forgetfulness
is the beginning of remembrance.

—ABRAHAM ABULAFIA

SAUL

"Gib mir ayn kush," said my aged Aunt Keni in a Yiddish made comprehensible by the fishy pucker of her desiccated lips. "Give me a kiss."

I made to peck her parched cheek, tinged with rouge, but she turned her head so that I found my lips pressing hers. A moment's suction and their flinty texture softened and became moist. Her spine elongated into a graceful swan's-neck curve and her dowager's hump disappeared. Her faded pumpkin dye job turned crimson down to the slate gray roots, her milky eyes behind their thick lenses cleared to an emerald green, and she was again a glimmering girl.

I'm lying. In fact, I was the one who was transfigured by the kiss, though the metamorphosis would take years to complete.

I was lonely in New York in 1969. I'd come from the South with great expectations, certain that the city would somehow change me from a timid misfit into an intense if melancholy young hero. A *poète maudit.* I longed, so I thought, for the reckless bohemian life, the *dérèglement de tous les sens,* and believed that New York City, through the crucible of its charged atmosphere, would effect that transformation overnight. Women, of whom (at the age of nineteen) I'd had no prior experience, would also be a natural appurtenance to such a life, though I seldom admitted the prospect even to myself. A homely kid with a wayward imagination, I'd managed to parlay my bare bones and pockmarked face into a self-image of authentic grotesquery. I was convinced that no woman of valor and substance could ever want me, and therein lay the source of the sorrowful nature that had wounded me into writing poems.

But New York in 1969 was not hospitable to my brand of wistful self-pity. In truth, I was tired of it myself, but the exotic character into which I was supposed to evolve had yet to show any manifest symptoms. I'd grown up in a squat brick ranch house on a flat grid of squat brick ranch houses in an otherwise barren suburb of Memphis, Tennessee, yearning for mystery and romance. My past? As a kid I tore up the floorboards under my bed to lower myself into the crawl space beneath the house and from there tunnel to the land of heart's desire. I hung my Zorro costume in a conduit space for water pipes behind the linen closet in the bathroom. From the attic I had a furtive access to this casket-size space; I could slide down the brass pipes to the bottom and, braving a native claustrophobia, don my black cape, hat, and mask; then, removing a small wooden panel, I would wriggle through the wall and burst out of the linen closet from beneath the bottom shelf with plastic sword drawn. I did this once when my little sister was in the bathtub, frightening her to the point of trauma, after which I took better care to conceal my secret life.

But in New York City, secrets were everywhere being divulged. Wild talents traditionally confined to artistic endeavors had spilled into the tawdry streets, and while there was rage in the air and a pervasive sense of imminent apocalypse (which no doubt served as a spur), there was also an ongoing carnival atmosphere. Wearing costumes like medieval jugglers, gowns out of pre-Raphaelite portraits, their flowing hair woven into elflocks and braids, my peers seemed shy of nothing in experience. They took the chemical sacraments that allowed them to duck deftly in and out of history. Although they might appear to be amorously cavorting in your very midst—on the leaf-dappled lawns of parks in the afternoons, in blacklit windows at dusk—you shouldn't be deceived; for they had escaped time for a season in eternity, abandoning rathole apartments to take up residence in music and dreams. It was a climate whose unbridled vitality intimidated me to near paralysis on my arrival from Memphis, which had always been a cozy place for wishing you were elsewhere in.

Now that I was someplace else, however, I was disappointed to find myself so out of tune with the spirit of the moment. Where I was audacious only in my fantasies, the young people of New York City dared to be antic in the broad light of day. It was a situation that prompted my

further retreat into diffidence, until I began to feel afraid of almost everything. Always a tolerable if uninspired student, I felt out of my element at
the Washington Square College of New York University, where I'd persuaded my family to foot the bill for a trial semester. The other students
seemed devilishly clever, the aggressiveness of the classroom dialogues
like games of crack-the-whip, which you joined by attaching yourself to
the stinging tip of the lash. Neither had I managed to make peace with
my sardonic suitemates in our Tenth Street dormitory, converted from a
residential hotel. (Along whose corridors you sometimes saw the few
surviving old residents scuttling beetlelike out of elevators and into stair-
wells.) Ambitious scholars—one a tightly wound mathematics wizard,
the other a paunchy economics savant, my suitemates liked to address
each other in the language of vaudeville comics, judging me for my sullen
disposition and slovenly habits "an unregenerate outsider, Mr. Gallagher."
This from the math wizard, to whom the economist would reply, "Belongs
among the unwashed Gypsy types overrunning our nation like locusts,
Mr. Shean." At first it was flattering to be identified with the allegedly free
spirits of Greenwich Village, and I sometimes went out of my way to try
to earn my suitemates' contempt—an attitude that only compounded
my loneliness.

     This was how things stood with me when I sought out Aunt Keni, my
single blood relation in the city. Though originally a Freischutz like my
mother, Keni Shendeldecker belonged to some remote hyperborean
branch of the family—was there such a thing as a "great-cousin"?—and
so hardly even qualified as kin; but the all-purpose title my mother had
conferred on her as a girl sounded reassuring to me now. I'd never met
the old lady, heard only veiled references to her from my parents: she was
"an eccentric," "a poor soul," "a nut," relatively meaningless categories in
a family where reading books was enough to brand you an oddity. Of
course I understood that it was a measure of my desperation that I should
seek out a geriatric stranger just because she had blood ties to my family.
I had never felt especially close to my family, preferring to think, despite
the unfortunate physical resemblance, that I was a changeling left in place
of my parents' real child, who'd been stolen by trolls. Still I phoned her,
and her voice at the other end of the line was as scratchy as an emery
board, with an accent of the type I'd heard spoken only by stage Jews in

maudlin old films. For her part she seemed less than delighted to hear from me, an unanticipated Johnny-come-lately, and her lack of enthusiasm gave me serious second thoughts. All the same, when at length she extended a perfunctory invitation, I accepted and, the following Saturday afternoon, set out to visit Aunt Keni Shendeldecker in her pensioners' high-rise on the Lower East Side.

Confirmed rather than bar mitzvahed in a southern synagogue that had refined all traces of Old World tradition out of the liturgy, I might as well have been a Methodist. (There was a pipe organ and a rabbi who wore ecclesiatical robes and an expression just this side of a rictus whenever he turned from the Ark to the congregation.) But I was Jew enough to know that the Lower East Side of New York had once had some significance as a sprawling ghetto, headquarters of East European immigrant culture; and there my knowledge (as well as my interest) ended. Nor did the blighted neighborhood, with its sooty tenements, zinc-shuttered shop fronts, and cinder-strewn lots, excite any further curiosity. To me the neighborhood looked like a place that had been ransacked by an invading army that had since moved on. Here you saw a shambling Chinese rag picker trailed by a three-legged dog, there a Hispanic family sitting in lawn chairs on the sidewalk, the father in holey underwear despite the crisp autumn air. An elderly couple waddled along the pavement: the husband in the lead wearing a skullcap like a crumpled cupola, the crumbs of his lunch in his beard, the wife following behind, putty-faced under the upturned jug of her wig. A circle of boys taunted a girl in platform shoes, while a pair of panther-sleek youths, slouched on a stoop in front of a derelict synagogue, looked on approvingly.

The building Aunt Keni lived in was one of a huddle of blood-brown monoliths looming above the congeries of bodegas and secondhand shops. Her voice over the speaker was a staticky bleat that asked me to identify myself twice before she sounded the buzzer, admitting me through an interior door. I took a shuddering elevator up twelve floors and walked down an ammoniac passage under a bulb that flickered like a dying moth, then knocked on a metal door with a mezuzah fixed diagonally to the jamb. On the other side locks turned, chains clanked as if a portcullis were being raised, and the door was opened a crack by a woman the image of a marzipan doll left in a cupboard to gather dust.

To her quizzical expression, I hastened to announce, "I'm Millie Bozoff's son." She made a face. "I knew when she was your age your mama," her throaty voice not so dissimilar from its bleat over the downstairs speaker. "An emotional girl."

That was putting it mildly; my mother was a veteran hysteric who'd spent the duration of my troubled adolescence facedown on her bed weeping disconsolately. But the accuracy of the old lady's appraisal did little to alleviate my sense of having made a grave mistake. What did I think I was doing by coming here? Didn't I already feel sorry enough for myself without complicating matters by inviting pity from some shriveled back number who'd outlived her allotted span? I was ready to admit my error and beat it back to my friendless condition, when what I saw beyond Aunt Keni's shoulder gave me pause. In fact, drawn helplessly into the small apartment, I realized I'd edged past the old woman without waiting for her to ask me in.

The room was crammed with ponderous furniture: a mahogany sideboard, a barge-size sofa, a pair of grease-stained morris chairs with cushions like craters. There was some cheesy bric-a-brac and lace-curtained windows (one with a cardboard insert to conceal a broken pane) and plaster walls of an indeterminate color practically obscured by a gallery's worth of garish paintings. Unframed and hung at drunken angles, the paintings masked the walls of what she quaintly called her "parlor." ("Take in my parlor a seat.") They were leaning on an easel that had collapsed against the altarlike sideboard, the paintings, wedged in dusty corners and stacked atop a dining table with folded wings. Those canvases whose surfaces were visible were mostly cityscapes, period street scenes with pushcarts and fire escapes, the kind of thing that, at first glance, you might have written off as nostalgia or ghetto kitsch; but look again and there was something extra. It was a something that declared the paintings in competition for their own brand of reality with the windows looking onto the pale afternoon. Rendered in custard-thick impastos drenched in rich primary hues, the buildings and figures alike appeared to be in motion, as if the atmosphere itself were intoxicated or viewed through a shimmering humidity. Fabulous details invaded the otherwise ordinary settings: a wrynecked fishmonger flanked by peddlers of pillows and eggs was hawking what looked to be a blowzy mermaid; a goose stood with its beak growing out of a barber pole around which a serpent was twined. A tar-paper rooftop was overspread by a tree in whose bare boughs Hebrew letters perched like predatory birds, and in an alley beneath clotheslines that crisscrossed like a sailing ship's tackle, a bearded man in a bloody apron wrestled an angel.

The only object besides the paintings that commanded any attention was an urn like an antique brass rocket atop the listing sideboard, about which the old woman was puttering.

"So this is *your* work?" was all I could think to say.

She didn't answer but began hobbling forward in her terry-cloth mules, bearing a clattering tea service with chipped porcelain cups. Myopic, she was on a collision course with an end table, which I lurched forward to shove out of her way, but, sufficiently familiar with the terrain, she managed to set down the tray on a leather hassock plumped like a toadstool between the two armchairs. "Sit already," she enjoined me, and, still transfixed by the paintings, I dropped into one of the concave armchairs, my knees risen to the level of my chin. She lowered herself by groaning degrees into the adjacent chair, then leaned forward endeavoring to serve the tea. Due to her faulty aim, she spilled at least as much into the saucers as she was able to pour into the cups, sloshing the lemon slices over their brims. I emptied the contents of the saucer back into my cup and took a sip, wincing at the astringent taste, and realized once again that I should have waited for my hostess. This was not an auspicious beginning.

"First the sugar," she told me, taking a cube out of the bowl with a hand like a badly pruned branch. She folded her turquoise tongue taco-wise about the sugar; then tilted the cup to her mouth with pinkie extended. Somewhere between fascinated and repulsed, I attempted to imitate her, scalding my own tongue as I swallowed the lump of sugar. Swallowing again to clear my craw (*uglmp*), I fanned my tongue, then sank into morose self-consciousness.

"Takes practice," she said tersely, and, having apparently heard my original question after all, added, "I don't do much no more the painting." Again I noticed her talonlike hands. It seemed to me at once inconceivable that this superannuated ruin could have been responsible for the circus of images swirling about us, while at the same time I thought ruefully, without knowing quite what I meant, Wouldn't you know it?

After that initial sally, conversation was temporarily stalled. I wanted to say something polite about her "art" without being too big a hypocrite. To my mind the stuff lacked all sophistication, though you wouldn't exactly have called it primitive either. What it was, her art, when you observed it with a cold eye, was frankly amateurish, if also—I had grudgingly to concede—somewhat arresting. Then there was the woman herself, shapeless as a haymow in her Hawaiian-print housedress, her spectacles dense as glass doorknobs, hennaed hair like gray shingles on fire. Her Old Country accent, though not terribly pronounced, seemed nonetheless vulgar to me, of a piece with the schmaltz and tobacco odors that enhanced the apartment's air of general decay. Sitting in that place with its ambience of a dime museum, I felt I had strayed off the map of the known world.

"My family sends their regards," I lied in an attempt to fill the dead air. Slumped in her chair with the trunks of her legs slightly parted, Aunt Keni fumbled to take an unfiltered cigarette out of the bead-strung bag that dangled from a handily placed aluminum walker. She flicked a butane lighter whose flame appeared to enter her nostril before she managed to light her cigarette. Inhaling, she coughed resonantly, clearly as unconcerned with my family as I was. I took a hard bite out of one of the ossified almond cookies from the tray.

"So how is college?" she finally asked.

I knew I was supposed to say, *Fine;* I was supposed to assure her I was thriving in my studies, enjoying the many cultural advantages the city offered. I should then engage her in half an hour's vapid small talk and forget about her for the rest of my life, which I had every intention of doing. Primed as always for disappointment, I'd already decided that, kaleidoscopic parlor notwithstanding, this obsolescent old party was not the wise woman who would turn my misguided life around. But when I spoke, after choking down the pebbly remains of the cookie, I was nevertheless unable to curb my tongue.

"College stinks," I confessed. It was the first time I'd admitted it to anyone, myself included.

"Nu?" The syllable implied a modicum of curiosity, and I was moved to continue.

"Okay," I said, as if she'd caught me out, "it's not school, there's nothing wrong with school. My classes are interesting enough, but I'm not, see . . . interesting, that is; which makes us, me and my classes, incompatible." There was not the least hint of comprehension in her bespectacled eyes. "Look, I came to New York to be some kind of enfant terrible. I was going to devour whole libraries, write dangerous poems all night. Drunk on ideas, and absinthe if I could get it, I'd be courageously self-destructive like a latter-day François Villon. The city was supposed to be my spiritual home; just breathing the air and walking the streets would change me. But I don't really think I belong here. To tell the truth, I don't think I belong anywhere."

The speech was more than either of us had bargained for, and, mortified to my fingertips, I decided to make my apologies and exit without looking back. But the old lady appeared unruffled. Merely harrumphing, she told me to calm down and drink my tea, asking in afterthought,

"You got a girl?"

"What's that got to do with anything?" I fairly snapped at her. She should understand that my problems were existential, not carnal, and it wasn't for an estranged relation, several times removed, to make such assumptions. Having detected a coquettish cast to her question, I was further disturbed when she offered this pensive non sequitur:

"Used to be I was a girl."

That's when it occurred to me that Aunt Keni might be crazy. Did she even know how old she was? "Uh-huh." I nodded idiotically, thinking that our exchange had advanced into unsafe latitudes.

"My second husband, Mr. Shendeldecker, may he be inscribed, used to say . . . ," she began, and I thought, Here it comes, the dime-store philosophy guaranteed to fix whatever ailed me. But instead the old lady paused, considering, then shrugged and cackled like sawteeth on steel. "What am I talking? He never said nothing. Not even to remark on his business—a factory that he managed, which the less I knew of it, the happier I was. This was my selfishness. Maybe a question I should of asked him sometime, but he was always with his *Tageblatt* in front of his face. He sat like that through two wars, so that now I only remember him below the waist, not that from that quarter there's much to remember." Again the cackle. "But he was good to me, a good provider. A father to my little *momzer*— you know *momzer*? A bastard child. And he never complained I didn't give him a kid of his own. A duplex he bought me in Astoria, Queens—that's the neighborhood where your mama grew up—and we had all the amenities; but he wasn't no fun. Me, I like a lot of fun. . . ."

This last was said so pointedly that I squirmed, thinking, Let me out of here. The old woman had received my confession and raised the stakes, and now I was ready to cut my losses and run. Hoping to divert the general drift of the conversation, I inquired as to the welfare of her son.

"Newman? A *macher*, a whatyoucallit—franchiser for a discount house, nationwide. Mr. Shendeldecker, that his practical nature rubbed off on the boy, but I always embarrassed him, my only son. Especially after his stepfather passed from forgetting to breathe, and I went back on my fixed income to the East Side, where I started up with the painting again. . . ." By then Newman had moved with his family to Texas or California, she couldn't remember which; he seldom called, but his checks arrived every month without fail.

It was clear that in the pathos department she had me beat hands down—I resented the competition. This time I insisted that I had to leave: I had exams pending, work due for the classes I only intermittently attended. "It's all right, I can see myself out," I assured her, but she wouldn't hear of it. She rose with me, following me haltingly to the door, where on the threshold she asked for a kiss. This unsettled me, but since I figured I'd never see her again, I made to buss her cheek, when she turned, causing me to give her a smack full on the mouth. Behind my hastily departing back, she barked another of her unsolicited remarks:

"You ain't so ugly as you think."

This from a woman who viewed the world through bottle glass.

A few nights later—one of the rare nights when I wasn't out wandering— the phone rang in the dormitory suite, and the math wizard, handing me the receiver, said with caustic disapproval, "Sounds like the Witch of Endor, Mr. Gallagher." Replied the economist, looking up from a scratch pad littered with freshly crunched numbers, "Which witch do you say, Mr. Shean?" I swear that was how they talked.

So tell me why my heart was palpitating so violently? If anything, my feelings of disclocation had intensified since my encounter with the old lady, who'd agitated me in ways I was unable to explain to myself. Since meeting Aunt Keni, I'd become even more remiss in attending my classes, falling into a sulk that made me increasingly the butt of my overachieving suitemates. I took long walks about the city, especially downtown around Battery Park and the harbor. Sometimes I rode the nickel ferry back and forth to Staten Island, staring into the quilted green wake, remarking the turreted wreckage of Ellis Island shrouded in cobwebs like Miss Havisham's wedding cake. I crossed the Brooklyn Bridge, leaned on a promenade railing over the brackish bay, whose bottom I envisioned as a garden of drowned gangsters asway like sea monkeys in cement overshoes. Gazing across at the stegosaurus spine of Manhattan, its spires wreathed in doughnut clouds, I pinched myself; I socked my temple with the heel of my hand but still couldn't quite conjure the city into actuality, or Saul Bozoff into its midst.

For all my drifting, however, I'd given a wide berth to the Lower East Side, so bedeviled was I by the memory of meeting my ersatz aunt. Toward her paintings I'd conceived what I thought of as a serviceable attitude: they were the clear evidence of a warped sensibility that had nothing whatever in common with my own. Nor was it the awkward farewell (or the flaky surface of her pursed lips) that bothered me so much as the fact that, in my entire life, old Keni Shendeldecker was the only woman I had ever truly kissed. And what was most troubling was that the kiss seemed to have awakened desires that had never more than catnapped at the best of times. With a degrading frequency, I succumbed to erotic fantasy, locking myself in the bathroom for marathon spells while outside the door my suitemates speculated on my activities. Then, in the throes of (excuse me) self-abuse, I would invariably see—attached to the body of, say, Jane Fonda as Barbarella the Halloween face of Aunt Keni; and the wonder (or horror) was that, instead of spoiling my absorption, her image seemed to hasten me to climax. Unbeliever that I was, I nevertheless associated these occasions with sin.

Distracted, I had to ask the old woman to please repeat what she'd said to me over the phone. She reasserted somewhat imperiously, "I need you should take me to the doctor Friday afternoon."

Since when, I wanted to know (though I refrained from asking), were we so chummy that she should feel entitled to demand such a favor? I was a student and might, for all she knew, have an active social life with its attendant obligations, though I knew that she knew better. In fact, before I could utter a protest, she challenged me:

"What else you got better to do?"

"Should I give to you a list?" I replied, falling involuntarily into her syntax. It was a transparent bluff that, despite my continued grumbling (funny that I felt free to grumble), could not disguise the fact that I was greatly relieved to hear her voice.

Our first expedition was to a clinic in a settlement house on Attorney Street that didn't exist. By the time we arrived, however, I wasn't especially surprised to find a parking lot instead of a medical facility, because none of the other sites the old lady had pointed out along the way had corresponded to her descriptions either. The pestilent building she indicated as housing the offices of *Di Morgen Zhurnal,* for instance, was a Puerto Rican men's club; the Lion's Dairy Restaurant was a soapy-windowed plumbing-supply outlet; Milstein's Bakery a beautician's; the butcher shop run by Karnovsky, a sweet-natured ritual slaughterer, now a furniture rental store. In her gravel-throated delivery, Aunt Keni conducted a nonstop narrative for the benefit (as it turned out) of my disorientation. Nothing was what her purblind commentary claimed it to be, and while I was ignorant of the Lower East Side of antiquity, I soon began to realize that her tour was at least half a century out of date. I felt as if I were taking a stroll with Rip van Winkle—though "stroll" hardly applied to our creeping progress. For my aunt, laminated in a wardrobe's worth of coats and sweaters against the October wind, proceeded like an inchworm. She would place the aluminum walker some feet in front of her before taking painful steps to catch it up, grunting huskily with every piece of ground she gained. Myself, I trudged alongside her at a pallbearer's pace, wondering when was the last time Aunt Keni had left her apartment.

I told myself I ought to be angry; after all, she had lured me into this pointless journey under false pretenses. She was using me to summon the courage to visit the world—the material world as opposed to the ethereal one represented by the paintings she could no longer execute. Well, if she thought I was going to play Virgil to her Dante. . . . The notion was admittedly grandiose, the analogy all wrong. For it wasn't the under-world she longed to visit (I imagined her already on speaking terms with the dead) but rather the once living past; and for that, instead of a psy-chopomp or guide, she wanted a gentleman escort. As the only candidate to present himself, I was automatically elected, though I wasn't sure that, even if I'd so desired, I was capable of accompanying her where she wanted to go. Our alliance, it appeared, was a pure case of the blind lead-ing the blind.

Occasionally I would take her arm in an effort to steer her through traffic, both pedestrian and automobile, but while she accepted the ges-ture, it was clear to me she had no urgent need of my help; for the geog-raphy she traveled, she was secure enough in her own bearings.

"This was Schreiber's Café," she announced, indicating a patriotically painted storefront advertising palm and tarot-card readings. I reminded her that she had a doctor to see, but she blithely deflected the subject, suddenly remembering that her appointment at the disappeared clinic was in fact a week hence—or had she already missed it? Never mind. I should know that Schreiber's "was where Louie Miller and that bunch from *Di Warheit* are advising how to make a revolution Leon Trotsky himself . . ." She spoke with a good deal of authority, fluctuating between tenses in a way that may have been simply a matter of improper usage. Or did she literally confuse the present neighborhood with the one that still endured in her mind's eye?

"This is the original bathhouse"—now a community rec center— "where I went when they came on me my monthlies; I was always a good Jewish daughter even if a bad girl."

I took the bait. "How were you bad, Aunt Keni?"

She smiled, showing the ravaged cemetery of her teeth. "I was a free-thinker and a artist," she boasted, making me to understand that such pursuits were scandalous in her day. "Out of wedlock I lived with a man, also an artist. You ever hear the Ashcan School? Well, Yanobsky painted the cans and I painted the ashes." Again her sawtooth cackle. But pleased as she'd been to be asked, she still reserved the right to be coy, satisfied for the moment to have teased me with a token confidence.

Then she reverted again to her role as cicerone, pointing out the candy store where she'd had her first charlotte russe, paid for with her winnings from a corner potsy game ("I was a tomboy"), and the dancing academy where she learned from Professor Fleg, his embrocated hair curled like a ram's horns, how to perform the turkey trot and the Haymarket rag. No matter that none of these places corresponded to her designations (one was Ozymandias Realty, another Fidelio's Bail Bonds); to each place along her trundling route, she assigned some sly personal anecdote, which helped compensate for the fact that the cobbler's shop or wine cellar had been given over to a restaurant-supply outfit, a nail parlor, an enchilada stand. There were also a few still-active vestiges of the original Jewish quarter, though they were aberrations now: a tallis shop, a lulav and esrog concession (it was nearly Sukkot), the Forward building with its neon clock, the Doric-columned Educational Alliance where Aunt Keni had taken life-drawing classes from the man whose mistress she would become. But these places were the exceptions, manned by skeleton crews and far outnumbered by the local vest-pocket businesses—the mom-and-pop stores operated by Caribbean families whose principal fixture was the ubiquitous stone-faced duenna seated beside a register telling her beads.

Aunt Keni showed no inclination to enter any of these businesses, succeeding as they had the ones that remained her points of reference. Didn't she perhaps need groceries or other provisions? I would ask, aware that I was needling her. But she assured me she wanted for nothing: "I got a neighborhood kid Manuel, he delivers me what I need." The information gave me a slight twinge of jealousy, though I suspected that the old woman had other reasons for her reluctance, because whenever I undertook to mention some fact about the current use of a particular address, she would practically clap her hands over her ears. Then she behaved as if the apothecary or the lodge hall in question must have been misplaced rather than converted. The past was more vital than the present for Aunt Keni, that much was apparent; she could see it with a clarity that effected a total eclipse of the foggy here and now. But even for her, time was a slippery element that made a companion, any companion, advantageous to the semiblind. I would do as a companion, though as a sighted guide I was entirely superfluous; I was an amateur at negotiating the caprices of the old lady's elastic calendar, how from one block to the next the decades might shift and alter their order. You couldn't count, for instance, on Chrystie Street's occupying the same vintage year as Grand; you should accustom yourself to change.

It was an attitude I came to share with Aunt Keni, as, during our subsequent walks, I began to observe the quarter through her eyes. Some of the streets we traveled, during excursions that became a habit for us both, were full of menace. Torched buildings smoldered like sleeping volcanoes; lurking dog-faced individuals with Giacometti limbs darted from pillar to post in the corners of our eyes. But nobody ever bothered us, and my impression was that together we constituted so pitiable a pair that it was beneath the dignity of even the most desperate fiend to do us harm. Or was it that, just as the sights in Aunt Keni's purview were invisible to others, so were we invisible as we went about inspecting places that were no longer there?

    I don't know at what point those mislaid sights started to assume substance for me as well. When it happened, I'd been stepping out with Aunt Keni for a couple of weeks, escorting her on the roundabout walks that seldom took us beyond the shadow of her subsidized-housing tower. Once she was certain of my willingness to accompany her, the old woman dropped all pretense of having any particular destination in mind and was content to toddle aimlessly about the quarter. I told myself these strolls were an extension of the exploring I'd done on my own; but where, in my solitary knocking about, I'd remained a stranger to the city, with Aunt Keni I felt I was finally entering it as a bonafide citizen. That the city I was entering existed in another dimension seemed immaterial to me; it was an authentic experience, wasn't it? And experience was what I had come to New York for. No longer choosy, I would take my adventure in whatever form it presented itself, however compromised. So nearly every day, in place of pursuing an unpromising college career, I squired my aunt through the same benighted arteries of what had once been known as Jewtown; I gathered tidbits of local history while Aunt Keni called the roll of missing real estate; and in time I learned to assist her in recovering what was lost.

"I think I see it!" I exclaimed one afternoon, when she'd pointed out a building that had once been the venue of the Pioneers of Liberty Yom Kippur Ball, circa 1908, a blasphemous affair Aunt Keni had attended to her shame.

"You see what, Nephew?" We'd begun to call each other, not a little self-consciously on my part, Nephew and Aunt respectively.

"The hand-painted sign for the New Hibernia Banquet Rooms," I declared. "It's on the wall next to the door."

Her response was characteristically dismissive. "Of course you see. *K'nacher,* what's not to see?"

"But there's nothing there."

"So *nu?*"

At first it was a sensation like double vision, as above some defaced tenement capital I would glimpse the visual echo of an equally crumbling gargoyle or the outline of a sagging mansard roof etched in the air over a weathered masonry eave. A kind of ectoplasm of carved entablatures and rusticated arches hovered about the sooty moldings and cracked cornices. Concrete dissolved into flagstone; stolen mosaic tesserae glinted again in the dark crannies between broken ceramic tiles; an evaporated mural of theatrical masks reasserted itself above the doorway of a burned-out music hall, which began by slow stages to reassemble itself out of rubble and fallen ailanthus leaves. Old Testament warriors stirred in their spectral frieze beneath a corroded fire escape, and an inlaid Hebrew cartouche shone from within the sandblasted cornerstone of the former headquarters of the Young Judea League. These were grimy ghosts peeking out through grimy façades, recalling ornaments that had mocked the destitute district just as cruelly then as now—the difference being that these features were revealed not through physical erosion, such as when asphalt is worn away to expose the cobbles beneath, but by threadbare areas in the fabric of time. Places worn thin by the intensity, as I came to believe, of my old aunt's misty regard.

I was always a little heartsick when we returned to her building and I deposited her at the door to her apartment. Each time, despite her near prostration, she invited me in, batting fake lashes that looked as if spiders clung to her lids.

"You ought to be ashamed of yourself," I would tell her point-blank, eliciting a blush like prickly heat, but the truth was, I was still a little afraid of her. Also, I understood that I'd been introduced prematurely to the weird intoxicant of her paintings; I'd imbibed the neighborhood's distilled essence before taking the *vin ordinaire* of its pedestrian atmosphere. In short, I'd been unprepared. With the walks I'd started again from scratch, learning under my aunt's erratic tutelage how to view the uncooked past before facing again her thoroughly baked version. Even as I washed out of NYU, I was matriculating into the College of the Lower East Side, or so I attempted to justify my delinquency. Meanwhile the abrupt farewells at her door lent to our relations the tension of a courtship: we were only just getting acquainted, the time not yet ripe for intimacy—that was my skewed rationale. The memory of my initial visit seemed like a clumsy intrusion, which our walks together had largely erased, and I was in no hurry to repeat the trespass of previous days.

Often, though, after dropping off Aunt Keni, I would nose about the quarter on my own, and once, as I poked along Rivington Street—or was it Ludlow?—I was accosted by an elderly gentleman, his stooped back encased in a coat like a bug's black carapace, who asked me if I was a Jew. He stood impatiently chewing a blubbery lip as I brooded over the question, finally concluding that yes, yes I was. I was a Jew.

"Mazel tov," he said, unimpressed, pincering my arm with his bony fingers. Then, *"Kim areyn,"* he enjoined me as you might a stray puppy, and began to tug me across the street. I felt I was being lured into some ghetto version of a rabbit hole but allowed my curiosity to overrule my natural resistance. Besides, I was developing an affinity for the hermetic community of the aged. He led me up the steps of a ruined synagogue, nudged open an unlocked wooden door, and shoved me through a vestibule and into a large hall skewered by shafts of moted sunlight. Some of the pews were overturned, the vaults above the women's gallery fertile with birds' nests, the air dense with urine and must. A chandelier had fallen on top of the bima, where it rested like a dead star under a rigging of spiderwebs.

Still grasping my wrist, the old man yanked me through an arched doorway to the left of the altar and down a flight of stairs into a stuffy cellar room. There a cabal of his mossbacked cronies with whiskers like kapok stuffing, their prayer shawls cowled over downy pink heads, were gathered around an Ark as unimposing as an open valise. At our entrance a couple of the men immediately shuffled forward to attend to me, one topping my head with a skullcap, another cloaking my shoulders in a blue-striped shawl, while my recruiter handed me a book. When they'd finished outfitting me like a candidate for sacrifice, they allowed themselves a little repartee.

"Ain't it prohibited, that he should be included in a minyan a *goylem?*" inquired a comical character with a goose-egg mole on his forehead.

"This you call 'included'?" countered my recruiter.

There was laughter like a cawing of jackdaws unspooked by the scarecrow in their midst—after which, promptly ignoring me, all faced the Ark to start in droning unharmonious prayers. Then it was every man for himself, a liturgical free-for-all, the daveners bobbing up and down like hammers striking chords on an out-of-tune instrument. When they removed the velvet mantle from the Torah scrolls, their horny hands trembled as if they were stripping a virgin of her gown.

Later Aunt Keni would enlighten me as to what had happened: The old men, seeking to complete their sparsely attended services, would conscript whomever they could find off the streets. "The *alter kucher*s, they operate around here a regular press gang. They think if they ain't got God's ear, they don't exist. Naturally, the same goes for God: if the East Side boys ain't listening, He got difficulty to hear Himself speak."

The problem remained that, long-lost clinics aside, Aunt Keni really was in need of medical attention here in the middle of the twentieth century. The smoker's cough that tore at her lungs, the arthritic pain that distorted her joints, the gout, dropsy, cataracts, shingles, and piles, which were only the afflictions she mentioned—never mind the others I couldn't even guess at—they all required urgent treatment. "Whatever happened to that doctor I was supposed to take you to?" I once tried to remind her.

"Ach, Nephew," she fairly purred, "you're all the medicine I need." But she dropped the tone soon enough if I persisted, beginning to bristle until I backed off. From time to time, I would try to make my case again: She wanted diagnoses and medication ("You know what it means, medication?"); there were real clinics in the neighborhood that cared for the indigent aged, and should unforeseen costs arise, she could surely rely on the conscience of her prosperous son.

"Feh." She waved a palsied hand. "Sick is what sick does; it's a state of mind. Look at you, a *mieskeit* that no friends he's got his own age—that I call sick. . . ."

Swallowing the insult, I took the occasion to ask her incidentally how old she was. "Two sweet potatoes and a sour gherkin," she replied, to my exasperation.

Of course, I wasn't so stupid that I couldn't see what she was up to— for couldn't I see further every day? With my help Aunt Keni had begun to reinhabit the past, where the insults of age couldn't reach her; this was her strategy. She could take shelter in her living memories, safe from the depredations of the advancing years. No doubt it was irresponsible of me not to have insisted more strenuously that she seek some manner of medical advice, though how could I force the issue? If I pushed it, she would invariably inform me, "Like a million bucks I feel; the walks, they give back to me my pep. . . ." So maybe I was complicit in her decline, but in my defense let me say that I, too, had come to believe in the healing powers of time travel. Our walks were restoring her health, she maintained, and I respectfully abetted that delusion.

So on we trudged, advancing one nippy fall afternoon into the previously unattained reaches of Orchard Street, where Aunt Keni remarked, "That was Pishkin's Ready-to-Wear." She was pointing to the onetime haberdashery (now a *carnicería*) where she had lived and worked with her Aunt Pesha Pishkin after her mother's death from some local pestilence in 1909. (Her sapless father had not survived the crossing from Europe.) I looked, and what I couldn't see for the flayed, rodentlike animals hung in the window, I imagined: the ragged awning and the glass-paned door with its sleighbell chimes, the rack of coats like a file of soldiers you had to push through in order to enter the sunken shop with its heavy camphor smell.

"A full-bodied lady, Aunt Pesha," my aunt was recalling, a tremor fluttering her wattled chin. "I used to help her to put on her corset. I would tug like I'm pulling the reins on a plow horse, while the clasps, like popcorn they snapped and flew off!" It was in this shop that her first husband, Nathan Hart, whom I couldn't remember her having mentioned before, had appeared one day to exchange some ill-fitting long underwear. That was one autumn evening on Orchard Street. Then, as we continued down along East Broadway, Aunt Keni indicated the Little Odessa Tearoom (now Carmelita's College of Cosmetology), where this same Nathan, clearly smitten, had turned up a second time and tried to enlist her interest in a story of his own devising.

"He was very persistent," she said a bit boastfully, looking as she leaned on her walker like some lumpish ship's figurehead. "It was a screwball affair, his story, about a angel that he comes to earth and has by a human girl a child. Feh," she spit *ptui,* a coarse gesture she some-times employed against the evil eye. Always assuring me that she wasn't superstitious, the old lady had me to know that demons, dybbuks, an-gels, and such were scientifically proven phenomena. (About God the jury was still out.) Shuddering slightly, she spit again. "Angels, they give to me a pain!"

But something about Nathan's angel must have intrigued her, because she'd begun, despite her relationship with the artist Yanobsky, to visit the young man in his Cherry Street garret (now a vacant lot) for further in-stallments of his fantastical story. This much I'd gleaned over the course of a dozen walks, collecting the crumbs of narrative that Aunt Keni dropped with increasing frequency, like a trail that (if we got lost) we could follow home. No matter that home was some sixty years ago.

"He was a newspaperman, Nathan Hart, which it means a liar by trade. Always he was with the *bubbeh mayseh*—you know *bubbeh mayseh?* A whopper. This is how he earns his living. Real? Make-believe? His whole life I don't think he knows the difference. Anyhow, we wasn't married six months when there comes one night a knock at the door. 'An anarchist, that he threw a bomb in Mulberry Street; your husband lays in Bellevue on a slab.' But when I go and see, no husband: they got there instead only a foot, a ear, an unmentionable item which I recognize it's his, but there ain't nothing he can't get along without. To this day I'm wondering is the rest of him somewhere alive and well."

The disclosure brought me to a standstill. "I should believe this?" I asked, as the old woman shambled on.

"So on my own I'm left to look after a infant child. I'm taking in washing, wet-nursing the neighbors' babies, goyim included, selling bath-tub schnapps—you name it. When comes along Mr. Solomonchik Shen-deldecker, I think as well him as somebody else. Besides, I already don't remember so good Nathan Hart. I'm thinking"—an asterisk of light twinkled in her left eyeglass lens—"maybe I made him up. . . ."

"So let me get this straight," I injected, overtaking her. "Newman is Nathan's son?"

She looked at me as if to ask was I born yesterday. "Newman is Yanobsky's that ran away from me to Paris, France. A *momzer*, like I told you." Yanobsky, I wondered, or the child? "Strictly speaking, he wasn't what you call marrying material, Nathan Hart. But in those days, try and have on your own a baby, they will skin you alive."

It was early November in Hester Street, the foxy leaves blown from Seward Park skittering across the sidewalk in front of Gertel's Bakery. In a handful of basement workshops, the remnants of a scattered community were stitching tallises and copying Torah scrolls, and in the middle of the street, accompanied by a phrase of rollicking music, I spied a leather gaiter strapped beneath a disembodied corduroy knee. Above the knee, which moved in a swiveling manner denoting a limp, I saw the corner of a scarlet box with a border of painted green grapevines. As I squinted hard to fix them in my sight, the knee and the box disappeared, though by then I knew what I had seen.

"There's a lame organ-grinder in the street," I announced to my aunt, wary of her possible sensitivity to reports of random body parts.

"That would be Picolomini the Italyaner, which didn't I just say so? What are you, Little Sir Echo here?" But she hadn't necessarily said so, nor could she snuff the delight I took in my perception; it was the first human figment (albeit the fragment of a figment) I'd glimpsed among so many phantom architectural details, unless you counted the old men from the minyan as ghosts. "The little girls," Aunt Keni continued, her rouged cheeks puffing like gills, "they would dance around him when he played his organ, Picolomini, then beat it before he could *patschken* their tushies. That's how from a stroke he died. . . . Did you see also his monkey? A very depressing creature."

No, I hadn't seen the monkey, but I did later on: or at least its dispirited face and the wilted anemone of its itchy behind; and as the elements remained favorable for the exercise of my fledgling visionary faculty, I saw as well the hem of a serge walking skirt dragging the pavement in front of Edelshtat the Furrier's (now Jimeno's Custom Cuts). I knew, because my instincts told me, that the skirt belonged to an operator girl with her sewing-machine case in hand, gazing longingly at a silver fox stole biting its tail; just as the pair of floating earlocks beneath a woolen watch cap on Division Street signified a fugitive from a nearby cheder— a young apostate who concealed forbidden texts behind his volume of Gemara, come to spy on the authors of those texts through the window of an absconded literary café (now a tong society). It was a café Aunt Keni advised me had once been the resort of famous Yiddish authors.

"Were there famous Yiddish authors?" I asked her, which provoked a litany of Moishes and Itzhaks previously unheard of by me. I sniffed a bit discourteously, wondering what could those folksy hacks (as I supposed all Yiddish writers to be) have to offer a modern reader? Didn't the old lady know that a generation of poets had just finished gloriously destroying themselves—leaping from boats and bridges, languishing in madhouses, drinking until they burst their brains? And a new generation, just as heedless in their fashion, were taking their clothes off in public and exploring the subterranean lairs of the soul. Could you seriously place beside them and their forebears—Baudelaire and Dostoyevsky, Nietszche and Franz Kafka (who, if I wasn't mistaken, was also some sort of a Jew)—names like Zalman Schneour and Moishe Nadir? Of course, my preconceptions were based on a total ignorance of Yiddish writers, never mind my sketchy acquaintance with the lords of modern literature. So in the end I was shamed into investigating some of the books themselves in their questionable translations.

I didn't get much beyond the jacket copy before learning that Yiddish writers rarely died in bed. If they survived the pogroms, they frequently perished for their seditious politics in the tomblike prisons of the czar; or if they survived the prisons, they died in the trenches of half a dozen fronts or in the chaos of the Revolution itself; or if they survived massacres, prison, war, and revolution and had managed to scramble out of Europe under the poison curtain that had by then begun to fall, they were routinely laid low by poverty and neglect on the Lower East Side of New York. Take the towheaded campaigner H. Leivick, who escaped on foot from Siberia and wrote lovingly of the ruined shoes and scraps of poems he'd left along the way. In America he hung wallpaper, contracted consumption, and had to check his brushes and ladder at the box office before being admitted to the premieres of his own classic plays. There was Moishe Leib Halpern—"Der Takhshit," the holy fool, a sign painter, pants presser, and maître d'—who, while waiting tables at the Café Royale, arranged his genitalia on a platter flanked by nova and potato salad to present as a homage to the actress Kamenskaya. There were the poets who leaped from windows and languished in madhouses.

From the volumes piled around my bed at Tenth and Broadway (prompting speculation on the part of my suitemates that I was going native) to the streets of the Lower East Side was now no distance at all. Whole scenes left their indelible imprint on the places where they'd occurred, and, thanks to my homework and developing extrasensory perception, I could apprehend them in their entirety, give or take the odd invisible limb. On the vacant steps of the old Eldridge Street Synagogue, I could see clearly—as I inched along beside my swollen-ankled aunt—the father in his miterlike yarmulke denouncing an errant daughter who knelt before him pleading forgiveness; and I could make an educated guess as to what she needed forgiveness for. I could see, in the corner grocery that once housed the Vinograd Café, a young Zionist upstart tugging the whiskers of an aged wedding bard. I could hear the old man, returning dignity for abuse, composing on the spot a macaronic verse in which *tsores* ("sorrow") was rhymed with *toig ahf kapores* ("pain in the ass").

On Allen Street, once the Jewish tenderloin under the demolished Second Avenue El, I saw, aided as ever by the chatty medium of my aunt, the ladies in their ruffled kimonos and nainsook peignoirs, dropping the parachutes of their laudanum-laced hankies. I saw a red light hung like an unholy *ner tamid,* an Everlasting Lamp, above a decaying doorway. Allen Street, the old lady had me to know, had been the special focus of much of her first husband's suspect journalism. Though she regarded his stories as crass sensationalism pandering to the baser instincts of the crowd (an opinion she assured me their purveyor would not have contested), Aunt Keni could nevertheless quote Nathan's articles chapter and verse.

" 'In the beginning,' " she had recited, a cigarette wagging between her crannied lips, " 'you had the patriarch Monk Eastman, him with his brickbat and the cockatoo on his shoulder, king of the lush-rollers and laundry thieves. . . .' " Pausing as she often did to catch her breath, which made the papery noise that might have worried me more had I not been so caught up in her performance. " '. . . And the Monk begat the white-slaver Max Zweibach, aka Kid Twist, who begat the archfagin Big Jack Zelig and his gorillas Lefty Louis and Gyp the Blood, who ran the arson and horse-poisoning trusts; and Jack Zelig begat the droopy-eyed con-niver Dopey Benny, who invented labor racketeering and consolidated the whole Lower East Side; and the Dope ruled the roost until the Tam-many bosses began to dip their beaks in, so that the syndicate found it more profitable to go straight. And these are the generations of the Jew-ish goons. . . .' "

It was the type of insider's reportage later made popular by newspa-per scribes such as Damon Runyon, and while my aunt disparaged the content of her husband's news items, she could never quite let their sub-jects go: she would carry on at length about the bloody Yid *shtarkers* and their adjustable rates for breaking heads. After which, her eyes moist as oysters in aspic, she would catch herself and offer a disclaimer.

"A tendency he had, Nathan Hart, for peddling moonshine."

Although I knew that Aunt Keni was no more reliable a narrator than Nathan himself, it was clear to me that in her day she had loved him. Then I found that my displaced jealousy for Manuel, the weedy kid who deliv-ered the chicken stock and halvah on which my aunt subsisted, had been transferred to the journalist. Keni Freischutz had loved Nathan Hart, loved him foolhardily in her youth, and, close to the age when they'd begun their affair myself, I craved the chance to engender such feelings in a woman. Though not just any woman. Mine must have artistic leanings and wild ginger hair, and a memory longer than her own meager years.

When I returned her to her door, I would leave the old lady dewy with perspiration, panting just this side of collapse from the strain of our walk. We would hug good-bye, and once in a while she would cling to me a little too long. Later on in the streets, minus the catalyst of my aunt, the phan-tom denizens would all have retired and the old squalor was again sup-planted by the new. Then I would miss how a dead rat in an oily puddle or an old man staring from a window at dusk partook of the pigments of Aunt Keni's besotted paintings. Alone but for the present-day inhabitants, I missed the stiff-necked Jews in their throngs, just as I missed the old Jewess who was as close to a reason for being in New York City as I'd yet to find.

Having entered her epoch past the point where I'd lost the desire to return to my own, I marveled at how tenuous was my connection to 1969, that I had slipped its moorings so easily. Of course I sometimes still felt the tug of current events; the times had after all never been more interesting. All around me my generation was violating the laws of God and man, sabotaging the body politic, blurring the line between high spirits and staged entertainments. In a storefront on St. Marks, agitprop puppets were immolated nightly in protest against the war, while in a theater (once a Yiddish theater, I was told) on Second Avenue, a disaffected Harvard professor lectured on the technology of ecstasy. A famous poet, incidentally a lapsed Jew, ate sacred mushrooms and chanted mantras in Tompkins Square Park. There were exhortations from the pulpits to the effect that universal media was reversing the fall of man—electronics would restore our innocence and make of our fragmented world one great egoless tribe. The whole of New York was a stewpot of intransigent energies, iconoclastic gestures, fiercely charismatic voices; and I was dwelling somewhat guiltily among ghosts.

The odd thing was that, though I remained in a fairly chronic state of rut, the girls of Greenwich Village no longer made me weak in the knees. They were a leggy clan, adorned in pagan fetishes and beads, so easy in their fluid bones that they seemed readily available, their nymphlike beauty welcoming scrutiny and admiration. Their lotus poses, to say nothing of their briny fragrance, made me feel, whenever I passed them, as if aqua regia had been poured down my pants. Of course it helped that, with the approach of winter, they had to bundle up, and I was no longer sandbagged by the sight of them sunning themselves in the parks, their gossamer dresses kilted to their *pupik*s. Anyway, I had become partial to modesty in fashion, tailored waists and worsted street skirts that showed to fine advantage the equine curve of a firm posterior. It occurred to me that it was for the girls of a vanished age that I maintained my protracted virginity; I was saving myself for the life that had long since passed me by.

Then Aunt Keni informed me that she couldn't walk anymore. I suppose I'd been expecting it; I was certainly aware that our excursions had been, for her, at the expense of great physical pain, each journey more hard fought than the one before. Lately I'd begun to feel almost sadistic, as if

I were forcing her to take walks for my sake rather than her own, because I'd noticed that, while she continued out of habit citing places and events, she was losing the battle for breath, running out of steam. More and more she alluded to her tennis elbow (forgodsakes) or her irritable bowel, trivial complaints by contrast to the one she never mentioned, the evidence of which she spit into her handkerchief after seismic coughing spells. Again I halfheartedly suggested a doctor, and this time, rather than reject the idea out of hand, she simply replied, "Not yet." Which ended the conversation. A few days later, when I called for her, instead of appearing dressed and ready in her several cardigans and dreadnought coat, she opened the door to her apartment in a flannel nightgown nubbly with lint. The off-kilter mascara and rouge that ordinarily made a totem mask of her face were absent, leaving her cheeks and chins terraced like a wax stalactite.

"I can't go no more for a walk," she said flatly, and turned to shuffle away.

Though I hadn't set foot in her apartment since my first visit, I followed her inside without ceremony, fully expecting her extravagant paintings to assail me all over again; but instead I felt as if I'd been inspecting them daily, novelty views of a country whose landscape (give or take the odd werewolf or siren) I'd come to know by heart. Her bedroom, which I'd never before laid eyes on, was no less airless than her so-called parlor, its livid walls unrelieved but for a single haphazardly mounted canvas—this one depicting a whiskery old man with chicken wings hovering above Hester Street, cradling a swaddled infant in his arms. The rest of the room was shoulder to shoulder with heavy furniture lowering about an iron bed. There was a standing wardrobe, a dressing table—its surface concealed by an Arabian skyline of atomizers and lotions—and a bureau sagging under stacks of old books. These were Yiddish books, and perhaps because I couldn't make out a single syllable on their well-creased spines, I begrudged their presence, another ghost minyan in which I was only marginally included.

With an affecting *oy*, Aunt Keni had crawled back into her unmade bed and pulled the afghan to her wispy chin.

That's when I voiced a woefully overdue resolution: "I'm phoning a doctor." The old woman lifted and let fall her carroty brows as if to indicate I could do as I pleased, thus calling my bluff. I marched purposefully into the parlor, where there was nothing so convenient as a telephone book, and began to broadcast my frustration. From the bedroom I heard Aunt Keni's voice, hoarse as a small engine underwater, telling me to call a number taped to her pantry door. That she would go so far as to help rather than hinder me made my stomach turn over with dread.

The number belonged to a local social-services agency. I was greeted by a harried, unfriendly female voice at the other end, who, when I stated my business, asked what made me think that my aunt's particular case was so special; there were any amount of old widows on the East Side dying unnecessarily of their own obstinacy when the programs that could assist them were in place; they had only to take advantage, and so on. When she was done giving me an unsolicited earful, I shook out the receiver and stated again irritably,

"My Aunt Keni needs a doctor to visit her at home."

She gave me the number of the Suffolk Street Elder Care Clinic and hung up.

The receptionist at the clinic put me on hold for a small eternity, until a nurse picked up and officiously presented me with a series of bureaucratic hoops to jump through. I lurched to and from the bedroom gathering information from the old lady, who turned out to be more conversant with her medical history than she'd previously let on. Then, just as the interrogation was about to exceed my endurance, I was informed that the appointment had been scheduled. It was only when I'd hung up, proud of a minor triumph, that I realized I'd failed to inquire when the doctor might arrive, but rather than run the risk of undoing what I'd done by further entanglements, I decided simply to wait with my aunt until he came. I waited all that afternoon and evening, making sure that Aunt Keni was resting comfortably, then turned in myself on a procrustean bed comprised of the opposing parlor armchairs. (They at least offered more support than the sofa, which was tantamount to lying in a sinkhole.) I woke at dawn racked with pain and surrounded by mounted images that made the transition from dreams to consciousness an arbitrary affair.

The doctor did not appear until late that afternoon. I'd hoped for Ben Casey, but this one was a rumpled sawbones with a dumpling nose and scuzzy jowls, fairly young but already rehearsing a tired-eyed middle age. With an air of having seen everything—including Aunt Keni's chimerical parlor—he pointed in the direction of the bedroom and, after an affirming nod from me, removed his trench coat, hefted his battered leather bag, and went straight in. At her bedside he asked the old lady, without any pretense of expecting a reply, how she felt.

"Like a million bucks," she said with no conviction at all.

I was standing at the doctor's shoulder when, with a careless wave, he signaled me out of the room, shutting the door behind him. Offended, I hung about outside, alternately pacing like an expectant father and pausing to listen for sounds of a struggle. Having invited the intruder, I resented his violation of my aunt's precious privacy, to say nothing of her passive surrender to his examination. He emerged about twenty minutes later, clasping the case whose grainy folds were repeated by his baggy jowls. Hovering at his side, I anxiously awaited the prognosis, but while he stood there frisking his own pockets, in search of (it turned out) the eyeglasses on his nose, his silence reinforced my reluctance to ask for what should have been forthcoming. Finally, unable to stand the suspense, I blurted,

"So what does she have?"

Turning his head as if he'd just become aware of my presence, the doctor shrugged, and I thought for a moment he might plead ignorance. "What doesn't she have would be more to the point," he said, his guttural voice half a belch. "Pneumothorax, arrhythmia, chronic pulmonary obstruction, for which the popular term is 'advanced emphysema'—you name it. I can see it in your face you want a second opinion? Okay, you're ugly, too."

I searched his expression for some indication that he thought he was being funny and, finding none, decided he was insane. Again he'd become taciturn, gathering up his coat, making me work for a word.

"Does she need a hospital?" I asked, feeling as if I were addressing a ouija board.

Puckering his rubbery face, he pronounced elegiacally, "A hospital she needed when you were in knee pants." I was working up to telling him I was never in knee pants, when he posed a question that took me completely unawares: "How bad you want to keep her alive?"

"What!"

"Look, you can put her in a hospital; they'll hook her up to hoses, give her injections, enemas, horse pills; she'll live maybe a month. Or you can keep her more or less comfortable at home, where she'll drop dead tomorrow. She got insurance?"

I believed so.

"What kind?"

I told him.

"With that and the president's endorsement, we can get her onto a charity ward where the rats nuzzle your toes and they force-feed you soup made from mucilage—or you can hire a nurse. You got any money?"

I shook my head.

Looking around: "These paintings worth anything?"

"What do you think?"

He sighed and said, "Tell you what," so that I thought he might offer some diabolical bargain: give me your shadow in exchange for your aunt's full recovery; and I asked myself if I were ready to make the sacrifice. But instead his meaty lips formed a humorless smile, his way (I assumed) of paying lip service to professionalism. "Talk it over with the old lady, and call the clinic when you decide what you want. Meantime"— scribbling something indecipherable on his script pad, tearing out the page which he thrust in my face—"have this filled for her. It's cortico-something, which is better than cortico-nothing, right? It'll help her cough up bile instead of blood." Then he drew on the dirty trench coat over his pear-shaped frame, saluted ironically, and was gone.

I reported to Aunt Keni that the doctor was a quack and was told— through congested lungs that outdid the radiator's squealing—that he seemed to her a nice young man, perhaps even a *lamed vovnik*. This I knew from my reading was one of the thirty-six hidden saints for whose sake God refrains from destroying the world; and while I was willing to withhold my judgment as to whether the doctor were madman or saint, it frightened me that, in her illness, my aunt should have become so suddenly complacent. But for once, rather than stymied, I was stirred by my fears to action, anxious to continue taking care of business.

I initiated another series of phone calls, first to the elder-care clinic that had dispatched the doctor, a knowledge of whom I half expected them to disclaim. But apparently fully apprised of Aunt Keni's case, they referred me to a nursing agency that had worked out of a nearby hospice for decades. The administrator, though not inhospitable, informed me that the service had recently forfeited its nonprofit status, making my aunt's minimal insurance inadequate to cover the cost of home care. Still energized by the urgency of my mission, however, I reached what I felt was an inescapable conclusion.

"Aunt Keni," I said in my capacity as rookie *nudzh*, "I think you should give me your son Newman's telephone number." I was a little disappointed when she relinquished the information without scruple.

Newman Shendeldecker of Pismo Beach, California (not Texas), was suspicious of me from the get-go.

"What did you say your connection was with my mama?" His voice was husky, belligerent.

I'm your long-lost brother, I had an impulse to tell him. That would have gotten his attention. But the rogue temptation gave way to a more diplomatic one, leavened by the realization that my feelings toward the old lady had in fact never been filial. So I explained that I was a nephew from the Memphis branch of the family at school in New York, who'd just learned of my aunt's serious illness.

"What Memphis branch of the family? The who? The Buzzoffs? How do I know you're not some swindler trying to bilk me in my mama's name?" he demanded. "You're a swindler, maybe a murderer for all I know. Where is my mama anyhow?"

I ground my teeth, aware that I was being tested but artless enough to ask what possible advantage he thought I might gain by lying. He made a list that demonstrated his intimacy with many types of deception and betrayal, so that I understood nothing else would suffice but that I drag Aunt Keni to the telephone. I asked him to please wait while I fetched her from bed, an event to which—like the doctor's examination—she pliantly conceded, though it took some time to facilitate her passage from the bedroom to a parlor chair. Once seated, the only vital sign she evidenced was the lighting of a tremulous cigarette.

When I'd determined that Newman was still on the line, I handed the receiver to the sick woman. "How's my *tateleh?*" she greeted him without enthusiasm. "And Inez and the kids? . . . Too bad. . . . So did Rochelle's husband have yet the embezzlement hearing? Ooh, touchy . . ." After that it seemed she was on the receiving end of the conversation, responding mostly in listless monosyllables. "Yeah," she said. "Yeah . . . yeah . . . no . . . yeah. . . . Dunno, dying, I guess . . . uh-huh, no . . . yeah . . ." It went on like that for a period, while I wagged my head this way and that in sympathy, until Aunt Keni, coughing her fruitiest cough, gave her warmest regards to Newman's family and handed the phone back to me.

"Listen." He was somewhat subdued, the dutifully troubled son. "My schedule won't let me come to New York right away, so do you mind if I leave you in charge?" But before I could respond to his generous injunction that no expense be spared, he was already reverting to type. "Naturally, I expect every penny to be accounted for, or, *heh-heh,* I'll hunt you down," trying to sound humorous though no one was fooled, "I'll take it out of your hide, *farshteyst?*"

"*A deigah hob ich,*" I knew enough to reply. "I should worry." Because I was confident his threat was an idle one: I was, after all, doing him a favor, saving him an onerous trip for which he should thank me. I assured him there was no need to thank me before I hung up.

Then I was floored by the enormity of what I'd undertaken, especially when I took stock of my diminished aunt with her bloodhound's dewlaps, her magnified eyes drooling like runny eggs.

"Don't be fooled," she was saying through labored breathing. "Beneath his gruff exterior, my Newman is—"

"A flaming asshole," I completed the sentence, as the old lady had already sunk into stertorous snoring.

Then, lest hesitation turn to paralysis, I again called the home-care service and hired a visiting nurse.

After the trials of the oddball doctor and Newman, I figured the nurse would be yet another: I pictured a truculent woman in jackboots, blundering in to forbid my unhygienic presence in the sickroom and treating my aunt like ailing livestock. Instead we were awarded the benefice of Nurse Daisy (I never learned her surname), a honey blonde of the type I was coming to think of as shiksa, neatly packaged in a crisp white uniform through which you could see the outline of her intricate underwear. Seemingly uncorrupted by modern attitudes, she appeared almost a throwback to the buxom nurses of old vaudeville routines; but notwithstanding her keyboard smile, her shapely calves further flattered by the nicely turned seam of her support hose, she was no bimbo. Personable and efficient, she had come prepared and, after reciting her credentials, wasted no time in producing an albuterol inhaler with which she flushed Aunt Keni's lungs. She consolidated that victory by hooking up the old lady to a machine she'd taken the liberty of ordering from a medical-supply store—a cylindrical contraption called an oxygen extractor, to which she attached her patient by means of a coiled plastic tube. The machine, also clear plastic and looking like some state-of-the-art whiskey still, featured a kind of concertina pump that seemed, at regular intervals, to heave bottomless sighs. It was a function that perhaps served as a substitute for the emotions my aunt—between the tube and the rounds of pills that left her comatose—lacked the energy to express. Brisk and attentive, Nurse Daisy was a marvel of industry: you could set the clock by her precise adjustments to the valves on the oxygen extractor and her administration of medications and meals. Humming popular airs, she filled the rancid atmosphere with aerosols, brewed spiced tea in the ivory-handled samovar, prepared a variety of fragrant soups and pabulums, which, seated on the bed with her splendid legs crossed, she spoon-fed my aunt. This while chatting freely about her church affiliation and the endearing habits of her several suitors.

Is it any wonder I hated her? I grew to despise her for her abrasive good humor and the constant provocation of her firm backside, whose inverted valentine I saw before me like an ill omen when I closed my eyes. I hated how she mussed my hair in passing and patronizingly called me Rumpelstiltskin. But more than that, I resented the alarming passivity with which the old lady submitted to her care. Aunt Keni's ready surrender gave me the impression that she'd already let go, that her soul had joined the shades of Orchard and Hester streets while her body lingered on in the cramped apartment only technically alive. Meanwhile I myself had become virtually redundant. True, under Nurse Daisy's benevolent dispensation, I was allowed a private audience in the sickroom whenever I pleased, but my aunt was hardly responsive. Observing me through slitted eyes stripped of their spectacles, with the afghan pulled to her chins, she was as inanimate as a mummy. Even as I listened to the wintry whistling of her lungs, I felt she'd abandoned me. Having harvested her memories thanks to my help, she was taking them with her, leaving me marooned in a low-rent project on the Lower East Side of New York.

"Look," I said to her with undisguised pugnacity, assuming that she wasn't listening anyway, "would you mind not dying quite so peacefully? Whats a matter, you never heard from the poet who said, 'Do not go gentle into that good night'?"

When her head moved slightly, I started, then took her nod as an indication that I should unplug the snorkel-like device from her nose—after which she issued a barely audible chirp as from a cricket at the bottom of a well: "You think that for me this is fun?"

Abruptly heartened, I replied, "And we know how you like your bit of fun."

That's when I made a decision. All this solicitude and intrusive technology, it did more damage than good. How was my aunt any better off than she would have been in a hospital? Call it rash, an impulsive act born of a mistaken sense of propriety, but I took it upon myself to fire Nurse Daisy. To this day I don't know where I found the gumption.

I was shivering as I delivered to that spruce-limbed young woman the line I'd rehearsed for a night and a day:

"We won't be needing your services any longer."

Looking more perplexed than offended, she inquired, "You find my work unsatisfactory?"

She seemed to be relying on the same corny script as I. In any case, I assured her that her work was first rate, no complaints whatsoever on that score; it was just that, given the limited funds at our disposal, I felt it in my aunt's best interests that I should take over from here. After all, hadn't I observed her routine until I knew it by heart?

She cocked her head prettily, the Cupid's bow of her mouth pulled taut. "You sure you know what you're doing?" she asked, challenging but sincerely concerned. Here was an authentic I-thou moment, and I nearly melted. Close enough to see a sprig of lace between the buttons of her bodice and inhale her blossomy scent, I wanted to fall on her breast and confess that I hadn't the least idea what I was doing. Perhaps she would take pity and give me succor, initiating me into fleshly mysteries that would make me, there and then, a man. But that was a scenario for another day; so I told her I could handle things just fine.

She left declaring the situation fraught with irregularities that she would have to report to her agency, which would in turn take them up with the proper authorities. But I was hopeful, once she was gone, that Aunt Keni's case would soon be lost in a thicket of paperwork that would fall between bureaucratic cracks, and there would be no further interference from outside.

When I broke to the sick woman the news of what I'd done, she took it, as she did most things these days, as a matter of course. She raised her unplucked brow as if in an effort to weigh the full significance of my actions, then let it fall under so heavy a load. "So tell me again," because her hearing could also have been better, "why did you let go the nice lady?"

"Nice?" I said. "There's that word again! Since when did you become Miss Congeniality? The woman was a total incompetent!"

Seeming to enjoy the transparency of my outrage, Aunt Keni's face was briefly lit with amusement. "Fine," she rasped. "Then take from out of my nose this *tsura*—you know *tsura* . . . ?" Yes, I did. ". . . and give to me a cigarette."

Grateful to the point of tears, I did as I was told. I removed the snorkel plug from her nose, tapped a cigarette on the nightstand, and stuck it between her lips. Then I flicked the daggerlike flame of her butane lighter.

But that, I promise, was the extent of my laxity. If anything, I overcompensated in my determination to be responsible; I had indeed paid vigilant attention to Nurse Daisy's ministry. Like her, I spoon-fed the old lady, holding her nose, which she turned up at the mashed vegetables I stirred into her chicken broth. I cooled her chapped lips with ice, gave her wedges of vanilla halvah to suck, along with the couple of cigarettes I rationed her each day. Periodically I irrigated her cloudy pupils with eyewash and stuck the thermometer under the salted slug of her tongue. Skeptical of their invasiveness, I nevertheless experimented with the inhaler and the oxygen extractor, which I credited with giving a certain musicality to Aunt Keni's breathing. I even insisted on the daily cocktail of two-toned spansules, albeit in less stupefying doses, that the nurse had dispensed to stave off pneumonia. I sluiced her insides with fluids to dilute the intense tangerine hue of her pee, which I caught in the aluminum bedpan along with the mustard-scented purgations of her gravy-like stools.

I clipped her toenails and groomed her hair, which had turned an iron gray; it came out in clumps with every stroke, so that the brush looked like a distaff when I was done. In what proved a delicate operation, I sitz-bathed her in the warm, Epsom saltsed water that I lugged from the kitchen in a sloshing enamel basin. First I would help her to sit up on the edge of the bed; then, folding her arms around my neck until my nostrils flared from her vulcanized smell, I lifted her enough to place a towel under her flaccid bottom. I pulled the flannel gown over her head and sponged her face, then sponged the translucent flesh of her arms and legs, whose parboiled texture appeared on the verge of peeling from her brittle bones. Inspecting for bedsores, I *toivel*ed her underarms and deflated udders, the ruddy sand-dollar aureoles around her nipples; nor did I shrink from making public her private parts. Scrupulously I scrubbed her tush and bush, lathering with disinfectant soap her clogged rectum and the goat-bearded mouth of her womb. It was an office I became fond of performing, unduly proud of my thoroughness, though there were times I wished she might have been more resistant; she might have flung me away from her, barking in aggravation, "What do you think, I'm some tchotchke for you to play with?" That would at least have been a sign that the plucky old lady I'd known was still in there. But cigarettes seemed the limit of her outlaw impulses, and to all my attentions she submitted without a peep, save for the rackety vibrations of her diaphragm.

At night I sat at her bedside listening for her fitful snoring to falter. Then I would crawl into the bed beside her and press an ear to her spongy chest to make certain the stuttering mechanism of her heart was still thumping. Later I would lie awake in my berth between the parlor armchairs, convinced that I could keep her alive indefinitely. She would regain her vigor, repossess her walker, and take to the streets again, where she would wait for me to outgrow my puerile longings and attain a venerable age of my own, by which time we would have become perfect complements. But even as I indulged them, I knew there was something terribly wrong with such thoughts, that my worries on the old lady's behalf were making me strange. Take for example the morning I woke up to the notion that her giddy paintings, like houseplants (of which Aunt Keni had none), were depleting the apartment of needed oxygen; so I covered the canvases with sheets or turned their loud surfaces toward the wall. After that, though she seldom left the bed, though she slept most of the day and brought up with her coughing discharges viscid as mollusks;

while she floundered sometimes like a fish reeled back from oblivion into a sphere she had no wish to be in, I was nevertheless satisfied that my aunt had begun to rally.

Since I had transferred my clothes and books to her apartment, my suitemates seldom saw me anymore—though on the occasions when I returned to Tenth Street for some forgotten toiletry article, they seemed to have grown bored with the entertainment I'd once provided them. The economist might make some insipid comment (to the effect that Quasimodo was back, Mr. Gallagher) to which the math wizard never even bothered to reply. Then, too, they may have been discomfited by my appearance—for in attending my aunt, I neglected myself, infrequently showering or changing apparel, losing weight I could ill afford to lose. It was a condition I noted with only the mildest interest in front of bathroom mirrors, where my naked body had the girth of a dragonfly. With my parents in Memphis, I'd ceased to communicate at all. This was partly owing to my guilt over having squandered the money they'd invested in my trial semester at NYU, partly because my current position vis-à-vis my aunt would have appalled them. Excessive devotion to people or ideas was considered unseemly in my family, and to have allied oneself so closely to another's suffering would have filled them with disgust.

Now that I had my own key to Aunt Keni's apartment, gone was the coy song and dance that used to give me pause about entering. I came and went as I pleased, having cultivated the habit of touching first the plastic mezuzah and then my lips as I passed over the threshold. (I felt the gesture somehow distinguished me, *kaynehoreh,* from the angel of death, whom I thought of as a frequent visitor to that tower of widows.) However, since the raccoon-eyed Manuel still delivered the groceries regularly on Mondays and Thursdays, frowning over his reduced gratuity— God forbid I should be spendthrift with Newman's money—there was little need for me to venture outside anymore. I was content with this state of affairs and—give or take the violent spasms that made me fear she might eject her own rib cage—optimistic about my aunt's slow but steady improvement. Only now that I'd managed to goad her into a few more hours of consciousness each day, we were sometimes at a loss as to how to pass the time.

Naturally, there was no TV, though, weaned on the thing as I'd been,

I never missed it; when in Aunt Keni's company, I forgot TV was ever invented. What I did miss, of course, and felt an acute withdrawal from, were our ritual stumblings into yesterday. I told myself that by now the whole culture of the Jewish East Side ought to have been contained in my head: what I hadn't experienced through the old lady's monologues, I'd encountered in my reading; and I still had the capacity (didn't I?) to summon the past out of thin air. So why did it all seem so suddenly distant, almost as if we'd never taken our walks at all? To jar my memory, I read aloud to my aunt from stories the immigrants themselves had told, especially those cris de coeur collected in a volume of letters received by the *Jewish Daily Forward*. But they failed to amuse the sick woman, who'd been there already, was perhaps there still, and required no further gloss on the subject. Nor could I persuade her to reminisce anymore. When I tried (with increasingly ungentle urging), the old lady disregarded my pleas, happy to snooze between periods of raucous coughing and fighting for breath.

If I pushed too hard, she would groan, *"Hab rachmones,"* and attempt to turn the tables, inviting me to talk about Memphis. Then I allowed as how I wasn't entirely proof against nostalgia: before adolescence had marked my face with a leprous acne, leaving me an unreconstructed sad sack, etcetera, I'd spent my childhood primarily up a tree. I came down to go to the movies, hardly noticing the *shvitz*-like climate, the snakes, red earth, kudzu, and bitterweed, the Colored and White water fountains, the Rosenbergs, Kennedys, Emmet Till, the imminent shadow of the mushroom cloud. I lived in daydreams, never quite certain where Saul Bozoff left off and El Zorro or Tarzan of the Apes began, until desire woke me up to my awful limitations.

"Satisfied?" I would ask after having spilled my guts, and if she made some affirmative noise, "Good," I replied, "now it's your turn." Though she pleaded fatigue, I refused to let her off the hook; nothing would do but that Aunt Keni should tell me more about her days with Nathan Hart.

"Ach," the old lady had sighed, the rattling in her throat like peas in a dry pod, "Nathan—" and that was it; because, away from the streets where the romance had first unfolded, the tale was perhaps too abstract to recall. Then there was an instance when it appeared that my sinking aunt was not quite done.

"Like I say . . . he didn't to me seem the marrying kind, *hnhhh* . . ." A
sound like a trounced squeeze box having emanated from her chest, I
fetched the inhaler to reinflate her lungs. "But when Yanobsky left me
shvengert with Newman . . . to go to Paris, France . . . where he died, I'm
told, of a social disease . . . and Nathan, the bad penny, he turns up
again . . . well, there was the baby to consider, *hnhhh* . . ." Once more I
pumped the inhaler. "As you know . . . he could be very persistent. But he
couldn't never finish what he started, Nathan Hart . . . which it included
his life . . ."

She paused, panting, her voice the faint burbling of an underground
spring, to suggest yet another type of diversion. This was late at night
(though I hardly bothered distinguishing night from day anymore), after I'd tucked her in and hooked her up to the sighing machine, when my
aunt asked me to take Nathan's manuscript down from the wardrobe.
Just like that: "Take down from on top the wardrobe his book . . . and
give to me." I hadn't known till then that such a thing even existed, yet
here she was asking for it as casually as she might have requested a tooth-
brush or a suppository.

It was wrapped in what back home would have been called a gunnysack, a burlap bag containing a ragged nosegay of irregular pages bound
in waxed string and reeking of age. Some of the sheets were standard
foolscap, others frayed butcher paper, cardboard stiff as buckram, wrappers limp as chammy leather speckled with mildew, their edges crumbling to the touch. They were scribbled over, those shelf-worn pages, in a
tortured cursive rendered in colored inks like tangled threads, in a Yiddish that may as well have been cuneiform for all its accessibility to me.
The characters had faded with time—or was it that the words had been
dulled by overmuch perusal? Whatever the case, this was the first tangi-
ble item I'd recovered intact from the dream of the old East Side, and I
handled it with the delicacy of a relic.

Bringing up some arsenic-green matter, which I received with a jai
alai player's dexterity in the bedpan, Aunt Keni took the manuscript
from me; she waited until I'd managed to untie the string, then held it
under her bristly nose, squinching her eyes behind the quartz-thick spectacles to try to make out the text:

" 'My son, Nachman, as you know,' " she began reading, her eyes at once starting to wander while her crooked fingers brushed over the words like braille, " 'was reared in paradise. . . .' " Lowering the pages, she informed me, "This is for us the ideal story . . ." a wheeze and a burble ". . . since it don't matter should I croak before we finish. Nathan didn't never finish the writing of it anyway." Then, prey to a sudden consideration, she gazed at me opaquely over the book, saying, "So, Nephew . . . why don't you?"

"Why don't I what?"

But she lacked the vitality to pursue the thought. Changing the subject, she announced with a mixture of vainglory and regret, "The title is called incidentally . . ." wheezing like a wolf whistle ". . . *The Angel of Forgetfulness.*"

Personally, I never liked that title. There were already enough angels in the card catalog: *Look Homeward, Angel; Desolation Angels; The Blue Angel; Teen Angel; Swamp Angel*—the list was endless. Nothing like an angel in the title to guarantee a book's mediocrity; that was my opinion. And as for completing the story, I wouldn't even have known how to proceed. Especially since, not long after she'd started to read it aloud— having struggled to the part where the angel, fallen in love with a mortal woman, begins to acquire the attributes of a human being—Aunt Keni, mustering more agony than I would have believed possible in one so frail, passed away.

NATHAN

On a chilly November evening in 1910, Nathan Hart, a timid young proofreader for the *Jewish Daily Forward*, entered Pishkin's Ready-to-Wear on Orchard Street to buy a pair of longjohns. He was waited on in the camphor-reeking cavern of a shop by a bustling, barrel-shaped woman wearing a wig like a round black loaf. She approached Nathan with what he perceived as aggression, gesturing with her thumb toward a tarnished brass cash register. Pasted to the back of the register was the rotogravure of a turtle-faced man in a collarless shirt clipped from the *Forward*'s "Gallery of Missing Men." Abandonment, Nathan was aware, had reached epidemic proportions in the Jewish quarter that season.

"You see *mayn* Pishkin," she said with overmuch familiarity, in the mingling of English and Yiddish that was typical around Orchard Street, "this to all my customers I tell them: you see Pishkin, say to him business is good, don't come back. What can I do for you?"

After the moment it took him to find his tongue, Nathan stated his wish to purchase a union suit. Mrs. Pishkin allowed her narrowed eyes to travel the length of the young man's scrawny frame, from the knotted woolen scarf at his throat to his beat-up bluchers. "I'd say you're a size . . . what? thirty-eight?"

Nathan nodded, though he hadn't a clue.

She heaped several pairs of folded longjohns on the beveled-glass counter. "We got here your double-breast lumberjack style," unfolding the pair on top which she made to sit up, tucking the neck under her chins. Then she lifted her head abruptly, allowing the longjohns to crumple as in a decapitation, and pulled out the pair underneath: "Australian fleece—this is very popular. . . ."

Uncomfortable with the intimacy of the garments and the manner with which Mrs. Pishkin displayed them, Nathan inquired which were the least expensive.

The woman seemed slightly irate. "Well, there's your so-called durable cotton, strictly a *shmatte*—this is forty-five cents; or you can have for another fifteen the Dr. Wright's worsted wool health suit. . . ."

"That one I'll take," blurted Nathan, anxious to get the transaction over with. Frowning when he didn't bother to haggle, Mrs. Pishkin nevertheless swept his coins from the counter into her pudgy palm. She rang up the sale, wrapped the union suit in brown paper, and tied it with string, then pushed it (a bit brusquely, he thought) toward Nathan. He thanked her all the same and, tucking his parcel under his arm, exited the shop beneath a curtain of Prince Albert coats and bell metal chimes.

The street was crowded despite the cold, its pavement lined with pushcarts lit by naphtha flares that made flickering Haman's masks of the vendors' faces. So fiendish did they appear to Nathan that they might have been hawking amulets and potions instead of umbrellas, nutmeg graters, and calicos. Head bowed, the proofreader made his way through the crush of pedestrians, averting his eyes from a pair of market wives engaged in a shoving match over the last spool of yarn in a peddler's bin. Here a man in a sheep's pelt with foaming lips extolled the sanctity of his braided candles; there a puller-in practically strong-armed a passing citizen outside a used-clothing shop. A pedal-pumping knife sharpener pressed a butcher's blade to his emery wheel and sprayed a comet's tail of sparks across the thoroughfare.

Nathan turned a corner into a gusting Canal Street and crossed Rutgers Square behind a furniture dray, its tired nag pausing to lift its tail and dump a steaming load onto the cobbles. On East Broadway parties of revelers floating from café to café forced the old men in patched caftans departing their *shtibls* to step off the curb. Nathan, too, stepped from the curb and took a right onto Clinton Street, where a gang of golf-capped urchins were twirling tin cans on strings. The cans contained burning embers that made lariats of flame whose loops the passerby had to negotiate at his own risk. With a sigh of relief, Nathan turned into Cherry Street and hastened to mount the unsturdy steps of the narrow frame house in which he occupied an attic room.

He climbed the four steep flights to his garret, unlocked the door, and lit—since the gas pipes didn't reach beyond the third floor—a spirit lamp that stood on the square deal table. Stoking the little Acme stove (shaped like a fireplug) full of wood chips and corncobs, anything that would burn, he sat down on the chirping iron bed to open his purchase. Though dank, the attic borrowed an illusion of warmth from the amber glow of the lamp and the scarlet ash grate in the stove. Poorly insulated, the place was made cozier by the books heaped against the low, peeling walls. Since his arrival in America nearly two years before, Nathan had boarded with a series of yammering families, sleeping on folding cots in the parlors and kitchens of their railroad flats. Only recently, since obtaining his job at the Yiddish daily, had he been able to afford the sanctuary of a room of his own.

Granted, it wasn't much: a table, a stove, a sagging bed, a sulfurous stink of cabbage rising from the apartments below. There was, however, a dirty casement through which you could view, beyond a vertical cluster of slate-shingled roofs, the smokestacks of steamers moored at the East River wharves. Not that Nathan was often given to looking out the window: the Lower East Side of New York, America, was a strident and menacing place, an evil-smelling Babylon. He much preferred to keep his nose in the pocket romances and novelettes he bought off the Essex Street stalls and read, despite the long days at his copy desk, into the small hours of the night.

Having opened his parcel, Nathan stood to remove his itchy rug coat; he peeled off the soiled celluloid collar and band bow tie, stepped out of his shoes, and stripped to the thin, worsted skivvies that had proven unseasonable. These he also discarded. Shivering in his nakedness, he unfolded the ribbed woolen health suit and pulled it on one snug leg at a time. The garment hugged his meager bones like a second skin, but for all the warmth the new *gatkes* provided, Nathan felt a slight draft between his legs. When he bent over to inspect, he discovered that the seam in the area of the crotch had come apart.

The purchase represented a sizable portion of his weekly wages, and it distressed him that the new drawers should prove as threadbare as the ones he had just cast off. But when he thought of having to face again the crass widow Pishkin with the complaint that she'd sold him inferior goods, Nathan shrank within. Never keen for confrontation, he would have mended the underwear himself, but he was one of the few Tenth Ward inhabitants unhandy with a needle and thread. Besides, didn't he have as much right as another to expect the quality he'd paid for? So Nathan resolved to return the defective garment the next evening after work.

He stood awhile on the sidewalk, buffeted by a brisk wind and the shoulders of heedless pedestrians, before steeling himself to enter the shop. Once inside, Nathan was relieved to find Mrs. Pishkin temporarily preoccupied, showing a squat column of bowler hats to a man in a flocky fur duffel; but as he waited, a scratchy voice called out to him from behind the necktie counter on his right.

"Can *I* help you?"

She was a young lady with an alabaster complexion, lightly freckled like a sprinkling of cinnamon in milk, and flame-red hair. Acutely aware of the nature of the defect in the goods he was returning, Nathan was doubly reluctant to point it out to a girl so close to his own age. Fighting an urge to back apologetically out the door, he placed his parcel on the counter, then stepped away as if to allow the garment to leap forth of its own accord.

"The *gatkes,* the union suit," he muttered, "they got in them a hole."

"A hole?" inquired the shopgirl, arching an eyebrow above the rim of her tiny oval spectacles. The word on her thin coral lips sounded slightly raffish.

"It split, the seam, when I'm putting them on."

Her mouth opened in a silent *oh* as she unwrapped the parcel and began to examine the merchandise, while Nathan furtively examined the girl. Despite her modest standing-collared waist and broadcloth skirt, she had about her a slightly untamed aspect, owing no doubt to her thick pile of crimson hair. Wisps of it, come loose from her topknot, were like the trails of rockets spiraling out of a bonfire—or so mused Nathan, not ordinarily given to such whimsical flights. The phrase "Hebrew lightning" came to mind, which was the tongue-in-cheek local term for arson; though were it not for her oval spectacles, signifying a strain of

Jewish bookishness, he might have taken her for a shiksa. Her high Dresden cheekbones were more akin to those of the Irishers who lived along the waterfront than of the dark-eyed Esthers and Rebeccas of the ghetto.

Then she'd located the rent in the fabric and, sticking three wriggling fingers through the hole, held the garment up for closer inspection. "Some morning pride you must of had," she hoarsely appraised. It was a remark perhaps not intended for other ears, but Nathan's dropped jaw indicated that he'd overheard all the same. Realizing as much, she covered her mouth, her pale face flushing the pink of beet soup. "You want a refund or an exchange?" she inquired through her fingers, trying to recover her professional aplomb. But the stunned expression on Nathan's face was finally too much for her, and she burst into a fit of cackling laughter.

"Keni," Mrs. Pishkin barked at her from across the aisle, "*vildeh moid,* behave yourself!"

Sniffling into a handkerchief, the girl once more attempted to compose herself. "Refund or exchange?" she asked again, and when Nathan mumbled the latter, she scurried around to a bin of longjohns, from which she selected another pair. But when she brought them back to the proofreader, his unabated embarrassment rekindled her amusement, and she succumbed to her screechy laughter again. Nathan snatched the underwear from her hand and fled the store, his dignity in tatters.

On the street, ears burning beneath the unfastened flaps of his plush cap, he tried to console himself that he knew her type—a "new" woman. The kind you saw at the labor bund rallies and Ethical Culture lectures at Cooper Union, or in the cafés plotting revolution with their male counterparts over tea *à la russe.* Often they were hatless and wearing hobble skirts, their crossed legs showing lisle-stockinged ankles above felt-button boots. They were a shameless lot, the despair of their pious fathers, who would frequently say over them a premature kaddish; and while he made no great claims to piety himself—he'd scarcely set foot in a synagogue since his greenhorn days—Nathan had little use for such boldfaced girls.

Returned to his attic, he tried on the new pair of *gatkes,* and, like the others, they fit him perfectly; like the others, they split instantly at the crotch. This time Nathan determined that he would mend them himself.

But his encounter with the shopgirl kept him from sleeping. For a while he thought that simple mortification was at the root of his insomnia, though toward dawn he realized it was something else. He could not give that "something else" a name, but he recognized it as dangerous. Of danger Nathan had had quite enough back in his native shtetl of Zitsk, where the favorite pastime of the local peasants was cracking Jewish heads. It was a place subject to the whims of fickle despots and the abiding ravages of poverty and disease. But America, to which his widowed mama had packed him off to save him from conscription into the army of the czar, was no less fearful.

Arriving wet and unskilled, Nathan had been able to find employment only as a schlepper, lugging piecework from the garment factories west of Broadway to the downtown sweatshops. From those makeshift workplaces in their sweltering tenement parlors, he collected the finished knee pants and wrappers, then, freighted like a wandering cloakroom, humped them back uptown to the jobber, who dispatched him to the department stores on Fourteenth Street. Along the way he got an eyeful of the Golden Land. His route might take him through the Hester Street market, where men in gory aprons sank their cleavers into meat seething with blue fly larvae. Rail-thin women fingered the entrails of hanging fowl to determine their kosherness, haggled with merchants who alternated between deference and poisonous invective. There were streets like Allen, known as "the street of perpetual shadow," lousy with pickpockets and strutting pimps. The whores, naked under their flower kimonos, spit out the husks of sunflower seeds as they beckoned from beneath the tracks of the Second Avenue El. Surviving one gauntlet, Nathan would be plunged into yet another, his progress often stalled behind the funeral cortege of some infant victim of cholera, its casket no larger than a bread box. He dodged the live cats the hoodlums dropped from rooftops, dodged the hoodlums who ran past with the bundles they'd snatched from evicted families shipwrecked on their stoops.

Having previously ventured no farther into the world than the tether of his mother's apron strings (or the thongs of his own phylacteries) would allow, Nathan had been desperate to get off those savage streets. Battling a lifelong timorousness, he'd presented himself as capable of a series of jobs for which he had no qualifications. His presumption had disastrous consequences in the Ludlow Street sweatshop where he dropped an eighteen-pound pressing iron through the floorboards, igniting a conflagration in the pillow-stuffing factory below. He fared no better at Lion's Dairy Restaurant on Delancey, where a bowl slid from his tilted tray to crown a patron with a bilious helmet of steaming lentil soup. Nor had he demonstrated a greater aptitude for rolling cigars or dipping candles or kneading matzo dough. Sacked from every position he held for an incompetence that confirmed his worst fears, Nathan succumbed to a crippling despondency. Had fear not outweighed his desolation, he might have followed the grimy caftan who invited him to audition for a local pickpocketing academy. This was his situation when he ducked out of an afternoon rain shower into the doorway of the *Jewish Daily Forward* in its new ten-story tower on East Broadway and diffidently peeked inside.

Up a flight from the street, the atmosphere was no less tumultuous than the traffic outside around Rutgers Square. Typing machines clacked like artillery, clothespinned messages zinged like raptors along a network of copper wires overhead. Warning valves sounded from the basement beneath the offices where the presses throbbed their prodigious heartbeat. Journalists shuttled up and down the stairs between the newsroom and the linotype shop, their ankles streaming teleprinter tape, while editors debated with rumpled reporters over union issues and the tyranny of Tammany Hall. Nathan stood on the threshold, too transfixed by the chaos to flee, when a tall, bushy-haired gentleman in leather suspenders emerged from an office to hand him a sheaf of handwritten pages.

"Take this, *mach shnel,* to the compositor!"

"What is it?" asked Nathan.

"Holy writ," the man barked, peering muddy-eyed over his spectacles at the former schlepper. "It's newspaper copy, what else?"

"But I don't work here."

The bushy-haired man seemed incapable of grasping the concept. "Then why are you holding my copy?"

Rather than return them, however, Nathan clutched the pages to his chest and answered experimentally, "Because I need a job?" It was the kind of gambit beyond the bounds of one's native reticence that survival in America could drive you to.

The man slid his spectacles up and down the long slope of his nose, taking a measure of the untidy kid. Squirming, Nathan tried with one hand to hoist a gartered sock, with the other to separate a caduceus of tangled curls. "Can you read?" the man asked him at length.

Nathan allowed that he'd done little else all his life.

The man snorted doubtfully but nevertheless offered him a trial run as a proofreader for the Yiddish daily. He was given a stool at a cubby-holed desk in a windowless corner of the vaulted basement. Drum-size rolls of paper stacked in a pyramid separated him from the printing presses, which thrashed and hammered with a sound like busy guillotines. There Nathan did nothing all the ten- to twelve-hour day but compare the pages of live-matter copy to the columns of dummy proof (crude as woodcuts) that were set up for the purpose on a small hand press. Occasionally the copy came in typescript, but more often it would arrive in the careless hand of the authors themselves, some of whom were the most illustrious Yiddish talents of the day. Nathan struggled to decipher their scribblings, to distinguish the spidery cursive of the gentle Abraham Liessin from the tea-stained hieroglyphs of the hotheaded propagandist Zametkin. In this way he played midwife to their rantings about pogroms in Russia, their sermons against graft and in favor of the strikes at Levy's Waist & Cloak; he saw their screeds translated intact from draggled holographs to handsomely mounted editorials and features. Aware that his corrections caused the lead matrices to be reshuffled in their heavy stone chases, Nathan could literally feel the weight of the word, which revived his old reverence for it.

For another the job might have been pure tedium, but Nathan was relieved to be studying Hebrew characters again as he'd done at his yeshiva back in Zitsk; they were soothing, the characters, especially in their bastard or bottle-assed type fonts, their beards, bellies, shoulders, and serifs so much more agreeable than the pinched faces of the fish-wives or the vacant faces of the quarter's wage slaves. True, the printers, compositors, and other proofreaders who inhabited that subterranean element were themselves a peculiar lot, begrimed and irascible, a bandy-legged, eyeshaded fraternity with whom Nathan felt no special kinship. Nor had they bothered to make friendly overtures toward the retiring young apprentice. But so long as his conscientiousness did not exceed the yet-to-be-recognized union standards, Nathan was tolerated, and for his part he was content in his molelike existence. Where others surfaced to take their lunches al fresco across the road in the sunshine of Seward Park, Nathan kept to his desk in the bowels of the *Forward*. There he regarded himself a kind of conduit through which observations on labor inequities, Jewish prodigies, bigamists, and yentas putting on airs reached the community at large. He was cozily ensconced in a place from which others steered the destinies and arbitrated the tastes of the ghetto. Though he seldom saw the actual authors—those penurious firebrands in their cheap waterproofs—their proximity in the editorial offices above made him feel privy to the East Side's most vital concerns. Having been brave enough to convince his employers that he was worthy of the position, Nathan relaxed in the feeling that he need never be brave again.

Then, too, his salary of four dollars and fifty cents a week was a substantial rise from the mingy wages he'd earned humping piecework. It enabled him to move out of the Moskowitz family flat on Rivington Street, where he'd slept at night on the same time-shared cot that Ellenbogen the watchman with his crab lice slept on by day.

Primitive as were his new digs—the bedbugs festered, the rafters groaned, the water closet was in a hallway two flights down—Nathan's attic room was his lofty retreat. He savored the privacy just as he'd come to savor the lockstep ritual of his days. There was a comfortable rhythm in their monotony: the long, cacophonous hours at the *Forward* followed by the short walk home, stopping at a vendor's for a liver knish or some dried herring and black bread, which he carried back to his attic in a grease-stained paper bag. Sometimes he might take a solitary bowl of barley soup at Maisel's Cafeteria on Division Street, where the fish-faced violinist serenading the tables kept him from lingering. Though it could be close to the point of unbreathable in Nathan's attic, the recent cold weather had dispelled the stuffiness, and each evening, upon returning, he padded the seat of the ladder-backed chair with his pillow and read by oil lamp at the scored deal table until his eyes began to close.

Sometimes he asked himself how a person could read all day only to come home and pursue more of the same at night, but Nathan had always been fond of the printed word. Never a gifted scholar, he'd been a dogged and assiduous one back in the moss-grown Zitsk yeshiva—where the symmetry of a page of Scripture, neatly distilling a disorderly world into black and white, tended to ease rather than irritate the eyes. Indeed, his affection for the word had always taken precedence over any interest he might have had in the flesh and the mischief it was heir to. Of course, the words with which Nathan had been most intimate were the arid legal texts of Talmud, whose connection to revelation was too distant to muddy the prose. Only lately had he contracted a yen for stories.

Not that Talmud wasn't replete with *aggadot,* with tales, but the young scholar had always shied away from them. Desire and fear, which seemed to constitute the bulk of human experience, were subjects too ambiguous to be described with any accuracy; they were changeable, elusive, resistant to language, unlike the more abstract considerations of the Law. Only since Nathan had taken shelter from the East Side schlepper's colony at his corner desk at the Yiddish paper had stories begun to hold for him any appeal. At first they were merely a change of pace from articles detailing proper etiquette and hygiene, or the endless attacks on sweatshop managers and tenement conditions. Then the occasional piece of narrative fiction—mostly slice-of-life chronicles rendered in the no-nonsense prose preferred by the editor in chief, Abe Cahan—would provide some distraction for the proofreader, who developed a taste for them.

They objectified the ghetto, those stories, extracting pity and drama from its apparent pandemonium, and, himself an East Side citizen in good standing, Nathan found that he sympathized with their subjects. Wasn't he, too, a type of *kleine menschele* as portrayed in the serial offerings of social realists such as Zalman Libin and Leon Kobrin? The characters in their stories were the unredeemed products of their sordid environment, their lives as narrowly circumscribed as Nathan's own. But while he might take solace in their grim predictability, Nathan also wondered why the protagonists of these stories (in which, theoretically, anything might happen) could not realize other possibilities. Why couldn't they achieve fates unavailable to their counterparts in the world? Though exactly what fates or possibilities Nathan meant, he couldn't have said. But why was it that, where the affluent Yankees peddled escapism on every newsstand, the ghetto Jews could only look at the hopelessness of their own circumstance?

Such fanciful thinking was a novel exercise for Nathan Hart, a function no doubt of his newfound security, but in some way it threatened that security as well. Change was not a thing he would have welcomed.

Still, he continued to read secular stories with the same concentration he'd once applied to sacred texts, having all but lost his sense of the distinction between the two. Lately, however, impatient with the claustrophobia of the lives depicted in the feuilletons, Nathan had turned for amusement to the more frivolous *shundromans*. He took a guilty pleasure in reading the sort of blood-and-thunder romances found in the popular tales of Shomer-Shaikevitch and Isaac Meir Dik, or the melodramas of Paul de Kock and Eugene Sue in their Yiddish translations. They were bupkes, of course, women's entertainments, their preposterous plots not so different from the kind of stories he'd had with his mother's milk; because his mama Froika Sara—"Froika the Troika" as she was called for her hardiness in the face of an impoverished widowhood—had herself been an intemperate teller of tales.

As a child, Nathan had rejected her stories wholesale. All those ghosts, homunculi, and wandering souls—they frightened him, multiplying the fears that were already so abundant in the Russian Pale. But recently, as Nathan's appetite for stories had increased, those distant *bubbeh maysehs* of his mother's again invaded his memory. Where had she acquired so many stories? Froika Sara herself always credited the source as Nathan's father, Reb Jakob Hart, whose grisly death she'd also converted into a tall tale: He had been a Hasid, Nathan's papa, a follower of the Medzibozher Rebbe and proprietor of a hole-in-the-wall general merchandise, murdered (while his son was yet unborn) by an angry mob for the crime of making a living. They'd slit him open, according to his wife, who was profligate in her descriptions, like "a *dershtekener chazzer*," a stuck pig. Fanatically pious, Reb Jakob had endeavored to die in a state of grace, taking hold of his spilled intestines to bind himself with them as with tefillin in a final prayer.

Froika Sara told the tale with a verve that carried it beyond plausibility into the realm of myth; but even so, even though he hadn't known the man, Nathan could never contemplate his father's end without being gripped by nausea and dread. Of late, however, he'd begun to appreciate the story precisely for its legendary quality and for the way he himself was distinguished by it. The fatherless Nathan Hart, as he saw it (through an uncharacteristically romantic lens), was the offspring of a union between legend and flesh and blood. Half a fiction himself, he was all the better suited for the company he kept with the figments of invented stories. They were the only society Nathan needed—though if ever he felt nostalgia for the community of the living, he might take in a Yiddish play.

This was his intention on the first Shabbos evening after his encounter with the redheaded shopgirl, who he had to admit had disturbed his peace. She had infected his brain with heretical notions, one of which was that, for the time being, he'd had enough of other people's stories. Even Nathan, it seemed, had limits to his tolerance. Putting down a novel of Marie Barbieri's full of duels and illicit love, he donned his knit jacket and plush cap and left the Cherry Street garret in a whistling wind. Steering clear of the clamorous dancing academies, the cafés and corner candy stores, places where East Siders traditionally sought their own kind, he headed north toward Second Avenue, which had recently come to replace the Bowery as the new Yiddish Rialto. His feet grown quickly numb from the cold, Nathan stopped at the first theater he came to: a chalk-white Greek revival affair formerly called the National but now the Tomashevsky in honor of its resident star. He bought a ticket for the second balcony, which was slightly pricier than the third, but the third balcony—the schnorrers' gallery—was too flyblown a place even for Nathan. The play, an operetta entitled *Rabbi Akiva and His Twenty-four Thousand Disciples*, starring Boris Tomashevsky (self-proclaimed "America's darling"), was already in progress, and Nathan realized he'd seen it before. In it the beefy leading man, in yellow tights that made his legs look like overstuffed wurst beneath his velvet robe, plays a Talmud sage who falls madly in love with a Gypsy girl.

This was a type of play commonly referred to as *shund,* or trash, by the playgoing public, who ate it up. Until the recent death of the earnest playwright Jacob Gordin, the Yiddish stage had enjoyed a so-called golden age; the fare had been largely *tseytbilder,* problem pieces drawn from life, depicting generational conflicts, political injustices, and so forth. But with Gordin's demise, the theaters, like the Jews at Sinai when Moses turned his back, had reverted to *shund.* They brought back the light operettas of Avrom Goldfadn, the hand-wringing *volkstuche* dramas of "Professors" Hurwitz and Lateiner. Instead of socially engaged studies of forsaken parents and conscience-stricken revolutionaries, the stage was made safe again for humbug. Jewish princes, biblical heroines, and mad sages decked out in garish costumes paraded across the boards in an utter disregard for historical fidelity; outlandish plots were resolved by multiple suicides or when brothers and sisters, estranged since birth, were deterred at the last minute from unholy marriages. Having arrived in New York in the wake of Gordin's passing, Nathan knew of the more sophisticated repertoire only by hearsay and so never missed it.

But the theater, it occurred to him, was perhaps an unlikely place to seek respite from a surfeit of stories. Ordinarily the spectacle, in striking contrast to his humdrum seclusion, would have held him spellbound, but tonight, despite the lavishness of the production, the size of the cast (which included a Roman cavalry on horseback), and the din of the orchestra, Nathan's mind was elsewhere. At intermission the gasoliers came up on the dusty filigree and the hall was instantly transformed into a brash forum of free enterprise. Vendors moved among the crowd hawking everything from seltzer to chickpeas and Eskimo Pies, while Nathan's eyes wandered over the whole obstreperous scene. From the second balcony, he surveyed the broad horseshoe of the first, scanning the multitude of off-duty seamstresses and shopkeepers, the disciples of various stars arguing with their detractors, the swank gentile curiosity seekers from uptown. Then his eyes lit on a circle of young men and women standing and reclining near the rail of the first balcony. The men, mostly beardless, wore the standard one-button cutaways that identified them as ghetto bohemians—artists and radicals, possibly even sometime contributors to the *Forward*. They belonged to the tribe that congregated in the Canal Street *kibitzarnias* gesticulating over glasses of tea, living on air or remittances from families in Europe, on the odd tutorial and fees from occasional essays or cartoons. They came to the theater, thought Nathan, to sneer at the plebeian gaucherie of it all, and he resented that the ladies seemed actually to admire their arrogance. He especially resented that among the ladies in their party was the flame-haired girl from the Orchard Street gents'-furnishings shop in her oval spectacles. Nathan realized that he'd been searching for her all along.

Seated, she was munching fried chickpeas from a paper twist in her lap and laughing appreciatively at the men's remarks, obviously more in her element than she had been in the haberdashery. There were a couple of other young ladies in their company, one a dark beauty in a tailored suit who sat among them in imperial tranquillity. But it was clear to Nathan, even from such a distance, that while they deferred to the sphinxlike beauty and her plainer companion, it was toward the shopgirl (toward Keni—wasn't that what Mrs. Pishkin had called her?) that they aimed their conversational sallies. Thinking he could hear her throaty laughter, Nathan recalled that it was she who'd kept him from sleep and cost him his appetite these past few days; although, for the feelings she inspired in him, he was still unable to find a name.

The curtain reopened, but despite the arresting stage effects (an electrical storm over the ruins of the Jerusalem Temple, a balalaika announcing a spooky Pepper's ghost) and the booming oratorios of the leading man, Nathan was practically unaware of the final act. At the close of the play, bobbing in the current of the exiting crowd, he was swept down into the street below; then, on second thought, he about-faced and fought his way back upstream to look for the girl, but she and her companions must have left the theater before him. He straggled along a windy Second Avenue, gazing through the plate-glass windows of several cafés in the hope of seeing her. The Cafe Royale was already filling with theater people, the players making grand entrances in their jewels and feather aigrettes, their fur-trimmed capes, trailing trains of doting sycophants; but farther along in the slightly less populous Metropole, under an elephant's ear at a marble-topped table from which a roving fiddler had just departed, there she was. She was smoking a roan cigarette, sipping tea, tilting her head pertly from left to right as she listened to the men holding forth. Occasionally she contributed some remark of her own, and there was laughter.

Watching her through the steamy window, Nathan felt a knocking in his chest, his heart like a prisoner banging his head against the wall of his cell. It was not a pleasant sensation, and, wondering how to relieve it, he toyed a moment with the idea of going inside. Only later, when he'd turned and redirected his steps toward Cherry Street, when he'd slogged up the stairs to his attic and plunked himself down at the table, was Nathan able to assign a name to the sensation the girl had evoked in him. It was loneliness.

He took up his fountain pen, glass filler, and a four-ounce bottle of ink from the drawer under the table and prepared to compose a letter to

his mama, an undertaking he'd always relied on to calm himself down.
Into these letters, which generally rehearsed the invariable routine of his
days, Nathan would sometimes insert a flourish. Now and then he concocted some innocuous fib to spice up the sameness of his reports—a
sighting of the celebrated author Sholom Aleichem in the *Forward* newsroom, say, or an excursion by ferryboat to Coney Island, which he'd yet
to visit. Then he would wonder what had compelled him to describe, almost involuntarily, such unfounded events. It was for the sake of amusing his mother and his two unmarried sisters, he decided; they should
get some enjoyment when the letters were read to them by the village
scribe. They should have some idea of the great adventure that was
America. But tonight he felt he'd been kidding himself all along, that the
embellishments were for no other purpose than exalting their son and
brother.

Did this mean he was dissatisfied? He hadn't thought so, though tonight something coaxed Nathan toward an extremity of invention he'd
never permitted himself before. As he wrote on his stack of thick octavo
pages (specially designed, according to the stationer, for foreign corre-
spondence), he started to take liberties with his own experience, liberties
that ultimately departed from that experience altogether; he assumed a
voice that ceased to resemble his own. The substance of the letter, if you
could call it a letter, seemed to Nathan as if dictated by a source exclusive
of himself. From his mother's fuddled tales, he was familiar with dybbuks,
the dispossessed spirits that occupied the bodies and minds of mortals;
he knew also about the *ibbur*, which took over your soul, enabling you to
accomplish feats of comprehension and originality far beyond your ordinary powers. But Nathan was not superstitious. He thought he understood what was happening—that, after so long a period of consuming
the stories of others, he had finally begun to write one of his own.

It began, after a formal greeting that degenerated into trivial references to weather and work, like this: *My son, Nachman, as you know, was
reared in paradise. I left him there, or rather here, to be brought up by his
dead mother, the laughing Hannaleh, who was murdered and worse by
Khmelnitzki's butchers in 1649. This was in the market town of Zitsk along
the pea green river Styr in what was then the Polish Ukraine. That's when I
decided the earth was no place to raise a kid, so I snatched him up and*

*made my way back to the Celestial Academy where Hannah was waiting. It
was some dreadful journey even then, I can tell you, though in those days
my wings were in better shape, and the distance, if I'm not mistaken, wasn't
quite as far. Of course I couldn't stay, nor did I feel especially welcome; I
guess I'd picked up too many bad habits down below. Saying so long to
Hannah and heaven a second time, I left for the world again, arriving near
the end of the nineteenth century on the Lower East Side of New York.
There, in reduced circumstances, I was eventually reunited with my son,
who, like his father in his own youth, had grown restless in the kingdom of
the blessed. . . .*

When he paused, Nathan looked at what he'd scribbled as if he had
just discovered it there on the page, rather than penned it himself. This
was not the sort of thing he did. Stories were written by uncommon
men, by visionaries if you will, or at the very least by the unwashed East
Side "intelligents," who leaped into the fires in their brains with, so to
speak, both feet—not by lowly proofreaders with a morbid fear of experience. Experience was the raw material of fiction, and Nathan had had
so little of it, nothing that he believed would translate readily into stories.
He had for his fuel only secondhand stories, though he couldn't recall
ever having read the one he found himself writing now.

What followed was the winter of Nathan Hart's perfect contentment. He
continued scrupulously performing his tasks throughout the long hours
of his six-day week at the Yiddish daily. After work he rested his eyes over
the barley soup at Maisel's Cafeteria, beneath the pearl gray surface of
which he might spy—his imaginative faculty working overtime—sunken
vessels. Then he returned to Cherry Street, boiled some water on the stove
for tea, and sat down at his table to confront the growing manuscript. The
rag-woven pile of pages, scrawled over in Nathan's crabbed hand with a
steel-nibbed pen, had begun to acquire the density of a novel, though he
was reluctant to call them such. It was a story pure and simple, and for
all his after-hours fatigue, once he began to write, the thing assumed a
momentum of its own. He would enter the narrative like someone entering an unfamiliar street that beckoned him to follow to its end, at first
proceeding with care, until his fascination with the curious turns of the
story began to carry him forward almost automatically. Then he wrote

with an increasing dauntlessness, holding his pen the way he imagined a boy on skates might hang on to the back of a careering milk wagon.

Outside, the winter of 1911 was bitter. Blizzards occurred with such frequency that no sooner had the neighborhood dug itself out from under one than it was deluged by yet another. The trolleys were mired in their tracks; washing left on the line would freeze and shatter in the wind like sheets of glass. Cops were stationed on corners by day to rub the ears of passersby, and at night the quarter, under its frigid blanket, was as hushed as the potter's field behind City Hall where the bums were buried three to a grave. Ice hung in walrus tusks from fire escapes and telephone wires, from the ceilings of basements where the pipes had burst; chimneys belched smoke like the mills of Gehenna, mantling the snow in black ashes, but Nathan's mood remained positively vernal. The hero of his story was irrepressible, himself a teller of tales, whose own tale was told by his father, a fallen angel. Mocky, the angel was called, which means "plague"; for at the time of the story, he'd fallen very far—Mocky narrated the history of his only son Nachman, his child by a mortal woman, who emigrates from paradise (where his slain mother has secretly raised him) to New York, America. There he becomes enamored of a star of the Yiddish stage known as Sophie the Red for her billowing crimson hair.

It was an eccentric and convoluted yarn, and while he eagerly looked forward to describing his hero Nachman's exploits, Nathan had yet to advance his narrative beyond the frame in which the angel's own story is revealed. Still, so long as the tale remained fresh and the writing fluid (and it always did), his exhilaration persisted; it endured through the whole of January and February and on into the blustering early weeks of March. But toward the end of March, as if in apology for so ferocious a season, the weather turned abruptly mild and springlike. Accustomed to coming and going in darkness, to spending his days belowground, Nathan now had the primrose sunlight to contend with on his walk to and from the paper; and while scarcely a blossom or blade of grass sprouted on the whole of the Lower East Side, the proofreader nevertheless had a sense of growing things. An ozone fragrance pervaded the streets, breezes overwhelming the less bracing odors released from under the melting snow. There were birdcalls over the roofs of Cherry Street and from the scraggly elms that bordered Seward Park, where the dissolving slush generated a morning fog through which the dawn broke like the yolk of a copper egg. And after work there was often a soft evening rain.

Nathan had never paid much attention to the changing seasons, so early had he been weaned from the world and bound over to the Word. The fields around Zitsk might run riot with marigolds, poppies, and sunflowers, while Nathan and the other cheder boys bent over their books, clinging to them like rafts in choppy water. "Nature is for the goyim," their gamy-breathed old *melammed* had admonished them, thumping with his thimbled finger any head that dared look up from its volume of Commentary. And even though Nathan had since made the transition from holy to profane texts, he had applied himself no less intently. Then he'd begun to claim words for his own, words plucked from the recesses of his unexplored interior, spiriting them into an expanding manuscript that grew fat on the contraband. But now it seemed to Nathan that the blotted letters of his Yiddish longhand refused to stay fixed to the page, that they detached themselves and beat about his head like furious birds; they darted at the casement window, jarring it open, escaping even as they admitted the bright world into Nathan's room.

As a result his concentration wavered and he was hobbled in the progress of his story. While the bleak months had kept his fancies safely confined to his garret, where he hunkered over his table in earmuffs and fingerless gloves, the advent of the sun subverted his thoughts. Nathan lost the sense of riding the flying coattails of his story and now felt he must drag the whole corpus forward by main force. It was work for which he suddenly lacked the heart. The months of fervid composition and little sleep, coupled with endless hours at the paper, had finally caught up with him. In his shaving mirror, his half-open eyes were bloodshot and the bones above his hollow cheeks gave his face the spectral shape of a bicycle seat. His frame was gaunt, his color ashen, and a deep weariness enveloped him like a cloak of lead. Still, Nathan felt he couldn't relax until he'd goaded his story toward some tentative conclusion.

He tried to take courage from the thought of the ghetto scribes whose ranks he had recently joined—men who lived on obsession and frayed nerve endings, their filament-thin bodies, often tuburcular, fastened to sewing machines or hampered with buckets and ladders, while their imaginations soared aloft. But their energy was evidently not contagious.

Nathan was stalled, and in the absence of an ability to move forward, he decided it was time to look back, having never before found occasion to read over what he'd written. He'd assumed that the pages he'd composed in a fever were as vital as the irresistible passion (his first) that had inspired them, but when he began to read the manuscript, he was mortally disappointed. The tale that had consumed his heart and soul in the telling seemed to lack both: the language, flat and unconvincing, was often as clumsy as the naïve appeals of the greenhorns in the "Bintl Brief" column of the *Daily Forward*. The voice that had thrilled Nathan to the point of feeling he was possessed, the voice of his hero's father, instead of inviting one to follow the cunning twists of the story, held the reader at an indifferent remove.

Sick with misgivings, Nathan spent a sleepless night and was barely fit for reading proof the next day. That evening, after toiling through scores of articles on fraternal societies and labor Zionism, tired as he was, Nathan was reluctant to return to his room. He was far from alone in this attitude, for, after so many inclement months, the warmer weather had enticed the whole quarter out of doors. Vendors and strollers glutted the streets; mountebanks, soapbox orators, and sausage-curled Hasidim waltzing their Torah scrolls through puddles of melted snow lent to the mercantile crush a carnival air. Families were gathered in front of the candy stores licking their hokey-pokeys and sipping soda water; solitary boarders leaned against arc lamps enjoying a private pierogi. Other appetites were also in evidence: pairs of lovers, with nowhere to go, bivouacked beneath a single oil slicker in a doorway or on a stoop, their heat aggravating the general itch. Nathan, who'd managed by and large to elude the itch for over a quarter century, was painfully aware of it now; and as he walked, aimlessly at first, he kept his eyes on his worn-out shoes, which made their way independently of his will (or so he told himself) toward Orchard Street.

He entered Pishkin's Ready-to-Wear with his heart in his throat, feeling as if he'd returned after a long journey, half expecting to be greeted as a prodigal. But the blockish Mrs. Pishkin offered him no such recognition. She was in any case busy totting up figures behind her till, chewing her pencil like a licorice whip, and so called to the back of the shop for assistance. Nathan braced himself beside a display of silk four-in-hands as the curtain parted and the shopgirl came in; but this one—a small, darting, mousy young woman with button eyes—was a stranger.

"Can I help you?" she asked.

Nathan's disappointment was palpable, as keen as when he'd read what he'd since come to think of as his misbegotten manuscript. He wanted to leave the shop, return to his attic, and wallow in longing, but there was a stronger impulse at work than his wish to surrender.

"Pardon me," he said to the assistant, who looked at him blankly, "there was working here the last time I come in another young lady . . ." The assistant continued to stare implacably. ". . . with . . ." Why was it so hard to say it? ". . . red hair."

The assistant only shook her head, but Mrs. Pishkin, overhearing from behind her register, shuffled toward them, scratching the whiskers at her chin.

"Why you want to know?" she asked suspiciously.

Fighting his urge to bolt, Nathan risked a lie. "I am acquainted with . . . Keni, from night school?"

"You paint pictures, too?" wondered Mrs. Pishkin in an accusatory tone that prompted Nathan to shake his head fervently. "*Keni,*" the woman sneered. "My sister, may she rest in peace, she names her daughter Chaineh Freyda, a lovely name, but Keni she calls herself—like an actress, like a *bumerkeh.* You want to know where she is? Gone to the Land of the Redheaded Jews, *a cholyerah.* You see her, tell her stay away, business is good. A wild one, for her to work is a sin. . . ."

Nathan had been backing away by degrees and, having reached the door, turned and made a hasty exit. He picked his way along Orchard, feeling that it was as crucial to find the girl as, months before, it had been so imperative to begin writing his story. Perhaps his fate would be to seek her the rest of his days.

"I am driven by desire," Nathan realized, savoring the phrase. "I am a ridiculous man."

He poked in other shops along Orchard Street and around the corner on Grand, sticking his head among flannelette bloomers and mercerized shirts in case she'd taken another salesclerking job; but her aunt's assessment of her relation to work did not make him hopeful. When the shops began closing, he headed north across Houston and walked up Second

Avenue, looking in the tonier cafés. He saw ghetto personalities seated according to their lights: the actors and their patriots holding court at the center tables spread with goulash, carp in sour sauce, and sparkling wine; the slouch-hatted poets and polemicists scheming behind columns and potted plants with glasses of quince yellow tea. But no *vildeh moid,* no Keni—Nathan exulted in the playfulness of her name.

For the next two or three nights, he continued making his rounds of the cafés, wine cellars, and dairy restaurants. He was living for the search, performing his tasks at the *Forward* with a mechanical mindlessness. Comparing the raw copy to the uncorrected proofs, Nathan may as well have been comparing grades of meat, so little did he care for the sense of what he read. He bided his time at his basement desk until the hour arrived when he could recommence his tour of public watering holes, looking for the source of his inspiration. Then came a night when, doubling back along East Broadway after having once again abandoned the quest, he happened to glance through the window of Glickman's Odessa Tearoom and saw her there; but so accustomed had he become to the false alarms of his senses that he continued several paces past Glickman's before retracing his steps. It was her—the only woman among a trio of local intelligents seated near the tea wagon with its eagle-crowned samovar. Two of the men were young, the other not so, and the older man (perhaps in his late thirties), who was regaling the rest, had an arm draped proprietarily over the back of Keni's chair. Nathan had expected to feel relief if not triumphant gladness upon finding her, or maybe even a little letdown, but this trembling from jealousy he could not have anticipated.

"She's *my* muse," he asserted under his breath, though he made no move to enter the café.

Nathan had always been shy of the cafés, having only ever peered into their rowdy interiors from the sidewalk, an impartial witness to their conspiracies and heated debates. As spectator he was perfectly comfortable, but to actually enter an East Broadway café was tantamount to stepping onto a stage: one should first have a clear understanding of the part he was about to play. Of course Nathan hadn't a clue as to what he intended, though, on the other hand, did he have any choice in the matter? Besides, it had started to drizzle, and the thought of returning to his attic, of lying alone in bed listening to rain on the shingle roof (once the most soothing of sounds), now seemed even more forbidding than step-ping into a crowded café. He opened the door and made his way through the talkers and kibitzers to occupy the single remaining table. It was situ-ated against the paneled wall beneath a lamp with a ruby dome, sand-wiched between two pairs of chess players and flanked by the table at which the girl sat with her bohemian friends. From that vantage, despite the general din and the kettledrumming in his chest, Nathan could catch whole snatches of the conversation of his neighbors.

"Don't give me no more your so-call Jewish Gothic," the older man was exhorting his companions, in a serviceable if heavily accented English. "Enough already with the characters that from the trees, which they sway like daveners under a sky like a wedding canopy, are all the time hanging themselves with their prayer shawls. Give me authentic—Ibsen, Gorky, Zangwill, ashes and soot. Give me Zola, who I hear they got writing for the *Forward* now he's dead. . . ."

Having cast a cautious eye in his direction, Nathan had to admire the man's brash delivery—to say nothing of the ivory sheen of his polished pate, the emblem of his smudge goatee like a tiny black heart. He noted also how the shopgirl listened to him with an astute tilt of her head: she drew on her cigarette, tilted her head, then swept from her forehead the wisps of hair slipped free of her heavy pompadour.

"The Art Students League, Jakie Epstein and Abie Walkowitz," the man went on, "they got the right idea, a new style idolatry: the Jews should wor-ship now the coal furnace and the Singer sewing machine. Put the Singer in place of the cantor, and I'll return to the synagogue. . . ."

While he envied the man his mordant authority, Nathan couldn't help thinking peevishly: a big noise. "Holy furnace, holy fire escape . . . ," the man was intoning, when the girl, flicking ashes into a plate of strudel crumbs, seemed to give voice to Nathan's thoughts,

"Yanobsky, what a windbag you are!"

There was silence at the table, as Yanobsky leaned toward the fellow on his right to inquire, "Windbag?" "*Ploiderzak,*" translated the liver-lipped fellow, and Yanobsky nodded his head, allowing an appreciative smile to spread across his face. Then he guffawed, which was the cue for the whole table to join him in laughing. Nathan marveled, wondering if, thus deflated, he himself would have had the equanimity to laugh.

A burly waiter in a soiled apron loomed impatiently over his table until Nathan obliged him by ordering a glass of tea. Outside, the rain was coming down harder, in sheets that staggered the broad windowpanes like breaking waves. Nathan turned back toward the girl's table to see that she had abruptly risen, while the others protested her threatened departure. "I need air," she announced, shrugging her shawl over the shoulders of her linen blouse, tinged yellow around the tucks like the tips of her nicotined fingers. "Air?" Yanobsky feigned incredulity. "But you said in here is already plenty wind. Out there it's only water, a second Flood." "They call it rain," she replied, bending swiftly to buss the top of his glistening dome. This left a mark resembling a scarlet butterfly, which Nathan coveted: he imagined throwing a net over Yanobsky's head to claim the butterfly for his own.

He knew that this was an unsound notion, but then what was there that was sensible about sitting in a café spying on a girl who carmined her lips and made public displays of affection? He turned in time to see her sauntering in her snuff walking skirt out the door. Though she wasn't tall, her stride was nevertheless rangy—she sauntered and she carmined her lips. Everything about his situation served to remind Nathan that never had he strayed so far from his own element.

Then he realized he was about to lose her again, but what could he do? The bashful Nathan Hart did not pursue strange women—though it occurred to him he'd done little else these past several nights. Nothing in his life was familiar to him lately. Taking perverse consolation from this fact, he clenched a sugar cube between his teeth and, as if to gather Dutch courage, took a long slurp of the tea that had just arrived; then he scattered some coins on the checkered tablecloth and hastily followed the girl from the café. On his way out, in the spirit of foolhardiness that had recently overtaken him, he snatched an umbrella from an elephant's foot near the door.

She was waiting under the awning in front of Glickman's for perhaps a break in the downpour, then appeared to take Nathan's emergence from the tearoom as her signal to proceed. No sooner had she pulled the shawl over her head and stepped into the rain, however, than the proofreader was beside her, opening the parasol above them both. She turned to him with a look of annoyance that even the shadow they shared couldn't conceal.

"Do I know you?"

"Nathan Hart," he had practically to shout over the rain that was beating a tattoo on the taut fabric—he'd selected, it turned out, a rather good umbrella. "By me you waited one time in Pishkin's Ready-to-Wear."

"Pishkin's," uttered like an execration. "And this makes us bosom companions?"

Again he relished the sandpaper rasp of her voice, how it complemented her silken skin. Her inflection seemed almost a formal refinement of an Old Country brogue, suggesting that she'd been in America a while.

When he remembered it was his turn to respond, he could only declare again stupidly, "I'm Nathan," as if the name might have some conjuring power.

"Very pleased to meet you, I'm sure," she replied without looking his way. "Now get lost."

"And you—*vos hayst* Keni, no?"

That he knew her name seemed only to stoke her irritation. "Like I said, how do you do? Now leave me alone."

She had accelerated her pace so that Nathan had almost to trot to keep up. The habit of fatal resignation was so strong in him that it took a mighty effort to surmount it, to continue matching her stride instead of merely halting to let her pass on. It would have been so easy to let her go. He rummaged about his mind for some way to engage her but could think of nothing, saw only the nuisance he must appear through her eyes. Couldn't she appreciate that he was in the midst of the most impetuous act of his life? When he finally spoke, in the language he still struggled to master, Nathan's own words took him by surprise.

"Can I tell to you a story?"

"No," she snapped, "but you can back into a pitchfork and grab for support a hot stove if you like."

"It's about a *gefallener malech*, a fallen angel."

She had stopped beside a canvas-covered tinker's cart at the corner of Henry and Clinton streets, where a passing motorcar splashed their ankles. They stood, thanks to the umbrella, in a tiny pavilion whose surrounding curtain was rain. "Look," she said, eyes narrowed to minnow slits behind their oval lenses, "what is it you want?"

"I told you, I want—"

"I know, to tell me a story. Are you just a harmless *nudzh,* or are you maybe dangerous? You don't look too dangerous. But can't you take from me the hint I don't want your company?"

Beneath the cowl of her merino shawl, her spectacles glinted with gilded raindrops, the cant of her lips made parentheses in her shaded cheek, and Nathan fought himself to keep from relenting.

"Mocky, the angel is called—you know, like a *makeh,* a plague; that he was a angel from forgetfulness, a whatyoucallit, a midwife of souls."

"I'll give you till I count three before I start to scream."

"It begins when on Canal Street he goes to the theater, this Mocky," words wrestling the tentacle of his tongue in his attempt to secure her interest. "He sees there a play which it's the story of his own *shlumperdik* life—"

"One."

"Makes him to remember, the play, because he didn't for a long time remember he's a angel; *azoi* he remembers how from heaven he fell on account of a mortal lady—this is Hannah that she laughs all the time. By her he has a son that they call him Nachman—"

"Two."

"Was in the market town from Zitsk on the river Styr, which it's then in olden days the Poilisheh Ukraine. But the Cossack Khmelnitzki and his butchers, should be blotted out their name, they did murder and worse by Mocky's Hannaleh. That's when decided, the angel, the *farkokte* earth, it's no place to raise a kid. . . ."

Something was happening as he spoke, the story starting to assume its old momentum, his zeal in the telling overcoming his anxiety. Nathan was excited to have an audience, however hostile, determined that she should hear his narrative, the whole of which he seemed to want to give her all at once. ". . . So he shucks off from him the sheepskin coat and the overblouse and takes then up the baby and spreads his wings which from disuse they are rusty. . . ."

Here she interjected something he didn't catch, and though he was building a head of steam, Nathan paused long enough to ask her to repeat what she'd said.

"I said it's better you should talk in Yiddish."

He could have wept. The realization that she was listening took his breath, made him want to rest upon that laurel and gloat a moment or two, having accomplished this much. But Nathan knew better than to take his progress for granted—he should seize the advantage and consolidate his success; he should summon his composure, which he set about with a squaring of the shoulders, and begin detailing Mocky's arduous return to paradise.

"It was some dreadful journey even then, I can tell you," continuing animatedly in the vernacular, "though in those days his wings were still in good shape, and the distance I don't think was as far. Of course he couldn't stay—"

"Couldn't stay?" She was puzzled but engaged.

"In heaven. He couldn't stay in heaven, nor did he feel especially welcome there. It seemed that he'd picked up too many bad habits down below. So, unable to readapt, he said good-bye to Hannah and the hereafter for a second time and departed—"

But before Nathan could advance Mocky the two and a half centuries it would take him to get back to the world, Keni interrupted again. "Tell me more about heaven."

They'd resumed walking, having leaped together from the curb over a coursing gutter to cross the street, heading in the general direction of the river. Amazed to find himself no longer in such a hurry, Nathan was pleased to accommodate the girl, backtracking as far as the angel's apprenticeship. "In his youth he would eavesdrop on the yarn-spinning minyans of the mortal dead (which were off-limits to cherubim), under the boughs of the Etz Chayim, the Tree of Life. There they entertained each other with endless tales of earthly heroes in amorous and martial entanglements. So intrigued was he by them, how could he know, the inexperienced Mocky—who was called Simcha then, which meant "happy" in heaven long before it meant "pander" on the Lower East Side—how was Mocky supposed to know that the stories were lies? Anyway"—Nathan had a sudden vision of a dry wooden booth in a cake-and-coffee parlor—"would you care for a glass of tea?"

The girl replied as if affronted, "I had already a glass tea. Tell me more. I'm confused how the angel met his wife."

Having modulated his voice along with the slackening rain, Nathan began describing Mocky's fall from grace: how he'd taken up with a mortal woman named Hannah Hinde Mindl's, whom he'd spotted while attending a birth in the breadbasket countryside on the border between Poland and Russia. "His task was to give the traditional fillip under the nose of newborn infants, which caused them to forget the wisdom they brought with them out of the womb. The idea was that a knowledge of paradise would make life on earth unbearable. . . ."

As they walked, Nathan had fleeting intimations of self-consciousness, when he saw himself as he imagined others also might: a young man with a girl strolling iridescent cobbles in the rain, the two of them oblivious to all but each other. Attentive, Keni had allowed the shawl to slip from her head, revealing her tousled hair and sharp-nosed profile, the gentle, horn-buttoned swell of her breast. Occasionally she tilted her head as she'd done while indulging Yanobsky in the café, sweeping the loose strands of hair from her damp forehead. It was a gesture so poignant that Nathan, watching out the corner of an eye, felt his throat constrict and had to clear it in order to proceed.

"So Mocky's presiding at the nativity of some shrill little *pisher* in the market town of Zitsk, when he sees her among the women assisting the midwife. . . ." She smiled—he'd made Keni smile—at his description of how Mocky was as attracted to Hannah's sweet disposition as to her bobbling *tsitske*s and sandy braid. "Fresh from the Garden, still mantled in an aura of more or less sanctity, he was as much drawn to virtue as sin."

"I couldn't tell you when was the turning point," Nathan was saying, while noting landmarks—a bill-plastered hoarding, a greengrocer's shop, a hydrocephalic child—that put them in the vicinity of Cherry Street, "when was the exact instant he realized he wasn't going back, but after some days of hanging around in hopes of catching a glimpse of her, his physicality had begun to assert itself. You see, if your mission on earth wasn't completed within a specified number of days, not only did you run the risk of being seen, but you were in danger of succumbing to the duality of mortals; they could infect you with virulent symptoms of gender. . . ."

Keni patted her mouth to stifle a yawn, and Nathan edited himself on the spot. "All of a sudden, he knew it was too late to retreat. He ate a she-goat's spleen and drank water leeches marinated in pickle brine, proven prescriptions for hastening the end of transparency, then daubed his still-immaterial parts with river mud. He swapped his glorious raiment for some sensible bast boots, a pair of moleskin trousers, and a turf-thick sheepskin coat. The coat hid his folded wings, giving him a somewhat crookbacked demeanor, but he thought himself otherwise quite appealing. He was fascinated by the novelty of being corporeal, not to say distinctly male, and took every opportunity to spy on his own reflection. In windows and barbers' basins, he paused to admire his auger-sharp eyes and dark forelock. And whenever convenient he stole a peek (forgive me) inside his pants—"

Keni laughed a discordant though nonetheless musical laugh, and Nathan, feeling never so intrepid, struggled to keep from yielding to its contagion. In his suppressed joviality, he realized that the rain had abated—who knew how long ago? He made a little show of folding the umbrella and handing it gallantly to the girl.

"A gift."

She inspected the partridgewood handle with its dented silver cap. "This belongs to Yanobsky," she said in alarm, and came to a full stop.

They were at the intersection of Rutgers and Cherry streets, within sight of Nathan's humble address, which he pointed out in the hope of distracting her. "I live in the attic of that house opposite the blacksmith," he submitted, indicating the skinny clapboard structure elbowed by tenements on either side. Above it the moon shone through a weft of parting clouds like a dirty penny. The familiarity of the street was somehow disorienting after heaven and the Ukrainian steppes, though Nathan wondered if he'd been steering them toward this destination all along.

Recalled to herself, Keni peered at him as if he'd made a rude suggestion. "What am I doing here?" she asked of a flickering gas lamp, then stated her intention to go.

"But"—Nathan was furious with himself for having waked her from the dream of his devising—"I only just begun."

"Another time," she said vaguely, turning her head this way and that as if to get her bearings.

"When?" asked Nathan, trying to contain his apprehension.

Her wandering gaze came back to light on the proofreader, giving him a wistful once-over, mouth tipped to one side like a boat riding a swell. Under her scrutiny Nathan shrank accordingly, the spellbinder reduced to a gawky immigrant in an out-at-elbows cardigan. "When the Messiah has finished tarrying," came her breezy reply, and, flinging the shawl back over her head, she sauntered away.

Disturbed as her departure had left him, Nathan could still take pride (couldn't he?) in what he had done. He'd made a frankly heroic if not wholly successful effort at captivating a woman. "*Dayenu!*" he said aloud on returning to his attic; it was enough that he'd made the attempt, and if he never set eyes on Keni again, he was nonetheless a changed man.

Physically spent from their encounter, however, Nathan was unable to shake the jittery excitement that kept him from sleep. Nor did that excitement diminish over the next few days, hampering his concentration at work. Word came down from an editor via a swivel-eyed compositor that Abe Cahan's own exposé of white slavery had appeared in the paper riddled with errors, and Nathan's colleagues, gloating over the lapse of Mr. Diligence, eyed him accusingly. But the proofreader was unusually cavalier with respect to his job, reasoning that if he were sacked, he could live out his term on pure inspiration. Because the story—it had a title now; he called it "The Angel of Forgetfulness"—was alive and kicking again, and where before he'd accommodated them only after hours, Nathan now entertained the exploits of Mocky and son during the day at his basement desk.

Which is not to say that he was adding much heft to the stack of pages on the deal table in his Cherry Street flat; that manuscript he already considered a corpse awaiting burial. Instead he was content to sit meditatively projecting the course of his saga, pursuing in his mind the further adventures of the greenhorn Nachman, as related by his inglorious fallen father. He envisioned scenes that had till now refused to come clear: as for instance the one where Nachman, terrorized by events subsequent to his coming from paradise to the Lower East Side, takes refuge in a disreputable Yiddish music hall. There he first sets eyes on the saucy female principal Sofia der Royte, with whom he falls deeply in love. To get close to her, he contrives to insinuate himself into the motley theatrical company she belongs to. Having endured their ritual hazing, he regales the company with the tales he's overheard about earth in the storytelling minyans of the Celestial Academy. Charmed despite their natural cynicism, the Canal Street troupe overnight patches together a play about a fallen angel, debuting Nachman Opgekumener (his own chosen stage name, meaning "the one who came down") playing opposite their resident star Sophie the Red. . . .

In imagining his story, Nathan felt he was more than himself; he was larger than his mother's son Nathan Hart, nebbish functionary of the *Jewish Daily Forward*. But even in the midst of an exuberance that seemed inexhaustible, he realized it was time he took up his pen again, though when he tried to apply himself to the act of writing, Nathan soon lost the impetus. His spiky script lacked the suppleness of the spoken word, especially as communicated to the variable young woman known as Keni; he missed the inducement of her proximity, the urgency of choosing the phrase that would hold her entranced.

An ache set in along with Nathan's distinct conviction that the story lacked validity unless the girl were there to hear it. So why shouldn't he simply go out and look for her? He knew the cafés she frequented; he could wait for her again on the sidewalk and, if she left alone, step up beside her and resume the tale. But as "The Angel of Forgetfulness" began to recede once more into mirage, so did the courage Nathan had rallied on the night of their encounter. For all the impassioned imagining their meeting had sparked in him, he could not now imagine confronting her again. In his attic he fanned the pages of his books as if strumming an instrument he had no interest in playing, while his mind kept on recollecting his walk with Keni. He remembered how she'd laughed at the tale's spicier episodes, and asked himself had it really been he, the shy former Talmud *bocher,* who'd recited them. That he'd been guilty of *loshen hora,* a wicked tongue, seemed trifling to Nathan, who thought he would give his soul without regret to make her laugh again.

Once or twice, in his craving to see her, he imagined a knock at the door and pictured himself opening it to her brassy countenance. Then he told himself he must not play such cruel tricks on himself as to wait for a knock that would never come. He put the notion out of his head so thoroughly that when it came, a peremptory staccato rapping as of a landlord or a cop, he assured himself he must be hearing things; no one ever came to his room. It was only when he heard her scratchy voice calling, "Mock . . . that is, Nathan—whatever your name is, let me in!" that he lurched for the door.

She swept past him over the threshold, after which, pulling up his suspender straps and buttoning his collar, Nathan uttered a belated "Come in." She was wearing the faded old rose shirtwaist and black merino shawl that were the standard uniform of East Side girls, though on Keni they acquired a somewhat Gypsy air. Taking her stance beside the table with hands on hips, her elbows stretching the shawl like porous wings, she looked angry, though whether with herself or with Nathan, he couldn't tell. He marveled at the way her breathing presence made his attic, which had never before received a visitor, shrink in size while increasing in wretchedness. He was painfully conscious of the cabbage stench, the clothes hanging like lynching victims above an unmade bed, the rats skittering behind the water-stained walls.

"What happens when they get married, the angel and Hanneleh?" she demanded to know.

Finding his tongue after a few false starts, he invited her to sit in the single chair in the room. This she conceded to do, meeting his stare all the while with a fierce expectation. She took her eyes off him only to tug at the drawstring of her suede reticule, bringing out a box of Sobranies and some lucifer matches. She lit a cigarette, inhaled, and, throwing back her head to release an arabesque of smoke, inquired of her still-motionless host, "So *nu?*"

Nathan thought to take the enamel basin from under the pitcher atop his weathered washstand and offer it to her for an ashtray. Her brow furrowed when, shoving the manuscript gracelessly aside, he placed the basin in front of her as if he'd fetched her a pan to be sick in. Then came the problem of what to do with himself. Briefly Nathan sat down on the iron bed, whose springs groaned agonizingly, and realized that the girl would have to crane her neck to see him. He stood up again, bumping his head against the low-pitched rafters, after which he feared he might actually weep. Finally he slid his backside onto the dome cover of the extinguished stove, which he straddled, his stockinged feet dangling to either side. He wanted to ask her so many questions (as for starters, what was her surname?), to express his gratitude for her return, but he knew that would somehow violate the terms of their acquaintance. Instead, with his hands tucked under his armpits to keep them from darting like sparrows, Nathan began to recount Mocky's courtship of Hannah, and no sooner had he begun than he was again under his own story's spell.

"After the nuptial feast, they led the bride and groom into the moldy festival booth behind her family's hovel. This was the ramshackle structure that was supposed to pass for both their honeymoon nest and newlywed dacha, where Mocky revealed to his wife his identity as a lapsed seraph. What choice did he have? It was either make a clean breast of things or let her believe, like everyone else, that his ill-fitting ritual garment concealed a deformity. Besides, although they'd become a needless encumbrance through long disuse, he was still rather proud of his wings; while his bride, for whom his buck-nakedness was a fresh revelation, reacted with typical mirth. She seemed to think that his downy pinions were another feature of the male anatomy for which her mother had failed to properly prepare her. When Mocky tried to explain that he was not a man at all but a member of an angelic order, she left off her tittering long enough to assure him, 'Nobody's perfect.'"

Keni, smiling, flashed teeth she'd apparently ground to the size of seed pearls. Touched by the imperfection, Nathan stumbled in his telling, hesitating long enough to remember that she was his guest. If he lit the stove, he could make her a pot of tea, a tedious process that would leave the attic hot as a steambath and himself nowhere to sit, or he could offer her the boolkie and herring he'd saved for tomorrow's lunch.

"Can I get you something?" he asked, and saw from the sudden curtailing of her smile that it was a mistake, always a mistake, to interrupt the story.

She shrugged. "Some schnapps?"

Alas, he had none, so she accepted a glass of turbid water from the cracked porcelain pitcher. She drank it down in one gulp, lit another cigarette, and asked what he was waiting for. Made dizzy by the smoke accumulating in his stuffy garret, Nathan experienced a momentary pang of obstinacy, almost of rebellion: who was *she* to be pushy? Then he continued describing Mocky's hymeneal rites.

"If anything, after she'd shrugged off the samite gown to rock him in her ample bosom, Hannah's hilarity increased; it reached a disturbing pitch when . . ." Nathan hesitated: for Hannah's father, Reb Berel Groysfuss, was a tanner, and exposure to his labors had left her entire family half embalmed, as a consequence of which . . . the detail was too juicy to exclude: ". . . when the angel, himself a virgin, punctured the somewhat leathery membrane of her maidenhood."

Keni laughed, and, thrilled by his own audacity, Nathan thought, So long, my soul. He shivered at the realization of how alone they were. As she sat smoking beside the sooty vapor lamp, her hair an ocher radiance in its glow, she could have been a creature born from its flame; he felt he'd conjured her in the same way that he'd conjured the story—which he must not stop telling again lest she vanish. But would she really vanish?

"So," he proceeded, slipping just this side of inadvertently into a first-person narrative voice. "Not so many months later, Hannah further assured me that for an angel I made a perfectly functional man and informed me that I was going to be a papa."

Keni pressed her hands together in a spontaneous gesture of pleasure, while Nathan paused to enjoy the sight.

"Why do you stop?" she wondered impatiently.

He pulled a face to ask himself the same question, then submitted, in English: "Because I want with you to make a *metsieh*, a bargain." Surely a devil had entered him.

Her brow clouded, and Nathan hugged his ribs a little harder but did not relent. "What bargain?" she practically snarled. "I'm here to be by you amused, not to be bargained with." Nathan felt the old quailing instinct start up in his gut, but something else was at work. Now that he'd drawn her into his story, they were together, he and Keni, in a story of their own, wherein, as in the tale he was telling, anything could happen. Here, it seemed, the limitations of the past no longer held sway, and rather than frightened—why should he be frightened?—Nathan felt free.

"More I would tell you," he said, "if you will take off from your nose the spectacles."

Keni colored; for such a spirited young woman, she blushed easily. "The cheek!" she snapped, but Nathan held his ground.

"I want to see how without them you will look," he offered.

"*Nishtikeit!*" she barked, risen to her feet. "You upstart nobody! It's not enough I give you my ear—now you want from me my eyeglasses as well? Go and catch already a nine-year cramp!"

With that she flounced indignantly out the door.

But she returned the next night. When the knock came, Nathan leaped for the door but opened it warily, then stood back as she burst in again without ceremony. Once inside, however, she composed herself, removing her shawl and folding it neatly over the back of the chair before taking a seat. Settled, she turned to her host, still half hidden behind the open door, and complained, "I'm blind as a bat without them." Then she took off the oval spectacles. She had difficulty maintaining her haughty expression, but, despite their chronic blinking, Keni's eyes remained provocative in their dreamy emerald hue, the color of glass in a window facing the sea.

"Vell, Nat'n, vot you vaitin'?" she asked with a forced jollity, looking at nothing.

Stunned, Nathan closed the door and moved over to the stove, upon whose lid he lowered himself gingerly. All day at work, he'd cursed his impertinence, asking what evil impulse had compelled him to overstep the mark. Why couldn't he have remembered his place: he was a simple *yold* who held her captive only by virtue of the story; he should never have confused the power of the story with that of the teller. But now she was back to acknowledge that the power had shifted, and he found that he admired her vulnerability even more than her disdain. There was a small, blue, scarab-shaped blemish on her downy cheek, perhaps a fleck of paint, and Nathan had a fevered urge to touch it, but he knew he mustn't push his luck. Again he told himself, *Dayenu,* it's enough she's here, and began to pick up his narrative where he'd left off.

"He became a *belfer,* Mocky, who at that time was still called Simcha, riding the kids on his shoulders to Hebrew class," he told her, dispensing with the short-lived complacency of the angel's married life. "Later on he diversified, joining the burial society and the local chapter of the Water Carriers Guild." Then the child was born, and they named him Nachman because . . . well, he was naked and had been delivered *bei nacht.*

"He was no more or less red and wrinkled than any other creature at whose birth the angel had presided," Nathan was saying, when Keni begged leave to interrupt, "I liked better when you spoke in Mocky's voice."

". . . at whose birth *I* presided," continued Nathan, slipping back into the first person as easily as into an old overcoat. "He had no distinguishing markings or disfigurations, no rudimentary wings or purple caul, nothing in short to identify him as half a seraph. Neither did he come out of the womb spouting Torah; so although I must have missed it, I guess some deputy angel had tweaked his nose. But while the baby's genius was not immediately apparent, at least his tiny *petsel* was intact, and I remained convinced that time would prove him (as in the case of the previous offspring of mortals and angels) mighty if not wise. In this I was supported by my wife and the neighbors—bearing plum brandy and amulets to his circumcision—for whom every male newborn was possibly Messiah. Besides, it was 1648, the year that by the kabbalists' reckonings we were slated for universal redemption. . . ."

Having cautiously replaced the spectacles on her delicate nose, Keni was fumbling inside her reticule, withdrawing along with her cigarettes a stem-winding hunting watch. Snapping open the gunmetal case, she studied the time with some concern.

"But before Nachman had an opportunity to reveal his messianic calling," Nathan continued, "the Cossacks came. What we got in place of redemption was the hetman Khmelnitzki, may his name be blotted out, and his demoniacal hordes. It was a great day for murder and mayhem, I can tell you, what with the Zaporogian berserkers settling scores with their Polish landlords and, while they were at it, the Jews they judged guilty by association. Then came a second wave of no-less-bloodthirsty Haidamak partisans, slaughtering anyone the Cossacks might have overlooked."

Though she'd lit a cigarette, Keni was visibly squirming, clearly torn between the need to leave soon and her desire to linger, while Nathan savored her discomfort.

"The fiends in their astrakhan caps and lobster-feeler mustaches stormed village after village, resting from rapine and torture only long enough to offer their victims a chance to convert. A stiff-necked people, however, the Jews went resolutely to their *kiddush ha-shem,* their martyrdom, in Tulczyn, Starodub, Czernigov, and little Zitsk, on a sunny day in the month of Elul."

Stubbing out the cigarette in the enamel bowl, the girl rose with a vague apology but remained otherwise unmoving.

"At first it was a noise you barely noticed, like water running underground; then you noticed, the sound swelling to a rumble, the cup clattering across the table to smash on the floor. A pressure built under your feet until the ground erupted thunderously around you and out poured stampeding horsemen with hyena cries. Suddenly they were everywhere, overturning the market stalls, heaving Torah scrolls into the street where their fellows set them ablaze. They were inside our houses, whose windows burst as from the breath of dragons, belching feathers and flames; they hauled out our heirlooms, the tea urns and menorahs, our wives. From where I stood beside the well, frozen by what for me was a recently acquired sensation (namely, fear), I watched Hannaleh battling gamely until they cuffed her with a saber hilt. Then she was quiet, my heart, as they dragged her along by the tuft of her shorn brown hair."

Sighing fretfully, Keni had sunk spraddle-legged back into the chair. Nathan could have crowed his triumph but managed instead to subdue the growing emotion in his voice.

"When I dropped the buckets, I ran, God help me, not to the aid of Hannah, whose fate was already in other hands, but to the child. The time was when I might have summoned awesome powers; I might have called on my angelic brethren to come to my relief. But, having lived as a man, I had grown just as helpless and had nothing left to attest my former station beyond a shriveled pair of wings. They lay limp from disuse beneath my sheepskin, passing for all the world as the camel's hump peculiar to those who practiced the water carrier's trade. Before I was able to coax them back into operation, I had first to witness the flaying and dismembering of half the town; I saw what they did to my wife, who for once was not laughing—whose braid lay in the dust like the broken cord of heaven's own bellpull. Is it any wonder that in those moments I concluded the earth was no fit place to bring up a kid?"

Now Keni appeared to be genuinely suffering, her blanched face pleading silently with Nathan to let her go.

"I'd taken the bundle of the three-month-old Nachman wrapped in a quilt of his mother's own making," he persisted, "and stepped outside the shanty door. Having shucked my coat and overblouse, I proceeded to flap, pumping an elbow to give the nudge to my rusty wings. At the outset the pain was unbearable, and I doubted that those appendages—their plumage molted to pinfeathers, the quills falling out like pine needles— could ever function again. But just as one of the sodden butchers reeled from an adjacent doorway, a plundered candelabrum brandished to brain me with, I rose with my burden into the air.

"It would have been some consolation to think that the sight of our climbing unsteadily aloft had inspired in the *pogromchiks* some degree of terror. But with their vision already distorted by bloodlust and vodka, what was one miserable down-at-heel angel (and child) in a sky already crowded with hallucinations? With the pink bears, flying troikas, and escaped souls of Zitsk rising from the carnage like dew, alongside of whom we also ascended . . ."

He prepared for her next appearance by laying in a bottle of schnapps, for which he sacrificed three nights of barley soup with soda crackers at Maisel's Cafeteria. It wasn't until the fourth night of her absence that Nathan's confidence in the girl's return began to waver. He sniffed the shawl she'd forgotten when she fled the attic and grieved that the scents he'd detected, rosewater and a hint of turpentine, had started to fade. Perhaps he should use the shawl as an excuse to seek out its owner, but by now it had become both a convention and a point of honor that he wait for her. So when he couldn't stand the waiting, Nathan told himself as he descended into the balmy street that he was merely taking a short constitutional.

Since it was too late to attend the theater, he wandered the quarter. The tinny pianos from the dancing academies and the blazing electric signs over the nickelodeons attracted the insomniac crowds like moths. That was the East Side for you: where it wasn't a malodorous trough or a gutter, it was a tawdry sideshow, and Nathan wondered that the whole yeasty scene, rather than distress him, seemed lately to lend him a tingling energy. He walked up Grand and down Canal Street, whistling a popular aria in the soft night air, resisting the urge to peer into the cafés. Though, as he passed the saffron window of Glickman's Odessa Tearoom on East Broadway, Nathan couldn't help but hazard a look.

She was seated at a table next to (what was his name?) Yanobsky, ever garrulous, his arm draped over the back of her chair. The others in their party, lank-haired youths in puff scarfs with their straw-hatted lady companions, paid deference to the bald man to whom Keni was obviously attached. Nathan observed how relaxed she seemed in their company, readily giving up the laughter that he'd had to breach barricades to win. It was unfair, he brooded, that she lived a life beyond his attic, out in the world where he was only a sloe-eyed proofreader instead of a fallen angel recalling paradise.

As he stood there in the wreckage of his buoyant mood, she glanced his way and the smile left her face. Instantly Nathan hurried on, assuring himself that she couldn't have seen him; from inside, all you would see in the glass was your own dark reflection. But he still couldn't shed his sense that a glimpse of his sulking person had spoiled her good time as surely as the sight of her had ended his. Once again he'd crossed an unmarked boundary, stepping outside his story's zone of influence; though wasn't it out here in the street that he'd first tempted her?

He was still fretting over her absence the next day, a rare Shabbos afternoon off from work, when there came the heart-stopping rap at his door. Though he knew it could be no one else, Nathan was nevertheless confused; having only ever seen her at night, he'd come to think of her as a nocturnal phenomenon, just slightly more real than the figments that populated his story. But in the chalky sunlight that streamed through the open casement, she was—when he'd stuffed the tails of his nightshirt into his pants to admit her—undeniably present. Her thick hair and marmoreal cheekbones, the yardarm of her clavicle beneath the washed-out crepe of her blouse, all impressed Nathan with a reality that it was no longer enough merely to behold. It wouldn't do, he decided there and then, to captivate her for brief periods; he must possess her for all time.

"Ach, there it is!" she exclaimed upon spying her woolen shawl, and for a moment he wondered if she'd come back only to reclaim it. But, having approached the chair, rather than snatch up the shawl, she took a seat. "A couple times I come back for it, but you ain't in," she said, which was all she offered by way of excuse for her truancy; nor did she mention having seen him the night before. Instead she folded her hands in the lap of her umber skirt and tilted her head. It was her signature tilt, which invited him to begin talking while at the same time seemed to defy him to say more.

Nathan smoothed back the helix of a curl from his forehead and took his place astride the stove. The sounds of river traffic, El trains, and peddlers' cries invaded the room through the open window, diluting the intimacy he'd felt with the girl on those other evenings. Not yet trusting himself to commence his narration, Nathan noted the particolored spatter of paint on her sleeve.

"Keni," he ventured, "you are a artist, no?"

She sniffed and said bluntly, "For conversation I didn't come here," as if to remind him of their rules of engagement.

Then he remembered the peppermint schnapps. Hopping from the stove, he fetched the sealed jade bottle from the washstand, cracked it open, and poured some of the liquid into a cloudy glass. He placed the glass on the table in front of her.

"Aren't you having some?" she asked.

"It's for me a little early."

"And not for me?"

Nathan was suddenly embarrassed that he'd expected her to drink alone. There was a dirty teacup on the floor beside the bed, and, retrieving it, he poured himself a little schnapps. But before he could bring the cup provisionally to his lips—Nathan was unaccustomed, though not on principle, to taking spirits—Keni raised her glass to propose a toast.

"To the angel and his boy, Nachman," she said, "who, *zeit azoy gut,* you might be so kind as to tell me some more about them." They clinked glass to china cup with a sound that was seconded by a clangor of not-so-distant trolley bells. The first sip burned Nathan's dry lips but warmed his chest and set a small propeller whirring in his brain. He took another sip and leaned back against the stove to begin describing Mocky's reunion with his dead wife in heaven.

"It was a foregone conclusion that by the time they . . . I mean *we,* my son and I, reached paradise, my guiltless wife would be waiting for us there. But after a journey that erased forever the memory of having once made the trip by leaps and bounds, I found it hard to hold up my end of a joyful reunion. Exhaustion aside, things were complicated by the fact that I was now an outlaw in the upper world. Not only had I forfeited my membership among the beatific by cohabiting with a mortal woman, but I'd compounded my first crime by smuggling its unsanctified issue into the Garden. This was strictly forbidden, undead creatures having been designated *treyf* in the realm of the sacred."

Having thrown back her first glass of schnapps, the girl poured herself a second, then slouched a little drowsily with her drink in the straight-backed chair.

"For the other victims of the massacre at Zitsk, those souls whose piety had spared them a period of wandering," he continued, "arrival in paradise was more congenial. Met by ancestors, they were awarded, hon-orarily, their own severed limbs and patched membranes, and congratu-lated on having made a brave immigration. They were introduced to an upper version of their native shtetl prepared for them in advance of their coming. It consoled the Zitskers to see that their destination contained the same familiar tumbledown roofs and onion domes as the town be-low, the same muddy streets, give or take a spangling of overripe jewelry fallen from empyrean shrubs. But for all its surface similarity, the upper Zitsk lacked the peculiar flavor of the original.

"In fact, the celestial landscape seemed more unkempt than I'd re-membered, the great Tree at its axis looking wintry despite a reputation for being evergreen. The afterlife, I concluded, was not what it used to be. . . ."

Watching Keni wreathed yet again in a luxuriance of acrid blue smoke, Nathan asked himself, Is she beautiful? Because, taken sepa-rately, her pinched nose and myopic eyes, the tiny yellow teeth, were not prepossessing—so why was it that their combination should result in so much more than the sum of their parts?

"Excuse me," she said in light of his hesitation, "all day I ain't got."

Why not? he wanted to ask her, but instead took an extra breath. It was a long story whose conclusion he didn't yet know, so where was the harm in lingering? True, he had still to arrive at the heart of the saga, Nachman's love affair with Sophie the Red; but, as the romance had re-fused to resolve itself in Nathan's mind, he was in no hurry to reach the point beyond which lay the unknown.

"*Vos iz?*" prompted the girl, and Nathan, snapping out of his reverie, surprised himself by responding brazenly,

"I will make with you a bargain."

His visitor sighed and assumed a put-upon face. "Again with the bar-gains." Then she removed her wire-rimmed eyeglasses, tossing them carelessly onto the table before her.

Scarcely acknowledging the gesture, Nathan swallowed and said,

"Unpin your . . . I mean, let to unpin your hair me myself, and then I will tell you more." There were a heady few seconds when he couldn't distinguish whether the first-person pronoun he'd used belonged to himself or Mocky.

The girl's mouth hung open, and, taking advantage of her disbelief, Nathan was on his feet beside the chair. Emboldened by drink and further intoxicated by the rose-and-tobacco scent of her pompadour, he reached for the hairpins. Keni made no effort to hinder him, nor did she offer to assist, at least not until she'd become frustrated with Nathan's clumsiness. Then, shooing away his hands, she inclined her head and removed the ebony pins herself. The hair spilled down like sluices opened at sunset, tumbling—as she shook her head to unfurl the tresses—in full flood over her shoulders and breasts. Stupefied, Nathan backed up uncertainly into the stove.

"What have I done?"

Said Keni tauntingly, "It's what you undone, foolish," and permitted herself the ghost of a smile.

Unprepared for the near delirium her liberated hair had released in him, Nathan slid sheepishly back onto the stovetop and retreated into his story.

"Once her husband and child, and . . . *um* her vaporous braid, were restored to her," he said, struggling to regain Mocky's voice, "so was my Hannaleh's good nature, her late martyrdom notwithstanding. In fact, despite having been translated into a condition of pure spirit, Hannah's carnal appetite persisted; her phantom vitals thrummed, and her female principle obtained. So, you see, the problem was mine. Because I could not expunge from my brain the picture of my wife's defilement, I was bitter; I didn't think her gleeful countenance conformed with the nightmare of what had gone before. Besides, what business did I have in the Upper Yeshivas anymore, where my fellow Zitskers were frankly no longer alive? Meanwhile, lest my estranged brethren, the seraphim, spot an interloper in their midst, I was forced to keep out of sight; I was housebound, sentenced to endlessly rocking the cradle, pacifying the baby with the rusty halo he used for a teething ring. . . ."

As he spoke, Keni rose trancelike from her chair, picking her way between the bed and the wall of books to the open window. Wishing she would sit back down, Nathan stumbled over a sentence or two but persevered. He told her how Mocky's restlessness had sometimes gotten the better of him, and, despite the risks involved, he would lurk about. He visited sights he'd largely ignored during his prior term in heaven— the magazine of storms, the incubator of souls—in the hopes of renewing a misplaced sense of wonder. But there was a neglected quality about such places: cobwebs in the spokes of the Holy Chariot, the curtain separating the Almighty from His angels dragging its hem in the dust. Fabulous beasts, such as the Messiah Ox (fattened for eons in anticipation of apocalypse), tottered on spindly shanks, their ribs like furrowed ground. The whole of Gan Eydn and its celebrated attractions, leached of terrestrial passions, appeared to Mocky no better than a ghost town. While he might elude the heavenly hosts, he couldn't manage to hide from himself the truth that he was bored. He'd become addicted to life on earth, terrors and all, and was homesick for a humanity he could hardly abide.

"Which is what you call a paradox," said Nathan, trying to give the words an emphasis that might induce Keni to turn around. " 'I don't belong here,' I complained to Hannah one night in our hovel, undistinguished in its meanness from our dwelling down below—though the hearth, burning some astral species of tamarind, was as radiant as an autumn bonfire, and the baby's quilt duplicated to scale the dusky pastures along the sinuous river Styr. 'I'm an outcast!' I cried, daring my spouse to contradict me. She was absorbed as usual in her handicrafts, Hannaleh, stitching costumes from Garden-variety materials to disguise our son as the fauna of paradise: a banana-beaked phoenix, a baby roc with a brindled horn. But as industriously as she prepared for the problems that might arise in rearing a kid under the rose, Hannah still found the patience to humor me in my rites of self-pity. The afterlife had if anything honed her talent for teasing, but her playful expressions of reassurance— 'Simcheleh, ain't I your footstool in *himmel*?'—only rankled me the more, and I recoiled from her touch, tarnished thing that she was. . . ."

Keni's body was coronaed in sunlight as she gazed out the window, a silhouette dissolving into translucency at its margins. Her loosened hair was more torchlike than ever, augmented by the cigarette smoke that made her appear to be smoldering.

"Don't think that for such an attitude I was proud of myself . . . ,"

Nathan continued, standing erect and starting to move diffidently toward her, ". . . which is why I resolved in the end that my misery should seek its own level, its rightful company. One morning, which was identical in its shopworn perfection to every other in the Garden, I ducked under a tangle of roots at the base of the Etz Chayim, the Tree of Life." He'd paused at her shoulder, close enough for his speech—as he explained how the Tree served as a ladder between the upper and lower worlds—to stir the loose ends of her hair.

"But I knew a shortcut," he asserted, "a back staircase condemned by the archangels since time immemorial. . . ."

Keni turned to face him, clearly irked. "Didn't you tell me already enough about the Tree?" Her expression bore a degree of impatience far beyond what Nathan thought his brief digression should have aroused. Her thin lips were pressed tight as a hyphen, making barbed dimples in either cheek. What's the matter? Nathan wanted to ask her, feeling suddenly apologetic for the angel's behavior—though he wasn't quite convinced that Mocky's inconstancy was the cause of Keni's mood. He wondered briefly what would happen if he crossed the charged space between them, then, getting hold of himself, stepped back a pace to resume his tale in a chastened undertone.

"I crept down the rickety back stairs without once looking over my shoulder, so confident was I that my son would follow his mother's example. He would grow up, please God, in heaven, free of the temptation to visit a homeland he wouldn't even remember. But, as you know, he took instead after me."

So it went during her next few visits: they played the game to whose rules each subscribed while each reserved the right to feign ignorance of the rules. Nor did it matter to Nathan anymore that neither had for the other a history outside their peculiar relation to his story. The precise nature of Keni's attachment to Yanobsky, her rumored artistic calling, her orphanhood—these issues no longer concerned him, or so he convinced himself, since her life in the world had no real connection to what transpired between them in his attic room. Meanwhile the girl kept up her habit of entering Nathan's apartment as if she were there against her will, though the pretense had begun to wear thin. It was betrayed by the readiness with which she warmed to the story, by the effort it took her to tear herself away. Still, Keni observed the unwritten contract that she'd come only for the next installment, but more and more Nathan dared to think there were signs that she'd come for the sake of the teller of the tale.

Initially it was always the same; always her physical presence spurred Nathan to such an affection for his subject that it seemed to him the girl's sole purpose was to serve as a stimulus. But somewhere during the telling (usually after his second schnapps, which muted his ears to battling neighbors and yowling cats), the balance would shift; then it would occur to Nathan that the story existed only for the purpose of exacting favors from the girl.

On this particular evening, he'd been describing just how far the angel had fallen from heaven during the couple of centuries it had taken him to get back to earth. "Of course," Nathan confessed, always in Mocky's ruefully fluent voice, "by the time my son, Nachman, turned up, I no longer even remembered I had a kid. I was living among the pimps and thieves on Allen Street, known as 'the street of perpetual shadow,' where I was a barely tolerated hanger-on of the mob captained by Dopey Benny Fein. . . ."

The name evoked a raised brow from Nathan's audience, who recognized the Dope as a famous Lower East Side felon, incarcerated in Sing Sing not so very long before. It pleased the teller to have advanced his story as far as their own historical moment, which made his characters into near contemporaries.

"In the hierarchy of the underworld, mine was the lowest rung," said Nathan, feeling happily consubstantial with his narrator. He told how Mocky had worn a number of caps over the years, descending backward through the ranks as age and the depredations of the hop pipe and bottle took their toll. From firebug he'd been demoted to horse poisoner, then to a cadet procurer of young women sold into slavery, but even for such inveigling he'd become too dissipated. Eventually he was reduced to a "caftan," a recruiter of apprentice pickpockets and thugs, and it was in this capacity that he stumbled, one December night, into a seamy Canal Street music hall.

"They were offering something called *Simcha's Fall*, which was billed as an 'original' production—though it was well known that everything at Uncle Shmuel's Playhouse (scripts, scenery, sometimes even actors forcibly abducted from respectable companies) was borrowed from elsewhere. Curious to see what constituted originality at this end of Canal Street, and perhaps entice a lost boy or two, I bought a ticket for the schnorrers' gallery and went in."

He sees a play in which a wayward angel named Simcha, bored in heaven, is seduced by the tales he hears from the dead about earth. There was a scene where Simcha, come of age, is dispatched to the world to perform his angelic duties; he mounts the pasteboard tree at the center of the stage and begins to climb its knotty trunk, but when he reaches the twisted branches, a surprising thing happens: while the angel hangs on, the tree begins, with a scraping of hydraulic counterweights, to revolve on its axis at midtrunk so that, inverted, the branches become the roots and vice versa.

"Crude as it was, the device of the rotating tree had its effect, which was to turn my world, like Simcha's, upside down. I reached into my pocket for the bottle of spirits and, attempting to fight fire with fire, took a swig to douse the ember of my brain. For a second I thought a fit was coming on, prone as I was to delirium tremens, to say nothing of cataracts, lumbago, incontinence, and every other mortal affliction save death. (For all my sins, I'd somehow remained proof against dying.) But while I fought to keep from realizing what had happened, I understood despite myself that my past had come back to find me. The *narishkeit* onstage I now recognized as a version of my own impossible story."

At that juncture Nathan judged, from the attentive tilt of her head, that the time was ripe for proposing yet another bargain to Keni. When he paused, she appeared to anticipate what was coming; she removed her glasses, released the firefall of her hair. Although she affected shock when Nathan dropped to his knees in front of her to state his request, she recovered soon enough, heaving an obligatory sigh of reproach before making her soft face available. It was that easy. The problem, though, was that Nathan was yet unfamiliar with the mechanics of a kiss: he'd only seen them executed from a distance, onstage or in murky doorways, and once in a nickelodeon where the flickering couple resembled pecking birds. But taking heart once again from his newly acquired temerity, on loan perhaps from his alter ego Mocky né Simcha, he was prepared to learn by trying, and Keni's lips—expectant if a little cracked and sour with alcohol—obliged by educating his own. Parting, they parted Nathan's, teaching him to nibble and graze, inviting his tongue to twine with hers in a slow serpents' waltz.

Though the window was opened on a mild May evening, the attic was close, the sweat streaming in rivulets from Nathan's forehead, dripping from his aquiline nose. At first he feared that the kiss might suffocate him, for it was unthinkable he should pull away. But when Keni drew back for air, he did the same, breathing deeply before seeking her mouth again. In that breath Nathan felt he'd inhaled the entirety of his past— from the lonely proofreader immersed in his penny dreadfuls all the way back to the yeshiva boy conning the texts that supplanted an ill-omened world; he held the past in his chest till his lungs complained of over-abundance, then let it go. Then Nathan breathed again and kissed the girl hard. His head was helium, his bones afloat in a broth of blood mulled with spices. Nothing in his experience was comparable, unless of course you included the inebriate excitement of relating his story to Keni, though this new sensation displaced the story wholesale.

Keni slid from her chair to kneel before him, folding her arms about his shoulders, stinging his nostrils with her piquant scent. Returning the embrace, Nathan pressed her fretted vertebrae through the damp lawn of her blouse; he crushed her breasts against his torso, felt the points of her hips meeting his own. Then it seemed to him that his stiffened spine was a taproot dipping into his loins and blossoming exquisitely at the base of his brain. The perception made him gasp and shove the girl away to arm's length.

"Chaineh Freyda," he said reverently.

She tried to puncture the tension by teasing him: "Who's afraida?" But her gaze was still veiled with the desire he'd aroused in her, and, trembling though he was, Nathan permitted himself the assurance that life had no limits and dared to think, She's mine. Then he started to tell her in a whisper how Mocky, or rather *he,* had turned detective in order to discover the origin of the play at Uncle Shmuel's.

These days Nathan had begun to enjoy a rare equilibrium, embodying in his person the ideal marriage of fact and fancy, though it was increasingly difficult to distinguish where one left off and the other began. Nor did his job performance at the *Forward* benefit from this internal harmony, and if his colleagues had kept aloof from the drudge, they were downright hostile toward the dreamer. Reports of Nathan's laxity had reached Krantz the city editor, who made an official trip to the basement to issue a reprimand. He informed the negligent proofreader that, owing to the embarrassing number of errors in his recent work (thanks to his oversights, girls had been *farkent* instead of *farbrent*—"ruined" rather than "burned"—in the devastating Triangle Shirtwaist Fire), he should consider himself on probation, his situation in serious jeopardy. Nathan nevertheless remained comfortable in his conviction that the world and his imagination were as fine a *shidekh,* a match, as were he and Keni.

The girl belonged to him now as completely as did "The Angel of Forgetfulness"; she was his for the taking—so why couldn't he swallow that notion without inviting ulcers? Well, for one thing, he'd never "taken" a girl before; and while it was clear that this one was a new breed of Jewish daughter, Nathan, having traveled thus far from his God-fearing boyhood, still felt constrained by its tug. In the small space in his head left unoccupied by amorous fantasy, there survived a residue of harsh Talmudic injunctions against unsanctified acts. And marriage, of course, was not an option. How to marry when they remained, in a sense, such perfect strangers? While in another sense, didn't he and Keni, in their curious relationship, occupy a precinct beyond the Law? This was Nathan's risky conclusion, but relishing as he did his role as un-fledged seducer, he was still reluctant to push for the final intimacy.

Instead he preferred to tantalize her with further episodes of his story, observing her shifting humors as he elaborated Nachman's obsession with Sophie the Red: how the angel's son had decided that it was for her he'd left heaven and not, as he'd previously thought, to chase after the rumor of a long-lost father. Of course Nathan still had no clear idea of where his story was headed or how it might be resolved (must stories be resolved?), but he rejoiced at finding himself in the midst of its developing complications. Now, if he walked the streets of the Lower East Side, he saw less a toxic stew of a district than the picturesque setting for his "Angel." Neither did he ask himself anymore where the story had come from: it was simply a gift he would not have received had he not been worthy to receive it. In his acceptance he was unlike the inquisitive

Mocky, who doggedly sought information concerning the source of *Simcha's Fall*. First, the reprobate angel had gone to Rivka, the daughter of Rabbi Mordecai the Blind, and threatened to reveal her secret unless she told him what he wanted to know. (Over the years, for the purpose of extorting favors, Mocky had made himself a repository of the quarter's dirty secrets.) A mournful-eyed, slatternly girl, her inky hair working out of its nickel clasp to fall in unwashed strands across her face, Rivka obliged; she said the play had its genesis in a tale told to the troupe by its leading man, who called himself Nachman Opgekumener.

And who, wondered Mocky, was this Nachman?

" 'Is your memory so short?' Rivka asks me," said Nathan, impersonating Mocky. " 'He's a greenhorn that you yourself brought him to Yoshke not a month ago.' Then she tells me how Nachman fled Allen Street and, looking all the time over his shoulder, ducked into the dingy music hall on Canal."

Since his audience, if she appeared, never came before evening (there had been no more daylight visits), Nathan had begun to take rambling walks home from work. He would have his soup and a crust of pumpernickel at Maisel's, then perhaps purchase strudel and schnapps for his guest and stroll the streets where his story unfolded. On Canal he passed beneath the marquee of a notorious burlesque house, which the cops, due to its mob associations and the indecencies flaunted on its stage, were forever targeting for raids. Then he might make a tour of Allen Street itself, reviewing the handkerchief ladies leaning against the Elevated stanchions, whose taunts ("Hot knish, fifty cent") no longer chilled his blood. For Nathan the sinister street now consisted less of substance than of make-believe, its sorry brick rookeries like great theatrical drops. In a stage effect, you could peel back their façades, exhibiting a hive of unswept rooms converted to *shtuss* parlors and cribs where the *nafkehs* brought their trade. You would also reveal the personal headquarters of the *shtarker* Dopey Benny Fein and the flat where old Rabbi Mordecai, protected by his blindness from the surrounding vice, was doted on by his dutiful daughter. You'd see the coal cellar where Mocky called Fargenish, when in residence, slept on a flea-ridden mattress, the rooftop where Yoshke Nigger conducted his pickpockets' institute.

When next she came, Nathan started in telling Keni what Mocky had gleaned from quizzing Miss Rivka Bubitsch: how the artless Nachman, dazzled by his first glimpse of theater, had searched high and low after the performance for the leading lady, with whom he was hopelessly in love. But just as the proofreader had begun to warm to his story, Keni, drumming her fingers on the tabletop, interrupted him to ask how all this information had come into the hands of a simple rabbi's daughter. Nathan stepped outside Mocky's character to gently scold her, "You shouldn't get ahead of the story."

The girl, however, remained unappeased. For a time she had seemed content to sip the sickly schnapps and smoke her Sobranies, munching a piece of poppy-seed strudel while Nathan led her through the desultory turns of his saga. Perhaps she felt more at ease since Nathan had stopped requesting favors in return for advancing the tale. In any case she had remained almost eerily quiet. But during her last couple of visits, Keni had shown increasing signs of restiveness, taking a well-whittled drawing pencil from her purse to doodle on the rough tabletop, and more and more her stretched credulity prompted questions. Just when Nathan had arrived at what he regarded as the heart of his chronicle, Keni—sketching again on the table, a cigarette dangling from her lips—suggested that the plot seemed to her a bit contrived.

"Tell me again how Mocky knows from Nachman's escaping Allen Street and the rest," she inquired without looking up.

Nathan stared at her, thinking she looked a little dowdy lately in her bleached shirtwaists and unpressed collars, though the paint spatters were not so much in evidence. "I told you already twice: what he doesn't find out by his snooping, Rivka tells him."

"But how does Rivka know?"

He sighed, unwilling to spill the girl's secret prematurely. "Nachman that by her he confides," he said, trying on English and finding it still a poor fit, "when he would come in her father's rooms." Then, reverting back to the mother tongue: "You see, all the Allen Street apprentices, by order of the Dope, were expected to attend prayer services in the rabbi's parlor. That's where Nachman met Rivka, who served them her potato pancakes dry as powder puffs and the *teyglakh* pastries that bound you up for a week. . . ."

"And why is it, again," Keni wondered, finally lifting her eyes from her drafting, "that she and her papa live in Dopey Benny's . . . what did you call it? A hot-sheet hotel?"

"You're not listening," Nathan accused her. Then he explained once more how the Dope, having taken over the building and strong-armed its tenants into moving elsewhere, allowed the rabbi and his daughter to stay on as his guests. A onetime *yeshiva bocher,* who liked to refer to his gang as his loyal *talmidim,* Dopey wasn't above an occasional mitzvah when it furthered his ends. He reasoned that the presence of a holy man on the premises was a sound investment, a hedged bet against the tenement's foundering in its sink of depravity. Since her father's health was failing—and from the certification of poultry or the sale of the odd magic word, nobody prospered—the sensible Rivka felt she had no recourse but to accept the offer. With her complicity the mobsters, who hung around Numbers 49–53 Allen, saw to it the old widower remained ignorant of the activities that festered beyond his daisy-papered walls.

But Keni still wasn't happy. "This is giving to me a headache," she grumbled while Nathan forged ahead, entertaining himself despite his audience's intimation that the tale was more than a little far-fetched.

He described how, even before the theatergoers had begun to tire of *Simcha's Fall,* the Shmuelers were already mounting a more ambitious production, also inspired by the stories Nachman had heard in heaven. *Der Meshuggener*—The Mooncalf, combined a whole complex of the greenhorn's confections braided together as intricately as challah bread, and all of them featuring Nachman as the male lead opposite Sophie. For despite the demi-angel's maladroit stage presence, the chemistry between him and his costar was nonetheless affecting, the impression made on the spectators profound.

"But how does Mocky know what Nachman feels for Sophie?" Keni asked to Nathan's irritation, because Mocky was no longer the primary focus of the story. In fact, Nathan had begun to abandon his first-person narrative in favor of an omniscience he made no apologies for.

"Didn't I just say the whole ghetto knows how he feels? In the galleries, where the matchmakers plied their trade alongside the other vendors, the people were excited to a friskiness their skins could scarcely contain. Hurrying home from the playhouse, they completed the business left unfinished onstage, as the skyrocketing rate of pregnancy in the ghetto that winter attested."

Unappeased, Keni persisted, "But how does he really know what his son that he doesn't yet know it's his son—how does Mocky know what Nachman feels for Sophie?"

The question seemed so irrelevant that Nathan momentarily lost all composure. "All right," he replied in exasperation, "so Mocky doesn't know. But *I* know!"

Then he wanted to go on explaining how Nachman had become so utterly satisfied with their onstage relations that he no longer felt compelled to seek out Sophie after each performance—the toothsome Sofia der Royte, whose coltish figure was redefining the standard in a theater where zaftig was à la mode; who every night, when the play was over, mysteriously disappeared. But Keni looked so disconsolate in her maidenly pout that Nathan had finally to stop and ask her what was wrong.

"I miss Mocky," she complained.

When she was gone, Nathan looked to see what she'd sketched on the tabletop. To the imbroglio of previous drawings, their outlines misshapen by the coarse grain of the wood, she'd added a humpback figure with a pair of magnificent wings—the features of whose craggy face had something in common with Nathan's own.

He tried to placate her at his next opportunity by describing how Mocky Fargenish stole backstage during a performance, the fourth or fifth he'd seen, of *The Mooncalf*. Sneaking into Nachman's dressing room, the angel had discovered, flung across the canvas camp bed, a limp crazy quilt purged of stuffing. It belonged, if he weren't mistaken, to the woebegone immigrant he'd met weeks before by the water stairs at Ellis Island and recruited for Yoshke Nigger's school for thieves. Then he was struck by the realization he'd tried to scuttle with vats of slivovitz and elude in a fog of opium, but the quilt quickened Mocky's memory of his meeting with the greenhorn and the heaven gelt he'd found on his person—and of a distant harrowing moment, before his last return and farewell to paradise, when he'd wrapped his child in the counterpane and, albeit with enormous difficulty, taken wing. So shaken was Mocky by the recollection that he never heard the ovations signaling the end of the play. It wasn't until the door opened behind him that he came back to himself and plunged into the rack of hanging costumes. . . .

Throughout the account Keni had sat silently smoking at the deal table—suspiciously silent, if you asked Nathan, given her recent protestations. But so long as the subject was Mocky, so long as Nathan related the fallen angel's covert investigations, the girl seemed reasonably attentive. She grew restless again, however, as soon as Nathan reintroduced Nachman, from whom Mocky had hidden behind the wardrobe rack. When Nachman, in the stylized rags of his Farfl Narish character, sat down at his dressing table and began to rub his painted cheeks with cold cream, Keni blew a languid ring of smoke. Then she stubbed out her cigarette in the ash-spotted basin and spoke up,

"Why doesn't Mocky say to him, 'Nachman, I'm your papa'?"

"Because he's ashamed what he became, a bum."

"Ah," said Keni, sounding less than satisfied but apparently lacking the incentive to press further. She sighed, removing her spectacles and placing them on the table. Noting the gesture, Nathan tried to ignore it and carry on describing the scene. It was a crucial scene, a turning point, in fact, and Nathan was determined to register it with his audience— who, in yet another unsolicited action, plucked the pins from her bun and shook out her tumultuous hair. Then she stood up and, disregarding Nathan's efforts to proceed with his story, began to deliver a speech of her own, which sounded at once spontaneous and rehearsed.

"My name is Chaineh Freyda Freischutz, but I called myself Keni, like the prima Madame Keni Liptzin, from the time we came to America when I was a little girl. I always had what you call a flair for the dramatic. 'Keni Horeh,' my mama, peace on her, would say to me when I was naughty, and I was often naughty. We left Kazimierz, me and Mama, with the money she made from the auction of Papa's smithy after he choked on a eel. In New York, Mama had a sweet-potato stall on Hester Street, but her health was never good, and sometimes I would relieve her after school—that is, when I went to school, because I mostly ran loose in the streets. Everything was always happening in the streets: You had the girls in dirty pinafores dancing circles around the lame organ grinder, the boys stirring the sparks from a bonfire into a storm of fireflies. You had the shylock in his pawnshop window with his forehead like a snake, the greener with his temple curls marooned on the island of his calico seabag, the lady by the curb that takes in hand her little boy's pet-sel to help aim the pee. They are the same faces you saw in Kazimierz but different, the people still poor but not so afraid. I myself didn't know to be scared from nothing. Then it wasn't enough just to look; I had to bring back home to our pesthole the faces. I brought them home in the pictures that, with grease-pencil stubs on butcher paper, soap wrappers— anything I could scrounge—I would draw. This was strictly forbidden as far as Mama was concerned, though my Aunt Pesha Pishkin, who we lived with over her shop on Orchard Street—this is after her *shtunkener* husband, my Uncle Bendit, disappeared—Aunt Pesha said in America, God help us, nothing is forbidden. Later on—who could stop me?—I went to night classes at the Edgies taught by Julius Yanobsky, a *paintner* of the so-called Ashcan School. He encouraged me when he wasn't mak-ing at me sheep's eyes, and I was grateful, but when Mama got sick, I gave up art to go to work. I worked in the shop of my Aunt Pesha—a shrew, though not unkind to me—but I couldn't stand to be in a shop, and after the white plague took Mama, Yanobsky asked me to come live with him. Funny that we never talked about getting married; we both read Kropotkin, heard Emma Goldman at the Cooper Union, and he was so much older than me, so it was understood I would become what he likes to call his 'spiritual bride.' Maybe I should be ashamed, but life with Yanobsky was interesting. I met all kinds people, and though I'm told my art is mediocre, I was happy—at least until you, a nobody that's got nothing but a *bobbeh mayseh* and a cheap bottle peppermint schnapps, came along and spoiled my peace of mind. . . ."

Nathan wished she would take it all back. Instead of appreciating her confession for what it was, clearly an effort to dissolve once and for all the artificial distance between them, he found he resented it: knowing the facts of her life impaired his freedom to invent them. It seemed to Nathan she was trying to compete with him, to overwhelm with her true story his make-believe, and he realized he had not wanted to hear it.

"S-so Nachman sits down to wipe off the makeup," he continued, his tone close to defiant. "He's in his Farfl Narish costume—this is Farfl the dummy ragpicker in *The Mooncalf,* who inhales the smoke from a dying rabbi's incinerated stories and finds his voice; he becomes for a time, like the rabbi, a genius storyteller himself, which I told you already. . . ."

As he spoke, Keni gave a quizzical tilt to her head, but if she was upset by Nathan's refusal to acknowledge her speech, she didn't show it. Instead she began slowly to unbutton the pearl buttons of her chiffon blouse, its brittle fabric aged the yellow of onionskin. With a kicking heart, Nathan gripped the cool cast iron of the stove and pretended not to notice.

"He's wiping from the greasepaint his face. . . ." Squinching shut his eyes. "I mean, he's wiping off his face, when comes a knock at the door. . . ."

Keni removed the blouse, revealing a lace-trimmed corset cover underneath, then let the blouse fall from an outstretched arm. Her shoulders were square and a little knobby, her nipples, which showed beneath the graying muslin, the old gold of antique coins. Kicking off a high-button shoe, she placed a leg on the seat of the chair, then nipped back her skirt and petticoat to unhitch a lilac stocking, unrolling it over her pink knee. She repeated the operation on her other leg, taking her time, as Nathan peeked through half-open lids, dizzied by the glimpse of her ivory thighs.

"'*Kum areyn,*' says Nachman," ejaculated Nathan, struggling hard to overcome the catch in his throat, "after which who should enter but Rivka Bubitsch, the blind rabbi's frump of a daughter. . . ." Risen, Keni had begun unfastening the hooks at the side of her melton skirt, then shoved the skirt along with her flounced petticoat down over her hips until they settled in a circular heap about her ankles. "Only tonight she's scrubbed for a change, she's scrubbed. . . ." His voice a phonograph disk running down. ". . . for . . . a . . . change." He attempted to describe Rivka's hair, disarranged as usual, though somehow meticulously so, but the words had thickened to a gluey mush in his mouth. "Like a scullery maid in a play," he pronounced soundlessly, then rested his jaw from overwork.

Clad only in the sleeveless bodice and her scallop-edged drawers, the stockings bunched at her calves, the girl stepped out of the heap of apparel and edged it aside with her foot. Then, leaning against the chair, she placed the heel of one foot over the toe of the other, lifting her leg to stretch a stocking that came away from her pointed toes like a peeled shadow. Bare-legged, Keni began to unlace the corset cover, and Nathan thought she must surely be bluffing: to go further was unimaginable. Then she did it; she parted the bodice, releasing her breasts, which swelled in their blue-veined fullness until Nathan nearly expected them to take flight. But rather than stop there (*dayenu*), she slid the drawers down over her narrow hips and knees, disengaging them from about her ankles. Aglow in the lamplight, her pale flesh appeared to Nathan as if, in a stuffy Cherry Street garret in late spring, heaven had snowed a woman. His heart beat like a clapper, while a nether ache begged him to tug at the binding crotch of his trousers.

Meanwhile, Keni had glided over to the bed, her buttocks alternately rising and falling, and Nathan, watching, adjusted his breathing to their pistonlike motion. She poured herself across the mattress, her breasts semiliquescent above a fluted rib cage, a knee folded over her scarlet fleece; she crooked an arm to prop her head in the palm of her hand, her cocked hip showing her tush to heart-shaped advantage, the half smile on her lips uncorroborated by her misted eyes. Astride the stove, Nathan pictured himself lapping schnapps from the ladle-shaped hollow of her haunch and clutched his chest. Having never actually seen a naked lady (not even in music halls where the chorines would sometimes remove garments to capture the lapsed attention of the crowd), Nathan thought that the girl had invented nakedness. Shifting his weight onto his unsteady pins, he felt bewildered to the point of nausea, a character adrift in a story of his own devising. Which way back to the world? he wanted desperately to know, and, having lost his sense of direction, he made for the attic door before turning abruptly back toward the bed.

He hadn't known what to do until she showed him, leading him well beyond the liberties he would have dared to take uninvited, and obediently he followed. Somewhere he retained a dim awareness that this was forbidden, though the rabbis were often at odds as to the gravity of the sin, and their jurisdiction, originating as it did on "the Other Side," seemed not to extend as far as this shabby attic room in America. But holding the girl, Nathan felt that, along with the code of ethics, he'd left behind the attic as well, having entered a dimension where nothing besides their bodies was true.

Arrived, he couldn't have recalled the route they'd taken to get there, though later on, in her absence, every stage of the journey would haunt him. He remembered, for instance, the moment when he'd closed his eyes before groping to kiss her, and her laughter had penetrated his chest like mild artillery; then he'd looked still unconvinced on her nakedness, as if, like a blind man, he had first to learn her body through touch in order to believe. That's when she took his hand and introduced him to the buff of her eyelids and the taut silk of her cheeks, her parted lips, the sea green tendon at the base of her neck, her breast whose distended nipple Nathan teased on his own initiative. He might have lingered there, had she not drawn his fingers, which she maneuvered like a divining planchette, further along the gentle slope of her abdomen.

But just when he felt he was ready to explore beyond her tender supervision, she suddenly pushed him away. Breathing heavily, Nathan slumped against the creaking bedstead, disappointed but willing to accept that they'd reached the limits of their intimacy. Then Keni sat up, her eyes (narrowed to feline slits) only inches from his, a distance from which she could presumably discern his features without magnification. While he worried that his weak-chinned *ponim* might not bear such scrutiny, she yanked down his suspenders and began with deft fingers to unbutton his pants, climbing over him to haul them off along with his clunky shoes. Underneath, he was wearing the identical mouse gray longjohns he'd bought the previous autumn, having trimmed the legs and sleeves for the sake of reducing them to a pair of summer drawers. Nathan was as fascinated as the girl to observe that the head of his rosy arousal was peeping through the torn seam at his crotch.

"Now I remember you!" declared Keni, swinging her leg over both of his to straddle his thighs. Watching her by the topaz lamplight that limned her wanton expression and shot her red hair through with gold, Nathan couldn't help but think, Succubus; yet while he waited for panic to grip him, he was gripped instead by Keni's deliberate hand, tugging willfully to take him into her body's lush confidence.

When he'd achieved his release (greeted by the girl with a ululation and an accelerated thrashing of her hips), rather than catapulted clear of his skin as he'd fully expected, Nathan felt he'd come back to where he belonged, surrounded by the blissful particulars of his imagined story.

On that night of their first union, she couldn't stay to hear more; then she missed a few evenings, her visits determined, as Nathan now understood, by Yanobsky's irregular habits of work and leisure. Nathan was patient, though, since the story now seemed to have assumed such a proportionate place in his life; it was under control, perfectly balanced against the depth of his feelings for Keni, together with whom he seemed to have tumbled into a period of pure grace. Still, when next she visited him, Nathan could barely contain his urgency until they'd made love—which was sweet, sweet, a sweetness beyond comprehension, beyond guilt, and somehow outside the Law. It was the culmination of what seemed like millennia of unacknowledged desire. And afterward, having dispensed with that turbulent digression, Nathan couldn't wait to give Keni yet another installment of "The Angel of Forgetfulness."

He told her in his bed, its mattress sagging like the hollow of a hand, how, at the height of Nachman's success, the actor's world came apart; it was almost bracing how quickly it happened. "Remember," said Nathan in the facile *mameloshen* he still reserved for his narrative, though his conversation in English (he'd been practicing) was much improved, "that the original Nachman-inspired productions on Canal Street had started something of a golden age at the outlaw playhouse. Nobody could say whether the attraction was the plays themselves—the Shmuelers had contrived yet another called *Tantzen Shikh*—Dancing Shoes—about a colony of Jewish trolls living under the city—or the erotic tension between the principals. So devoted were the fans of the rehabilitated music hall that few even noticed the change that had come over the premier player Sophie Kush; or if they noticed, they no doubt assumed that her character was supposed to be cool, if not a little distracted, in the face of her costar's clumsy overtures. No one, it seemed, wanted to wake up from the enchantment of such singular dramatic fare, whose spell endured long after the play was over.

"Then a seemingly unrelated event made mutual the distance between the two stars." Nathan paused for effect, leaning over to inhale the narcotic of Keni's tousled mane upon the pillow. "Rabbi Mordecai the Blind," he announced, and lay on his back again with his hands clasped behind his head, "passed away—his soul plucked from the world as easily, so they said, as a hair is removed from milk. . . ."

With her cheek nestled in the cavity of Nathan's funnel chest, an arm and a leg flung across his reclining form, Keni Freischutz played the passive audience; though lately Nathan was more disposed to think of her as his collaborator. True, in the peacefulness that followed their thermal embraces, their limbs entangled until it was hard to know what belonged to whom, she seldom interrupted anymore; in fact, there was evidence that she no longer heeded so closely the wheels within wheels of Nathan's narrative. (She'd even fallen asleep once or twice during his renderings, leaving Nathan to wonder how long he'd been talking to himself.) But the catalyst of the girl's adhesive nearness, in a small room where their mingled odors overwhelmed the schmaltz reek from below, allowed Nathan to enter "The Angel" as if the story were a physical place and to take (or so he believed) Keni with him. Indeed, her body now seemed to him a means of access without which he could not enter his story at all, and in her absences he was as lonely as he'd been before she came into his life. So it was odd that he still had the capacity, when relating his story, to forget about her altogether.

But when it came time for her to return to Yanobsky, who'd begun to assume ogrelike proportions in Nathan's mind, he had difficulty letting her go. Of course he had no grounds to delay her departure, not unless he was prepared to offer her something more than a tall tale and a groaning bed.

One night, however, in his growing unwillingness to let her out of his sight, he left the attic to follow Keni at a distance. She walked west in the muggy late evening on East Broadway, past the cafés, sandstone walk-ups, and storefront synagogues, and stepped through the bill-strewn arches of the Educational Alliance, which the locals called Edgies. This was the institution erected by the uptown Jews to instruct their Russian cousins in the ways of the West, lest those *ostjuden* embarrass their betters with nasty habits; it was also the building that provided Julius Yanobsky, in exchange for his nominal teaching duties, with studio space. Skulking across the street in front of the library, Nathan wondered if, upon greeting her, the artist would smell the proofreader's scent on the girl. Before leaving the attic, she always made, while Nathan watched admiringly, an impromptu *shvitz* in the basin he fetched her from the common faucet. (This after discreetly removing the rubber pessary that resembled a small pink jellyfish from between her legs.) But perhaps enough of his essence still clung to her person, like an olfactory echo, to alert the artist that she belonged to another. Was that what he wanted? Nathan asked himself, as Keni and Yanobsky emerged from the Alliance arm in arm.

He had an easy way about him, Yanobsky, Nathan had grudgingly to admit; he carried himself with a settled assurance, and beside him Keni, the aspiring amateur, seemed girlish, her typically bluff manner mitigated by respect. With him she was tame, less the changeable, *chutzpedik* maiden of Nathan's garret than a worshipful student, all of which served to aggravate Nathan the more. In his string tie and inverted-teardrop goatee, a brass-knobbed walking stick in his hand, the artist was clearly someone to be reckoned with; and Nathan, working himself into a tem-per—he seemed of late to have a temper, to say nothing of an abundance of unwonted nerve—imagined planting himself athwart their path, and saying . . . what? *She's mine, and I'll fight to the death any man who says different!* Which was precisely what, having crossed the street before rea-son could overtake him, Nathan did.

It was a line worthy of one of Professor Hurwitz's melodramas, but, once blurted, it was too late to take it back. Brought up short, Yanobsky granted Nathan a coolly quizzical expression, then looked to Keni to in-terpret. Flustered, she managed an awkward introduction.

"Yanobsky, Nathan; Nathan, Julius Yanobsky. Nathan here . . ." She hesitated in search of a plausible explanation, "I knew him already from Orchard Street. He was always a joker."

Yanobsky nodded his head and asked archly, "So, Nathan, you like a bit of fun?"

Seized as powerfully by an acute self-consciousness as he had been by jealousy moments before, Nathan was at a loss for words. "I . . ." He, too, appealed silently to Keni, whose scowl implied that he'd made his own bed.

"You . . . ?" Yanobsky prompted helpfully, turning again toward the girl for enlightenment. Keni swiveled her head back and forth between smiling nervously at Yanobsky and staring daggers at Nathan; then she whispered something to Yanobsky that made him roll his eyes in sham sympathy and grin, the arc light glinting off a gold-capped incisor.

"Well, Nathan," said the artist with good-natured condescension, "I'm glad we had this little interview," and, taking his free hand from his pocket, he tendered it toward the proofreader. Nathan grasped the hand reflexively, then quickly pulled away, feeling doubly chagrined at finding that a coin had been pressed into his palm. He was studying the two bits as if he had suddenly developed stigmata, when the girl and her escort brushed quickly past him.

The next night Keni irrupted through the attic door without knocking. "Just what did you think you were doing?" she demanded to know.

Ashamed of himself, Nathan nevertheless assumed the tone of the injured party. "I was trying to come in your life."

"Well, you can't!" she barked.

He made demurely to challenge her, "But it's all right you should come in mine?"

"You didn't want me to?"

Nathan confessed that he'd wanted nothing more.

Keni sat down on the bed and began to rifle her drawstring purse for cigarettes, making an effort to prolong her scornful displeasure, when a sudden bubble of levity escaped her diaphragm and exploded the tight edges of her frown.

"I had to . . . ach, I told him . . . Julius, I said . . . *hee-hee* . . ."

It was ultimately revealed, between peals of laughter, that she'd confided to the artist that Nathan was the resident meshuggener of Orchard Street: he was a pathetic case with no fixed abode who believed himself to be a fallen angel, and had for years carried a torch for Keni. Mortified, Nathan fell to sulking but, having glimpsed his own absurdity through her eyes, could not maintain the pose. With an audible sigh, he dropped onto the bed beside her and surrendered to Keni's hilarity. At length they collapsed into each other's arms, where they succumbed to a gleeful combustion, and afterward Nathan, more complacent than it seemed entirely ethical to be, told her the consequences of Rabbi Mordecai's demise.

"Understand, the old man had been the unofficial chaplain to the mob since the emergence of Allen Street as the seat of East Side vice; so when he died, word came down from the almighty Dope that no expense should be spared for his funeral."

There was a motorcade to the Mount Hebron Cemetery in Brooklyn, where the elect of the Jewish underworld (whose ranks included a tag-along Mocky Fargenish) arranged themselves in their bearskins and muskrat cluster scarves about the open grave. As the rosewood casket was being lowered by thick leather straps, Rivka stepped to the lip of the grave; she undid the knot at her chin and let the wind whip the cowl from her head and send it flying. Then, having revealed herself as another—a playactor in point of fact, with painted lips, powdered cheeks, and dense crimson hair—she tore off the crimson wig and flung it into the rabbi's grave, announcing the end of her long masquerade.

"'Today,' she declared, shaking out her own dark tresses, 'along with my papa I bury my own wicked deceit. From now on I am what you see—my father's daughter, Rivka Bubitsch, first lady from the Uncle Sam's repertoree.'"

The assembled mobsters and their gin-soaked paramours stood with jaws uniformly hanging, until their sleepy-eyed captain shook himself out of his stupor.

"'L'chayim La Rivka/Sofia!' piped none other than Dopey Benny himself in his adenoidal tenor, tipping the narrow brim of his hat. 'The little lady's got, begging the rabbi's pardon, beytsim. . . .' Clutching himself purposefully between the legs."

Then the mazel tovs went up all around, and even Mocky, saying so long to any extortionist designs he might still have had on the girl, extended his congratulations. The only holdout from the prevailing conviviality, standing apart from the knot of mourners behind a monument in the falling snow, was Mocky's lurking son. It wasn't so surprising to find him there; the boy had always had a soft spot for the rabbi, in whose parlor he'd perhaps felt closer to heaven than anywhere outside of Shmuel's, and old Mordecai's spinsterly daughter had shown him every kindness. So why, instead of raising his hat like the others, did he hide behind the wing of a granite angel burying his face in his hands . . . ?

That night Nathan had broken off his narrative with the sudden disquieting realization that he might have shot his bolt. Lying next to a drowsy Keni, among ruined sheets sprinkled with ashes and poppy seeds, he remembered that he hadn't intended to give away this last episode quite so soon. He'd meant to take it slow, draw it out, perhaps return to the salad days of Uncle Shmuel's, back when Nachman and Sophie were the most talked-about twosome in the ghetto. The funeral scene should have been postponed, because it was after Rivka's revelation in the cemetery that Nachman begins to lose his powers; and subsequent to that, the story, so far as Nathan had conceived it, went cold. What he'd related to this point he had imagined before he knew Keni, before she'd been transformed from muse to flesh and blood. She was different now, as was he, but the story remained the same, and though he would have liked to turn it around and make a few changes, it had acquired its own suicidal velocity.

So even as Keni had showed signs of beginning to warm to Mocky's son and to cheer his onstage romance, Nathan told her how the fugitive from heaven turned Yiddish thespian (never, truth be known, much of an actor) began to falter. He became little better before the footlights than a stilted clay *goylem*.

"You see," explained Nathan, nearly ashamed to divulge it, "he couldn't in his splitting head contain it, the idea that she was the same person, the rabbi's daughter and the actress, so he lost his way."

Meanwhile, having closed for a week in deference to its leading lady's bereavement, Shmuel's reopened with what was billed as the "debut" of Rivka/Sofia—for Dopey Benny's tandem handle had stuck. The house that night was standing room only, word of Sophie's double life having spread like an influenza through every cafeteria and speaking tube. But for all the company's exploitation of their star's notoriety, her public was not let down. The girl shone as the raven-haired Lula, the soubrette in *Dancing Shoes,* who becomes involved with Velvl, king of the *shretelekh*, the Jewish trolls. (Velvl's tribe, displaced by a subway excavation, had surfaced from their cavern beneath the city to become performers in a third-rate music hall.) "Like reading the Song of Songs by the light of a magician's flash paper" was how one overheated reviewer described her performance, but in the end the actress's strengths only served to heighten the audience's awareness of her costar's ineptitude.

Lackluster at best, Nachman maintained such a skittish distance from his leading lady that you would have thought she had something catching; you'd have thought they were playing a game of Rivka's cat to Nachman's mechanical mouse. He fluffed his lines and seemed generally incapable of returning in kind even the measured affections the girl expressed toward him. Watching from the gallery, Mocky could detect in his costumed son the immigrant from the Upper Yeshiva fallen out of his element, a hybrid angel pretending to be an actor pretending to be a troll disguised as a man: a player at least thrice removed. For some nights, however, Nachman got away with it, if only by dint of the loyalty of his patriots and the universal admiration for the girl. But after only a couple of weeks, apparently fed up with carrying the planklike burden of Opgekumener, Rivka/Sofia, to the astonishment of Canal Street, flew the coop. All the respectable theaters had made bids for her, including a couple of Broadway companies, though Yiddish stars, limited as they were to "ethnic" parts, had never fared well uptown. So she went to Adler's opulent Grand Street, where she was guaranteed not only a benefit performance and a percentage of the gate but the title role in an upcoming production of Gordin's classic *Mirele Efros*. She was going forth in her prime to embrace her destiny: that was the popular wisdom, though Mocky knew well enough she was running away from Nachman.

After her departure the Shmuelers tried to put the best face on things: they took solace in the fact that they still had the matchless resource of Opgekumener, whose slump would surely pass. But with Sophie's emergency replacements, Nachman was never able to establish any rapport. Without the prima's galvanizing presence, he was not only next to useless on the boards but was also fresh out of stories for ready conversion into hit plays. The company nevertheless held out the hope for his revival, refusing to believe that the vital fund of energies that had altered for a time the landscape of the Yiddish stage was irredeemably bankrupt. Meanwhile the playgoers, for all their sworn fidelity, began drifting—first at a trickle, then in droves—to the other theaters, many following La Rivka/Sofia to Grand Street. Eventually the Uncle Sam's repertory, bowing to the inevitable, resumed staging the old lewd warhorse operettas that had formerly been their staple; and almost as an afterthought, they gave their fallen star his walking papers. . . .

After a long silence, during which Nathan had drawn the smelly sheet to his chin, Keni asked him, "So then happens what?"

Said Nathan, embarrassed, "I don't know," and pulled the sheet the rest of the way over his face.

Keni tugged it back down to his chest. "What do you mean, you don't know?"

"That's as far as I got it, the story, when I would write it down."

He anticipated her fury, felt he deserved it, having strung her along all these weeks as if together they were headed toward a sure destination. But beyond the slight pooch of her lower lip, Keni seemed not to be especially disappointed. She slid down onto her side, crooked an elbow to prop her head, her breast lolling like spilled cream.

"So maybe that's the end," she suggested thoughtfully.

Nathan looked at her in disbelief, waiting for the other shoe to fall. "You ain't going to ask why the half angel Nachman, that he can't accept Rivka and Sophie is the same?"

"You said it already," she replied, and as Nathan still appeared to be waiting, repeated his premise as if she were being catechized: that unable to reconcile plain Rivka Bubitsch with Sofia der Royte, fixed constellation of the Yiddish firmament, Nachman (schmuck) could no longer accommodate either.

"That's right," agreed Nathan, amazed at how well she'd followed the twisted logic of his fable; it was a testament to his storytelling abilities. But was she also right that the story was over? He'd hoped their romance, his and Keni's, revelatory in so many ways, would reveal to him some promising alternative for his onstage lovers, some event that might reunite them in the world beyond the playhouse. But if Keni Freischutz was satisfied, who was he to question further?

Nathan was still considering this when she swept the heavy hair back from her forehead to kiss his temple before reluctantly saying good night. It was a gesture so tender that you'd have thought that "The Angel of Forgetfulness" was the least of her reasons for coming to visit him.

When she'd gone, Nathan quickly got dressed and followed her home. He trailed her first to the Alliance and again waited across the street until she emerged arm in arm with Yanobsky; then he shadowed them with the stealth he imagined that Mocky employed in following his son. At Clinton Street, sidestepping a furniture dray, they turned left and mounted the stoop of an Old Law tenement. Nathan stood on the opposite curb until he saw a light come up in a third-floor apartment. He thought he could make out bodies passing an open window, and an irrational anger came over him: the girl was no better than she should be; a *veltz kurveh,* she belonged to anyone. Then he asked himself what was he thinking, didn't he have with Keni the best of at least two worlds? More disposed now to rescue than curse her, he crossed the street and approached the building.

For all the clambering that occurred in "The Angel," Nathan had never been athletic himself—in the shtetl an athlete was he who *shukele*d longest at prayer—but there was much he'd never been before meeting Keni. A narrow ladder hung down from a fire escape, and when no hucksters or passersby seemed to be looking—or what if they were?—he leaped for the lowest rung. The ladder slid abruptly to the ground with his dangling weight, jarring his frame from the impact, but when his bones ceased their rattling, Nathan commenced a shaky ascent to the bottommost platform of the fire escape. He climbed a few flights, scrambling over a raft of airing mattresses, to the window he'd sighted from below and, peeking in, saw an apartment whose drab interior was a poor advertisement for the artist's trade. The combined kitchen and parlor was sparsely furnished with only a table, a horsehair sofa leaking stuffing, a stove with drying stockings and a razor strop draped over its elbow flue. It was a dinginess only slightly subdued by the unframed paintings that hung about the damp-stained walls. They were cityscapes, mostly, with duffel-bosomed women leaning out of handshake windows, aproned storekeepers in skullcaps raising candy-striped awnings, boys on a rooftop releasing homing pigeons from a coop. Certain objects in the paintings—a chicken crate, a sandwich board, a burnt-sienna *karnat-zlach*, a damask swagger coat hung on crossed staves—seemed to pulse, as if they might be the abode of trapped souls. Rendered in broad strokes and richly saturated earth tones, heavy on the shadows, the eloquence of the paintings muted by contrast the starker composition of the room.

At the table beneath a singed gasmantle, Yanobsky sat in a tasseled nightcap reading his Yiddish daily, while Keni served him tea with lemon. Nathan grimaced at their domesticity and was a little relieved when, instead of joining him, Keni pulled a paint-stippled smock from a hook on the wall. Drawing it over her shirtwaist, she retired to the adjoining room, as Nathan edged along the catwalk to regard her through a second window. She turned up the gas flame on an L-shaped bedroom occupied in large part by an iron-framed double bed. The bed was flanked on one side by standing wardrobes, while, in the blind space on the other, a wooden easel had been erected over a tarpaulin drop cloth. Hunkered beneath the window, Nathan watched as Keni removed a sheet from over the easel, then knelt to retrieve a palette and some scattered paint tubes from beside a jug of turpentine. She squeezed a dollop of indigo onto the oblong palette and snatched some brushes from a jar, a couple of which she clenched in her teeth as she rose. Then, cocking a brow, she stirred a brush in the blue and began to dab at the canvas, whose surface, owing to its angle, was hidden from Nathan's view.

Observing her, Nathan thought she looked like so many others he'd seen about the ghetto who set up their easels in Seward Park and the Hester Street "pig market," or on the roofs alongside the tents of the tuburculars. They were fresh-faced ex-*bocher*s flouting the laws against idolatry, seeing in the teeming slum their own brand of pastoral; they were cutters and basters and Ethical Culture girls, the first generation among the Jews with artistic pretensions. What was in the noxious air that compelled them, these poor Yids released for a spell from the shops and factories, to take to their canvases, their writing desks, rented pianos and violins? It was as if in America, far from the Old Testament God and His original works, they were driven to participate in an orgy of new creation. Nathan didn't know whether he counted himself proud to be among them or if he merely felt sorry for them all.

But this one, wiping her brush in a wadded rag as she stepped back to admire her work, this was his own inspiration, his Chaineh Freyda. So what was she doing looking so much at home in the household of another man? Seized with the sudden urge to get a glimpse of her painting, Nathan leaned out over the bird-beshitted railing, craning his neck around the corner of the building. At some considerable risk to his safety, he spied through a grimy pane what she was working on. It was a street scene in the manner of those in the parlor (which Nathan assumed were Yanobsky's), though Keni's was cruder, the colors bolder but laid on with less precision of technique. The street, which could have been Orchard or Eldridge or Clinton, was littered with browsers and peddlers, above whom floated an old man in a dented bowler, his shoulders sprouting a paltry pair of wings. Folded in his arms was a scrawny child looking bewildered at having been snatched into the chrome yellow air. This fantastical touch, if set beside the sobriety of her mentor's productions, seemed to Nathan (disturbed for reasons he didn't care to examine) self-indulgent, the kind of thing they would have labeled neurotic and counterrevolutionary in the talkers' cafés. Though what, Nathan reminded himself, did he know about art?

Suddenly he felt he was losing his balance, and in an effort to save himself from pitching headforemost into the alley, jerked his body backward in the nick of time. In so doing, he lost his hold of the railing and fell to the iron slats, banging his leg. He yelped, then ducked below the windowsill, trying his best to disguise his outcry as the yowling of a tomcat in rut.

A few nights later, Keni returned to the attic and waited until they were in bed to drop her bombshell—though she first asked somewhat suspiciously how Nathan had bruised his thigh. She accepted his excuse readily enough, that he'd stumbled over a compositor's stone in the print shop, then announced that she was leaving Yanobsky.

Nathan froze in midembrace. "What for?"

Stiffening in return, Keni shoved him roughly away from her. "Because always I wanted to live in a room so small we will have to take turns breathing," she snapped; then, evenly, "Because it ain't in me I should be a two-timer." And softening, "Because, what else, *a klug tzu mir?* I want to be with you."

"Me?" He was puzzled—since now that his story was spent, so, it seemed, was his confidence. Nathan no longer felt certain of who he was supposed to be.

Keni nodded her head in the affirmative.

The proofreader forced his lips to curl at their corners in the semblance of a grin: So this was victory. His long shaggy-dog serenade had finally paid off, and he'd won the girl after all; he was chosen. So why, instead of jubilant, did he feel only a tightness in his chest, as if his rib cage were a trap sprung about his heart? It occurred to him that, rather than grateful, he was actually annoyed with Keni Freischutz—though why annoyed when she'd come around to wanting the very thing he wanted most himself? Or did he? Then Nathan realized what it was: He was irked at how freely she'd accepted that "The Angel of Forgetfulness" should simply fizzle. He blamed her for having failed to rekindle his incandescent vision, that he might see past the place where his story had petered out.

It was a resentment he'd felt from the moment she'd reappeared in his room, clinging to him in the frowsy crepe de chine that, for all he knew, bore the paw marks of his rival. Of course he'd taken some initial comfort from her touch, as together they tumbled, notably without benefit of narrative, into the squawking bed. There was the preliminary tussling, not without its playful aspect, the furious tugging at buttons and braces, and the always original shock of flesh upon flesh. Then she'd interrupted their sport to make her announcement, and Nathan had responded with the foolish ambivalence that Keni, nearly naked, tried to dismiss, saying, "Please, just take me already."

The invitation was at once thrilling and cordial, the girl temptation itself, the unwrapped gift of her orchid pink pallor awaiting his ardent embrace; but Nathan found himself unable to summon the courage.

"What's the matter?" she asked, tracing a bead of sweat along his knitted brow, and in his shame Nathan understood a harsh truth: He could enter his story only so far as his life allowed and life only so far as the story would let him. The real and the make-believe were equally unattainable, and, stuck in the space between, Nathan felt his will, along with his organ, gone limp as an empty sausage casing. So why hadn't Keni's declared affections lent him the strength to break free of his tethers? But while the girl tried impishly to excite him, pretending that the tip of her tongue was a brush she must dip in the pot of his navel before painting his parts, Nathan would not be revived.

"*Tei yerinkeh*, what can I do for you?" she wondered in the sandpaper voice that was years too old for her, and Nathan heard an echo from a long-ago evening in Pishkin's Ready-to-Wear, when the milquetoast proofreader had been afraid to state why he'd come in.

On her next visit, the fear still had not left him, nor had it abated by the visit after that. Helpless to conquer his failure of nerve or to take refuge in his played-out narrative, Nathan was desolate. He was further frustrated by the mortal irony of having gotten the girl at the expense of his story and deemed it fitting he should now lose them both. For her part, Keni made to reassure him that his impotence was only temporary, though the more she tried to convince him it didn't matter, the more adamantly he insisted it did: he had nothing left to give her.

"Didn't you love me?" she asked, and Nathan inclined his head as if endeavoring to recall.

When she finally lost patience, a vein beat like a turquoise fuse in Keni's forehead, and her fretfulness took the tone that Nathan remembered, nostalgically, from the time he'd first accosted her on the street with his crazy tale. The following week, during which the girl did not return at all, Nathan was informed that his job at the *Daily Forward* had been officially terminated, his supervisor grown tired of correcting his thoughtless corrections.

MOCKY

My son, Nachman, as you know, was reared in paradise, et cetera.

By the time he turned up on the Lower East Side, some two and a half centuries after I'd left him in heaven, I'd forgotten I had a son. I was living among the Jewish bandits of Allen Street, sleeping in the coal cellar of Number 49 under the din of the Second Avenue El. Mocky, they called me around the neighborhood, meaning "plague," or sometimes Mocky der Hoyker, the Humpback, for the scaly protuberance that split the seams of my coat. They called me Shnoz when I stuck my varicose nose where it wasn't invited, and Fargenish because I couldn't recall where I came from. I had many names but answered to few, which was why I was a barely tolerated hanger-on of the mob captained by Dopey Benny Fein.

Over the years I'd served in a number of capacities, from firebug (known in the trade as a specialist in Jewish lightning) to badger and dip. While your current run of punks were still pishers in Hebrew school, I was procuring young women for Rosie the Factory's *shandoiz*. My method was to accost them in the dance halls and at the porphyry counters of candy stores, enticing them with avuncular assurances and promises of steady work and benefits. But due to my age and destructive habits, I lost my knack for attacting the girls and was reduced to the role of a bearded recruiter of apprentice pickpockets and thugs.

I would take the steam launch over to Ellis Island, where I searched in the melee of recent arrivals for the newly processed immigrant boys that no one else claimed. Such was the fate of those ungreeted by family or *landsmen:* they fell into the hands of sweatshop contractors, boarding-house sharks, labor gangs, or Mocky Fargenish. With the lure of instant loot and community, I would shepherd them back to Allen Street—a pair of Lit-vak orphans, a harelipped oaf in a Ruthenian goatskin—and hand them over to the pock-faced Yoshke Nigger, resident Fagin of the Jewish Black Hand, who gave me for my troubles a little *tish gelt.* Then I would brush off my bowler hat, don the Prince Isaac cutaway, and douse my whiskers in benzine to kill the lice; I would head for Sid Boske's hop joint in Bottle Al-ley via Max Schnure's concert saloon at Chrystie and Grand.

I was making the above-mentioned rounds on a December night, the wind snatching at my pant legs with icy fingernails, when a marquee pro-claiming a unique entertainment at the Uncle Sam's Burlesque caught my eye. A former Pantages music hall in a crumbling Beaux Arts building on Canal Street, Uncle Sam's, affectionately called Shmuel's by the locals, had been converted in recent years into a Yiddish theater of bad repute. When I entered the *shnorrers'* gallery, the play was already nearing the end of the first act, the curtain open on a two-dimensional tree. The tree looked like a misshapen menorah hung with lit candles, foil harps, and six-pointed stars, its exposed roots resembling a gnarled fist—a third-rate set even by Shmuel's primitive standards. The action, which lacked the trademark raunchiness of most Canal Street fare, involved a young angel whose head has been turned by the tales he overheard in the minyans of the mortal dead. It was a frankly preposterous plot, and the kid who played the hero, Simcha, dragging around a pair of wings like barroom doors, was little better than inept. So why was it that I, along with the rest of the ordinarily rowdy audience, was so transfixed?

There was the scene where Simcha, graduated to the rank of full ser-aph, is sent to the world to carry out his celestial duties. He climbs the flimsy tree at center stage, which begins to rotate at midtrunk with a screaming and ratcheting of gears, so that above becomes below and vice versa. Then the ass-over-elbows angel, clumsily correcting himself, climbs back down to the stage, upon which scenery flats depicting a Russian market town have been wheeled. It was a cheap effect, that re-volving tree, which nevertheless set off a corresponding revolution in my amnesiac brain; and though I fought hard against remembering, I was clobbered by the realization that the play was in fact a version of my own sad story.

My story: First, understand that in olden times you had more traffic between here and there, so there were more temptations for a young angel. Naturally I'd heard the cautionary tales from our august arch-seraphim, a severe and unbending, not to say humorless, lot. Always they insisted on a strict separation of the races: above should go with above, below with below. They liked to hark back sanctimoniously to their original censure of God's creation of man, "I told you so" being their favorite refrain. It was a criticism the Lord Himself had not disputed, having since retired into His mansion, which looked, when you scaled the wall to spy on it, like some deserted old plantation house shuttered up and overgrown with snaky vines.

What they schooled us in, in our angelic cheder, was the wisdom we were supposed to impart to unborn souls. There was a pointlessness to this operation, since why would you fill a vessel with learning in one world only to empty it in another? It was a cruel and unusual process, which made your immortal souls reluctant to assume their mortality, just as later, having forgotten on earth what they'd learned in heaven, they were unwilling to return to paradise. The whole program was enough to make you wonder: Why heaven and earth in the first place? What was so remarkable about the lower world that the upper should be mindful of it, and vice versa? Anyway, when we weren't getting educated, we were getting indoctrinated, admonished not to follow the bad examples of our fallen ancestors. These were the Nefilim, the first to have succumbed to temptation, who bred monsters off the wanton daughters of men in the time before the Flood. There were Uzzah and Azazel, the Weber and Fields of fallen angels, who shed their splendor for the sake of a pair of designing females and came to unfortunate ends. But all such tales, tired as they were and told with so little conviction, only whetted my appetite for more.

Maybe I didn't know when I was well off, but where rapture and ecstatic devotion were the order of the day—a day in heaven being equal to scores on earth—you're likely to long for something less rarefied. Of course there were a number of things to keep us amused in those ethereal reaches; I don't mean to suggest I had an unhappy childhood. But I was content to let others boast of their baiting of fabulous beasts: the *zis-shaddai* whose broad pinions are responsible for turning day to night, the *re'em* that in its indolence *shtups* only once every seventy years, the sea-goat, the infinitesimal *shamir*—all of which remain rumors to me still. It was the same with the fabled cellar of smoke and the mill for grinding manna, which I'm told is no longer in operation. Nor did I see the Bird's Nest where Messiah waits for the optimum moment to come forth and redeem us. ("What's wrong with now?" I hear you say, and do heartily concur.) Reports of such phenomena only served to oppress me; their prodigality deepened my yearning for more *haimesheh* haunts, a desire that led me to the lowlier precincts of the mortal dead.

I hung around their unpaved streets and untended arbors, the outdoor quorums in which they spent eternity studying Torah. Or pretending to study, because they took every opportunity to digress from the text at hand. Indeed, Holy Writ often functioned as nothing more than a triggering device to put them in mind of exemplary tales about earth. That's what they did with their everlasting tenure—they debauched themselves with apocryphal gossip about heroes and dangerous amours. So how was I to know that the stories, forgive me, were lies?

Put it down to too much time on my hands, but for as long as I can remember, I was hungry for news of the world. A born kibitzer, I neglected my chores to spend more time in the yarn-spinning sessions of the celestial *landsmanshaftn*. I became a familiar figure in that part of the Garden that had been allowed to go to seed—the part reserved for the formerly tellurian, where places on earth were duplicated in their heavenly knock-offs. Thatch-roofed villages, as dilapidated as their originals though purged of want and fear (items about which I was particularly interested), huddled under the boughs of a titanic shade tree, which some call the Tree of Life. Since the Tree also served as a ladder between the upper and lower worlds, there was considerable coming and going, and sometimes you had a situation where, out of the traffic in the lower branches, the odd living being would tumble.

Among them was, naturally, the prophet Elijah, ushering souls on reprieve from Gehenna, from hell, for a Shabbos celebration among the righteous. He often appeared in one of the many disguises he wore below, removing an eye patch or a false nose, peeling off a leper's sores, to don the fancy dress he sported in paradise. Then there were those who trespassed without a proper dispensation for entering the Garden alive, as for instance the rabbis who stumbled in by means of their mystical transports. But such characters were routinely struck dead, blind, or insane by the radiance (or was it the disappointment?) they encountered on entering. Once a married couple, by virtue of their zealous Sabbath-eve union (an act that, when performed with intent, was said to speed the coming of Messiah), found themselves elevated through sheer bliss to another world. But having made such an immodest debut, they were sheepish in the face of my questions—especially when I asked them (at a stage in my own development when I belonged to neither gender) what was it like, their copulation. I also wanted to know why, for them, heaven was such an awesome place and, while I was at it, why were humans afraid to die?

So you can see that, even before I came of age and was entrusted with missions below, I was already leaning in that direction. Sometimes it happened that one of my kind was spawned by some mortal's halfhearted mitzvah, a good deed so trifling it was half a sin; so that, even among the angelic orders, you occasionally got a bad seed.

At first I could negotiate the journey almost effortlessly. Like the other hosts, I traveled from branch to branch of the Tree of Life with a leisurely hand-over-hand brachiation, saving my wings for the final stage of descent. You know, of course, that the Tree is shaped something like Siamese twins joined at the crowns of their heads, their feet planted in either world. Thus, in climbing up the Tree from its serpentine roots in the Garden, you found yourself, at its apex, climbing back down. When you reached the bottom branches, too high for most mortals to grab hold of, you had to fly the rest of the way. It's written that it takes the angel Gabriel six flaps of the wings to get to earth, Simon four, and the Angel of Death only one, but I was lucky if I could manage the distance with a couple of dozen.

Also, I knew a shortcut. Under the roots on the unmoonlit side of the Tree, the side in need of a surgeon and subject to rot, there was a hole in the ground, a crimped colon of a tunnel terminating in a dim back staircase. Rickety, tortuous, and steep, without railing or candle sconce, the stairs had been condemned by the archons since time immemorial; they cautioned (always they cautioned) that the stairs led to Sitra Achra, the kingdom of demons. Never superstitious, however, I suspected what I later confirmed, that our governors had forbidden us the easy access in order to save it for themselves. Because the back stairs turned out to be merely a less kosher route to the lower world. Ultimately it became an open secret that the Tree and the staircase led to the selfsame place, give or take a couple of miles; both debouched you over that part of the planet where the Jews were thickest on the ground—in biblical times the neighborhood around Solomon's Temple, say, or later the Russian Pale of Settlement and, in Nachman's day, Ellis Island, or the Allen Street tenderloin if you happened to take the stairs.

In keeping with the duties assigned me after my commencment, an event much delayed on account of my chronic delinquency, I was making a routine tour of birthing beds; I was presiding at nativities in my designated district around the Polish town of Tchertkov when it happened. My task was to give to newborns an initiatory nose tweak, which erased any lingering wisdom they might have brought with them out of the womb: God forbid their prenatal knowledge of paradise should prejudice them against life on earth.

I was attending the delivery of some squawling *kaddishel* in the market town of Zitsk when I saw her among the women assisting the midwife. Her complexion was the dun brown of doeskin, her agate eyes moist and aslant, hips lush, bosom generous, plaited hair uncoiling from under her shawl like a rope of brass. Holding a rushlight for the old *vartsfroy* to work by, she couldn't keep the flame from stuttering, so risibly amused was she over the bloody wonder of the new arrival. As a creature fashioned from the sloughed light of the Shekhinah, the garment discarded by God when He went into seclusion, I was imperceptible to mortal eyes. Still, it didn't pay to linger. Prolonged contact with the lower orders could permanently impair an angel's sublime constitution, never mind the toll it took on your sexual neutrality. For all that, I continued to put off my departure. I hung about the *shtot* hoping for a glimpse of the girl—who was called, I learned, Hannah Hinde Mindl's. Meanwhile my physicality had begun to assert itself, until I realized it was too late to turn back.

After making discreet inquiries, I went through the customary channels to court her. I engaged the services of Menachem One-Lung, a match-maker of questionable character, who arranged a meeting with her family in their ancestral hovel. An accomplished liar, Menachem introduced me as Simcha Opgekumener, Talmud adept and grandson of the Pshishker rabbi, come from Izbitze in search of a wife. Why? Because, as everyone knows, the women of Izbitze have the faces of lizards. In support of the *shadchan's* claims, I spouted sufficient commentary—hadn't I breathed the stuff in the upper world?—to reduce Hannah's father, an unlettered tanner, to tears. I flatter myself that the rest of his tribe, including my intended (who stood behind her mama chewing her braid) were not un-moved. They were lined up in a chronologically descending row of seven dirty siblings, all male but for their retiring sister, fidgeting under beaver hides hung from the rafters while rank breezes wafted in from the court-yard vats. From prolonged exposure to their industry, they'd become a tawny lot, the Groysfussers, graduated in leatheriness according to their ages. Noting this, I felt it even more incumbent upon me to rescue my prospective bride from her half-embalmed household before her flesh lost its pliancy and was cured to the vellum-stiff state of her older brothers'.

Because the impoverishment of Hannah's family had discouraged suitors, and because a scholar was a sought-after commodity in a town unblessed with a surplus of same, the bargain was soon struck. Her father even threw in some miniver pelts for a dowry. I was lodged until the date set for our nuptials on a hard pallet in the study house but took my meals at the Groysfussers' board. The derma was stuffed with gristle and the groats tasted like the tannery smelled; nor did the prevailing aroma of her people exclude my moon-faced fiancée, though even by her pungent bouquet I was aroused. And through her sauciness of attitude, Hannah led me to believe that the feeling was mutual. But as our wedding night approached, I grew apprehensive. After all, we were both of us virgins, and despite the desires I'd nurtured since assuming my physical condi-tion, I was anxious about my ability to perform. As it turned out, however, I needn't have worried, for no sooner had I shed the last vestiges of the sublime than I came into another kind of wisdom. Far sweeter than the abiding bliss one enjoyed in the Garden was this immersion in an ele-ment of want and fear, where your only access to paradise was through the body of your beloved.

Some months later I was cast into anxiety again, when Hannah informed me I was soon to be a papa. Raised as I'd been to believe that the fruit of the unions of women and angels were monstrosities, I wondered if we shouldn't try to obtain a philter from the speaker woman. On the other hand, I'd heard in the storytellers' minyans that such offspring sometimes turned out, against all odds, to be sages and mighty men; and heartened by my Hannaleh's buoyant spirits, I looked forward to seeing what I had spawned.

Meanwhile I grew bored with being a kept man, tired of my role as feather in the greasy cap of Berel Groysfuss, while my expectant wife peddled skins. Also, I was fed up with our unsanitary quarters in Berel's courtyard, which in no way could I feature as a nursery. So I became a *belfer,* riding the kids on my shoulders to Hebrew school through streets knee-deep in Polish gumbo. Looking back, I might have set my sights higher; the artisans of our community—the glassblowers, millwrights, and blacksmiths—did all right for themselves. But what skills did I have other than instilling in the unborn the knowledge I'd been obliged to revoke at birth, a knowledge I'd already begun to forget myself? Not that they weren't exacting, my labors, which barely kept my wife and me in barley soup, to acquire a taste for which I'd had to wean myself from manna. But life—how should I say it?—was good; *tahkeh,* it was life, an event I was forever making the acquaintance of.

You had snow on the steppe in winter, sleighs drawn by jangling ponies bearing gentry under thistledown, and spring announced by sassafras and linden trees, jessamine bushes and lilacs, forget-me-nots sprouting from the rotten thatch above our heads. There was market day when the Jews came in caravans selling fabrics, bottled spirits, tubs of buttermilk, bales of flax. They came wearing voluminous skirts underneath which they'd smuggled a hundredweight of game across the border; they sold mushrooms from the surrounding forests, deers' teeth for suckling infants, kiddush cups, Hanukkah lamps, editions of the illuminated Lublin Talmud. There were bloodletting booths outside the bathhouse, where an attendant sold charms to childless women. Scribes wrote bills of sale, marriage brokers drew up contracts on the doorstep of the synagogue—which looked small from without in order not to antagonize the goyim, though inside its floors were sunk deep, its rafters raised high, carved with stags, lions, and signs of the zodiac. If it was something less than the world depicted in the storytellers' minyans, it was something more than the world I'd left behind.

Above all there was my darling wife, my Hannaleh, protégée of the angel of laughter. Her I liked to watch by hearth light in the hand-me-down headdress of Odessa lace, her forehead filleted in hemp, her broad face aglow, a belly so gravid I thumped it for ripeness like a melon. And I was her chosen one, her Simcha; you should have seen me then: the husband and almost upright provider in calico trousers and linen shirt, its seams rounded to exempt it from ritual fringes. We made a fine pair, Hannah and I, as we strolled the crooked streets of our town, which in those days believed it had reason to rejoice. For hadn't there just commenced a Cossack rebellion, signaling—or so said the pious—the war between Gog and Magog that would herald Apocalypse?

Then the child was born, and we called him Nachman, relieved that he seemed to be normal, while anticipating like all parents his glorious destiny. But before Nachman had a chance to reveal his messianic calling, the butchers came. It's better I should spare you the details, about which our rabbis said in the pinkas register, "We are ashamed to write down what the Cossacks and Tartars did to our people, lest we disgrace a species created in the image of God." As you know, my wife was murdered and worse, which was when I decided the earth was no place to raise a kid. So I took up my son and made my way back to the Upper Eden, where his mother would be waiting. It was some dreadful journey even then, et cetera. I stopped awhile with my family in the hereafter, but of course I couldn't stay, and, saying so long to Hannah and heaven a second time, I left for the world again, arriving near the end of the nineteenth century on the Lower East Side of New York.

After the shock waves from viewing *Simcha's Fall* had subsided, I went to Rivka Bubitsch, daughter of Rabbi Mordecai the Blind, and threatened to expose her unless she told me what I wanted to know. Later on she would reveal her secret to everyone, but for the present she was fiercely protective of her private life. She assured me my threats were unnecessary, the information was not classified, then told me that the play had its genesis in a tale told to the Shmueler troupe by its leading man, who called himself Nachman Opgekumener.

And who, I wondered, was this Nachman?

"Is your memory so short?" Rivka asks me. "He's a greenhorn that you yourself brought him to Yoshke not a month ago." Then she told me about the greenhorn's undignified flight from the school for thieves. This was the rooftop institution directed by the ambidextrous Yoshke Nigger, in whose care I had apparently entrusted my conscript—where, according to Rivka, for his bungled efforts to pick the pocket of a bell-hung manikin, Nachman was strung out on a clothesline above an alley alongside the shantung kimonos and umbrella drawers of the pleasure girls. At no small risk to life and limb, he managed to escape, running away from Allen Street to take shelter in the darkness of the gallery at Uncle Sam's Burlesque. It was there he first set eyes on Sophie the Red, playing a racy version of the good niece Mina in a farcical production of Gordin's *God, Man, and the Devil*, and was smitten.

After the play he searched high and low for the leading lady, scouring the ghetto to no avail, then returned the following day to the music hall, where he stumbled into a company "rehearsal." Drawn largely from the ranks of local chippies and desperadoes, the Shmuelers were never that keen on rehearsing—which to them meant gathering to congratulate themselves on the outrageous liberties they'd taken with a given script. So they always welcomed distraction, and this one— in the form of a draggle-tailed intruder with a quilt like funny papers draped over his shoulders— looked to be especially interesting. Encouraged by their director, Lazar Waxman, himself a renegade from Second Avenue, they prepared to haze the *yold*, as would-be theatricals were sneeringly called. They sat him down on a three-legged stool at center stage, shone an olivette lamp in his face, and retreated to the stalls to be amused, while the greenhorn (who'd had little enough practice speaking to souls in heaven, never mind on earth) did what came naturally. He began to tell a story.

"Then, before you know it, they're hooked," Rivka tells me. "Well, maybe not all of a sudden; but once Waxman stops heckling long enough to catch the drift of the immigrant's tale—about a angel, no less—he shushes Tillie Taub, the wardrobe mistress, who's dallying with the ham

Shlomo Fertig, who makes a righteous show of shushing the others. Then everybody's all ears. Before Nachman can even reach the climax of his *mishegoss,* the Shmuelers, they don't know themselves if they're horsing around or what, they're talking how let's make of his story a stage business, a *shpiel.* They're on their feet fighting already over who will play which part, when Waxman, that looks like a goat in a China silk dressing gown, speaks up to settle the debate; he announces that nobody but the greenhorn himself (who hasn't asked) must take the role of the fallen angel, with Sophie of course as Hannaleh, his giddy bride."

After that I was at the theater every night for the run of *Simcha's Fall* and for *The Mooncalf,* which the Shmuelers mounted even before the public had tired of the previous play. Then one night I stole backstage. Thanks to the frenzied activity of players and stagehands, I was able to slip into the wings and climb the spiral stairs unnoticed; I crept down a narrow passage past the green room, which was painted red, until I came to a door with the name OPGEKUMENER embroidered on a knitted sampler. I reached for my steel-shanked jimmy, but a preliminary twist of the knob proved the door to be unlocked. The ripe odor of the airless cell suggested that its occupant used it for a dormitory as well as a dressing room. The table with its smoky mirror was cluttered like a shrine with gifts from admirers, spilling onto the carpetless floor. There were clocks and cutglass decanters, a morose songbird in a cage, stacks of letters—some tied with ribbon, some leaking petals and fancy garters from their opened envelopes. A plate of half-eaten whitefish sat atop a small hardwood icebox next to a wardrobe rack containing, among various costumes and accessories, Simcha's folded wings. Across the canvas camp bed, beneath which squatted a covered chamber pot, lay a crazy quilt emptied of stuffing.

It belonged, I now recalled, to the kid I'd met some weeks before on Ellis Island. So crestfallen had he appeared—mantled in his tattered patchwork, wearing moleskin leggings above his toeless top boots, tags fluttering from his overblouse like feathers on a baby bird—that none of the other predators bothered to approach him, which left me to pad forward and inquire,

"How did they ever let you past the customs?"

The boy turned from surveying the harbor with an expression so forlorn that I thought he'd mistaken the Statue of Liberty for Lot's wife. In an accent I identified as the Volin dialect, a brand of Yiddish common to east-ern Poland and the Ukraine (though listen closely and there was a subtle inflection you couldn't quite place), the kid guilelessly volunteered, "I gave them some of these."

He turned out a pocket, opening a fist full of what looked at first to be fruit, strawberries, and dwarf pears, and crumpled autumn leaves. But look again and you saw that the fruit might be precious stones, the leaves shards of coruscating gold. I snatched the baubles from the kid's hand to weigh them in my own, squinting to speculate how they would fare beneath the jeweler's loupe. The stuff exuded a musky scent that went straight to my head, kindling a fire there compared to which the one in my hand was nothing, a stray couple of sparks.

"From where did you get these?" I demanded, then, before the boy could reply, told him never mind, suddenly not wanting to know. I thrust the heaven gelt into a pocket, withdrew the slab bottle from another, and took a swig to douse the brilliance that had infected my head. Then the kid asked me humbly, indicating the towers of Wall Street, their windows glinting like fish scales across the bay, "This is *di goldeneh medinah?*"

"No!" I snapped, still trying to recover my wits. "This is *di treyfeneh medinah,* the trashy land. The Golden Land, now, that would be up past the end of the horse-car line."

He sighed, clearly exhausted, his chin sinking to his sparrow chest. I studied him: a sad-eyed, hook-nosed sack of bones, come to America de-fenseless and (now) empty-handed, without even a hat to protect him from the November wind. This one was definitely damaged goods, better to throw him back in favor of some other Moishe, one more suited to braving the trials of the New World.

"The Golden Land, he wants," I said to the sulfur yellow sky swarming with gulls, " 'the land that I show you,' eh?" I grabbed the front of the kid's frayed overblouse, appreciating its crewelwork between thumb and fore-finger, thinking, All the same, your ready-made stuff was *shmattes* by com-parison. "You want Golden Land?" I asked a touch menacingly. A gust of wind off the harbor mussed the greenhorn's hair, a mop made of scorched *lokshen* noodles. "C'mon," shoving him in the direction of a steam launch about to depart its slip for the Battery, "I'll give you Golden Land."

From the Battery we rode the Elevated to Allen Street, where I consigned my charge to the good offices of Yoshke, thereby washing my hands of him. I took the tchatshkes to Cohen's Loans in the Bowery, where they brought only a measly finif, having already lost their luster in the ghetto's corrosive atmosphere. Still, the sum was enough to finance a short vacation from Number 49. I made the rounds of the dives operated by Dopey Benny's bankroll boys, Harry Blinder's Café and Billiards on Delancey Street, Simmie Tischler's Sans Souci on Broome. I put in an appearance at Sid Boske's hop joint and was thrown out of a *nafkeh bias*, a cathouse, run by Paula the Horse Car, who claimed my presence dampened the ardor of her clientele. I kipped under the chromo of a Yid pugilist in Max Schnure's Chrystie Street saloon, where I was pished on by an ape named Samson who swabbed the spitoons. Eventually, via the bucket shops along Water Street and the dead houses under the Brooklyn Bridge, I fetched up half frozen, with empty pockets and a pickled brain, on an ash heap under the Brooklyn Bridge. Managing somehow to get myself back to the island, I rounded up a few more recruits for Yoshke's academy, in exchange for the cash that would enable me to repeat my routine. It was at that point when, cold and idly curious, curiosity being a stimulant I was as susceptible to as schnapps, I'd stumbled into an original theatrical offering on Canal Street.

So shaken was I by the memory that I never heard the ovations signaling the end of the play; only when the door opened behind me did I come back to myself in time to plunge into the costume rack. Nachman had entered dressed as Farfl Narish from *The Mooncalf* and sat down to wipe the greasepaint from his face, when there was coincidentally a knock at the door. *"Kum areyn,"* he says, after which who should straggle into the dressing room but Rivka Bubitsch, the rabbi's frumpish daughter, who had been Nachman's first audience. This I'd had from the girl herself: how, in her father's flat, after the old blind man led the apprentices in afternoon prayers, Nachman would tell her the stories he'd overheard in heaven, where he'd always had to keep them to himself. Then he would ask, because he'd been disappointed by the bleakness of the Lower East Side, if there were a place on earth where such splendid things happened. It was Rivka, whispering so her ailing father (who disapproved of it) wouldn't overhear, that set him straight: "In the theater," she said.

Not having seen her since he'd run away from Allen Street to become an overnight sensation, Nachman was surprised by the visit. "What do you want?" he asked a bit flatly, because he had scarcely thought of the girl from the moment he'd begun his onstage romance with Sophie the Red. Rivka apologized for disturbing him, but her father's clarion cough kept her awake nights, and she'd thought it might calm her down if Nachman told her one of his stories. It would be like old times.

"Who gets out of bed and walks five blocks in the night for a story?" Nachman wanted to know, suspicious of her motives though not unreceptive to her request. It was what kept him calm when he wasn't onstage with Sophie, spinning his bootleg yarns in the cafés and coffeehouses for anyone who would listen. Otherwise he was wandering the streets (incognito to discourage idolatrous fans), looking with only half a heart for a long-lost papa. So, despite his postperformance fatigue, he started in, "*A mol iz geven*, once upon a time . . . ," when Rivka, perched on the edge of the camp bed, said please could she have *The Mooncalf*.

"How did you know that's not the one I'm telling?" wondered Nachman testily, and proceeded with the tale of the ragpicker who sniffs the smoke from the fables an old rabbi has asked his daughter to burn. ("They are from my soul its private parts," the rabbi confessed with his dying breath.) Then Rivka butted in again: he should hurry up and get to the good part, the scene where Rokhl the rabbi's daughter, delighted with Farfl Narish's spicy version of her father's own stories, becomes enamored of the transformed ragpicker. "I thought you didn't see the show," said Nachman to Rivka, who assured him she'd only read about it in the papers; her papa would never allow her to go in the theater. Nachman reminded her that she was in the theater now, but she told him please to just get on with the story.

"Why should I bother to tell you what you already know?" he grumbled, while Rivka composed herself in a more responsive attitude on the cot and waited for him to continue. Tentatively, he went on to describe how Farfl was reluctant to tell Rokhl he loves her for fear he'll turn back into an idiot.

Said Rivka, "Which he does anyway, no?" Then Nachman: "Yes, but first he and Rokhl—" Rivka: "They fall in love, and he says to her, this Farfl, he says . . . Well, what are you waiting?" Nachman was nettled: "Since when did you need me to tell you anything?"

At Rivka's supplicant urging, however, Nachman hemmed and began again: "So Farfl says, 'I'm afraid I should love you,' and Rokhl replies—" Here Rivka beat him to Rokhl's line, "Who's afraid from love?" Snapped Nachman, "Am I telling this story or you!"—though, despite his annoyance, I could see he was impressed by Rivka's deep-felt delivery. She sounded almost professional.

"Then what do they do?" nudged Rivka, kittenish again.

Said Nachman, "Farfl says, 'You don't understand,' then Rokhl—" But again Rivka usurped Rokhl's line: "I understand better than you think." "*Gevalt!*" cried Nachman as, indifferent to his aggravation, Rivka coaxed him, "Then what?" "Then nothing," barked the actor, and fell to muttering, "He's still scared, so . . ." Nachman hesitated as if daring Rivka to give him the cue and, satisfied that she was silenced for the moment, persevered: "So she kisses him."

Asked Rivka, "Like how?" Nachman: "Like you kiss. What do you mean, how?" "Like this?" asked Rivka, rising from the bed to lean over Nachman, still seated astraddle his chair, and kiss him. Nachman sputtered, "You kissed me!" Said Rivka, blushing to the lobes of her ears, "*Nu,* so I thought you maybe wanted to rehearse." Nachman was incredulous. "This play I'm performing already in my sleep! What for did you come in my room?" Pouting, Rivka sat back down on the bed, rearranged her drab skirt, and said, "You couldn't just humor a girl that her papa is sick and she has also insomnia? The great Opgekumener that used to come in my papa's parlor before he ran off to be the heartthrob of the ghetto, who would tell by me his stories that he claimed he brought them from paradise. This Nachman couldn't just for tonight pretend I'm Sophie Kush? I'm Sophie that's playing Rokhl in the show I didn't ever see? Just the scene I heard about where Farfl Narish says, 'You don't understand. . . .'" She moved her lips in a voiceless invitation for him to repeat.

Nachman relented enough to mumble a perfunctory, "You don't understand," upon which Rivka, back on her feet, put a finger to his lips in an unscripted improvisation: "Shah!" Then she bent from the waist, experimentally removing the finger, replacing it with her warm mouth, her moist lips once again pressing Nachman's in a crushing kiss. This time, however, Nachman didn't resist; he rose, knocking over the chair in his haste to enfold the girl in his arms. He squeezed her as fervently as he'd been known to squeeze his costar, the kind of embrace that caused spectators to reach for their fans in midwinter. But just when I—remember I'm still spying on them from the wardrobe rack—just when I thought, So good on him, my son! Nachman abruptly broke away to come up for air.

"Rivka, for shame!" he cried, shoving the girl to arm's length. "You know I love only the *shauspieler* Sofia der Royte." Rivka stared at him with a look that fluctuated, with each blink of the eye, between pity and outrage. "Sophie!" she shouted. "That Jezebel! A *finster mazel*, bad luck on her, the bride of cholera, that she don't even exist but on the stage!" Then, gathering her ratty plush cape about her, she stormed out of the room in a dust-raising huff. Equally disappointed, I surfaced from the cover of the wardrobe rack, sniffed "Feh!" at my son, and slammed out the door behind Rivka.

Shortly after, I detected a new detachment in the stage attitude of Sofia der Royte with regard to her male counterpart; though you couldn't have proved it by the cloakmakers, shoelace peddlers, and horseradish widows who packed the place out every night. It was around this time that Rabbi Mordecai the Blind passed away. Of course his death had been anticipated for so long that its indefinite postponement had become a fact of life on Allen Street. Chronically moribund, the old man—his sightless eyes like pearl onions, lips like jelly babies in the excelsior of a beard perpetually flecked with blood—had continued leading his skeleton faithful in prayer. Even bedridden, he prayed with his phlebitic leg tethered by a velvet cord to his davenport, lest in his transports he should be lifted up to the Celestial Academy before his time. But just when it seemed that the pious old party might carry on in extremis forever, he expired, and, always a sucker for the pomp of a gangster funeral (never mind that this one was occasioned by the death of a holy man), I secured a seat in one of the limousines.

The motorcade of freshly waxed Arrows and Panhard touring cars set out through the slush of a leaden February afternoon; it crossed over the Williamsburg Bridge, beneath which tugboats sundered the ice-choked river like scissors through rucked green paper, and wound its way up the snowbanked avenues of Brooklyn. At the Mount Hebron Cemetery, its frosted monuments dwarfing from their higher ground the towers of Manhattan in the distance, a short procession accompanied the casket to the half acre reserved for the worthies of vice and capital crime. A snowflake or two leaked from the clouds like down from a torn pillow slip, as the allrightnik rabbi (snatched from some uptown temple to lend legitimacy to the proceedings) made his eulogy, and Boss Dopey Fein, spruce but unassuming in an ankle-length astrakhan, prized a crust of mud from the heap beside the pit. Then he handed the spade to the rabbi's daughter, who removed her shawl to reveal herself as the notorious Mademoiselle Sophie, before flinging her wig like a wad of flame into her father's grave. As she declared her true identity, the mounting storm swirled around her like flour from a sifter, and my son hid his face in his hands.

Not long after that, Rivka/Sofia accepted an offer from a respectable theater, and Nachman, reduced to a cipher in her absence, was shown the door.

SAUL

By the time I returned home from New York City, my hair had grown to resemble a burnt shrub, and my parents hardly knew me. At my unannounced arrival on their doorstep, my mother, always quick to turn on the waterworks, retreated into the kitchen to weep. "Sammy," she keened to my father, who, with yeoman powers of denial, was in the den showing me slides of their recent Caribbean cruise, "I can't look at our son!" "That was Port-au-Prince," my father informed me, scarcely lifting the walnut shells of his heavy eyelids, "or was it Santo Domingo? Your mother took these while I was locked in the head with the squirts. . . ." This to the eldritch accompaniment of my mother's keening.

At some point my younger sister, puffed with righteousness, threw in a much-rehearsed two cents: "Somehow I'll make it up to our family for your disgrace." "I haven't begun to disgrace our family," I replied, uncertain as to whether I was objecting to her aspersion or issuing a threat.

My moping presence lent our tidy ranch house the atmosphere of a plague ship becalmed in a Sargasso Sea. Several weeks passed, and I still showed no signs of emerging from my funk, nor did I give any indication of returning to school. What school? NYU was now out of the question, and, even allowing for some probationary arrangement, the last resort of a state-funded university would not accept me in the midst of an academic year. Gainful employment was the obvious solution, but when I failed to respond to my parents' gentle persuasion, all patience spent, they suggested I visit a psychiatrist. This was a radical development on their part, given my family's association of mental disorder with shame, and, affected by their compassionate resolve, I made no protest.

Why should I protest? Bereft as I was, it was all the same to me. Also, I was aware there was a war going on; the draft lottery was in place, and, my number being relatively low, it wouldn't hurt to have some history of emotional imbalance on the books.

On the way out the door to visit the shrink, flanked by my mother and father, I passed through the living room, where a gilt-framed mirror was hung above the mantelpiece crowning a fireplace with no flue. In the mirror my old high-school graduation portrait watched me from the opposite wall, its buttoned-down visage leering over my shoulder with smug disdain.

The shrink, porcine and perspiring in midwinter, his face a scarlet doily of broken capillaries, set great store by his frankness of speech. A quick study, he confirmed with knuckle-crackling satisfaction that I was miserable. ("This is news?" asked my beleaguered father.) A period of rest and therapy in the psychiatric hospital to which the good doctor was attached was recommended, and a decision (without recourse to my opinion) was made. My head swam from the swift dispatch of my fate. I had visions of *The Magic Mountain,* but the hospital itself turned out to be a no-frills, state-run institution locally legendary as a kind of junior Bedlam, though the reality was much less Gothic. Behind a façade of ferro-cement and tinted glass, there were four antiseptic floors, each graduated according to the desolation of its inmates. I was placed on the third floor among the lost souls designated as Chronics, a catchall term embracing a range of patients from recovering alcoholics to depressives and benign psychopaths. We were one story beneath the terminal Acutes, creatures so unsalvageable as to have been reduced to mere rumor. At our parting my father shook my hand as if to say, *Today you are certifiable,* while my mother wept so unconsolably that you'd have thought they'd pronounced me criminally insane. I was more or less indifferent to the proceedings, but for the slight romantic pang that tweaked my heart at the prospect of being incarcerated.

Once the doors slammed behind me, however, the romance dissolved. I was conscious of the hallowed tradition of breakdown and confinement among literary types, that to have been in a madhouse was a badge of distinction. But my dull melancholy hardly qualified me for the ranks of those driven to madness by an excess of genius. Even as

I wallowed in my unhappiness, I thought of my condition as symptomatic of the merely weak and spoiled. At the outset I was confined to a private room and subjected to a regimen of narcotics that left me in a vegetable state. I was surprised at how readily I adapted to perpetual stupor and would have been more than content if allowed to drop into an interminable sleep. ("Sleep cure" was a phrase that reprised itself in my brain like a soothing melody.) But no sooner had I begun to surrender to sluggishness, my body as if fed on buckshot, than my medication was abruptly reduced and I was driven from my room onto a ward with half a dozen beds. Thereafter I was made to spend the hours of forced consciousness in the sterile, fluorescent snake pit of the dayroom, where it was believed that mingling with my own kind would aid in my recovery. Recovery from what? I wondered, feeling no more desire to come out of depression than I had to persist in it.

A sampling of the society I was compelled to mingle with included a fat lady in a sequined housecoat who fancied herself a species of walking fish and always carried a carafe of water as a symbol of the medium that sustained her; a hairless ex-priest who'd lost his faith and literally girded his loins in a breechclout of institutional bath towels, flaying himself with electrical cords until orderlies confiscated them; a middle-aged lady of pleasant features and sapphire hair who laid claim to the sovereignty of the planet Toximania, where a pretender sat on the throne, and wore at all times the mantle of her sensible tweed cloak; a flinty-faced old gentleman with knobkerrie legs, who stood rigid as a sentry for days, only to fling himself without warning onto some unwitting female patient who'd ventured within range. There were the hollow-eyed spectators who sat in perfect tranquillity most of the week, until the effects of their electroshock therapy wore off, leaving them to fidget and writhe like a gallery of Uriah Heeps. And there was Billy Boots, about whom more later.

At intervals over the next few weeks, I was hauled into the presence of the psychiatrist who had advised my admission to the hospital. In the absence of witnesses, he exchanged his professional detachment for an attitude of outright hostility and let it be known that he regarded my depression as narcissistic self-indulgence. When I told him I was inclined to agree, his scorn intensified. "Why, you supercilious little bastard," he declared, and recommended that I enlist in the military. It would, he

contended, make me a man, which to his mind I clearly wasn't. He himself had been a fighter pilot in the Korean War, and having presented his
brute demeanor as evidence of the manhood to which I might aspire,
rested his case. For all his antagonism, I gave him the benefit of the doubt:
the aggression was part of a strategy to bully me out of my despair. (Later
I would decide that he really did hold me in contempt.) But if anything,
the doctor's tactics backfired, and I clung more tenaciously than ever to
the sadness that had come to define me.

By the time my medication had been downgraded from a stunning
Thorazine cocktail to a relatively innocuous three or four Valiums a day,
I'd begun to adjust to the hospital routine. There was, after all, some
comfort in its structured boredom. There were the odd group-therapy
sessions led by a young nurse with thinning hair and no apparent expertise in such things. For all her good intentions (and a uniform so
starched that it squeaked), there were days when she was unable to elicit
a single word from the assembled circle, days when she couldn't stop the
defrocked priest from exhorting us all into slumber. There were the
"privileges" awarded to the compliant, among whom I was included on
account of my apparent harmlessness. These might involve an afternoon
stroll under strict supervision about a gravel-paved hospital courtyard;
or if you preferred, you could use the "gymnasium," which consisted of a
padded chamber that contained a punching bag and a medicine ball.
There was a seldom-used billiard table in the dayroom, which, when its
accordion panels were opened, also functioned as a cafeteria, where the
meals—powdered eggs, overcooked vegetables with the consistency of
viscera, mystery meats in a snot-gelid gravy—were a caricature of institutional food. There were the weekly visits from my family, who had begun
to treat me as if I were Gregor Samsa, and then there was, as I mentioned,
Billy Boots.

Though I'd done my best to remain aloof from the general population, having assumed a misery that was its own caveat, Billy, perhaps attracted by the novelty of someone reading a book, approached me during
my first week on the ward. Without bothering to introduce himself, he
stood over my chair in the dayroom, angling his large, square-jawed head
to read the title of my novel.

"I used to like Hermann Hesse in my callow youth," he commented in a molasses-slow southern voice (he couldn't have been more than a couple of years older than me), "but I find the stuff too, I dunno, tendentious anymore. I prefer your madder music these days." This said somehow without pretense or condescension. When I looked up, he asked jauntily, "What are you in for?" as if we were on a cell block instead of in a loony bin.

Though solidly built (with the kind of unapologetic good looks that always made me squeamish), he gave the impression of someone whose hard edges had been buffed and burnished, like a sculpture changing into a human being. His eyes, soft and bovine, kept cutting away, as if distracted by something on the room's (or the earth's) periphery. He had a slightly splay nose and a shock of thick chestnut hair falling over his forehead in a breaking wave, an easiness in his skin that made him especially conspicuous among the shuffling and stationary wounded. The rolled sleeves of his faded lumberjack shirt revealed powerful forearms.

Such a robust presence seemed almost criminally out of place in the hospital dayroom, and, squirming under his observation, I answered his question with a shrug, as if my condition were self-evident. Billy nodded, apparently satisfied, and introduced himself, extending a hand that clasped my own in a bone-crushing grip. I felt for a moment like a captive leprechaun whom he wouldn't release until I'd divulged my name, which I did. As I reclaimed my hand, Billy announced without a speck of self-consciousness that he had tried to kill himself. He lifted his chin to show me a recently healed scar like a lopsided grin the pale echo of his own and boasted almost boyishly, "I cut my throat ear to ear." Then, though I'd said not a word to invite him, he plopped himself down in the chair opposite mine and launched into a graphic replay of the whole incident, including those parts of which he couldn't have had any clear recollection.

He'd taken the drug LSD, "which gives every sensation about seven dimensions and will transport you to a zone beyond time." Casually, in his mellow Delta accent, he alluded to Franz Kafka's "Before the Law" parable, commencing a digression on Kafka's history until I muttered that I was familiar with the author and his work.

"Wellsir," he continued undaunted, "unlike the character in the parable who spends his life waiting to be admitted to the Palace of the Law, acid gives you the . . ." He paused to take stock of my features and broadened his grin. "It gives you the *hudspah* to slip inside." Recounting the experience after a fashion that may or may not have been figurative, he told me how he'd eluded a series of gatekeepers, racing through all the chambers of the Palace until he had only one more threshold to cross, which was: "You guessed it . . ." Though I'm not sure I had. Anyway, in what he described as a pragmatic decision, he'd taken out his penknife under a sap-green moon and opened his throat. Miraculously, he missed severing his jugular, and the frigid February evening further cooperated by temporarily stanching the flow of blood.

"But how was I to know I wasn't dead?" Billy asked in all earnestness, describing his subsequent inspection of what he supposed was a transmundane world. He was gazing through the windows of houses—at a girl whose bone-white beauty could petrify the beholder, a patriarch in striped pajamas warming his hands at a blue philosopher's stone—when the cops, alerted by reports of a Peeping Tom, arrived in force. "It took six of those suckers to wrestle me into a squad car," he boasted, "but I think I gave as good as I got." He smiled and gestured to show off what he'd "got"—a missing molar and some angry abrasions above his eye—shaking his head over the memory of such youthful folly.

Later on in the lockup, his wound thawed and the blood spilled as from an open spigot, after which he was transferred to the police infirmary and thence to Tennessee Psychiatric for "observation" pending a court hearing. All this he related in a tone of guileless enthusiasm, as if he were at once the hero of and spellbound audience to his own adventure.

Needless to say, his story terrified me. Billy Boots seemed to me more dangerous and deluded than any of the other more or less subdued lunatics on the floor, and after our initial encounter, I tried my best to keep my distance from him. But he continued to seek me out, and the circumstances of our confinement made it impossible to avoid him. At some point he'd even persuaded Mr. Eubanks, the gibbering retiree who slept in the bed next to mine, to swap places with him in exchange for some smuggled-in pornography. During mostly one-sided nocturnal conversations, until the night nurse came in to threaten us with forced injections, he would regale me on diverse subjects. One moment he might be praising the virtues of the local wrestler Sputnik Monroe (or Elvis Presley, who he swore had lived for a while in a house down the street and saluted young Billy whenever he passed), the next conjuring some obscure Flemish poet of centuries ago. He seemed completely unabashed by my feigned indifference to his blather, an attitude his friendly overtures were starting to wear down. The truth was, though still wary and intimidated, I was beginning to be a little intrigued by Billy Boots, not to say flattered that he'd singled me out for his confidences. Despite the perceived risk of letting him get too chummy (as if it were up to me), I conceded from time to time to ask him some tepid question, which never failed to trigger an elaborate response.

"So what kind of name is Boots?"

"Cracker," he informed me matter-of-factly. He'd been an orphan (why was I not surprised?), adopted by a family of rural people recently moved to the city from the Arkansas Ozarks, an uncultured hillbilly couple, but not stupid (the husband was a land surveyor) and reasonably kind. For all that, he'd always felt a stranger in their house, a member of a lost tribe who might at any moment recall him to their fold. While he couldn't be 100 percent certain of his true heritage, he had reason to believe that his birth father was a Jew of Sephardic descent, a sugar magnate who'd had relations with a Creole demimonde who had in turn given up Billy for adoption. "There's Jew and nigger both in my woodpile." I asked where in the world he'd gleaned his information and was given a tale of implausible research and hearsay. This confirmed me in my suspicion that Billy Boots was a compulsive liar or, more generously, that he was a kind of alchemist of happenstance, distilling credible falsehood into pure moonshine. That said, there was in fact a Mediterranean cast to his complexion, and his high buttocks and fleshy lips gave some indication of Negro blood.

He was casually conversant in a bewildering array of subjects, which he discussed without any perceptible transition from one to another. I wondered how he knew so much and ranged so far in his mind when, thanks to barbiturates and melancholia, I could barely think beyond the hospital walls. But Billy Boots, who declared on some days never to have left the South—while on others he made reference to mysterious journeys—could imagine an absinthe binge in the labyrinth of the Paris streets before Baron Haussmann razed the slums or picture himself shadowing a rooster-legged Nikolai Gogol along the Nevsky Prospekt at dusk. He recalled the levee camps on the Mississippi River, where he claimed to have spent his summers with his adoptive father, who worked for the TVA; described the hoodoo practices of the bayou Negroes and compared their playing the "dozens" to the backchat in Aristophanes. He spoke of his drug trips as if they'd been personally superintended by Havelock Ellis and Jean Cocteau. Between life and learning he acknowledged no special boundaries, so that the books he referred to had the urgency of actual events, while events assumed the contours of theatrical productions. In his table talk, he seemed composed of equal parts Huck Finn and William Blake, one moment earthbound and innocent, the next slipping off to paradise.

The largeness of the world Billy inhabited excited me to the point of exasperation, and there were nights when I pulled the sheet over my head and stuffed my ears. While you couldn't have detected a trace of posturing in his runaway discourse (he seemed always to assume that his listener was as effortlessly erudite as he), I tried to convince myself that he was finally just a dilettante. Then there was his irksome way of refusing to take seriously what I liked to believe was my incurable unhappiness. When he tried to cajole me out of it, I bristled and attempted to defend myself, even hinted at having come through an ordeal of my own, but Billy never gave much credence to my grief. His judgment was harder on me than the shrink's, for while Dr. Glasscock (that was his unfortunate name) merely browbeat and insulted me, Billy Boots, with his undiscriminating appetite for life (and death), made me feel ashamed. Consequently I began to try to conceal in his presence the depth of my misery, which resulted in my becoming less miserable.

The efforts I made under Billy's influence to overcome despair were apparently noted by the authorities. In our increasingly rare interviews, Dr. Glasscock had stopped calling me names and begun alluding to my imminent release, though he continued urging me to consider joining the armed forces. Billy, for all his excesses, had also finessed the doctors and charmed the hospital staff, but just as the powers were prepared to bestow on him his provisional freedom, he decided he would prefer not to leave. It turned out that, like me, Billy Boots was enjoying his holiday from the quotidian. He was entertaining a parade of tricked-out visitors bearing tributes: outré books and stuffed animals, some of which hid caches of dope and (coals to Newcastle) pills. Also, he'd initiated a liaison with a self-described nymphomaniac recently arrived on our floor. This was Deirdre, a whey-faced, bedroom-eyed confection whose postage-stamp skirts were discomposing the ordinarily sedated male population of the dayroom. (They had become the central issue of our group-therapy sessions, those skirts, where the defrocked priest insisted that the girl be made to wear a shapeless garment like a *sambenito*.) An inveterate exhibitionist, Deirdre was in the habit of playing a card game with herself in the dayroom that amounted to strip solitaire. While the most comatose among the male patients were provoked by her to tentlike protrusions in their pants, only Billy dared approach her and was thus rewarded with an intimate knowledge of her charms.

"I thought you told me you were spoken for," I said, recalling the willowy visitor who'd clung to him on the dayroom sofa.

"Call it a rehearsal for my return to civilian life."

Was he, I wondered, rehearsing sex or infidelity? In any event, they would meet, he and Deirdre, with minimal discretion in the men's shower. Physical relations between patients were of course unacceptable—they were a major breach of hospital policy—but the unofficial judgment of the doctors was that Billy's exploits were an indication of an improved mental attitude. (Not to mention physical vigor, since he'd also shown himself proof against the antiaphrodisiacs that seasoned our powdered eggs.) Realizing he was about to be discharged, Billy mounted a campaign to convince all concerned of his abiding dementia. The problem was that, despite his extravagant imagination, Billy Boots was a dud at pretending to be nuts. "The CIA has implanted censors in my brain," he would complain, or, "Dr. Melersh has antennae under his toupee," delusions so conventional and transparent that they scarcely warranted attending. Nor was anyone fooled by his claims in group-therapy sessions that he was the incarnation of an eighteenth-century necromancer called the Count de St. Germain. Such assertions were regarded as what they were, desperate acts. Having long since assessed his throat-cutting incident a fluke, the result of a bad drug trip—the sort of thing they saw routinely these days—the doctors gave Billy a clean bill of health and, with the consent of the court to release him on his own recognizance, sent him packing.

I admit to having felt relieved at his departure. It was bad enough that my reawakened libido had been subjected to those parts of Deirdre's anatomy made visible to all, but that I should have to be regaled by Billy concerning those parts no one else had seen was intolerable. Jealous as I was, I might even have found the backbone to offer myself to her now that he was gone, but Deirdre had since been medicated into neutrality for her own protection and removed from the floor. Also, in Billy's absence, I was thankful not to have before me the constant challenge of his vitality against which to measure my own. But I missed him, and I missed those aspects of myself he aroused. In any case, whereas Billy's part had been to sham craziness, mine was, for Billy's sake, to simulate mental health, which I managed perhaps more effectively than I intended. As a consequence I was soon made to follow Billy's lead. About a week after his ouster, I, too, was dismissed by Dr. Glasscock ("dismissed" being the operative word, since the doctor seemed to have grown bored by my presence) and returned to the custody of my parents.

Before his exit from Tennessee Psychiatric, Billy Boots had invited me to come live in the house he shared with friends—the very characters whose operatic attire had caused such a stir among the inhabitants of the ward. Great experiments, he assured me, were being conducted at his domicile daily: "Think the Bateau Lavoir. . . ." That was all I had needed to hear to be sure that I wanted no part of his improvised household. I thanked-but-no-thanked him, looking forward to I didn't know what, certain only that mine was a solitary destiny. But no sooner had I returned to my parents' house and their persistent interrogations regarding my plans than I was grateful to have another option, however temporary. Exempt now from the draft (ironically, in light of my psychiatrist's sage advice), I could look forward to a career of feeling sorry for myself and wanted only a refuge where I could pursue that activity with all my heavy heart.

Doubtful that Billy Boots's urban compound was that place, in the end I felt I had no other alternative. I redisposed my mind to include the possibility that there was an element of kismet (*bashert,* as my Aunt Keni might have said) in my meeting with the failed suicide. Resist though I might, the time came—came, in fact, in little more than a week—when

I turned up with my meager belongings on the front porch of a narrow frame house in a cul-de-sac called Idlewild Street.

On my first night in the house, Billy Boots, acting as host, introduced me to the others as a genius of despondency. This was a dubious distinction, but I learned soon enough that everyone else who lived there was, by Billy's lights, some sort of a genius or hero. Christopher Nimitz, cool and piratical in balloon sleeves and pin-striped pants, his features as chiseled as a stone knight on a slab, had held some clerical post at a supply base behind the lines in Vietnam but was nonetheless a bona fide war hero. "A survivor," Billy had whispered to me within Christopher's hearing, adding that he'd been endowed by his experience with a rigorous conscience that made cowards of us all. Muhle, too, with his dark glasses, reptilian complexion, and shady past, had returned Lazarus-like from distant shores; resurrected from a heroin overdose, he'd come back as a minstrel and confidence trickster for whom the common moral laws did not apply. Finbar, oddly epicene despite his size and fame with women, who drank like a fish and was given to wicked bouts of dejection (and whose real name was Hugger Pugh), was, as Billy put it, a saint of depravity. He was Little John to Billy's Robin Hood, a vamping Falstaff to his friend's Prince Hal. Billy's lissome, long-suffering girlfriend, Lila, with her onyx eyes and the rainbow highlights in her midnight hair, was a creature of instinct and fathomless wisdom, as were practically all the women that passed through Idlewild Street, though I sometimes suspected they would have been happier to be counted as mere human beings.

After my reception, during which my back was repeatedly slapped by the ham hand of Finbar and my cheek bussed by Lila, they all went about their respective business. One minute I was surrounded by official greeters warmly assuring me that their dump was my dump, the next left entirely to my own devices. In a gesture toward orientation, Billy had previously shown me to a windowless alcove that could serve as my bedroom. The alcove was off what should have been a dining room but was instead an extension of the parlor, which was illumined by a rose-shaded floor lamp no brighter than a candle. There were heavy velvet draperies that I was told had been liberated from a condemned movie house, layers of throw rugs that made the floor heave like a pitcher's mound. Frayed posters of a blues diva and a revolutionary cynosure hung side by side like ancestral portraits. There was a tall bookshelf containing an insanely eclectic library and an elaborate sound system with a blinking panel that looked as if it might receive messages from outer space. In the alcove was a camp bed covered by an ash-strewn tapestry, which I sat upon gingerly, for the furniture did not inspire confidence: the cot, the armchair, the dragonesque chaise longue gave the impression of the sort of props that collapsed on hinges in Hollywood houses, spilling you through a trap into a dungeon or catacomb.

Satisfied that the cot was just a cot, I'd begun unpacking my bag, searching for maybe a closet where I could hang my clothes, when there came a knock at the door. This was a merciful event, since it both distracted me from contemplating the mistake I'd made in coming there and gave me the opportunity to take some initiative. I shoved the bag under the cot with my foot and went to answer the door.

A tall man, still young despite deeply creased cheeks and steel gray hair to his shoulders, stood on the porch wearing a duster like Wyatt Earp.

"Where's my wife?" he wanted to know.

The insinuation aroused in me an immediate (if premature) sense of loyalty. "I'm sure I don't know," I answered, sounding a little priggish to my own ears. Of course, I wasn't being entirely honest. Meeting Christopher, I'd been introduced as well to a dishwater blonde with liquid blue eyes, referred to without apology as Bateman's wife. It was therefore a simple matter to deduce that this was Bateman himself.

"I know she's upstairs with Numnutz," he persisted.

"Then why did you bother to ask?"

He gave me a moment's hard scrutiny, then sniffed as if I weren't worth the trouble, stepping into the room so that I was forced to take an awkward step backward. "You can tell Numnutz for me that he's a dead man."

My stomach cramped and my mouth went dry. An hour into my Idlewild Street debut, and already I was presented with a chance to prove my mettle, though exactly what mettle would that have been?

In any event, I replied, "Who do you think you are that you can come into our home [admittedly stretching the definition] and make threats?"

Having issued what I hoped was an adequate rejoinder, I turned my back. Did I really think he would give me the last word? Instantly I felt his fingers squeezing my throat, tearing off the recently acquired fetish of a glass-bead necklace, symbol of the new life upon which I was about to embark. Unstrung, the beads spilled onto the mound of carpets and scattered. But just as my knees began to buckle under the burden of the man on my back, his weight—to the accompaniment of thundering hooves—was abruptly removed. Maybe they'd been alerted by my gagging, or did the house have a sixth sense about such things? Whatever the case, Billy and Finbar, egged on by a whooping Muhle, had flung themselves into the room to break Bateman's death grip on my throat. Gasping for air, I stood upright in time to see them lift him bodily, carrying him like pallbearers dragging an uncooperative corpse to the open door, where they cast him out. Then, not content with having tossed him down the front steps, they bounded from the porch to administer a battery of kicks to his fetal form.

This sort of thing was new to me. But while Bateman's drubbing left me shaken and nauseous, the *whump, whump* of fists on flesh still reverberating in my gut, it also quickened my heart, and I felt as if, rather than a helpless victim, I had myself been a participant in a brawl. When my housemates slammed the door on the intruder and began to ask after my welfare, I accepted their compliments as if I deserved them. By then the rest of the household had reassembled in the parlor, curious to find out what had happened, and Billy presented me as the man of the hour. Proud but embarrassed to have been twice in one night made the center of attention, I complained,

"But he broke my love beads."

For reasons that at first eluded me, the company found this utterance hilarious, and with it I seemed to have launched my new identity. I was a type that had thus far been conspicuously missing on Idlewild Street: the sad clown. No matter that I wasn't particularly funny; from then on, my least whining plaint—"I lost my Valium prescription" or "Has anyone seen my acne scrubs?"—elicited incontinent laughter. And as Billy laughed loudest, my role as jester in our makeshift family was confirmed. Strange that, given my history of solitary habits, I should be so suddenly delighted to find myself a member of a family.

It was, despite appearances to the contrary, a functioning family with a working economy. The economy was based chiefly on drug traffic—marijuana, hashish, methamphetamines, LSD—a hazardous and complicated business of which I was left in near-total ignorance. Why should I, whose part was to entertain the house with a parody of despair—which was how my behavior was viewed—trouble my unpretty head with matters that needn't concern me? But drugs were an erratic and unreliable source of income, which required supplemental funds during the lean periods, funds to which I contributed not a whit. Meanwhile Lila worked a day job as a dentist's secretary, doffing her peasant dresses to ride a bicycle each weekday morning disguised in pantsuits as an ordinary citizen. It was thanks to her steady salary, and to the government food stamps we finagled every month, that we survived those times when the dope market was dry. Add to that Finbar's occasional blackjack winnings and his leaning on tardy debtors, Muhle's independent ventures in extortion and deceit, and Christopher's precise accounting and budgeting of the monthly take, and you could say we lived pretty well. Feast or famine, however, the rhythm of life on Idlewild Street remained much the same: Finbar alternated between his virile and distaff activities, one moment brooding over the puzzle of his disassembled VW engine, whose parts lay scattered about his room, the next transforming a minimal larder into lavish casseroles and soufflés. Muhle, in his daylight role as valetudinarian recovering from various addictions that had left him thin as a gibbet, entertained underage girls on his guitar, while Christopher kept the books and plotted social revolution between extraconjugal visits from Bateman's wife. Then night would fall, skirling music would play, and the house begin to undulate like a cartoon edifice to crescendos of chirruping bedsprings.

During my first weeks on Idlewild Street, the honeymoon period, Billy Boots seemed to be making up for his sedentary time in the hospital by seldom sitting still. Despite all his far-flung erudition, I never once saw him reading a book, which might have led you to conclude he was some kind of idiot savant. Though on any given day, peeking into the master bedroom that Lila had decorated like a fin-de-siècle salon, you might observe beside the canopied bed, wreathed in a froth of Lila's intimate garments, volumes by Louis Aragon, G. K. Chesterton, Yukio Mishima,

Claude Lévi-Strauss—strange bedfellows whose limp pages looked as if sucked of their contents like artichoke leaves.

Once I asked him if, having assimilated so much miscellaneous literature, he wasn't moved to try to make some of his own. Grinning, Billy took down a cigar box from a closet shelf and opened it, revealing a sheaf of neatly typed onionskin pages. They appeared with their unaligned margins to be poems in free verse, though the language, describing rustic mysteries and bizarre initiations, had an immediacy beyond artifice. I sampled page after page from the box, reading greedily and wondering how Billy had managed to endow such homely materials—carpenters' tools, catfish heads, barbers' strops, crushed japonica blossoms, and cypress knees—with the numinous quality of icons. There was a swatch from a young girl's nightgown hung on a barbed-wire fence, a shotgun kicking the heart, death in a dozen maverick personae; a boy suffering a rite of passage, standing against an outhouse wall as another boy threw knives with names at him. As the knives flew by, the boy dreamed himself into other countries where houses clung to cliffs and souls were extracted like syrup from trees. But while I bit my lip in concentration, the pages I was holding burst into flames. My first thought was that the poems had spontaneously combusted under the intensity of my regard, but, dropping them, sickened at the sight of the words curling into black ash, I heard him snicker and looked up to see Billy blow out a match.

"Writing is a rotten footbridge you better hightail it across," he said, looking through me with his fox-colored eyes, " 'cause the slats break with every step you take."

"I'm sure that's very deep," I replied, nevertheless inhaling the smoke from the burning pages like a healing vapor.

At his court hearing, which had come and gone, Billy Boots explained to the judge in his earnest manner that, distraught following a fight with his girl, he'd met an acquaintance who gave him a pill he was told would make him feel better. "That's the last thing I remember, Your Honor," he said, and the judge actually bought the story and threw out the case. Since then Billy had been traveling a lot. Sometimes with Finbar playing the trusty sidekick, sometimes solo, he flew to Austin, then traveled by bus to jerkwater towns along the Mexican border to score shipments of cannabis, which he then transported to receivers in select northern cities. Returning home, he would perform a slow striptease in the parlor, peeling down to underwear pinned all over in a feathery panoply of dollar bills. Once or twice, violating his own rule against fouling the nest, Billy had brought back the dope to Idlewild Street to peddle locally. He and Finbar would lug in a strongbox or a sticker-strewn steamer trunk, whose lid Billy opened with the pride of an undertaker showing off his handiwork. Then we would pay our respects to seventy-five pounds of tufted green marijuana neatly packaged in clear plastic bags.

As much as he enjoyed the risks involved in moving contraband, Billy exulted in his function as principal provider to the household, though, for all his professed allegiance to its members, he seemed anxious to be often gone. In residence, he tended to stay either in motion or out of sight. When not frolicking with Lila, who was sullen in public but given to hilarious trilling behind closed doors, he liked frequenting the shadier watering holes of the city. In his capacity as smuggler and trafficker, Billy saw himself—saw all of us, in fact—in the tradition of desperate men, "Like the James boys, Frank and Jesse, William and Henry." It was all a charade, of course, Billy's public-enemy stance; there was always about him the sense that he contained in one person the boy who was playing a part and the man who played that part for keeps. At any rate, to travel with Cap'n Billy and company, to enter with them some ill-lit barroom or fly-by-night coffee house, was to belong to an elite society, respected and maybe even a little feared. It was a feeling I was almost ashamed to find myself enjoying so much.

For a while Billy took me under his wing, introducing me to the city I'd grown up in but seldom explored beyond my desert suburb. He showed me Beale Street, or what was left of it—because, in the wake of last year's assassination and ensuing riots (events that had happened along with so many others while I was looking the other way), the city fathers, in the name of urban renewal, had razed the buildings, leveling the surrounding neighborhood for several square miles. Nothing remained of the heart of the old Negro district but what looked like a carpet-bombed waste. "Used to be," said Billy, "you had your honky-tonks at one end and your Jew pawnbrokers at the other. I got this from Mr. Boots," which was what he called his adoptive father, "that before they built the levees, the bayou behind Beale would back up every spring. The street would flood, and there would be this lagoon that the blacks rowed across in skiffs. . . ." We visited cinder block nightclubs under viaducts, roadhouses in malarial swamps, places so disreputable that the bands played in chicken-wire cages to protect them from bottles flung during free-for-alls. We drove the Chevy pickup that was the common property of the household out onto a sandbar in the river, behind which moldered a graveyard fleet of sidewheeler steamboats camouflaged in kudzu.

Despite the charge he clearly got from these excursions, Billy nevertheless maintained that, since the flight to Las Vegas of Elvis and the martyrdom of Dr. King, the party was over. Such pronouncements notwithstanding, nearly everyone we met deferred to Billy Boots, and as his associates we enjoyed, through no industry of our own, a certain local fame.

Discovering the city's underside, I felt I was being weaned from the middle class and would forget for days on end to be unhappy. Still, I was never so content that I neglected my part on Idlewild Street, frequently uttering the mournful expressions that defined my role in our household and invited gales of inexplicable laughter. In this way I became a kind of mascot, cosseted and indulged, and even visitors treated me accordingly. So what if the role was a little demeaning, if not downright emasculating? It was comfortable; though there were times when, wanting to make a more substantial contribution, I offered to apprentice myself to crime. I was relieved when my proposition was greeted with the same levity prompted by almost everything else I said. But while it was true that my lack of muscle and business savvy would have made me a liability as a felon, I was determined to carry my own weight, and toward that end I undertook a series of menial jobs.

The first was as a mail sorter in a nearby post office, struggling alongside broad-shouldered men with prison tattoos who slung the heavy parcels like partners in an apache dance. I lasted less than a week, after which I worked in a local car wash—a tedious, mind-numbing activity punctuated only by the appearance of a club lady who drove through at irregular intervals and, in the safety of her locked Lincoln, while leering men carressed her windows with wet rags, slowly unbuttoned her blouse. After that I got a job washing dishes in a greasy spoon. All day long in a back room behind the counter area (I'd been told it was better the patrons didn't see me), I stood at a sink receiving an endless succession of dirty dishes through a rectangular window; I scraped the leavings into a barrel, scrubbed the plates, and placed them in the rack of a wooden dish drainer. By midafternoon of my first day, exhausted, I was ready to pack it in, when a gaunt old man in a soiled raincoat appeared at my side.

"Put yer foot in thar," he said, pointing to the barrel of garbage.

Since he spoke with some authority, I did as I was told, swinging my foot over the barrel rim to tamp down the offal inside.

"Rat," said the old man. "Now t'other'n."

Thinking this was illogical, I nevertheless obeyed, as what did I know of waste management? When I was standing upright in the trash can, the swill seeping into my sneakers, the old man said "Rat" again, then confided, "Twenny-fie years I've et here. Six times they done try to p'ison me. Can you blame 'em?"

I left without even bothering to collect my pay.

The tales of my exploits consolidated my position as house clown, and the pittance I'd earned and turned over to Christopher, our treasurer, squared me to a degree with my conscience. Taking an early retirement from the workforce, I borrowed Billy's Underwood manual, its carriage velvety with dust, and commenced a meandering narrative about a lonely centaur, a hybrid creature belonging neither entirely to myth nor to the race of men. It was a lukewarm exercise, but since it was my first creative impulse in recent memory, I pressed ahead—until the tolerant condescensions of my housemates (Christopher proposed "The Heart Is a Lonely Centaur" for a title) caused me to abandon the project after a week. Then, just as I'd begun to warm to my old hometown, with stirrings I hadn't felt since my sojourn among the ghosts of the Lower East Side, Muhle swapped a half pound of Jamaican weed for some Owsley acid freshly imported from the West Coast, and the city, like a port from the deck of a ship, began to recede from view.

For all the various endeavors of Idlewild Street, both real and imaginary, were just a marking of time between the ingestion of controlled substances. Drugs were the raison d'être, and while I'd known all along that the moment would come when I would take the sacrament or else be perceived as rejecting my new friends, I was full of apprehension. Though

I had no real sense of what to expect, I was convinced that, in light of my history of depression, an artificially induced, mind-altering experience could derail me for life. On the other hand, had I traveled this far from inertia and sorrow only to turn back again, or was a leap into the unknown just the thing to complete my intitiation into a new order of being?

I had not expected to leap so far. Whereas in New York, my Aunt Keni had led me slowly across invisible borders and back again, the Idlewild brotherhood jumped into the melting pot of the collective unconscious with the blind glee of kids cannonballing off a pier. Where I'd had a dread of letting go, of losing the little stability the household provided, I was amazed at how swiftly "letting go" ceased to be an issue. Here was an experience in which your mind was the least of the things you lost. In the end, call it foolhardiness or peer pressure—for it would have taken more courage to refuse the drugs than take them—but like the others I swallowed the capsules and pastel tablets, dissolved the sugar cubes and cellophane windows on my tongue, ate the blotter paper stamped with the impressions of dragons. Then I waited: at first nothing, perhaps a faint hummingbird flutter in the belly, the awareness of a previously undiscerned edge to the atmosphere, then the slow awakening of the arteries of sensation, listless rivers uncoiling their oxbows to release the lost memories and dreams that clogged their backwaters. Set loose, these memories, not necessarily one's own, were washed downstream in a rising flood. For a time you enjoyed watching them pass, snapshots and furniture from your life and the life of the race, and this counted for euphoria, until you realized that you yourself had lost your purchase on the bank, the bank collapsing into the flood, and, somewhere between sinking and swimming, you rode the selfsame current. There was white water, the terror of being swept over rapids and falls, of crashing into a pool of elastic time. Then came a period of learning to breathe underwater, of viewing the subaqueous world with a fishy eye, with a falcon's eye, with the hundred eyes of Argus transplanted to the fan of a peacock's tail. This is the place where everything is momentous and mercurial; the eyes of animals and objects have fingers, the nose a sandy tongue; taste is melody and melody a many-colored raiment. Holiness partakes of the satanic, and the devil has alabaster wings.

It was an experience whose trajectory overshot every coordinate on the map of my consciousness. And when the effects of the drug finally began to subside and my body to reconstitute itself, the fragments of my psyche as they settled back into my brain never assumed quite the same disposition. On acid, mescaline, psylocybin with a soupçon of speed, I understood everything, though the wisdom was erased as swiftly as it was perceived. What stayed with me was how the inhabitants of Idlewild Street were held captive, voluntarily or no, by the roles that Billy Boots had assigned us. No one seemed to have any choice in the matter, nor did anyone think to protest, since, through the prism of Billy's Homeric imagination, we all gained in stature, all acquired (at perhaps some expense of the human) a mythic dimension. We were the art form that Billy had elected after abandoning his poetry, the puppets—satyrs, tricksters, sirens, knights errant, and fools—in his toy theater. By virtue of the woeful countenance that had become a performance piece even for myself, I was a natural as the fool. In fairness to Billy, I admit he tried to assure me that I wasn't really ugly anymore; "it's just that ugliness has a half-life in you that's still active." But even though it was true that my cystic acne was in remission, both Billy and I had too much invested in the conjuring power of my present personality to scrap it. If anything, the drugs had given a cosmic significance to the image of myself as a sort of subspecies of troll.

Then, too, there was some currency in being unhandsome in those days; it was almost a counterculture statement in itself, though it did not translate into winning fair ladies. My enduring virginity in a house I'd come to view as the capital seat of sex was itself the central joke in my repertoire. Of course the drug experience was very large, prompting spiritual ejaculations that diminished for a time all bodily concerns. Afterward the world would appear a little raw and discolored, a little parched, until a trickle of desire began to irrigate the barren landscape, and soon enough the house was saturated in erotic activity again. Lila would be warbling away in the master bedroom, Finbar pleasuring Regina, a barmaid from a local dive, standing up in the clawfooted bathtub, the two of them going at it like stampeding buffalo. Later an insatiable Regina would pick her way over the cylinders and flywheels in Finbar's bedroom to service Muhle in the rear of the house, while Christopher and Bateman's wife rode his galloping bed in the attic above me. Sometimes in the small hours, wrapping a dirndl around her generous hips, Regina would sashay past my cot—where the claw marks on the wall beside it bore witness to the extremes insomnia had driven me to—and bid me a cordial good night.

I had them about me night and day, the tactile presences and lingering scents of the ladies that traipsed through our narrow house. They came to Idlewild Street for its renown as a guilt-free zone and climbed into bed—or into the bathtub or onto the butcher's block in the kitchen—with whoever was available. Naturally they were aware of me and my flagrant longing, but as my reputation had perhaps preceded their visits, the ladies took for granted the untouchable's role I'd assumed. They laughed at my unfunny remarks and treated me generally like a house pet, an attitude that, to my shame, I took some pleasure in. So hungry was I for their attention that I took what I could get, even at the forfeit of being viewed as a man. Occasionally I inspired pity, such as when Finbar, struck with fraternal feeling, persuaded a crop-headed girl in a paisley smock reeking of patchouli to hop into my camp bed; but when I returned her playfulness with an uncurbed intensity, she exclaimed in alarm, "God, you're serious!" and bolted from the cot.

Lila, too, acknowledged my condition with the sympathy she reserved for all the members of our household, an attitude no doubt essential to her survival as sole female resident. It also helped that she was Billy's girl, which incited in us a chaste devotion akin to that of the dwarves toward Snow White. Still, I was painfully conscious of her lithe body in tight jeans and the T-shirts stretched over her perfect breasts, plus the fact that she, too, was a participant, however reluctant, in the orgies that rocked the house. As time wore on, I began to think that the longer I remained a virgin in the midst of that running bacchanal, the more proof I was against ever getting laid, the anguish of abstinence having become my signature shtik.

Then it was May, and I'd been dwelling among the outlaws for more than two months. I was a veteran of several drug odysseys, and, though psychedelics were reputedly nonaddictive, I was addicted to the experience—not so much the rush and wild ride of it as the fear. It was a biblical fear beside which my own native anxieties were reduced to the mildest itch.

On this particularly sultry evening, with the humidity breeding mosquitoes that haloed the lampposts, the house besieged by a riot of growing things, we'd taken LSD, which was seldom pure, often cut with additives—amphetamines, even toxins—that increased the unpredictability of the trip. It was an aspect of the drug that my fellows, who delighted in misrule, seemed to enjoy, and their recklessness made good company for me to be frightened in.

No matter how turbulent the stimuli, however, everyone remained more or less in character—everyone, that is, but Billy Boots, the exception to every rule. While he enjoyed and sometimes instigated the high jinks of his friends, telling stories that would have embarrassed Baron Münchausen, on drugs he tended to keep to himself. Often he seemed to be watching us from afar, or not watching at all, but looking in another direction entirely. Finbar, wearing a codpiece to highlight his advantage, might be performing a dervish dance, lashing some breathless partner with his golden hair, Muhle encouraging him on staccato guitar; Christopher might be developing some crackpot theory with a deadpan delivery that made it impossible to gauge his sincerity—when a look askance at Billy Boots, who'd lost interest, would stop them cold. For to lose Billy's attention was practically to lose oneself, just as conversely: the source of Billy's power over us (my theory) was that we must love him unconditionally or risk his becoming untethered from the world.

On this lavender-fragrant night, a party was in progress, in celebration of a full moon, or a half-moon, a new or a blue moon. Christopher, who remained astonishingly single-minded under the influence, was playing disc jockey, alternating rock 'n' roll and country blues with *The Rite of Spring* in a mix that seemed always to anticipate the mood of the house. Or was it that our moods were dictated by the crossbred music? A few of our colleagues in crime were also in circulation, some of them with prison records, characters with quicksilver dispositions that Christopher liked to stir to a boil with his unorthodox blend. Then, just before tempers flared, he would lower the flame to a civilized simmer with some sweet canticle.

Myself, I was seated cross-legged on my cot, which, along with being my bed of travail, served also as a kind of snug harbor. I had beside me some volumes by the masters of altered perception—De Quincey,

Baudelaire—whose words might provide an escort as far as the limits of language allowed. From that point on, I was content to let the vehicle of Christopher's music carry me to farther ports of call. His seamless orchestration of the journey could preserve your white-knuckled acid freak from the type of interior glance that might cause him to lose momentum and spiral downward like an Icarus. Though I hadn't seen Billy for a while, I can't say that I missed him, having assumed that he and Lila were in their bedroom otherwise occupied. Then I saw Lila wander through the parlor in a diaphanous caftan, apparently looking for her man, and realized that I, too, could do with a beaconlike glimpse of Cap'n Billy. No sooner had I wished it than he appeared.

But rather than radiating assurance, Billy looked troubled, wearing the thoughtful expression that had made me so uncomfortable in the hospital. He was sporting a silk vest and red neckerchief, a pair of flared trousers pied with bright patches—his party attire, which only heightened the contradiction of his abstracted air. Lowering himself beside me on the cot, he flipped through the pages of one of my books, then snickered slightly as he shoved them aside. Across the room Muhle, seated on the downhill slope of the carpets, was pantomiming a serenade for Becky Le Bon Bon, ripest of the teenage girls who came to dote on him, strumming unheard music overwhelmed by the stereo.

Without turning his head, Billy Boots, clearly in the throes of making a decision, said to me, "I've gone about as far as I care to go, y'know, toot ensemble . . . ," and he drew a heavy breath.

I was a universe away from engaging in such a conversation, and in that moment when I was compelled to turn around and begin the long trek back to Billy, I think I hated him. "What do you mean?" I asked reflexively, though I knew perfectly well what he meant, even if I couldn't conceive what chain of logic he'd followed to get there.

"Look," he said, "we're in either Bluebeard's or Bluebird's Castle, whichever, but there's one door that still remains shut." I made a face to show he'd lost me, while the room spun like a tumbler on a safe. "Time I opened it, no?"

"No!" I blurted, and felt my heart squirt black ink throughout my system. The intimacy with your own mortality that lysergic acid afforded was no longer thrilling, and I was scared of the resignation that made

a vacuum of Billy's handsome face. Why had he chosen to inflict his rid-
dles on me? I resented having to muster enough concentration to confront what, in an ordinary light, would have been considered claptrap.
Nevertheless, I made a stab at addressing at least the Bluebeard part of
his analogy, which I believed I in some fashion understood.

"We already know there's just skeletons in that closet."

"*We* know?" Billy sniffed, which was doubly disturbing, since when
was scorn a facet of his temperament? "What do we know?"

The question seemed intensely personal, the room become stationary
again, the house as if it had just dropped out of a funnel cloud. No match
for the commotion of my heart, the music faded to so much white noise.
"We know," I began on a hopeful note that fizzled in the delivery, "that
life puts death in the shade?"

Billy regarded me with a benign but thinning patience, while, in the
front parlor, Christopher, sensitive to any change in the atmosphere,
lowered the volume on the stereo. The sounds of strings and snares subsided, their grace notes swirling about our ankles as if down a drain.
Straggling in from the kitchen with a beer in her hand, Bateman's wife
crossed the floor quickly, giving my cot the wide berth you might allow
for an accident. She crouched next to Christopher, who was hunkered on
his footstool beside the sound system, and hid her nose in his flossy hair.
Lila had entered as well, but, sizing up a situation she may have witnessed
once too often, instantly withdrew. Also aware of the sea change, Muhle
had ceased whaling his instrument and swiveled about, so that all eyes
were now on me and Billy, which made it clear I was expected to continue what I'd begun.

"Think of what you'll miss," I added to an already weak argument.

"Like what?" asked Billy, seeming tired, calipering his temples between his thumb and forefinger. The black ink pooling in the pit of my
stomach threatened dyspepsia. I wondered again how it was that I had
been designated attorney for the defense of existence, a thing I was ambivalent toward at best. It was an unlikely role for a jester, but, as Billy
had bequeathed it to me for the evening, to shirk my part would be to fall
into disgrace.

"Like us?" I ventured.

Sighed Billy, with a tenderness like a laying of hands on my frontal lobe, "I miss you already."

"What about Lila?" I said, and Billy moaned softly again, his unspoken response perfectly apparent: his attachment to her was as tenuous as his attachment to the rest of us; he could not have loved us half so much if he loved not oblivion more. And because I knew this and the peril he was in—what didn't I think I knew in the eye of a drug trip?—I felt it was up to me to rescue Billy. "What about the starry night," I went on, "and your smuggling adventures and our own pleasure palace here, where you take a pill, lean back in an armchair, and slide down a chute into caverns measureless to man . . . ?" Which actually caused a bolus of sentiment to block my windpipe until I cleared my throat, but Billy only smiled wanly at so obvious an effort.

"Saul," he said after contemplating me a long moment, "do you believe in God?"

I swallowed. "Is this a trick question?"

There was cautious laughter from the bystanders, which now included a newly arrived Finbar, his mustache waxed for the occasion like a bison's horns, and Regina practically decanting herself from her milkmaid's corset. Instinctively she'd switched on the floor lamp, which left us all blinking and vulnerable. Risen to his feet, Christopher was shaking hands and hustling out the door the odd guests who'd yet to perceive ("Here's your hat, what's your hurry?") that it was time to go. I attempted a grin myself, remembering despite the gravity of the situation that I was still the joker. But Billy was not amused. So I backtracked, offering a pathetic, "Sometimes?"

"Some say the world's absurd because God up and took French leave, but I don't believe it." Billy ran a hand through his upstanding chestnut hair. "What's absurd is that He insists on hanging around, even though He isn't wanted here anymore. . . ."

A ridiculous thought occurred to me. "Are you trying to say that the world isn't big enough for the both of you?"

Again there was measured laughter from the spectators, and this time Billy's features admitted a degree of mild appreciation. I let myself relax for the instant it took his brow to furrow again, signaling the immense distance between us. There was nothing to bridge that distance with but words, and one wrong choice might open an abyss deeper than history.

"Problem is," offered Billy, pursuing his own rationale, "I don't think I ever got all the way born, and the unborn part of me, that's home. There's this Kafka parable. . . ." And he proceeded to tell me the one about the man who's a citizen of both heaven and earth, but the chain that fastens him to earth makes heaven inaccessible and ditto the chain that attaches him to heaven; which was when, in my capacity as court fool, I interrupted—because I was permitted to, wasn't I? I wore the fool's motley of my pockmarked cheeks, the fool was the card I'd drawn from the tarot pack, and it was my prerogative in these circumstances to play it.

"Kafka, shmafka," I declared. "I like New York in June, how about you? I like those screwball movies where Carole Lombard falls for the butler and Cary Grant runs around in drag, and the kind of novel that starts in a room with a hearth and sleeping mastiffs and ends up in a wilderness on no known map. I like the myth of Orpheus and a nice piece pastrami and Jean Shrimpton's breasts exposed to moonlight on top of that mountain Yeats is buried under. . . ."

Then I seemed to have opened the floodgates. Even as dread cut the strength of the drug, words boiled out of me, my mouth like a fireplug tapped by a prophet's staff. I was buoyed on a froth of words, all nonsense and free association, but somehow involving thoughts and sensations that didn't necessarily belong to me. "I like the twisty streets of the Moldavanka in Isaac Babel's Odessa and the cedar smell of the closet where Gatsby keeps his shirts. I like when Sidney Carton climbs up the steps of the guillotine, which correspond to the *sefirot,* the branches of the Tree of Life, but even better I like when Edmund Dantes is tossed in his shroud from the parapet of the Château d'If, because, like the rabbis say, 'The seed of redemption is contained in the fall.' Nature you can have, which—let's face it—is anti-Semitic; though I like the first blast of winter when it comes in like a salvo from an armada offshore. How about you?"

My babbling, like a torch held to cobwebs, burned away any lingering veils of psychotropic mirage. Aware I was playing a dangerous game, I persisted in my folly, confident that so long as I talked, Billy Boots, Cap'n

Billy, would be powerless to act or speak himself. I could save him if only I kept on talking. But in actually feeling attached to what I said, I experienced a curious side effect: I was speaking both my own mind *and* Billy's, as if through me he were giving himself reasons to live. Then I thought, heretically, Billy be damned; I'm falling out of love with fear, and I like it; I like feeling brave!

"I like hiding in a culvert in Paris where you look up through a grate just as Colette steps over it in a ballerina skirt, and I like how my penis, marked though it is with the sign of the Covenant, sprouts like a blossoming olive branch when I whack off. . . ."

Which was when, during the beat I missed in order to breathe, Muhle, reclining sultanlike on the carpets, threw in offhandedly, "I like a pus-y discharge, or the mustardy scent of a freshly squeezed cyst in the morning. . . ."

Silence like an abruptly cut chord, and a universal intake of air. Then Finbar, bending over to rub my scalp as he might have rubbed a hunchback's hump for luck: "What about headlice? I like picking nits and grubs out of kinky hair: fry 'em up in sesame oil, serve 'em in a garnished pocket of pita bread. . . ."

"I like waking up in the morning with a touch of leprosy," added Christopher, leaning poker-faced against a doorpost with arms folded, while Bateman's wife leaned against him. "You know, when you find your lips and eyelids on the bloody pillow beside you. . . ."

"Or your genitals," tendered Muhle.

"But they would be under your pillow," Finbar advised, "where you put them the night before, in the hope that the genital fairy might leave you a woman."

"Which," reasoned Muhle, "you can't do nothing with on account of you got no balls. This is the paradox. Course, she can always hold your hand and inspire you to write a story about a guy who can't have a woman 'cause he's got no balls."

"Hemingway wrote that already," said Christopher, his impassivity thinly veiling his waggishness. "But maybe the fairy doesn't take his unit at all, because it doesn't look right. It's got olives growing on it instead of balls. Very decorative, a miracle really, and when the word gets out, the rabbis come around and declare you a saint," gleefully conflating traditions as he warmed to his narrative; "you're the patron saint of dermatology. They hang your johnson—"

"Your jonah?" suggested Regina, proud of her Old Testament acumen.

"Your jonah." Christopher stood corrected. "They hang it in the Synagogue of the Holy Syphilitic, and the pilgrims come from all over to worship at your shrine. You're a big man until the dermatologists—they're such sticklers—they declare you a fraud. Seems the olives aren't olives after all, but some rare form of herpes zoster—"

"Herpes Foster," said Finbar, kissing his fingers, "served à la flambeau. Flambée? flambeau?"

"À la Rimbaud." This from Billy Boots, which caused all heads to turn, not so much shocked that he was participating in such idle banter as that they had perhaps forgotten for a moment he was there.

Then everybody was in the act, proposing competing scurrilities that took in a variety of targets other than myself, though the damage was already done. Of course I'd been used to ribbings at my expense, since I was first and foremost a figure of fun, but, given my efforts to rescue Billy—efforts that had already begun to seem insipid—I felt persecuted and betrayed, as if I'd risen above my station and my so-called friends had been obliged to put me back in my place. I wondered if Billy had really contemplated suicide at all, or was the whole thing just a setup to put me through my paces and make me, the joker, the butt of a joke?

In the last faint flickerings of the drug trip, words were blunt instruments rather than pyrotechnic flares—which didn't stop the company from laughing like loons, Billy Boots included. Now that the coast was clear, Lila had returned, wedging her compact bottom between me and Billy, folding him in her arms, while I sat there mute, a victim of heartburn or "acid" reflux as Christopher would have it, despising my friends.

Christopher was mouthing off about the coming Marxist utopia. "Until then," he said, with his habit of mixing idealism and disparagement, "you can stick around in this world while still enjoying all the benefits of being dead."

"But, Christopher," Billy gently reminded him, "there are only miracles."

Said Christopher, "Oh, yeah, I forgot."

The morning had begun to seep through the burgundy curtains, a single thread broadening to a ribbon of filmy light, and Christopher retreated to the stereo, where he cranked up the Beatles singing "Here Comes the Sun." It was a tongue-in-cheek dawn chorus meant to cleanse the mental palate, but the bitterness remained, and as Finbar rubbed my head once again for good measure, I fought down an impulse toward gratitude. Then every male but me grabbed a girl and went to bed. I lay back on my cot, exhausted, my brain stiff and porous as a dry sponge. To my litany of reasons to live, which had already grown obscure, I said good riddance; they had after all been mostly gleaned from secondhand sources, and though I dimly recalled having touched on things Jewish, I realized that I'd neglected any mention of the old Lower East Side. I supposed it was too late to mention it now.

After that night I ceased to trust my friends. I suffered their tolerant shakings of the head like *you just won't do* and smiled sheepishly to show I remembered my place; I forgave them their loutishness, blamed it on the drug, and even felt a creeping return of the old allegiance. But I knew better than to trust them. As for Billy Boots, him I no longer wanted to let out of my sight. It was a skewed impulse, since I was much more likely to receive Billy's protection than give him mine, but in the days following his dark night, I became his shadow—or, as Christopher put it, his stooge.

When he was in town, I would lobby to accompany him on marijuana runs. The depleted dope market had made local sales irresistible, and if the delivery were routine enough that Finbar's muscle wasn't needed, I was allowed to replace him. Then we would drive the bilious green pickup with its eight-track blasting to a cold-water address in midtown, where the goods were turned over to some nickel-and-dime pusher for a previously agreed-upon sum. The exchanges were usually courteous and swift, since Billy, never fond of the society of pushers, kept the transactions on a strictly professional basis. Once, however, a piggy character in a silk kimono and Samurai queue, instead of tendering payment, picked up a baseball bat. That's when I saw the basilisk glint come into Billy's eyes, an expression that made me think I didn't know him. "You'll look silly with that thing shoved halfway up your ass," he said, in a tone that balanced reason and menace; and the kimonoed guy, in lieu of turning to stone, put down the bat and relinquished a wad of cash.

The pleasantest junkets were the ones involving straight retail sales, when we would travel to local colleges and enter dormitory rooms appointed in hookahs and strobes, where nervous students greeted us in store-bought hippie gear. Then I would feel a pang of regret, wondering how it had happened that I was on the supply side of the negotiations. Billy continued to acquaint me with the city of my birth, though it was too late now to view it with any real sense of habitation; we'd already severed the chain that attached us to a place in time called Memphis and held only that other chain with its faulty connection to paradise. We were citizens of a low-rent eternity inspecting the fallen world, and no place seemed to have fallen further than Memphis, Tennessee—as evidenced by the domestic tribes who had begun to abandon hallucinogens in favor of needles, which they used with unconcerned exhibitionism in the bars and clubs. There was one especially sordid establishment called the Roaring 60's, a shooting gallery with a mirror ball in the crumbling shell of an old Orthodox synagogue downtown. The synagogue, as Billy pointed out, was off North Main Street, a skid-row district that in the years before the Second World War had been a thriving East European ghetto community. I received the information with only passing interest.

Meanwhile life on Idlewild Street continued with its ordinary round of chicanery and excess. After a trip to a urologist, Finbar returned home with his hoselike member wrapped in bloody gauze and tied in a sling around his neck. When Christopher was bitten in the thigh by a neighborhood dog, Finbar and Muhle, instead of offering solace, surrounded their beds with crumpled newspapers to warn them in case Christopher became rabid and attacked them in the night. One saturnalian evening in June, Billy Boots was moved to perform an extempore dance in the parlor, a tortured solo freestyle during which his unfluid limbs responded to astral music as if stung by whips. But beyond our throbbing house, there was continuing unrest in the land; there was trouble close to home. The police were conducting the latest in a series of citywide crackdowns on drug offenders, rounding up more than the usual suspects, and several of our associates either awaited trial or had jumped bail and fled to points unknown. Every day we remained in Memphis, we were tempting fate— that was the consensus, though no one had as yet proposed a plan to avoid what all agreed was inevitable.

Then Billy called a council in the front parlor for the purpose of making a decision. He and Finbar had recently moved a shipment of Colombian dope from Austin to Chicago, the last in a series of major operations intended to ensure our solvency for an unspecified time. Moreover, as Christopher revealed, we had been squirreling away a portion of our profits all along, and, owing to forced austerity and Christopher's own prudent handling of accounts, we were in the black, our liquid assets amounting to "a substantial nest egg." As proof Christopher nodded to Finbar, who upturned a fat pillowcase to spill a staggering sum of bundled bills onto the floor. For all its drama, the demonstration did not thrill me; I'd seen impressive sums of cash on Idlewild Street before. Neither did the word "family," so often invoked with regard to our household, fill me with a sense of security anymore. Having fled one family only to be entangled in another, I wondered if a period of absence from Idlewild Street might help my heart grow fonder. Christopher's theory was that the cumulative effects of acid would eventually meld us all into a single organism, a kind of revolutionary centipede, but I still harbored a sentimental attachment to the idea of the individual. Our dependence on one another (and the lot of us on Billy Boots) for our very identities was not healthy, and while an exodus from Idlewild was attractive, I thought it might behoove us to go our separate ways. But in Billy's mind it was a given that we find a solution collectively.

Various impracticable plans were put forward, some so self-defeating as to make me wonder if others shared my secret wish for dissolution. Muhle, who enjoyed courting disaster, envisioned a last stand with the cops, or perhaps a flight to some desert outpost like Libya, there to sell ourselves as mercenaries or trade in slaves. Announcing that the reconstruction of its engine was imminent, Finbar proposed we travel the country in his VW bus till the thing gave out, then turn it into a brothel. The enterprising Christopher had an idea of some relative feasibility: There was a resort town in northwest Arkansas where—and here he turned the floor over to Bateman's wife, who in her raggedy voice told us of a gutted turn-of-the-century hotel that could be had for a song. We could fix it up and operate it as—Christopher: "What else?"—a hotel. Fired by the fantasy, Finbar volunteered himself as head chef and began proposing elaborate menus; Muhle advised us on rigging the rooms for what he termed "the badger game." Christopher himself envisioned the whole thing as pure theater, with all of us rotating hats as burlesque bellhops, desk clerks, and chambermaids in a nonstop anarchic romp. I admit that the notion had some appeal for me as well and pictured myself as a tummler working the bar mitzvah and wedding crowds. But having suffered our frivolity long enough, Billy called us back to order with what he viewed as the logical conclusion to our urban episode.

"Arkansas might be the promised land, but our destiny don't lie in the towns. What we need is a place of our own in the country, a nice piece of land in the back of beyond, situated just outside of recorded time."

"You mean, like a farm?" asked Muhle, sounding slightly appalled.

Billy nodded thoughtfully. "For lack of a better word."

Then Christopher offered the better word, savoring it like a melting wafer on his tongue—"A commune"—and Billy Boots did not say no.

"So you're saying we're about to turn field hippie?" wondered Finbar, for whom Billy's judgment precluded all argument, and, adjusting to the prospect with a prodigious shrug, he let go a holler: "Jump down, turn around, pick a bail of cotton!" Then Muhle came on board with the confidence that he already had in cultivation a store of seeds that might be the basis for a cash crop—which sparked a debate concerning the standard of legitimacy to which we should adhere in our future endeavors. Perched on the arm of Billy's sagging morris chair, Lila remained silent as usual, though it was assumed she would follow Billy whithersoever. Then it was my turn to weigh in, but, seated beside the stalk of a dead amaryllis with my back against the wall, I couldn't bring myself to confess how unexcited I was.

"Sauly," inquired Billy, "what do you say?"

I sighed, well aware that back-to-the-land was the prescribed next stage of the counterculture diaspora, that strung-out drug veterans all over the country were mounting an exodus toward rural environs to test their utopian zeal. But we were no textbook hippies, and the earth in its rock-girt, scrub-brushy aspect was not necessarily our home, was it?

Taking a deep breath, I said, "It occurs to me you're all deluded, and if we isolate ourselves on some remote dirt farm, we will end by eating each other. So why don't we just call it a day, tear a dollar bill in four or five pieces, and meet at the Statue of Liberty in, say, fifty years . . . ?"

There followed vociferous laughter; I was still the joker, and, on the strength of my negative endorsement, it was agreed that back to the land was precisely where we must go. Then, as happened so often on Idlewild Street, they all departed in their several directions, already on their way to the next chapter, and I was left alone in the parlor hugging my knees. Moments later Billy Boots, whom I credited with having detected the seriousness of my speech, strayed back into the room and laid a hand on my shoulder.

"If it wasn't for negative capability, Sauly, you wouldn't have no capability at all," he quipped; then he said, "You know we can't do this without you." And that—God help me—was that; I could scarcely believe I'd dared to flirt with the notion of setting out on my own.

Of course, the land had first to be located, and, with this as their goal, Billy and Finbar took off for the nearest authentic wilderness, Billy's ancestral Arkansas Ozarks, where there was a bruited 360 degrees of reality.

Once I'd resigned myself to the project, I began looking for ways to make myself useful, casting about for some area of specialization I could call my own. Eventually I hit on the idea of growing herbs. I managed a measure of enthusiasm over the prospect of cultivating a formal patch of color and fragrance, which might be distilled into condiments, physics, medicinal teas, products with both practical application and aesthetic appeal. I saw myself years hence, a stooped figure living in a hut beside my garden; men and women would come to me for poultices and drafts, and I would cure them of warts, barrenness, the indignities of age. The fancy never really caught fire, but while I had no particular interest in botany (or agriculture in any form, for that matter), I liked the Elizabethan music of the plant names: sweet woodruff, star jasmine, johnny-jump-up, yarrow, creeping thyme, elecampane. I thought that around the herbs I would also place hives of bees.

Then came the misty morning when I was reclining on my cot poring over some medieval herbal, and the house began to shake. This I was of course accustomed to, but as these were ordinarily quiet hours, especially with Billy and Finbar away and Lila at work, I leaped to another conclusion. The city of Memphis sat atop its river bluff on a famous fault line, and in the midst of all that rampant fornication, I'd sometimes imagined that the big quake was in progress. Now I was convinced it had at last arrived—and not, I thought perversely, a moment too soon.

I rushed onto the porch anticipating fissures in the earth's surface but saw instead our old enemy Bateman, rival dealer and cuckolded husband, along with a brawny accomplice in the tire-rutted front yard. Each had hold of one of Christopher's upper arms and was using his head for a battering ram, swinging him repeatedly into the stuccoed foundation of the house. As I stood rooted to the spot, wishing that Billy and Finbar could somehow be paged, Muhle appeared on the porch beside me. Having performed the daily phoenix routine of rising from his semi-invalid's bed, he flung himself without hesitation from the ivy-twined steps onto the shoulders of the stranger. Thus assaulted, Bateman's crony—a black man with a puff of hair like a maroon dandelion and a hewn torso beneath his leather vest—let go of Christopher to begin spinning Muhle propeller style, until they both went sprawling. In an instant, however, the black man had swarmed over Muhle's rattle bones and held him pinned to the damp ground. But Muhle, whose murky past had made him a living repository of dirty secrets, muttered something in the ear of the stranger astride his chest, something about (if I heard correctly) some prior unpleasantness to which Muhle alone was privy. The black man stood up as if bitten and backed off a few paces, showing coral pink palms, while Muhle propped himself on his elbows, assuring him, "I never saw you, okay? You weren't even here." And with a jingling of bells on horizontal fringes, the stranger was gone.

This left Bateman still holding the wrist of a stuporous Christopher, who was slumped in a daze to the earth, which grew soggier by the second as the mist gathered into a shower. On his feet again, Muhle, whose eyes (for once deprived of his tinted specs) were cornflower blue, looked briefly to me for the support I as yet withheld; then he swung around to paste Bateman (a head taller than himself) a clout to the temple. Bateman crumpled, and while Muhle massaged his stinging knuckles, I was finally impelled to action; I hadn't lived five months on Idlewild Street without learning a thing or two. I stepped off the porch just as Bateman had begun to raise himself to his knees in the mud, and made to kick him. But the moccasins I was wearing had no traction, and the kick—aimed in the vicinity of Bateman's kidneys—went awry when I slipped and fell in the mud myself. Soaked to the skin, I scrambled to stand before Bateman could counterattack, swelling my ribs in an effort to recover some dignity; but the defeated husband of Bateman's wife remained on his knees in what was becoming a cloudburst.

"Please," he begged, actually locking his fingers, the rain lashing his Rasputin-like hair across his face, "don't take my kids away. You can have my wife, the ungrateful whore, but forgodsakes leave my kids!" There were two of them, a nine-year-old girl, dark like her father, and an impish, fair-haired seven-year-old boy, whom their mother intended bringing along with us back to the land. That's what we called it: not promised or golden, just "the land."

Behind the praying Bateman, neighbors in the apartment complex across the street were peering through parted curtains. There was a Catholic day school beyond the swollen drainage ditch where Idlewild dead-ended, the very school Bateman's children attended, and in every rain-beaded pane of every window was framed the saucer-eyed face of a summer-school kid.

Later that evening, washed clean of the front-yard mud, I was again bent over my seed catalogs, though the image of the broken father staggering away in the rain spoiled my concentration. The storm had played itself out by late afternoon, the clouds parting in time to admit a neon sunset, the summer expelling its musk like a civet cat. Muhle was off entertaining Becky Le Bon Bon, whom he'd persuaded to run away from her family to join us. With his head rakishly bandaged, Christopher, mildly concussed, had dropped his trademark implacability to ask if he'd survived 'Nam only to be mauled by animals and madmen at home. When last seen, he was being escorted upstairs by Bateman's wife, still complaining, though the words had dwindled to a singsong delirium. I was slouched at the long kitchen table, thoughts of hyssop and lemon balm giving way to a consideration of how far I had degenerated during my tenure on Idlewild Street.

This was my mood when a corn-fed, ash-blond girl in hip-hugging sailor pants came into the house. (While we slept with pistols under our pillows, we never bothered locking the doors.) She passed through the kitchen hardly sparing me a glance of her dilated eyes, searching, I supposed, for some unattached party, which by now I was used to; I was used to my own near invisibility. But, having presumably toured the house and found no one available, she returned to the kitchen and stopped at my shoulder. I looked up and asked if she were lost, but, ignoring the question, she asserted a touch regretfully,

"I guess you'll do."

I wasn't ready. The day's events had more than distracted me from my unremitting preoccupation with carnality, and the possibility of realizing so fundamental a need on such a night was quite simply out of the question. There was no avenue from my base condition to that of a man capable of making love, and my first impulse was to tell her to leave me alone. But the ribbed undershirt clinging to the upstanding buds of her breasts, her exposed navel, and her odor of incense and sweat constituted an imperative that my brain struggled to accommodate. Then all my tacit objections suddenly seemed to me nothing but a coward's excuse—so when she took my hand, I let her haul me to my feet. She had a soft, tallowy face made dreamier by whatever drug she was on, and while it occurred to me I was taking advantage of her vulnerability, I reserved the right to believe that the reverse was the case.

"Are you a virgin?" I felt nevertheless compelled to ask, which prompted a quizzical tilt of her head.

"Are you a hedgehog?" she replied, all taxonomies being equal. Then, having scouted ahead, she led me down the hallway to the entrance of the master bedroom. I hesitated at the threshold of what was, after all, Billy's domain. But Billy was away in farthest Arkansas, and Lila was out with old friends—a curious notion, that any one of us could stray outside the group when I no longer thought of our group as having an "outside" anymore. The girl tugged again gently but firmly until I yielded, stepping into the room to admire the antique four-poster at the still center of a swirl of stray garments and open books. It was too grand a stage and I was too humble a player to trespass here, but the girl, all business, shoved me backward until I was seated on the rumpled crazy quilt. (The very quilt, in fact, that Billy alleged his birth mother had wrapped, then abandoned, him in.) Without overture she began methodically to unbutton my shirt, to unzip my pants, which she pulled to my ankles along with my grungy underwear. Though my passivity embarrassed me, I couldn't overcome it, feeling as if I were submitting to an operation that was ultimately for my own good. I thought of the girl as a specialist, perhaps a miracle worker, and, unable to contain my gratitude, said, "Bless you," which earned me a level gaze.

"Did I sneeze?"

Kneeling, she scooped my forlorn manhood into her hand like a wounded thing in need of resuscitation, and toward that end, with up-turned eyes to gauge my response, she took me into her mouth. The humid warmth was its own element, and my soul, seeking the heat, raced headlong from some remote corner of my being to enter it. Instantly I was engorged, and the girl made a slight choking sound, emitting a muf-fled chuckle without relaxing the hold of her lips, which she proceeded to slide up and down my shaft. I half expected music to pipe from my nether parts. Certain now that I functioned, she released me, so that I fell through space for the time it took her to stand and shimmy out of her sailor pants. She was wearing olive drab undies whose masculine cut ac-cented, as she stepped out of them, the contrast with the milky curve of her hips. I shuddered at the sight of her nakedness, my teeth chattering despite the general swelter, while the girl—the hint of a smile betraying her enjoyment of my agitated state—stepped forward to fold me in her arms. I wondered that I did not melt or ignite but instead, with my penis grazing her electric fur, found the temerity to return her embrace. Be-cause I perspired so freely, she blew on my forehead to cool me, but her breath was hot as well, and the squeaky ceiling fan did little to disperse the infernal air. Though I knew nothing of the girl beyond her chunky anatomy, her plum-size breasts, and the pastilles of her nipples (which I'd raised her undershirt to blindly suck), I was in love.

With a gesture that had the authority of ritual, she turned her head to spit into her palm, then rubbed the spittle between her legs as if applying a salve. She lifted a downy thigh to straddle my lap, and I closed my eyes, welcoming the little death I'd ached for throughout all my sap-risen days. But just when it seemed that nothing could interrupt the long-delayed fi-nale of my innocence, there came an emphatic knocking at the front door.

We'd been living the past month or so with the expectation that at any moment narcotics agents would break down the (unlocked) door and storm the premises. There was no doubt in my mind that this was that moment—though, on the other hand, maybe they would grow bored and go away. . . . But the persistent pounding finally roused me from an impossible dream, and I actually pushed the girl aside in my haste to pull up my jeans. My instinct was to bolt for the back steps and beat it over the battered board fence in the yard; then I took a breath—possibly the first I'd drawn since the girl had entered the house—and lurched through the parlor toward the front door, attempting to strangle my erection along the way. Opening the door, I was greeted by a dour man in a pin-striped jumpsuit with a company insignia on his breast. I recognized him as one of our neighbors, who, when parking his produce truck in his drive, had always avoided looking our way. In an even drawl, the kind he might have used to announce the delivery of a shipment of cantaloupe, he informed me of what I could plainly see.

"Your house is on fire."

My initial thought was that it was my fault. The near attainment of a desire turned flammable from so long a suppression had resulted in a sympathetic combustion; my enflamed loins had put the torch to the termite-infested timbers, and the fire that had engulfed the porch was now starting to consume the parlor. In a panic I alerted the occupants. Muhle said so long forever to his phony sickbed, and Christopher was temporarily persuaded to leave off bemoaning his aching head, as, together with Becky and Bateman's wife, we scrambled to remove guns and illegal substances and to salvage whatever we could before the fire department arrived.

It was suspected at first that Bateman was responsible, that vengeance must be exacted. But it was just as likely that Muhle, accustomed to smoking dope in the disabled chesterfield on the front porch, had dropped a still-burning roach between the cushions; this had happened before. (There was even speculation that, in his trickster mode, Muhle had set the fire deliberately, which wouldn't have surprised anyone.) The ash would have taken its time to convert to flame, the flames lapping the clapboard that gave way to the interior walls, the fire increasing in intensity until—despite the uninspired efforts of firefighters, who showed evidence (along with the neighbors) of enjoying the burning of so disreputable an abode—the walls collapsed and the roof caved in. Billy and Finbar arrived the next afternoon to find us picking through rubble. They fell over each other in their hilarity, Finbar performing a spontaneous hornpipe in the ruins, Billy declaring the fire a sign and a benediction:

for hadn't they just completed negotiations on an eighty-acre dirt farm in the Arkansas Ozarks? Not only was it time to leave, but now we would have less baggage to haul across the river into the mountains.

Our landlord contacted us via the mouthpiece of a bow-tied attorney, who, with alligator briefcase in hand, tracked us to the fleabag motel we'd holed up in before departing, threatening us with a criminal-negligence suit. In the end, though, the landlord was placated by the insurance, which paid more than the market value for so decrepit a house; and besides, no sooner had the threats been delivered than, in one of those satirical rites that characterized us as a group, we'd sown the ground of Idlewild Street with salt. Then, enjoining one another not to look back, we were on our way. We traveled northwest across the flounder-flat Arkansas delta in a caravan that included the Chevy pickup equipped with a camper, a rental truck containing rescued books and clothes, and Finbar's hiccupping Volkswagen van. (Demonstrating a degree of inge- nuity no one would have credited him with outside the kitchen, Finbar had reconstituted the engine in a matter of days out of the parts we'd re- trieved from the flames.) The van, with Finbar at the wheel, was crammed full of refugees including Regina, who'd quit her bartending job to take her chances; Bateman's wife, cradling Christopher's still-sore head in her lap; two cranky children; and a lame black dog that the boy had be- friended the day before and refused to give up. Muhle drove the rental truck with Becky Le Bon Bon (still wearing her private-school uniform) beside him, about whom it was rumored that an all-points bulletin had been issued. In the cab of the vanguard pickup manned by Billy Boots were also a pensive Lila and myself enjoying the change of scene. It wasn't until we'd passed Little Rock, heading north toward higher ground, that I thought to mention my ministering angel, who, in the excitement of the fire, had vanished without a trace.

NATHAN

A train clattered over the tracks above Allen Street, and, shuffling between the gas lamps below, Nathan Hart, newly dispossessed from his attic room, ducked under a shower of sparks. He coughed from inhaling the soft coal fumes and wiped his tearing eyes on a raveled sleeve. Lurid ladies in thin kimonos, despite the biting breeze, lounged about the sidewalk in an open-air seraglio. With a confection of slips and cami-knickers showing beneath their unfastened gowns, they sat spraddle-legged on the stoops; they leaned in gauze petticoats against the Elevated stanchions, calling out to furtive men who pretended not to hear them. The men pretended that they had only chanced along the "street of perpetual shadow," having urgent business elsewhere; then, dropping their pretense, they paused to negotiate with the whores.

But the whores were not wasting their unchaste overtures ("A nice piece knish, for you a bargain . . .") on Nathan, gaunt as a shepherd's crook in his grubby rug coat; for him the handkerchief girls didn't drop their handkerchiefs. Ordinarily the ex-proofreader might have been relieved by their disinterest, but tonight circumstances had conspired to make him feel otherwise. Tonight his invisibility seemed an affliction, and in his desire to overcome it, he viewed the flesh of women as a means to that end. With a lolloping heart, he approached one of the less brazen ladies—spindle-shanked in a wilted tea gown with a helmet of thinning, marcelled hair—and asked if she would take him inside. (The word "inside" thrummed agreeably in his vitals.) At first the girl seemed dismayed, then affronted that such an unsightly *oysvurf* should choose her;

then she sighed, perhaps remembering that degradation was the essence of her trade.

"Fifty cents the *yentz,*" she said without expression, "plus for the room fifty cents." When Nathan nodded in agreement, she turned and trudged wearily up the steps of Number 96. Nathan followed her into a dingy hallway, past doors behind which muffled noises—banshee moans, hysterical laughter—could be heard. There was a narrow staircase where the women, like a louche version of Jacob's ladder, were squeezing past one another with their clients in tow. On the first landing, Nathan's *nafkeh* entered a fulsome parlor where a chicken liver lay sizzling in a pan atop a one-burner lamp stove. A man with a full beard, wearing a yarmulke and ritual tassels, his hands clasped over a belly like a medicine ball, sat sleeping at a collapsible card table. In front of him on the table was an open *Tanakh,* with a dope sheet tucked inside, and a cigar box full of cash.

The girl padded past trying not to wake him, and Nathan (when in Rome) endeavored to do the same. They entered a windowless compartment off the parlor, bare as a doctor's examining room, furnished with only a chair and a woven-wire cot, a gas jet the girl never bothered turning up. Over the chair hung a dirty towel and a rubber enema bag. The girl kicked off her mules and removed her cheap floral gown with an apathetic shrug; then she stood before Nathan in a shapeless gray shift, her spatulate feet protruding from under its hem.

"You got now to pay me," she said, and held out a raw, red palm, adding somewhat guiltily, "and also for the room."

Swallowing, Nathan turned out his empty pockets, and the whore stepped back in alarm, her raisinlike nipples shrinking behind the flimsy nainsook of her shift. "What if," he tendered, "I should tell to you instead a story?"

The girl backed up as far as the wall. "What will I want with a story?" she asked, anxious despite her outward show of disdain.

"It's about a fallen angel," submitted Nathan, taking courage from her apparent unease, and straightaway he began to unfold the cockamamy conceit: how the angel's son by a mortal woman, *vos hayst* Hannah, was reared in paradise, where the angel had dumped him after a pogrom on earth.

"I'll scream," threatened the girl, her lusterless eyes gone wide as poached eggs.

"Mocky, they would call him, the angel, on the Lower East Side of New York, like a *makeh,* you know, a plague," checking her face for some sign of the transport that wasn't forthcoming, "that he lives in a coal cellar where it keeps, the mob, its bottles phosphorus and diamond drills. . . ."

The girl had begun to bite the fleshy underside of her thumb.

"So he goes one night on Canal Street, this angel, to a music hall, and sees there a play which it's the story from his own life. . . ."

The girl screamed.

After the final departure of Keni Freischutz, Nathan had relaxed again almost wistfully into his old routine. This is me, he thought, dismissing the tumult of the past year as a kind of protracted fever dream. He was Nathan Hart, sedulous proofreader for the *Jewish Daily Forward,* enthusiast of secular literature and Yiddish theater; he lived alone in a pantry-size attic on Cherry Street, where he observed a quiet, thrifty little life that need never be disturbed again. And that was enough. Then, abruptly given the sack from the *Forward* for chronic incompetence, Nathan was a proofreader no more, his world diminished to the space between his garret walls; but for the time being, that, too, was enough.

The few dollars he had in reserve, however, were soon spent, and the discharged wage earner had no choice but to look for immediate employment. Yet he hesitated, idling in his room as he reviewed the events that had led to his current straits. He recalled that, sometime during the preceding year, he'd begun a letter to his family; that the letter, infected by hokum, had evolved into a megillah, a long, aborted narrative he'd finally pitched into the archive of his unlit stove. So maybe he ought to return to the letter, to try to splice the interrupted sequence of his days. But, faced with the prospect of a blank sheet of foolscap, Nathan decided it was too late: his mother and sisters had begun to recede along with his murdered father into myth. The empty page invited nothing but the start of an unlikely story about a reprobate heavenly host and his son.

There had been a drop or two remaining in the bottle of schnapps on the washstand, but though he imbibed, the familiar warmth in his chest never reached Nathan's brain. Taking a peek at the deckle-edged manuscript he'd stashed in the stove's unemptied ash pan, he couldn't summon—he was almost proud of it—a single distinct memory of its composition; and in its inspirer, the girl Chaineh Freyda, Nathan was no longer sure he believed at all. Of course he wasn't so disaffected that he didn't remember the title he'd given the tale, and how the whole thing had dried up at the point where his character Nachman, the half-a-seraph, begins to prowl the quarter looking for he knows not what; while Mocky, the *gefallener malech,* trots at a distance behind him, keeping his son in his sights. For his part, Nathan was content to leave them wandering that way for all eternity.

In the meantime there remained the problem of his own survival. If only he'd had the skill to take in piecework like everyone else, to rent a machine and perform his labors by the light of the little window that looked over the slate and tarpaper roofs toward the river. But the suffocating heat of his attic would have driven him out of doors in any case. He made a few vain inquiries at some of the other Yiddish dailies but was refused work on account of his lack of references. For every available position—grocer's assistant, synagogue beadle, bathhouse attendant—there were dozens of experienced applicants; there were a multitude of driven apprentices for every trade. But for a young man with no particular calling desperate for cash, there were only last resorts. And in the end, much as he dreaded the shrill exposure of the streets, Nathan appealed to the straw-boatered contractor at a Broadway rag factory and went back to the garment schlepping of his greenhorn days. Again he humped the bales of yokes and buckram-stiff collars to the downtown sweatshops, carried the finished waists, wrappers, and knee pants back uptown to the jobber who dispatched him to the department stores. His back bent like a poor man's Atlas under his alp of fabric, Nathan slogged through butchers' shambles, across platforms over subway excavations; he staggered among drummers and draymen and sidewalk scribes, past ladies in dainty frocks on uptown pavements showing trim, white-stockinged ankles and holding parasols. Though he kept his head bowed under his burden, Nathan was alive enough to his surroundings to feel both assaulted and oppressed. The world—a place of clashing disharmonies beseiged by smokestacks and towers, hedged about by bristling masts, lofty palisades, troubled seas—was better left to the imagination.

Sometimes en route he passed bookstores where scores of titles, disgorged from their basement shops, overflowed the sidewalk stalls and bins. Browsers stroked the bindings and sniffed the print almost pruriently, while Nathan, who could walk by cafeterias with impunity, felt his parched mouth water at the sight. But back in his stifling attic, where every breath filled his lungs like damp wool, his own books in their torn dust covers had lost their savor. If he hungered now, it was with an appetite he had no idea how to satisfy. Meanwhile the weather had rallied in an infernal end-of-summer valedictory. By day the clammy air was thick with bluebottles, their hum competing with the drone of sewing machines in their lofts. Colicky babies wailed, meat spoiled before you could carry it home from the market, rats surfaced from the sewers to gnaw at the carcasses of fallen truck horses; they bobbed and drowned in the gutters around open fireplugs. At night the ghetto's population camped on their fire escapes and rooftops, some carelessly rolling off in their sleep. Throughout the heat wave, Nathan, recent conscript to the general travail, struggled with buckling knees under his ponderous load. But where others, on the eve of the Days of Awe, may have thought they were enduring a penance, Nathan felt merely outcast. He was slaving for wages that barely kept him in herring and black bread, forget about paying the rent.

Cataloging his regrets, he might ask himself: The story that had been his undoing, the *bubbeh mayseh* of Mocky and his halfbreed son, had it been only a ploy to entice an auburn-haired girl? Or was the girl simply a useful device to spur the progress of the story? It all seemed so long ago, back in the days when he'd had a special dispensation that allowed him to live in two worlds at once. Now, Cherry Street notwithstanding, the toil-weary Nathan felt that he lived nowhere at all.

By the time the heat broke, both the story and the girl were virtually forgotten, replaced by only a dull and nameless longing (spiced with misgiving) that had dogged Nathan for much of his twenty-four years. Then, on an evening in late September, with the first hint of an autumnal nip in the air, he'd arrived back at Cherry Street to find his books and belongings piled on the bowed front steps. It came as no real surprise, the hand-scrawled eviction notice pinned to the bundle of his clothes; the landlady, herself an indigent old beldam fed up with her tenant's tardiness, had been threatening him for weeks. Curiously numb to this new development, however, Nathan nosed about his meager possessions, trying to recall what was missing. When he'd determined as much, he plodded into the house and up the stairs to the top-floor apartment, where he imprudently pushed open an unbolted door.

Inside stood a man in his shirtsleeves, his bullet head inclined beneath the sloping ceiling. He was holding a kettle like a weapon, with a fist as big as a sledge. "What you want?"

"Um, please, is in the stove, *mayn* . . ." The word lost its purchase on Nathan's tongue, as he observed the crackling cast-iron heater ablaze with perhaps its first fire of the season. Closing his eyes, he inhaled the smoke as if to breathe in the manuscript before its contents escaped up the flue.

Prior to slouching away in no particular direction, Nathan had the presence of mind to recover his flea-bitten rug coat from the heap of his belongings. He might have stood beside his remaining effects with a beggar's bowl, as was common among the East Side evicted, or flogged them to an old-clothes peddler had he cared to make the effort. Instead he set off meandering the quarter, conscious of unquiet sensations stalled in their transit toward his brain by the knots in his nerves. There was a magician on Second Avenue, he recalled to no discernible purpose, whose entire act consisted in making knots disappear, but magic, fake or otherwise, was not Nathan's province. When next he thought to take stock of his whereabouts, he discovered that his aimlessness had led him into Allen Street.

Even as the door flew open and the bearded parlor custodian, roused from his slumber, burst into the room, Nathan persisted in regaling the whore.

". . . Makes Mocky né Simcha to remember, the play he attended, how from heaven he fell on account of a mortal lady, which is Hannaleh that she laughs all the time. . . ."

"What happens here!" the custodian demanded, hoisting suspenders over the nap of his ritual garment. Other whores and their clients, some clad only in singlets and unit suits, had gathered to gawk behind the custodian's furry shoulders.

The girl was backed into a corner, her patron in his question-mark posture still fully clothed beside the cot, falling silent by degrees as he turned to acknowledge the intruders.

"Uncle Rhody," exclaimed the girl, taking heart now that help had arrived, "this *grober,* he wants for a shtup to tell me a story."

The custodian's tiny eyes squinted from behind their bloated lids. "You I settle with later," he warned the girl, aware that she had stiffed him for the room; then he took hold of Nathan's coat collar and yanked him toward the door. *"Loch-in-kop, aroys!"*

"Wait a minute!" cried Nathan, attempting to dig in his heels. He was shocked by his own resistance and the unaccustomed fervor of his voice; but, having gotten his foot in the door—any door—he couldn't bear to be so soon cast out again. "I'm by Yoshke one of his boys!" he declared.

Ignoring him, Uncle Rhody continued to remove Nathan from the room. He bum-rushed him, still protesting, through the clump of onlookers, dragging him through the parlor and out onto the landing, where he paused to ask the kid on second thought, "What you said?"

"Yoshke Nigger . . ." Nathan repeated the name of thc head of the Jewish Black Hand, which he'd borrowed in the past to lend authority to his cock-and-bull. Now that he was being heeded, however, his voice had lost some of its conviction, though still he prattled on. "Him that's from Dopey Benny his fagin, who would teach me when I was apprentice to pick a pocket." Scratching the chin beneath his beard, Uncle Rhody harrumphed and proceeded to hustle Nathan down the stairs, while the ex-proofreader continued embellishing his fib. "By his rooftop academy, with the warbling of the fantails in their cages, he would demonstrate us the decoys and dodges—"

"Pisher," said Uncle Rhody, drawing up short with his charge at the fanlit front door. "You think in a *nafkeh bayis* is legal tender, the name Yoshke Nigger? Just say Yoshke, *lang leben,* for one free ride?"

Captive though he was, Nathan succumbed to a rash of gooseflesh: as if Yoshke's name on Rhody's lips had constituted a password. Humbly he replied, "He told me, Yoshke, I can make here a swap?"

The custodian let go of his coat collar one stubby finger at a time. "What you think, Rothschild that he made his millions from trading in grandmother's tales? You want your *biseleh peeric*," his broad face admitting a malevolent grin, "you got first to earn it." Then, instead of tossing the interloper out on his ear, Uncle Rhody opened the door to another apartment and shoved Nathan in.

A party of men, the majority in late middle age, sat in subdued conversation around a card table littered with bottles and wooden counters. The room stank from a medley of noxious odors (pomatum, plug tobacco, human gas), its only nod to ornament a *mizrach* of the Holy Land high on the wall beneath the pressed-tin ceiling. On the credenza a disk-playing graphopone with a trumpet speaker blared a syncopated rendition of "Dos maidl fun der vest." As the disk wound down and the voice of the matzo-soprano dropped to baritone, one of the men— bespectacled, with a mudslide of unshaven jowls—leaned from his chair to turn the crank. He revealed as he did so a revolver tucked into his waist. The dealer, pockmarked face like a trodden colander, called, "Gentlemen, buck the tiger," as he slid a card from an open-ended shoe box; then he slapped it down on the tabletop, to which was pasted a complete suit of spades.

They were a sundry lot, the players, most of them in open-necked pinstripes minus the rubber collars—though one, beetle brow athwart the ridge of his broken nose, wore a starched bib without a shirt over his thickset torso; another sported a pencil mustache, an oily kiss curl inching from beneath his crusher hat. So this, thought Nathan with a booming in his chest, is your authentic *shtuss* parlor. He'd read about such places in the muckraking columns of the *Forward* and had visited them on several occasions in his waking dreams. Tonight was another of those.

"Soda card's dead as I am to my papa," declared the dealer, slapping down another. "Nine of hearts forfeits [slap], the trey from clubs takes the turn."

A babble of contented and disgruntled voices swelled about the table as the wagers were relinquished and gathered up. A couple of beer bottles, knocked over in the commotion, were righted just in time to be toppled again by a passing El train. The beetle-browed player bit off the end of a cigar and spit it into a cuspidor that tolled like a muted cymbal. Next to him the man with the jowls and nickel specs was advertising his wife's culinary skills.

"Her gefilte fish, light as foam . . . ," touching fingers to puckered lips.

". . . from a mad dog'sh mouf," ragged the beetle brow through his gnashed cigar. "I sheen your wife, Shalo," hazarding a chip on the seven of clubs, "a *mieshkeit*." Across the table a younger man with an orange cowlick concurred. He cut the deck and passed it back to the dealer, flipping a penny. "Copper the jack to tumble."

"That may be," conceded the doting husband, "but her brisket is more tender than . . . ," struggling for the analogy.

"Than Sadie the Chink's mattress back," completed the rooster comb, clearly a wit. "I recall you had me one time by your house for Shabbos. The derma I gave to a cat who licked its tush to get the taste from its mouth."

Grumbled Salo, "*Gai in drerd!*"

Shifty-eyed under his leather shade, the dealer popped a chickpea into his mouth and chased it with a swig of celery tonic. Then he slapped down another pair of cards. "An embarrassment," clucking his tongue as he raked in the split wagers for the bank, "that the king and knave should wear the same suit. So, Yutch," addressing the rooster comb, "what's the condition of your sister?"

"Her price is above rubies," replied Yutch, "but you can have her for a cut of the bakery shakedowns. The Kid here'll come out of retirement to break her in."

Sitting beside him, the "Kid" was an aging cadet whose features, beneath his nutria crusher, appeared to have been cosmetically enhanced. He bet on a "square jack," shoved forward his chips, and fixed a Russian cigarette in an ivory holder. "Could use some tweaking, her *tsitskes*," he pronounced with a connoisseur's license, "but the keister, please God, is ripe."

"*Putzayim!*" exclaimed the dealer, doffing the eyeshade to run a hand over his sloping forehead. "I meant how is she since she got burnt in the tenement fire?"

"Ahh," Yutch considered. "She's all right, though her *ponim* looks now like a roasted chestnut, and they say she won't ever see again."

The beetle brow called the turn and, while the dealer sucked the interior of a pitted cheek, gloatingly claimed the pot. As he collected his winnings, the old dude beside him sighed audibly, bear grease and hair dye runneling his sunken temples.

"So bring her 'round, Yutchie," advised the dealer, still charitably disposed despite the game's reversal. "We'll make terms."

The uxorious Salo seconded the dealer's judiciousness. "They're a novelty, your blinders, a regular cash cow."

At that juncture a flatus from Uncle Rhody fouled the air in Nathan's vicinity and called attention to the newcomers. The dealer shifted his slitted eyes toward Nathan, appraising him like a dish he hadn't remembered ordering, while Rhody, as if to make him more presentable, plucked a louse from the top of Nathan's brow.

Said the dealer, "*Vos machst a yid?*"

Frozen in place, Nathan didn't trust himself to respond.

"Allow me to present . . . ," began Uncle Rhody. "Pardon me," turning to Nathan with exaggerated courtesy, "that I didn't catch it what they call you your name. . . ."

Nathan remained speechless in the face of an assembly he suspected of being locally august. Their titles had rung bells: Yutch might be Little Yutch, onetime prodigy of the disbanded Dopey Benny mob, and who knew but that the Kid was Candy Kid Phil, chief pander of the Allen Street vice trust. The *shtarker* with his bib and simian brow was quite possibly Cutcher-Head-Off Rothkopf, protégé of the legendary Monk Eastman. (Though the froggy-voiced dealer, whom he'd yet to hear addressed by name, was anyone's guess.) Hadn't Nathan once appropriated bits of their biographies from the tabloids to season his own incinerated saga? Once he'd felt as if they were his personal property—while now, though he ought perhaps to be more frightened, Nathan somehow took solace in the knowledge that the tables were turned: he belonged, for the moment, to them.

"I said I didn't catch it yet, your *nomen* . . . ," repeated Uncle Rhody.

Nathan took a breath, then let it out as if expelling a soul. "Nachman," he replied.

"Like the Bratslaver, may his name be for a blessing?" asked Rhody, and when Nathan nodded his head, proclaimed, "This is Nachman, who learned the yegg trade by . . . who did you say was for you your *melammed?*"

"Yoshke Nigger."

The voices around the table fell hushed, all heads having turned toward Nathan. He squirmed under their scrutiny, conscious of his uncomely appearance: a dustmop in an outsize rug coat. Still he congratulated himself on his choice of sponsors: who'd have guessed that a random sobriquet from the annals of gangland would have such conjuring power?

Uncle Rhody spoke again. "He wants to do with us a swap, Reb Nachman, his services for the services of the house."

There was some initial clearing of throats, then a flurry of suggestions from the floor as to what services "Nachman" might provide. He could start by assassinating the heads of the Kehillah, broker a peace between the Mugwumps and Tammany Hall; he could wash by hand the soiled knickers of the ladies of Allen Street during their monthlies. Said Cutcher, "He should go and bother the bedbugs." Then the dealer, with a tic in his cheek that tugged his eye like a string tugs a kite, called the room to order.

"Bockso Weiss," he said to a sharp-featured youth in an open waistcoat, seated on the crippled divan. He was dandling on his knee a young whore in lace skivvies, who was in turn paring her nails with a stiletto blade. "Bockso, didn't you need tonight in your business some assistance?"

The kid on the sofa looked edgy.

"Comes recommended, this one," continued the dealer, his left eye aflutter, "from . . . who was it? Oh, yeah, Yoshke the Nigger."

Taking the hint, Bockso relaxed his put-upon air and lifted the corners of his pickerel lips. "Why not?"

"So let come along with you Nachman to earn his piece pleasure."

Snatching back his dagger, which he stuffed into a boot, Bockso dumped the girl from his lap as he rose from the couch. (She landed on her backside but showed not the least discomfiture.) The kid gave the nod to Nathan, who hoped to disguise his internal unrest by adopting a suitably brash expression. He was about to follow Bockso from the room when he was apprehended by the dealer, clutching his sleeve with an outstretched hand.

"So how is old Nosh . . . I mean, Yoshke?"

Nathan started a moment, suddenly unsure whether Yoshke's existence had preceded his own fabrications. "In the pink," he replied.

"Glad to hear it," said the dealer, his colander face further distorted by a lopsided smile as he let Nathan go.

In the hall Bockso was pounding on a closed door. "Lighthouse Freddy Bialy!" he shouted in his native Americanese. "Get offa Tillie the Toiler already! We gotta jobba woik."

Eventually the door opened, and out stepped a hulking fellow with a rufous complexion that gave his skin a peeled effect. He wore only a long-bosomed shirt, from beneath the tails of which his prodigious organ dangled like a nozzle. On seeing Nathan he frowned and peered inquiringly at Bockso.

"Nachman," said Bockso by way of introduction, "meet the Lighthouse"—Freddy caused his member to rear up, presumably in salutation—"and his educated *schlong*. Freddy, this is Nachman, who's a all-round mayhem-man, ain't you, Nachman?"

Nathan was still stunned from Freddy's greeting.

"Nachman belongs to . . . who did you say was the boss of your outfit?"

Why was the name so hard for them to remember? "Yoshke Nigger."

Lighthouse Freddy chewed his lower lip in confusion, until Bockso reminded him, "You remember Yoshke, don't you? He was head of . . . what did they call it in olden days, the Yid Black Hand?"

Freddy arched a hairless brow. "Sure," he muttered without emphasis. "So how fares the old Nig?"

Nathan assured him he was in the pink. Toddling back into the apartment, Lighthouse Freddy emerged shortly thereafter wearing pants and an ill-fitting reefer jacket, his cropped head led by his lantern jaw. Bockso had taken a woolen cap and sack coat from a peg on the wall, pulling the cap down nearly to the bridge of his gimlet nose.

They headed north along Allen Street under the trestle, Bockso and Freddy crowding Nathan on either side. Practically trotting to stay abreast of them, Nathan was aware of a residual fear in the pit of his stomach, but rather than ominous, it seemed to imbue his innards with a hearth-like warmth. Of course it wasn't sensible, that he should take comfort in the company of thugs, but he couldn't help it; he felt that their proximity actually insulated him from harm, that even as they inducted him into a new order of experience, they kept him safe. That was on the one hand, while on the other, Nathan was not yet convinced this was happening, as if he were making up these characters and events as he went along.

Just below Grand Street, a sporty gent in a belted Norfolk jacket and lemon spats came strolling toward them, and Bockso (whispering to Nathan, "Is this how Yoshke taught you?") made a sign to Freddy to pick up the pace. Leaving Nathan temporarily behind, they approached their mark, Lighthouse Freddy barging into his shoulder with an impact that spun him around into Bockso's arms. Bockso apologized profusely to the gent, who, extricating himself from the boy's embrace, brushed the dust of the encounter from his person and walked away fuming. Then, their maneuver accomplished with balletic precision, Bockso and Freddy fell back into formation beside Nathan—where Bockso began to handle the freshly pinched turnip watch.

"Napoleon gold hunting case," he judged, "with an eleven-jewel movement, which should fetch us . . . ?"

The Lighthouse squinched up his baby face knowledgeably. "A double sawbuck."

"A double sawbuck at Cohen's Loans."

Nathan fairly swooned with admiration.

On Delancey they stopped at a produce cart, where Bockso sampled an apple, made a grimace in midchomp, and (*phwhaa*) spit it out. Then he offered to take the whole rotten bushel gratis off the peddler's hands. The old peddler made toothless objections but stood helplessly by as Freddy toppled the pyramid of apples to scoop them into a burlap sack. He slung the sack over his shoulder while Bockso said, "Don't thank us," to the peddler, and the threesome set off again. They crossed Delancey and proceeded as far as Rivington, where they turned east, entering an alley paved with old headstones in the middle of the block.

The alley dead-ended at a whitewashed gate, padlocked from within, its weathered boards scrawled across with a peeling logo: LEVINE'S A LIVERY. Without a word Bockso placed his foot on the heavy steel chain twined through the wings of the gate and nimbly hoisted himself up; he turned to receive the sack of apples from Lighthouse Freddy, which he then heaved mightily over the gate into the stableyard. Then he offered a hand to Nathan, whom (lest he hang back) Freddy also boosted from behind. He needn't have bothered; Nathan had no intention of hanging back. Regarding himself fortunate at having so soon exchanged his desolation for such intrepid fellowship, he was resolved not to disappoint them.

At Bockso's urging, Nathan scrambled over the top of the gate and dropped alongside his comrade into a packed-earth wagon yard reeking of stale garbage and dung. On the far side of the yard, crisscrossed by the shadows of scuttling vermin, was a neglected teamster's dray parked beneath a cankered brick wall. The wall ran perpendicular to a row of stables, above which sloped an eroded gallery that fronted a ramshackle clapboard living quarters. Of the four horse stalls, only one was occupied, and that by a woeful old jade, its dull coat resembling hoarfrost under the light of the three-quarter moon.

Nathan assumed that their business here must be theft, so be it—though what was there to steal in such a place? And why the apples? Nevertheless, though his teeth clacked like a linotype, he told himself that out here, beyond the reach of the rabbis if not the cops, he would show himself equal to whatever task lay at hand. Still, Nathan was puzzled when Bockso, picking up a bruised winesap from the ground, invited him to restore the rest of the spilled fruit to the sack; then he should carry please the sack over to the horse stall. Glad of an assignment, Nathan complied, lugging the apples that Freddy (straddling the arched ridge of the gate in his function as lookout) had hauled so effortlessly from Delancey Street. At the half door to the stall, he stood muzzle to muzzle with the aged beast, its head shaped like a battered bass fiddle, runny eyes misted in cataracts.

Bockso sidled up next to him. "She didn't never in her life have enough to eat," he alleged with overdone sympathy, "so give her why dontcha a napple."

Having uttered scarcely a word since Allen Street, Nathan took the opportunity to try to sound tough. "This bag of bones that's got already one hoof in the glue factory?"

"The more reason we should be to her humane," said Bockso. "Whasamattah, you never heard from *mitzvot?*"

Nathan knew better than to believe that his newfound chums were bent on good works, but neither was it his place to inquire further; so he reached into the sack and offered the mare—for Bockso had referred to her in the feminine—an apple. The horse inspected the fruit incuriously and farted, rubbing her bony haunches against the splintered pinewood stall. She nickered and cropped the ground skittishly, flattened her ears; then, having exhausted her repertoire of agitation, stretched her neck over the half door and practically inhaled the apple.

"Don't be a piker," advised Bockso, and Nathan offered the animal another, and yet another. Soon the horse was consuming the fruit at a rapid rate with a minimum of ruminative chomping, well on her way toward emptying the whole bushel sack. In the process her glaucous eyes had begun to bulge from their crusty sockets, her nostrils to exude a porridgelike substance; her swollen belly dragged the ground. It was then Nathan began to have qualms.

"Maybe it's had enough," he ventured to Bockso, who'd withdrawn from the folds of his jacket what looked at first to be a bug sprayer but was in fact a needle-nosed syringe. With a swift stabbing motion, Bockso bayoneted the apple in his hand, pressing the plunger with his thumb, injecting into the fruit the entire chartreuse contents of the glass cylinder. Then he tossed the apple to Nathan, saying,

"Let it be for dessert."

Nathan was aware, as who was not, that the energies of the Jewish underworld were divided largely between horse poisoning and arson. (Says Perlmutter, "Mr. Potash, what is to the Jews more offensive than pork?" Says Potash, "Asbestos, Mr. Perlmutter.") But eager as Nathan was to prove himself worthy of the company, murdering a defenseless nag, and by such an unkosher method at that, deeply repulsed him. In the Talmud that Nathan thought he'd outgrown, it was prohibited even to pluck a feather from a living goose for a quill. The rabbis were suddenly at the gate, and Nathan Hart was farther from his attic than he had meant to stray.

Though, wasn't there another way of viewing his predicament? Having adopted for the night the name of a figment of his own manufacture, didn't Nathan feel partly a figment himself? If Nachman was half a seraph, then wasn't Nathan, his begetter, at least one-half a Nachman? And Nathan knew beyond a certainty what Nachman would have done in his shoes: he'd have fled the wagon yard. He'd have vaulted the gate, eluding Lighthouse Freddy, hotfooting it as far as Canal Street, where he'd have taken refuge in a disreputable music hall. There he would have discovered the sullied but sublime Sofia der Royte, fallen in love, and commenced a fabled romance. But as desperately as Nathan wanted to steal a page from Nachman's book, in hesitating he'd already revised the page; and on this one Nachman Hannah Hinde Mindl's, recent emigrant from paradise, offers a poisoned apple to a swayback mare.

In vain he hoped the horse would reject it, and that would be that, but the unglutted animal scarfed the tainted fruit as greedily as she had the others. She snorted, champed the ground, and began to shake her great head, spraying the ropy soup from her nostrils, her lips peeled back to show blasted, foam-flecked teeth. Then she emitted a single whistling whinny and went rigid. Muscular tremors rippled in waves from her withers to her rump, the veins branching over her distended belly like spreading vines. Making a feeble effort to kick, she rattled the hanging horse tack and caused a collar shaped like a toilet seat to fall from the knotholed wall. Nathan stepped back, half expecting some fearful display: the beast would rear up breathing flames, charge headlong from its stall in an attempt to escape its own end. But so finally accustomed was the creature to indignities that she seemed to accept the choking and shuddering as her due. Trickling blood from her eyes, she gave at the knees as if genuflecting before an executioner's uplifted ax.

Bockso, a head shorter than Nathan, nevertheless extended a fraternal arm around his shoulder, as if together they were witnessing a momentous event. "Y'know, it can't *oysbrechn,* a horse," the boy informed him, "it can't spew." Then he leaned over the half door and grabbed a fistful of the animal's mane, yanking it free with the sound of uprooted turf. "Makes a nice souvenir for the judies," he explained.

Meanwhile a light had appeared on the gallery above, and from his perch astride the gate, Freddy cried out, "*Zechs,* the *balagoula!*" Because a limping, chicken-legged old man, no doubt the teamster Levine, had emerged in his nightshirt holding a lantern.

"What you do don deh?" he hollered.

The dying jade exhaled a final stertorous whimper and rolled over. Its rib cage, no longer heaving, looked to Nathan like the curved trusses of a beached ark that had sprung viscous leaks at its seams. Sickened, he began to back away, when Bockso detained him with a hand at his wrist.

"Next time they send 'round to you from the Tenth Ward Amusement Commission a delegatz," he shouted up to the grizzled old man, "I recommend you should buy a ticket or two to their shindy." And, on a congenial note, "You owe it to yourself a good time."

Having by now divined what had happened, the teamster, as likely inured to misfortune as his exterminated nag, said only,

"But I dun dance."

Once he'd flung himself back over the gate alongside his fellows, Nathan was ready to call it a night. He retreated the alley with them as far as the street, out of earshot of the old man's lamentations for his fallen "Hagar!" and then tried to beg off.

"If you don't need no more my services . . . ," he began breathlessly, wanting to make himself scarce, to beat it to some obscure place where he could give himself up to shame and disgust; though exactly where that place might be, he couldn't have said.

"Don't be a ninny, Nachman," interrupted Bockso, hooking an arm through Nathan's. "You got first to get your reward for a job well done— *nu*, Freddy?" The Lighthouse, with viselike fingers, pincered Nathan's other arm.

As they frog-marched the ex-proofreader up the avenue, Bockso announced that they would make a small private party before repairing to Allen Street. His tutors having become his captors, Nathan felt again the tension in his gut; it was a palpable thing, this lump of fear, like a sick organ in danger of rupturing, of swamping his system in a marinade of nausea—though not quite yet. For hadn't Bockso called him by another handle? "Nachman," Nathan repeated under his breath, as if trying on the name for size, and for an instant it seemed to fit, exonerating Nathan Hart of any wrongdoing. But it was a dicey proposition, Nathan's identifying with his make-believe hero, since Nachman, no stranger to faintheartedness, had accumulated sins of his own.

After a couple of blocks, they arrived at a low, unmarked threshold on Stanton Street. Ushered down spoon-shaped steps through a tinplated doorway, Nathan was introduced to a dreary basement with a sawdusted floor. There was a bar consisting of gutter planks laid across a couple of barrels, some tables around which ill-kempt men and women were huddled over mugs of needled beer. The exposed-brick walls were bare but for some framed newspaper clippings of sporting events and a chromo of Teddy Roosevelt's charge up San Juan Hill. A salmon-lipped Negro in a derby sat at an upright piano playing a rag-time dirge, while an underfed monkey groomed itself on the bench beside him.

Stepping ahead, Bockso placed an order at the bar, giving a wink to a brilliantined barkeep with a beauty spot; then he parted a hanging tarp over a literal hole in the wall and bade Freddy escort their guest into the stygian backroom. Until his eyes adjusted to the faint light of the cellar, Nathan thought he might have been back in steerage again. Human beings were strewn about the floor on coarse pallets, crammed into cantilevered shelves against the walls, suspended from the ceiling in hammocks like furled shrouds. Draped over the red points of scattered spirit lamps, a scrim of green smoke smelling as tart as burned almonds overhung the entire scene. A warehouse of jackstraw bodies waiting to be animated by souls, was how the room impressed itself on the dumbstruck ex-proofreader. He could see they were mostly men, the majority of them roughshod, though here and there was some swell in a negligee shirt. There were also a handful of women, faded baggages likely from the Five Points district, their squashed faces hidden under the brims of leghorn hats. While most of the patrons appeared to be unconscious, lying on their sides with knees folded to their chins, a few reclined on their pallets like pashas, drawing serenely on the stems of bamboo pipes.

"Take a pew," invited Bockso, while Lighthouse Freddy busied himself with rousting a logy tenant from his berth against the wall. With no apparent choice in the matter, Nathan plunked himself down on the straw-matted berth, hunching his back to keep from hitting his head on the shelf above. "So," said Bockso, settling in beside him with drink in hand, "you know already from Sissy Sid's?" Fresh out of bluff, Nathan shook his head. Freddy went lumbering off through the litter of prostrate humanity, reckless of his tread, while Bockso, relaxing into the role of pedagogue, started to acquaint the novice with the protocol of the opium den.

He had barely begun his disquisition, expanding on the culture from "ice-cream eaters" to celebrity dope fiends like Anna Held, when the Lighthouse returned with a tray of paraphernalia. Squatting beside the berth, Freddy spread the layout on the bug-infested mat between Bockso and Nathan. There were a number of exotic items for which Bockso enthusiastically provided the nomenclature: the drum-shaped box containing the dope he dubbed *yen hop,* the miniature brass and porcelain bowls were *dow,* the flute-size bamboo pipe the *yen tshung.* There was a bell-globed spirit lamp, *yen dong,* which Lighthouse Freddy lit with a lucifer struck on his massive thigh. Sliding the shiv from his boot, Bockso opened the tiny *yen hop* and speared the pill inside, which looked like a plug of earwax, then held it over the guttering lamp flame. "First you cook it, your Fountain of Happiness," he explained, enjoying the demonstration, allowing the opium to melt into a molasses-like goo. As it dripped from the knife blade, Freddy deftly caught the droplets in a small brass receptacle, then scooped a bit of residue with a thin metal scraper into the ceramic *dow.* He screwed the *dow* onto the end of the pipe, lit it with the lamp, inhaled, and passed it along to Bockso, who inhaled and passed the "joint" to Nathan, directing him in a clotted voice to take a suck.

"This is what they call banging the gong."

Nathan did as he was told, taking a feeble pull from the pipe and coughing. Bockso slapped his back and enjoined him to "Fill your lungs," and Nathan, with no will left to resist, made to obey. He felt instantly as if an umbrella had been opened in his chest: he had leaped from a great height, and the umbrella sustained him in midair. He was deliciously giddy, his brain a warm twist like a sponge from which all traces of virulence have been wrung. But as his body, not quite lighter than air, seemed to float slowly downward, the contents of Nathan's stomach—an undigested piece of flanken, barley soup from a forgotten repast, stark fear—rose up into his gorge. Convulsing, he thanked God for small blessings: at least he wasn't a horse.

With marvelous dexterity Bockso snatched a bowler from off the face of a nearby sleeper in time to hold it under Nathan's nose as he heaved. He returned the hat, filled and steaming, to the Lighthouse (who placed it on the heedless sleeper's chest) and lifted Nathan's shirttail to pat the strands of flecked saliva from his chin. Then he offered him a sip from his tumbler of rust-colored liquid. *"L'chayim,"* he said as Nathan guzzled the libation in a long, greedy pull, after which he let loose a tortured groan from his scalded diaphragm.

"That's the hair from the mare you done in," said Bockso, a slight chilliness having entered his voice, "pure grain laced with camphor and benzine, cocaine scrapings, and what else . . . ?"

Offered Lighthouse Freddy sagaciously, "Chloral hydrate and rectified erl of turpentine."

Bockso chuckled. "He don't talk much, Freddy Bialy, but he's deep."

A carousel had begun to revolve about the interior of Nathan's head, its painted ponies dragging their bloated bellies along the ground. Their swaybacks were straddled by angry Cossacks lashing their mounts for their stubborn lack of motion, until the whole gaudy roundabout swerved dangerously on its axis.

"So, Freddy," Nathan heard Bockso through the ringing in his ears, "think we can make it back to Allen Street before Yoshke deals the last turn?" Then the two hoodlums rose and started for the exit without so much as a *gezunterhait.*

Collapsed supine on his berth, Nathan rested his throbbing head against a hard pillow like a square rolling pin. He fell in and out of consciousness, images seeping from his semidreams into the world at large. During one wild revolution of his brain, a riderless pony careened through the tissue-thin wall of his skull, blundering out into the hop shop, where it grew instantly old. Its heavy wings drooped in the people-cluttered dust, the limp crest along its bowed neck bursting into flame. Then its mane was a torch spewing ashes in the shape of Hebrew characters, the letters darting about the cellar until they lit again like carrion crows upon the fallen horse. With no standard left against which to gauge his perceptions, Nathan clung to what shreds of logic remained to him; to wit: if Joseph Toblonsky, alias Yoshke Nigger, was really alive, then why not Mocky der Hoyker and his mongrel son, their existence proof, he reasoned, that Nathan Hart was pure fantasy. In the near distance, an old man was picking his way among the layouts and lamps, his back hunched over from the large earthen jug strapped to his shoulders. From one palsied hand dangled a wicker hamper, his other hand fingering a string of sausages looped across his puny chest like a bandolier. He moved among the more or less conscious with muggy eyes gleaming beneath the rim of his bowler hat, dispensing lemonade through a hose from his tilted jug into a single dirty glass.

"Penny refreshment," he croaked over the sibilant dreamers and the rolling piano from the blind pig outside, "*tayglakh, shnecken, nuchspeissen . . .*"

Eventually he made his way as far as the berth where Nathan had labored to prop himself on an elbow.

"Lemonade, for you a penny, pastries, *kichel,* have a nosh. . . ."

"Is that you, Mocky Fargenish?" asked Nathan, wanting and not wanting it to be true.

Pausing before his questioner, the old man parted his lips to show the stumps of his teeth. Then, like some superannuated snake charmer, he began to unwind from his shoulder the sausages (which appeared to Nathan to be glossy with blood), dropping the hamper to wrap them phylactery-wise around a fidgeting arm. He swayed from the waist as he chanted a penitential prayer.

More perplexed than unnerved, Nathan wondered, was it better to have encountered in the flesh a chimera of one's own invention or a ghost of your own flesh and blood? And which was this? "Papa," he asked tentatively—as what did he have left to lose?—"can you . . . take me home?" The question hung in the air a moment, greeted at length by the old man's wheezing laughter, as he offered Nathan the brackish glass of lemonade. That's when the full dread of his situation announced itself to the former proofreader. Fighting vertigo, Nathan managed to rise from his berth, knocking the glass from the old man's hand as he lurched past him. He stumbled over insensate bodies, seeking light, plunging through the drapery into the barroom and thence out the spy-holed front door.

Though he recognized the names of the streets he floundered through—Rivington, Chrystie, Grand—they did not impress him with their familiarity. They were, he decided, the streets of America as described in heaven by the dead, who had never seen them. They were formal streets of stylized refuse and squalor, once removed from the real: tenements that, for all their decrepitude, might have doubled as music boxes, the pushcarts like pulpits and scaffolds, wattled wives that could as well have been rust-bucket barges or lemures or barnacle geese. Counterfeit streets that, if you followed them as far as their source, might lead you back to the original. Back to the familiarly menacing streets he'd traveled as schlepper and employee of the *Jewish Daily Forward* and as lover of a redheaded girl. But was *back* where Nathan really wanted to go, or wouldn't he rather escape the bowels of the ghetto altogether and make for paradise? Once there he could retrieve more stories, then funnel them back again to the Lower East Side for ready conversion into hit plays. Then the girl would return to him forever, and they would perform together in newly contrived theatricals, and she would love him as she had before. Because ultimately that was what he wanted, wasn't it? The girl?

He was on East Broadway, aka Newspaper Row, this much he was sure of—though the shop fronts and the offices of the Yiddish dailies kept alternating, with every breath he took, between two and three dimensions, and the throngs drifted or danced, between each blink of his eye, past a dairy restaurant whose string quartet painted musical pinwheels in the evening air. Across the way from a palpitating Educational Alliance, Nathan plopped himself down on the granite steps of the library, feeling both inside and outside of his own skin. Both an actor in and a passive witness to his own tailspinning decline.

"Nachman," said Nathan beneath his breath, the follicles of his scalp prickling with heat, "sat down on the steps of the Seward Park Library."

In time, which meant nothing to him now—he was merely a tourist in time from a timeless sphere—she came along. She sauntered as usual, her head covered in a tight mull turban, hair plaited into a ginger braid that switched behind her like a scorpion's tail. She wore a flounced wash skirt to the ankles, and over her shoulders, completing her Gypsy demeanor, the loosely wrapped merino shawl.

"That's when he saw Rivka Sofia," Nathan said aloud to no one at all, his narrative faculty reengaged.

No longer bothering to conceal her beauty, neither did she augment it as she had onstage. She was a slight, raven-haired girl with large, sorrowful eyes, on her way to her job in the chorus line at a Canal Street music hall.

Her progress since Nachman had last seen her had been circular. At Adler's Grand Street Theater, she'd disappointed her fans in the brief run of Mirele Efros. *The army of admirers that had followed her to Adler's play-*

house let it be known they had little interest in Adler himself. The Nesher haGadol, the "Great Eagle," sultan of Second Avenue, whose personal harem rivaled the fleshpots of Allen Street—him they could take or leave. But the real anticipation they reserved for the heroine of Uncle Shmuel's, who, untethered at last from the kerosene circuit, was poised to soar.

So they scarcely believed that the costumed dolly going through the motions in front of a painted drop was the same vibrant actress they had come to adore. This one was equivocal, almost dithering, with none of the sauce and whimsicality that had characterized the underworld star. Thinking perhaps the piece was not right for her, that the gravity of Mirele's temperament impeded the girl's natural exuberance, Adler changed tactics: he cast her in the lead of Lateiner's three-handkerchief melodrama, The Jewish Heart. *This was the role that had made a star of Mrs. Liptzin, earning her the title of the Yiddish Duse, and was generally judged an ideal vehicle for aspiring primas. A fine supporting cast was assembled, some of them making guest appearances on loan from other companies, so much did they want to hitch their wagons to the new phenomenon. But if high drama was not her strong suit, how much less was the standard* shund? *When she didn't appear to be sleepwalking, the girl looked literally lost, as if she'd waked to find herself in an unkind place bombarded by lights. Her gestures were so mechanical, her voice so strident, that even her staunchest supporters felt betrayed.*

Fleeing the Grand, she found temporary shelter in Tomashevky's People's Theater, where her rudderless interpretation of Esther von Engedi made her a laughingstock. Out of pity, or perhaps making a show of noblesse oblige, Mrs. Liptzin took her on for a spell at the Thalia; but there were limits to the grand dame's beneficence, and instead of the principal part, the rabbi's daughter was given a minor role in a hackneyed operetta. A few steadfast admirers still believed that La Liptzin's high-handedness would backfire and the girl's comedic talents win the day; but despite all the operetta had in common with the vulgar spectacles that had been her bread and butter at Shmuel's, a fish out of water, Rivka Sofia flopped.

By the time she returned in disgrace to Canal Street, she had been labeled box-office poison by every respectable Yid theater in town. Nor did her erstwhile company welcome her back with open arms. In a gesture like a

*stripping of rank, Lazar Waxman dropped the "Sofia" from the errant
actress's double-barreled stage name. Reduced to plain Rivka, she was sentenced to the supporting cast, surfacing thereafter only in walk-ons such as
the nurse (bustles fore and aft) in a Dr. Kronkeit routine. To her credit, it
was said the once willful first lady accepted her fate without protest, thankful as she must have been to be home. . . .*

Across the street where a stick man in a one-button cutaway was
hawking sheet music and bags of dirt from the Holy Land, Keni Freischutz was about to enter the Educational Alliance. That's when Nathan,
having recovered some fugitive piece of himself, got experimentally to
his feet. He wobbled out into the street, oblivious of electric trolleys and
motorcars, lunging onto the opposite sidewalk to take hold of the girl's
slender wrist.

"Come back to me already!" he beseeched her.

Keni appraised his scruffy countenance with much the same distaste
as had the men around the *shtuss*-parlor table. "Do I know you?" she
asked, trying unsuccessfully to reclaim her hand, so that Nathan couldn't
tell if she were teasing him. Impulsively he began to tug her toward the
steps of a basement area below the offices of *Di Morgen Zhurnal*, where
he might plead his case in more privacy. At first she resisted, braking on
the heels of her button shoes, but, rather than make a scene in the
crowded street, Keni allowed herself in the end to be led. When they
reached the bottom of the steps, he let go of her arm with the idea of embracing her, but, once released, Keni shoved him hard in the chest. Unsteady on his stems, Nathan stumbled backward, falling on his behind
over a trash-strewn drain. Then, even as he made an effort to rise, the
girl had planted her legs on either side of him, kneeling astride his knees
to pin him to the paving stones.

With brutally scrupulous fingers, she began to unfasten his trousers,
and before he could stop her—though why should he want to stop
her?—she had thrust a probing hand into his fly. Like, thought Nathan, a
fishwife invading the innards of a carp. While the traffic clamored above
them, she pulled out his dispirited member and set about vigorously trying to revive it. To Nathan's own astonishment, she succeeded in relatively short order to pump the mettle back into his manhood. Then she

raised her skirt and petticoat and clamped them between the pips of her teeth, thus freeing her hands to drag down her cambric drawers. She clutched him with one hand, moistened herself with the other, and parted her teeth to let the skirts fall tent-wise over Nathan's uncovered parts. Lifting her hips to settle herself upon him, she grunted once and began to rock back and forth with the abandon of a runaway metronome.

Nathan wished he could enjoy the miracle of his risen virility, but, in his baffled condition, the achievement seemed to have little to do with himself. Nor was this girl the muse he remembered—or was it that she was muse and something else? She was a painter and wayward Jewish daughter and, when he blinked, a once versatile music-hall soubrette. Then blink again and she was a demon out of the stories that Froika the Troika had inherited from her disemboweled spouse: a Lilith from Sitra Achra, the Other Side, who visited men in the night to steal their seed. Having mounted him, she cursed him with every thrust of her churning hips: "Lily-liver milksop, india-rubber *goylem* (unh), no spine you got and for a brain (unh) a lump anthracite, a shriveled gonad for a soul! *Pishakhtz*, with your angels and coward sons of angels, you should *shtupn zay in toches arayn*—I shit on them, a dark ending (unh) for you all!" She continued her litany of abuses, the chant becoming almost melodic, the music quickening until the moment the girl went rigid, her eyes clenched, her mouth wide open but mute. Then came a spastic shudder the complement to his own, and she slumped as if stricken across Nathan's heaving chest.

She remained there holding on to him only an instant before sliding away, discarding his spent body to stand and rearrange her dress, correcting her turban and pushing the spectacles back onto her nose. Looking down at her victim, she kicked him once in the side for good measure before ascending the steps to the street.

Reaching for her cast-off drawers as for a lifebuoy, Nathan hugged them to his aching ribs; then, with no previous talent for weeping, he surrendered to sobs. Sepulchral sobs wrenched his chest, dislodging his heart, which broke apart and dissolved in the acid flood of his tears—the tears welling up, spilling over his lids like scarlet streamers unscrolling down his cheeks. One moment he was hemorrhaging tears from a bottomless cistern, the next they had ceased, the waters subsiding, leaving

Nathan to wonder from what source they had sprung. Becalmed, he was perfectly empty save for the words that occupied the hollowness where his longing had been.

"Rivka kicked Nachman once for good measure," said Nathan, releasing the words like doves in search of dry land, "before ascending the steps to the street."

MOCKY

Rivka kicked Nachman once for good measure before ascending the steps to the street. He might have lain there like that indefinitely with his limp putz exposed, clutching the quilt he'd carried with him from paradise, if I hadn't forsaken my role as spy to go down into the area and help him up.

"Have some dignity," I told him, hauling him to his feet, upon which he stood unsturdily, looking like he might prefer to lie down again. He stared at his drooping organ as if the thing had only just sprouted there beneath his belly, then fumblingly tucked it back into his unbuttoned trousers. Scarcely seeming to regard my presence, though I'd draped his filthy quilt cloak-wise over his shoulders, he started back up the stairs.

I followed and was ignored when I asked him where he thought he was going. "Where you going?" I repeated, catching him up as we were pelted by the inaugural dollops of a late-evening shower. So many umbrellas opened along the avenue that the pedestrian traffic resembled a traveling field of burgeoning mushrooms.

"I'm looking," he replied at last, studiously *not* looking at me.

"I can see you looking. What you looking?"

"I'm looking," he frowned in pain or deliberation, the rain plastering the hair in quarter notes over his brow, "for the back door from kingdom come."

"You crazy?" I said, as if it weren't already self-evident. "There ain't been for years no back door. It got blew away like in that play, *Der Meshugener*, where they made in it dynamite for a subway. From here to there you can't get no more—at least not alive."

Nachman digested the news with some consternation but neither questioned its source nor broke his jolting stride, and eventually he offered this considered alternative: "Then I'm looking for my papa, he should teach me to fly."

I laughed a hollow laugh and swallowed the guilty lump in my throat. "You got a papa?" His nod was barely perceptible. "So why you think you would find around here your papa?" I probed. "*Di farshvoondn* papas, they scatter to the winds. In China he might be, or the North Pole. Why you don't look in the North Pole? New York ain't the whole of the world."

Said Nachman, not without a measure of logic, "Ain't this the type place a angel would fall in?"

It was the first time he'd alluded to his celestial parentage in my hearing; but as the mention sounded more careless than confiding (discretion was never his strong suit), I chose to leave it alone. Besides, I suspected another, less filial reason for his sticking around the quarter: because, whatever the unpromising particulars of their last encounter, I would wager he wasn't yet willing to leave the vicinity of the girl.

"How you going to know him when you would find him, your papa?" I continued to press him, and Nachman asked me in turn if I didn't think a fallen angel would stand out among ordinary men.

Though he had a point, I nonetheless groaned aloud, "Angel, shmangel, you make my kishkes ache." Winded and getting drenched in the now steady downpour, I couldn't keep up with him any longer, so I grabbed his arm and forced him to halt. "Go away from here already, why don't you," I advised, concerned that for the crucible of ghetto life, he was wholly unfit. "Go in the mountains where they got there a better class Hebrew. You'll rent a *kukhaleyn*, take a bath, play shovelboard. This ain't the only place they got Jews . . ."

We were standing in front of Saperstein's Secondhand, its rolled-up awning leaving us unprotected from the rain that was coming down harder. "Give a look at what by America you become," I said, indicating his soggy reflection in the streaming plate glass. "Ain't you a shame?"

Nachman turned his head toward the window, dimly illuminated by a corner streetlamp. "You should talk," he muttered in reference to the other, more stunted reflection; and it was true that we looked in our beaded translucence like a pair of souls done in from wandering.

Shaking off the remark, I raised my voice above the Niagara drumming my hat. "Clean yourself up and you ain't such a bad-looking fellow. You got a nice bone structure." For didn't he favor his father? "The ladies that they cared for the actor Opgekumener will care again for Nachman. You should try already and be a person."

I was aware, of course, that half a person was the most he could aspire to, my paternity having sentenced him to remaining betwixt and between.

Nachman's reply was unexpectedly hurtful. "Listen on him, the Plague. What business is this of you?" He was no longer staring at the window but into my face, asking pointedly, "Ain't you a nastiness that's hardly himself a human being?"

"What did you say?"

Nachman: "You didn't hear?"

It was clear he was trying to get rid of me, the ingrate, and I had half a mind to abandon him then and there; though the tired old memory of my prior defection kept me in place. "Well, for once you got it right," I assured him, galled despite myself by the insult. "I ain't a human being!"

"Like I said."

"Paskudnyak!" I was livid. "You watch it how you talk to your papa. . . ." Then right away I'm backpedaling: "That is, a mortal man who like a son he thinks of you." But in view of all that had transpired since the day I'd discovered him by the water stairs on the island, the truth now seemed largely superfluous. As heaven held no secrets for either of us, where was the point of preserving them here on earth? "Because," I submitted, waiving all caution, "what I mean to say is, I'm your papa."

So there it was: the thing had been that simple all along—and, having said it, I felt I'd discharged my duty. He could do with the information as he pleased. Myself, making a face like he should put that in his pipe and smoke it, I turned into the sheeting rain.

When, after a few steps, I glanced over my shoulder, Nachman was right behind me. Indifferent to the torrents, he looked neither shocked nor forgiving, or even skeptical—only curious. It was apparent he meant to follow wherever I led, a liability that (since I had no particular destination in mind) caused me to stop in midstride. When he trod on my heel,

I turned around to bark my displeasure but ended by pulling the quilt over his naked head. Then I aimed my dripping beak in the direction of Division Street and Mushy's Rumanian Wine Cellar, across the car lines and down six soapy stairs.

At this hour the place was full of prophets without honor, disaffected scholars, and armchair provocateurs living on peddled pawn tickets and public relief. It was a clientele so seedy that even the likes of Nachman and Mocky Fargenish could enter undetained. I chose a wooden booth toward the back, near a stove, under a heroic portrait of Theodor Herzl draped in a Zionist flag. Removing my hat, I poured the moat of rainwater around its rim into a brass spitoon. I took off my Prince Albert coat, wrung the sleeves, and hung it over the back of the booth to dry—and, while he kept a weather eye trained on my every movement, did the same with Nachman's soaking quilt. Then I motioned him into the booth and slid in opposite.

A waiter in a long, shmutz-stained apron and brush mustache approached the table looking unfriendly, as if we might give the place's bad name an even worse one. To appease him I ordered a cup of hot schav and asked Nachman if he cared for a spoon, but he only shook his head.

"When was it the last time you had to eat?" I inquired, though I could see that he currently hungered for something other than sourgrass soup.

"Tell me again to my face," he said.

I settled back and cleared my throat stentorianly, composing myself for the lengthy disclosure. "Understand," I stated for the record, "that you had in olden times more traffic between here and there . . . ," thus proceeding to relate the tale of my otherworldly origins. It was, of course, a rehash of the story Nachman himself had brought to Uncle Shmuel's, whereupon he had initiated a revolution in theater. The fact was, there being no real difference between my biography and the plot of *Simcha's Fall,* who knew whether I relied more on faulty memory or the music-hall version of the tale? Still, I was annoyed when Nachman interrupted the narrative I'd only just begun to demand of me,

"*Nu,*" the raindrops dangling like plumb bobs from his wet black curls, "so prove it."

"Prove what? What '*it*'?"

"Prove it you're my papa."

Summoning what remained of my moth-eaten pride, I asked him, "It ain't proof enough I give mine word?"

He sniffed like I shouldn't make him laugh.

I fetched up a sigh from the bottom of my heart and began to describe his mother. I described both her jovial good nature and her bountiful anatomy, perhaps lingering too long over attributes better omitted in the presence of one's son. But even in the face of such generous (not to say poignant) details, Nachman again voiced his discontent.

"This is proof?"

"Like it or lump it," I snapped, feeling I'd divulged enough for one night—since where did it say I had to convince the *nudzh?* Besides, wasn't my acknowledgment of our kinship an argument in itself? "Who else would even want to be your papa?" I wondered aloud.

Nachman dismissed the remark with a wave. "If you're my papa," he said, worrying the thought, "then you are also a angel?"

This I was forced to concede.

"And a angel has got by definition a pair wings?"

Again I was obliged to admit the reasonableness of his assumption.

"Then show to me your wings."

The waiter, having returned just in time to overhear Nachman's request, allowed his tray to tilt forward as he bent an ear. The soup bowl slid off, landing spectacularly upright on the table but sloshing a viscous broth over the oilcloth, which the waiter made no move to clean up. Instead, despite his air of having heard everything, he joined me in my incredulity, folding his arms to wait and see what happened next. I glowered at him till he shrugged and departed, then said to Nachman, "Come again?"

He repeated his request with an urgency that further unsettled me. My angelhood was a property as abstract to me now as my fatherhood had so recently been. The wings—is that really what they were? those shriveled appendages crusted just this side of petrifaction, which I thought of (if I thought of them at all) as a deformity—my wings were as useless as was Nachman's faculty for recalling stories. Furthermore, despite all the dishonorable things I'd done in my time, never for love or money had I stooped to exhibiting my long-retired pinions. There I'd drawn the line.

Then it wasn't up to me anymore. Risen and come around to my side of the booth, Nachman started in tugging my waistcoat over my head. I tried to resist, asking him was he nuts, there were people all around, though the truth was that nowhere else could have afforded us more privacy. The waiter was off kibitzing a quarrel at another table (something about the most efficient means of exterminating the capitalist cockroach), while everyone not involved had his head in a journal or was brooding over a game of chess. Moreover, for such career dreamers as the patrons of Mushy's Rumanian, nothing was ever really out of the ordinary. Still I struggled, as Nachman, seeming as if possessed of a preternatural strength, dragged me from the booth.

Like the good student he'd never been at Yoshke Nigger's lush-rolling academy, he deftly yanked my suspenders and tore my shirt free of its studs. Squinching his nose, he peeled to my waist the union suit I hadn't removed in living memory. Then, having exposed my sunken chest, its skin the texture of cheesecloth, he turned me roughly about and shoved me toward the wall.

I was unpleasantly surprised to find that when he touched them, my feathered parts, they still had some feeling left in them. In fact, when he began to unfold them (irreverently to my mind, like manhandling a holy text), I got a sensation as if he were peeling a scab. Not happy with having parted my wings, however, he had to manipulate them in a vigorous flapping motion, which made a chirping sound and set up an unsavory breeze. All this caused me no small amount of pain.

"Oy!" I exclaimed in protest, while Nachman wanted eagerly to know, "These things, do they work?" He was diligently testing a linty scapula, careless of hollow bones as brittle as bread sticks.

"Not in centuries," I grumbled, and, having had enough, turned around in a temper and pushed him away; then I covered up and resumed my seat. Nachman made no move to stop me or to conceal his disappointment.

"But"—he looked perplexed—"when you took me when I was a baby back to *Gan Eydn,* you didn't fly there like in the story?"

"I flew—but wore me out the journey, and that's the truth. When I came back in the world, you think that like a leaf I glided?" I fluttered my fingers airy-fairily. "Down the backstairs I tumbled, *toches* over teakettle. The wings, they are only a nuisance now; some *mohel* I should have made him to clip them a long time ago."

But Nachman wasn't so easily discouraged. All of a sudden he seemed to have come to a decision, recovering his resolve of a moment before.

"They look to me hunky-dory," he said, sliding back into his side of the booth. He leaned toward me—with a wink, no less—and, noticing the soup, took up my spoon and began to eat with relish. "In the joints a *bisl* lubrication," he suggested between gulps, "some exercise, a proper diet, and you'll see, they're good as new."

The storm outside had turned the front window into a shimmering, iridescent curtain, and for an instant I could hardly remember what was on the other side. That's how agitated he'd made me, the rag mop, who actually believed he was being sensible.

"Excuse me," I was almost afraid to ask, "but just what it is you are getting at?"

Nachman ceased his slurping, allowing the spoon to stir what was left of the soup like a feathering oar. "Papa," he said, the word prompting the few remaining hairs on my scalp to stand at rigid attention, "I was thinking you could take me back."

"Take you back where?" I inquired.

"To paradise."

I suggested that his overstimulated condition had disordered his brain, but Nachman was unflappable.

"You'll take me, see, and I'll get from there more stories that I can make from them, when we return to earth, theatrical presentations. Shows for Rivka that by them she can again be a star. Then again she will love me, no?" I told him no, even as he was asking, "So what do you say?"

"I say *vos nisht geshtoygn, nisht gefloygn*—it won't fly! Didn't I tell you already that from here to there you can't get? It ain't possible."

"What for a angel ain't possible?"

"*Vey iz mir!*" I cried, and began to point out the many shortcomings of his plan. First there was the great unlikelihood that my wings would ever again be operational. But suppose they were; say we were able to reach *Gan Eydn*, then what? Then directly the archangels, they're showing us the door. Or, for the sake of argument, suppose that everything went according to plan: we get an earful and come back with a fresh stock of bunkum ready for quick conversion to the Yiddish stage. *Mazel tov.* Only by then who knows how much time has elapsed on earth? By then the East Side is maybe ashes; maybe there's no more Jews. By then Rivka and America have passed into history.

"This is for us the chance we would take," replied Nachman with stubborn conviction, and something in the sound of his "we" made my bowels churn like cement in a mixer.

I wanted to shout at him that, if he still wanted Rivka, he should for Gods sake go and get Rivka—though I knew it wasn't plain Rivka he was after, but a Rivka transported into one of his *farshlogener* plays. I was on the verge of saying as much but didn't like to belabor the obvious.

"This scheme," I queried him nevertheless, "you don't really expect me to take it serious?"

Nachman relaxed the intensity of his expression to submit the ghost of a grin.

I could have wept for both our sakes. The whole business of heaven and angels: it'd had some currency during the great days at Shmuel's, but those days were over, and heaven had since retreated into superstition again. Of course, only a superstitious mind could have hatched a scheme as thoroughly crackpot as Nachman's. The poor schnook, he'd lost his knack for remembering stories just as I had lost the knack of believing in the place where the stories came from. We were even: he was a deluded pipe dreamer and I a worn-out, homesick old man, infected—God help him—by his son's blind exuberance.

SAUL

In Arkansas we toiled and we spun. We inhabited a rugged parcel of land excrescent with shacks, lean-tos, a patchwork Indian tepee—the whole place resembling some jerry-built mining camp surrounded by scrub woods and once-great mountains eroded to hills. We called it, alternately, Cockaigne, Klopstokia, the Vegetable Kingdom of Thumbumbia, the Nature Theater of the Ozarks, the Gulag, and Brigadoon, depending on our mood, though, for the sake of convenience, we tended to fall back on "the farm." This designation may have lacked the irony that was a hallmark of our crowd, but now that we'd become dependent on one another for food and shelter as well as clever remarks, irony was not our first priority. Besides, a farm was what we'd bought, and had we not set about attending to its practical operation, those baked yellow acres would have seemed all the more hostile and forlorn. So we turned our hands to husbanding animals and tilling the rocky soil, to reinforcing the ramshackle structures that already existed and improvising new habitations. We performed these tasks literally by the book, since our only knowledge of rural survival (notwithstanding that all the men but myself had once been Eagle Scouts) came from literature ordered through a counterculture wish book called the *Whole Earth Catalog*. We labored each day until exhaustion overtook us, then burrowed into our down-filled bags and dropped off into unconsciousness as if from a precipice. We crawled out at dawn through a detritus of dreams to labor some more, all the while pretending, until the pretense became second nature, that this was the life we were destined for.

When we arrived, the mean hovel that had been the widowed farmer's home before he sold his property and opened a small-arms shop, was uninhabitable. The smashed windows were invaded by creepers, the walls pocked with hornets' nests, the roof a fractured spine. The interior stank from the spoor of both human and animal trespassers, which crunched underfoot, the whole house seeming from a distance to revert to a feature of the natural landscape. So we pitched tents intended for weekend campers in a hollow chosen for its pastoral setting along a creek bordered by goldenrod—never mind that the site was a quarter mile from the cinder-block wellhouse up the hill. In this way we thrust ourselves without preamble back into the Stone Age, hauling the five-gallon water jugs down the long hill in the August sun to the campsite, where we cooked our stir-fry over an open fire. We had taken possession of the place too late in the season to put in a garden but nevertheless spent our first weeks rolling boulders out of a field to prepare for its cultivation. I thought of building pyramids or hauling stones to reinforce ghetto walls, but such thoughts were counterproductive; so improbable were our exertions in any case that they resisted translation into nightmare or romance and were too taxing to be other than what they were. At the end of the day, our fatigue made us practically indifferent to the plagues of mosquitoes and wasps that attacked our camp, the snakes and scorpions that may have preceded us into our sweltering sleeping bags. We likewise ignored the summer storms that hammered our tents until they came apart like damp paper.

In the beginning we were staggered by the magnitude of what we'd undertaken: how could we have deliberately marooned ourselves in such inimical surroundings? We were overwhelmed by the persistence of nature, with its venomous plants and reptiles, the bloated blood ticks that clung to our armpits and ears like paste pearls. We were disappointed in Billy Boots, who, having brought us here, refused to play the part of leader and instead kept his own counsel. There were tarantulas and wolves, no-necked neighbors who burned crosses and barns; there was a wilderness that defied our best efforts to find soothing precedents, *Lord of the Flies* being the most obvious literary model. We felt alone in all creation. "First things first"; we repeated this brainless mantra, though we hadn't a clue where to begin. But there was the fire to build and the tents to secure, the coffee to boil; there were children, no less, in need of assurance and shoes. So we grimly set about the necessary tasks as if, though there was no immediate danger, we were locked in a life-and-death struggle with the elements.

In time, however, an awareness of the absurdity of our situation began to subvert our sense of urgency, and the environment surrendered some of its dominion. Slowly, with several steps backward for every one forward, we began to learn a thing or two. For one thing, we learned we were not alone. There were other social castaways dwelling in the secluded pockets of those piney hills, tribal communities embracing various fuzzy dogmas willing to barter and offer advice. They advised us that we might overcome the natural distrust of our neighbors by offering ourselves as a cheap source of labor. Owing perhaps more to curiosity than charity, some of the locals did allow us to swap bunglingly executed chores in exchange for the loan of machinery: a tractor with which to bush-hog (bush-hog?) an overgrown pasture, a shark-toothed chainsaw for cutting dead wood, a rifle to threaten interloping wildlife—implements whose mysteries we approached with the caution of aborigines inspecting a downed cargo plane. Or am I speaking only for myself? Because Finbar, chameleon to the point of schizophrenia, demonstrated an uncanny ability to adopt whatever skills were needed for a given operation. He was carpenter, plowman, and engineer by turns, trades he practiced with an aptitude based more on delusion than any practical experience he may have had. In pursuing so many traditionally masculine tasks, however, Finbar was forced to cut back his efforts on the culinary front, ceding kitchen duties largely to Regina and Bateman's wife, whose name—we eventually took the trouble to discover—was Norma. In his stead Regina and Norma performed as adequately as our austere cupboard would permit—whose staples were brown rice and lentils garnished with the odd green pea or yellow squash, rations guaranteed to bind your bowels and too pedestrian in any event to inspire a chef of Finbar's caliber.

Christopher seemed to have lost something of his imperturbable nature en route to Arkansas, possibly due to having had his skull stove in by Bateman and friend. Given now to seizures of irrationality, he was no less doctrinaire, praising the proletarian life in a running discourse ("Bolsheviki, put your egos to the wheel!") that was its own impious lampoon. Blurring the line between self-righteousness and perversity, he nevertheless practiced what he preached, digging postholes and hammering roofing shingles with exemplary zeal. As for Muhle, his scrounging talents, which had seemed so peculiarly urban, discovered their ideal milieu on the farm. Shortly after our arrival, certain "found" objects of varying utility began turning up in the dirt-floored garage that doubled as our sitting room. Vintage items, such as a wheelbarrow seeder, a walking plow, a spinning wheel, a device like a torture rack that even Muhle could not identify, would appear, until the garage had the air of an agricultural museum. From Muhle, who kept his ear to the ground, we learned that derelict houses in a nearby town, if you were willing to knock them down and cart them away, could be had for a song.

So we bought a couple for recycling materials, then proceeded to dismantle them—the once stately Queen Anne cottage with its widow's walk, the octagonal dance pavilion on rickety pilings over a bone-dry reservoir—with clawhammers, wrecking bars, and burlesque turns. It was how we had begun to manage our unlikely labors, by assuming the identities of those for whom we imagined such tasks were comme il faut. In this way we parlayed a joke about home wrecking into a concept of ourselves as a family of wreckers, in the demolition business for generations. We were the Benvenuto brothers—Vito, Gino, Angelo, and Pasquale (the names were arbitrary and interchangeable)—lusty young men full of filial allegiance, rivals for the affection of our mama by whom each of us claimed to be loved best. Billy Boots, who'd declined to offer a name of his own, we dubbed Benny Benvenuto, the crusty immigrant patriarch of the family, but Billy preferred not to join in our theatrics. While we'd begun to realize how our portable role-playing could domesticate the extremest drudgery, Billy remained withdrawn. He seemed never to have entirely arrived at the farm, as if some critical aspect of himself had been lost in the translation back to the land.

Despite the provincial lore he'd learned in the levee camps of his youth (if you could believe him), Billy Boots seemed reluctant to share his skills, occupying himself in furtive projects that turned their back on the collective ethos to which we subscribed. (An ethos that Christopher, as self-appointed minister of propaganda, would never let us forget.) When he deigned to enter into the communal labors, helping topple a house or dig a bathing pool in the spring below the watercress, Billy did so with a fervor that was almost forbidding, as if we should all stand back and be warned. The rest of the time, he was barely present, hanging about the periphery of things until he seemed in our minds to be half a mirage, and, as on Idlewild Street, he was absent for long hours when no one knew his whereabouts. Since he offered no explanations, on principle we declined to ask. Meanwhile Lila, left much to her own devices, spent her time looking after Norma's children, whom Norma herself tended to neglect. In her solitary fashion, Lila seemed to take to the life of the farm, hunkering beside the creek to rinse her clothes, kneading them against the rocks with a casual peasant grace. But you could also see how she pricked up her ears at the *ka-thunk, ka-thunk* that echoed from the woods at the back of the property, where Billy was building something we made a point of refusing to investigate; and I wondered if, like the rest of us, Lila were trying to wean herself from Billy Boots.

Meanwhile we clung to gables overlooking a dry lake bed, pried nails that exited the creaking joists with a pinched-sphincter squeal, and, on a signal from Christopher, kicked in walls (freestanding once the roof beams were removed) so that they tumbled like Jericho in a simultaneous, dust-raising heap. Then we hauled the wood back to the farm on a three-ton flatbed borrowed from a local farmer with a prosthetic thumb (in our county there were many men missing digits and limbs) in exchange for helping him drive fence posts and listening to his fantasies about a thousand-dollar whore. Back at the farm, we used the aged lumber to shore up the structures already standing and to erect a few impromptu follies among the trees. Before fall the widowed farmer's shack, which now included electrical outlets, a working sink, an iron woodstove, and no end of accumulated error, was ready for occupation. It was designated the abode of Christopher, Norma, and her offspring (who were becoming increasingly feral despite Lila's attentions), though we used it as a cramped dining hall and general headquarters in the evenings.

There was a two-seater outhouse papered with pages torn from interior-design catalogs and fashion magazines, where I was once joined in my meditations by a blasé Regina. "Isn't this taking togetherness a step too far?" I muttered, but she only told me to get over it and finished her business with a bestial grunt. A sensualist for whom bodily functions merited no special privacy, Regina might at any instant raise her sarong, drop to her haunches, and, making a cork-popping sound with her thumb in her mouth, pull the string on a tampon; she might lower her bodice to offer her voluptuous breasts to the sun. But she'd also proven that her energies were as available to the daily grind as to the pursuit of pleasure. For it was Regina, assisted by a sometimes somnambulant Norma, who organized the kitchen and oversaw the ritual of the evening meal. Though there was no official division of labor, jobs tended to fall along traditional lines, the men doing the heavy lifting, the women performing the distaff chores—we were hypocrites to this extent. But Regina worked alongside the men, accompanying us on our wrecking operations, becoming Lucia, the Benvenuto brothers' immodest sister. Provocative in her cutoffs and loose psyche knot, sweat pasting a sleeveless jersey to her swaying jugs, she looked, wielding a sickle or a chain saw, like a poster girl for the workers' revolution.

Though they made no special claims on each other, Regina and Finbar bunked together on a raised platform of Finbar's construction back in the cedars: a plank-walled affair lashed to the living trees, with a Coleman stove and a roof shingled in old license plates. There they welcomed the nocturnal visitations of Muhle, who was temporarily on his own, since Becky Le Bon Bon's parents, with the aid of the state police, had finally tracked down their stray daughter. (For a time, violation of the Mann Act and the charge of statutory rape had hung over Muhle's head, but in the end, due to Becky's special pleading, the charges were waived, though the ensuing stink took a toll on the respectability we tried in vain to project among our neighbors.) When he wasn't sharing their bower with Finbar and Regina, Muhle slept in the tepee he was stitching together from scraps of salvaged tent canvas and animal hides—materials that looked from afar like the lifted homespun skirt of a lady with eight spindly, peeled-pine legs.

Until such time as I should build my own retreat, I slept in an uninsulated cabin like a boxcar on stilts, which we'd thrown together with the spare wood from our house razings. I occupied a loft to which you gained access by a rope ladder of my own design, a swashbuckling if impractical device that called for some acrobatic dexterity to ascend. In the adjacent loft slept Billy Boots and Lila, an unsatisfactory arrangement for all concerned. I knew I should suffer the inconvenience of seeking other accommodations, that I had put myself in the way of more of the same torment I'd experienced on Idlewild Street; but, having feathered my nest with a foam pallet and some select books arranged about a Visqueen porthole, I was cozy. Moreover, Billy's uncommunicativeness and my reluctance to try to draw him out tended to simplify relations. Of course, though they had no alternative, it irked me that he and Lila should carry on across that narrow gulf with such complete disregard for my presence; it further bothered me that Lila should be so willing to take whatever crumbs of affection Billy tossed her way. But I devoted astonishingly little time to fretting about it. Their bumping and moaning only yards away became my lullaby, rocking me into a slumber more sound than any I'd known since my days in the asylum. It was only on the nights when Billy (who Christopher suggested was turning into a lycanthrope) stayed away, and I was alone in the cabin with a restless Lila, that I might lie awake a little longer than was usual.

So we spun—Norma overcame her listlessness to restore Muhle's liberated spinning wheel and began spinning the yarn she planned to peddle in town; she stood to make, according to Christopher's calculations, in the neighborhood of six cents an hour for her labors—and we toiled. We had heated debates over how to spend what meager funds remained to us after the purchase of the property. As usual, it was Christopher, still a moral authority despite being intermittently addled, who determined the ways we could best apportion our expenses: We should of course conserve on food, though our already ascetic diet consisted of a minimal fare. (This was food bought in bulk from a market run cooperatively by a local tribe in the nearby town of Eureka Springs, a once fashionable Jazz Era watering hole gone to seed, its storefronts commandeered by hippie entrepreneurs.) We should, recommended Christopher, invest the major portion of our capital in corporate securities and (seriously) spend whatever was left on livestock. There were structures existing from the prehistory of the farm that demanded habitation: a wire chicken coop, a rabbit hutch, a barn to house milking goats (cheaper and easier to care for than cows), a cedarwood sty for pigs. We should buy what we could and acquire the rest through labor; the hay-hauling season was upon us, and a farmer down the road, the one from whom Norma acquired her wool, had offered to give us a couple of angora goats in exchange for our help in the shearing.

Impressed with Christopher's ad hoc knowledge of the rural economy, we followed his advice, and I, with the lingering sense of having something to prove, became a swineherd and milker of goats. I rose at dawn to spread chicken scratch and collect the eggs; I fed the rabbits and cleaned the pellets from their cages, fed the goats, clamping their heads in the pillory-like stanchions and squeezing, as they chomped their feed, bitter milk from their doughy dugs. (The sound of its stream hitting the tin pail was my tardy alarm clock.) Trudging into the foul slush of their pen in the rubber Wellington boots that had become my all-purpose footwear, masked in a kerchief against the smell, I slopped the hogs, whom we'd dubbed Abelard and Heloise on account of the male's having been gelded. I tossed scraps to the black dog with the withered leg that the kids (in rare high spirits) had named Spot, made the porridge and coffee before the others had roused themselves from their beds.

I wielded the double-edged ax with a headsman's resolve, pitched hay until my hands, already raw despite heavy work gloves, became horny with calluses from the rub of the baling twine. Staying in constant motion, I outran heartache, longing, and fear, eluded them so well for so long that, when I met them in chance encounters, we were estranged. Labor had hardened my body, its thin skin cured by the sun, and, thanks to a scarcity of mirrors on the farm, I was able to view myself for days on end in the image of a frontiersman. It was not an image I had ever before aspired to, displacing as it did the ragged remains of the jester, but I warmed to my hale and sanctimonious new self, capable of titanic tasks and independent of the designs of Billy Boots.

By the end of the summer, we had a reputation around the county for, among other things, our willingness to perform jobs for nominal wages, if only to demonstrate our fortitude. The farmer most eager to exploit us was our neighbor, the one-armed Gideon Benbow, whose sheep we'd helped to shear. Although we left the animals multiply lacerated, their blue hides flayed with wounds, the loquacious old farmer, whose sight was not keen, hired us again to help bring in the hay. Tottering atop four tiers of baled alfalfa piled in the back of his oxidized pickup, he conducted the labor with a vicious hay hook held in his solitary hand, all the while endlessly telling bad jokes. On the ground we stumbled alongside the truck, endeavoring to hoist the rain-soaked bales to a height he could reach with his hook.

"Preacher's giving this gal a buggy ride home," he cawed, leaning over to snag another bale with his hay hook and drag it to the top of the stack. "Sez Preacher, 'Gal, I long to sin with you.' 'Cain't,' sez the gal, 'I got the curse.'"

Grumbling throughout that exposure to Farmer Benbow's jokes was a greater occupational hazard than the blazing August sun, we hoisted another waterlogged bale to a height at which—relieved by the sweep of his hook—the hay became weightless.

"Preacher sez," Farmer Benbow continued, "'Gal, I long to sin with you canine style.' 'Cain't,' sez the gal, 'I got the piles.'" Reeling perilously, he bent over to snag another bale. "Preacher breaks a branch off a overhanging tree . . ." At which point, having leaned over too far for a bale we'd failed to raise high enough, the old man pitched headforemost from the top of the stack. He hit the ground with a sickening thud but scrambled immediately to his feet, remarkably unimpaled by the hook he'd yet to let go of, blood flowing freely into his collar from a split-open ear. "'Gal,' sez the preacher," said Farmer Benbow without missing a beat, "'tell me you got a sore throat and I'll switch you to within a inch of your life.'"

We built a hay barn in the employ of another old duffer, who'd been the first to discover us in the hollow where we'd initially laid siege to the rest of the farm. Having hunted down rumors of misfits in the area, he had followed his bilberry nose and staggered one night sodden and bandy-legged into our camp. "Name's Beck, Leonard Beck," he announced, approaching us ambassadorially, "but you can call me Windy. I can tell a snake by his scent, speak seven languages, including Cherokee and Australian. See this gut"—thumping the gravid protuberance of his overalls. "Full of cancer. Doc don't give me three months." This by way of engaging our sympathies. Later we realized that, thanks to his patented pickling process, Windy Beck would probably dance on our graves. He was a shrewd man, with a touch of the romantic, and the first to recognize in us a potential pool of slaves.

It turned out that he was also the county pariah, notorious for having been the only man to walk away breathing from a dispute over a three-way blackjack game in his youth—or so he claimed, and his treatment by the locals bore it out. Since there was little law to speak of in those parts, he'd been forbidden entry by community consensus to the only general-merchandise store in the area. It was a condition he'd endured for several decades while sponging off relations and making frequent forays into town; but, after cultivating our acquaintance, he prevailed on us to run errands for him and perform odd jobs. Not all of the jobs were strictly legal, nor did we get much in the way of compensation beyond the plea-sure of his company, until his grass-widowed sister, Opal, contracted him to build a haybarn. The project was not especially ambitious, but it came at a time when Windy was receiving shots to his reputedly malig-nant stomach as a result of having been bitten by a rabid coyote. Finbar agreed to lend a hand in the construction for a token wage, but a job ex-pected to take no more than a week had been extended to two, then three, until it seemed that Finbar had indentured himself to Windy Beck. Since Finbar was needed on the farm, I volunteered to help secure his manumission; then I understood that the job offered fringe benefits that made it desirable to prolong the labor.

Our days began around seven, when Windy came to fetch us in his sputtering Ford pickup. Finbar would be waiting in the drive, brushing his straw-colored mane and waxing his mustache. "I want to look my best for Leonard," he would say. The old yokel would drive us to the back of his sister Opal's property, where his shack perched on an eminence surrounded by generations of rusted trucks. Finbar's theory was that, whenever a pickup anywhere in the world felt its time was near, it would limp thousands of miles just to die at Windy Beck's doorstep. In his mi-asmic kitchen, we chewed elastic flapjacks, listened to his fibs, and drank his pal Shorty Izett's green-sick beer. Periodically Windy and Shorty's table talk would be interrupted by squeals from the closet in which Windy kept his pet pig, Boy-Boy.

Around nine-thirty we would wander over to the site of the new barn, a concrete rectangle demarcated by a stand of sentinel studs. Windy, who regretted that, due to his treatments, his role must remain supervisory, would take up his station on his unbitten buttock beneath the shade of a walnut tree. Claiming the status of professional carpenter despite the missing digits of his paw-shaped left hand (he was left-handed), Shorty would worry over his calculations, like—Finbar opined—the contractor for the Tower of Babel. Then, with an electric handsaw, he would trim a few boards as best he could, while Finbar and I made gestures toward erecting the frame. We proceeded in this for a couple of hours until the dinner bell rang, when we would stroll up to Opal's kitchen, where she'd prepared a meal as handsome as she herself was homely. The table would be spread with pork chops, field peas, mashed potatoes and pan gravy, red applesauce and glazed carrots, hot cornbread with butter and wild-flower honey, followed by peach cobbler and coffee cut with fresh cream. It was a board beside which our typical farm fare seemed unworthy of even the livestock. After lunch (called dinner) we dragged ourselves onto the breezy back porch to digest the feast, where Shorty lulled us into cat-naps with his reminiscences. Cradling his cockleburr head in his good hand, he might recall the distant morning when, as a boy in the streets of Hayes, Kansas, he had seen Jesse James rob a bank. . . .

As a sop to her minimal wages, Sister Opal was apparently willing to indulge our indolence. Horse-faced and dressed like a man, she would sit over us in her rocker, rolling cigarettes and sipping whiskey, flicking her flyswatter above our slumped bodies as if to shoo away untoward dreams: on our salaries we were entitled to sleep but not to dream. After the siesta we confronted the hay barn again, while Windy and Shorty, uneager to have their sinecures revoked, ceaselessly discussed strategies and antici-pated problems. Then, as a last resort, having charged their apprentices to resume their former positions among the timbers, they might take a few steps toward putting theory into practice. Careful not to overdo it, they generally knocked off around three o'clock.

The routine was at first offensive to my developing conscience; there was too much to be done back at the farm for me to waste time among the lotus-eaters. But Finbar would tell me, "Relax," passing me a lotus-leaf cigarette; it was his idea that, beyond building a barn, we were helping a pair of codgers feel useful in their twilight years, and after my resistance was broken by Opal's lunches, I became a reluctant convert to Finbar's reasoning.

But despite my corruption and our efforts to the contrary, the work progressed. In fact, after I'd been on the job only a week, we were sad to realize that the barn had entered its final stage of construction. Earlier that week, seated in the shade, sallow from a combination of alcohol and injections against hydrophobia, Windy had been seized by a visionary impulse. "Boys," he'd announced, tears welling in his bloodshot eyes, "I'm gone build that barn, and on the last day, when I climb them rafters and hammer the last nail, I'm gone fall to my death." And on an afternoon with the barn all but completed, Windy had taken up a hammer and mounted a ladder toward the fulfillment of his prophecy. His hat was blown off, and the wind meddled with the two or three strands of his hair as, stepping onto a tie beam, he gained for a moment a miraculous equilibrium; he pounded a rafter in the vicinity of a tenpenny nail like a clockwork burgher come out to chime the hour. Then, teetering upon the beam, which wobbled in turn, Windy dropped the hammer and leaned backward in the direction of eternity.

We caught him in the nick of time. Lying on either side of the pitch as the sun ricocheted off the roofing tin into our eyes, Finbar and I grabbed his flabby arms, thus effecting an abortion of destiny to which Windy willingly acquiesced. "You boys are my two good right arms," he professed, venturing a vertiginous glance over his shoulder. We had then to become his legs as well, which had turned to jelly.

Sometime during the fall, our sow, Heloise, came into heat, and poor Abelard was helpless to relieve her frustration. Night and day she emitted a pitiable squall and exuded a palpable musk that misted the air and rivaled even the reek of the mire. Jokes were made, though not appreciated, that in my capacity as swineherd I should service her myself; it would be a union of two virgins. There were unwelcome speculations as to the fruit of that union. But when I turned my back on the sow to face my detractors, a wild pig came out of the woods and battered the sty to try to get at Heloise. This was an interesting development, as we had not known there were such things as wild pigs; though this one, neither tusker nor razorback, was apparently not bred to the wilderness, but a foraging fugitive from a neighboring hog farm. His courtship of our sow, a pedigreed black-and-white Poland China, consisted in ramming his snout (which bristled like a lunker with half a dozen brass rings) against the soggy planks of the pigpen until they began to give way. Since I didn't like to see Heloise in distress but nevertheless felt obliged to defend her chastity, I was torn, and called a council to decide what should be done.

Measures were debated, most of them frivolous. Perhaps there was some homeopathic remedy that could quell Heloise's ardor and discourage her suitor; or should she be allowed, under supervision, to satisfy her lust? Who knew but the wayfaring hog came from a good family? Christopher posited a fantastic connection between the wayward pig and the Wild Child of Aveyron. Lila cautioned that we ought to take poor Abelard's feelings into consideration, a view with which I secretly concurred. It took Regina, undoing her topknot and shaking out her tawny hair as if for action, to propose the self-evident solution: "I say we shoot the sucker and eat his bacon and tenderloins." All agreed save Billy, who was not available for a vote.

There was the rifle Finbar had borrowed from Berl Booker, the lickerish neighbor of the artificial thumb, who frequented our holdings in the wan hope of snagging some "hippie nookie." It was a turn-of-the-century Remington repeater, or "fowling piece" as Finbar liked to call it, with notches on its scorched wooden stock. On three consecutive November nights, while Heloise rent the air with her caterwaul, Finbar fired at the stray pig unsuccessfully at point-blank range. Then the randy old boar would eye the lot of us as if surely we could do better than that, before showing his behind to trot back into the woods, only to return on the following evening.

"Gun's got a barrel like a dog's hind leg," complained Finbar in defense of his marksmanship. "Must be designed for shooting around corners."

On the fourth night, stationing himself around the corner of the sty with me and Muhle rubbernecking over his shoulder, Finbar succeeded in putting a bullet in the hog's left flank. The animal reared, squealing like a whizgig, and careened down the slope toward the stock pond in a gadarene slalom. As we watched the old runagate escaping yet again, a figure darted from the shadows of the juniper grove to the right of the pig's zigzag trajectory to give chase. The sun was down, and the figure— running swiftly alongside the hog with purposeful strides before leaping onto its back—appeared in silhouette like a creature out of regional folklore: some species of hillbilly Caliban, say, or yeti. This was an easier sell than the truth, which was that the figure who rode the pig, and drew the knife that he plunged beneath the pig's right ear, was our own elusive Billy Boots. Insufficient light from a honeydew sliver of moon prevented us from seeing what we couldn't help but imagine: the bloody crescent described by the blade that Billy dragged across the hog's sable throat; though we heard clearly enough the blaring skirl that thinned to a whistle before dissolving in silence and saw the animal shudder and stumble, then capsize with its rider, who rolled neatly to his feet with the blade held triumphantly aloft. What we couldn't tell from our vantage was whether this gesture were made in earnest, or was it merely a caricature of triumph?

By now we'd grown used to Billy's dwelling in shadows, though we'd never forgiven him for his withdrawal nor had any of us, to my knowledge, made any attempts to ferret out the reasons, which was a source of some guilt. But weren't we living the life Billy Boots had bade us live? While he, who should have been at its center, had removed himself to the margins like—one of his favorite phrases—a *deus absconditus*. In our resentment we'd virtually sealed his exclusion—but, after all, we were busy, adapting ourselves to circumstances that Billy, for all his touted resourcefulness, had failed to embrace.

Now here he was leaping out of the wings to slay a marauding beast, waving the weapon over his head like a banner, prompting Muhle to say, "If he beats his chest and makes with a Tarzan yell, I'm out of here." But instead he beckoned us to come help. Tentatively we approached him, noting how gaunt and wiry he'd grown, his thick hair matted as old thatch, his flannel shirt nearly in shreds and caked with blood. Most of us were pretty threadbare by now, our clothes held together by constellations of Norma's patches, but Billy was ragged as a mendicant. He was nonetheless animated, enjoining us each to grab a leg of the pig's still-twitching carcass, which we did, gripping its ankles like oars. Feeling that we had at last become savages, we dragged the animal in its final spasms up the hill toward the barn, as along the way Cap'n Billy, convivial again, reminisced about the ceremonial hog butcherings of his youth.

When we'd deposited our steaming prey in the harsh glow of a floodlight hung from the front of the barn, Billy proclaimed, "We got first to scald him." It was a raw night, occasional snowflakes drifting like eiderdown, which further motivated us to set about building a fire. Finbar called to the shack to roust out Christopher and the women, who, once they'd absorbed the shock of their encounter with the stone-dead pig, attacked the project along with the rest of us as one body. We rinsed out a zinc garbage pail and filled it with water, then placed it on a trivet of bricks in the midst of a now roaring fire fed with freshly split logs. While waiting for the water to boil, we fetched the block and tackle that Finbar had used to hoist the engine from his bus in order to color-code its various parts in Day-Glo paint. Attaching the rope-and-pulley device from a horizontal joist jutting gallowslike from beneath the hayloft, we skewered the hog's hind feet (at Billy's instruction) with a thick wooden peg and raised it by its stretched ankle tendons above the cauldron. Then, with Billy and Finbar manning the rope like a scene from an auto-da-fé, we immersed the entire hog in the rolling boil.

A keen stink of burning hair suffused the barnyard, causing Simon, Norma's towheaded little boy, to retch down his front. The dripping hog was hoisted again and left suspended above the rim of the pail, where Billy commenced scraping its bristles with the blade of his hunting knife; while others of us, following his example, swarmed over the dangling animal like a college of demonic barbers. I myself employed a serrated steak knife, until I discovered that you could speed the process by snatching up hanks of stiff black bristles by the fistful. As we exposed the bulk of albino flesh beneath the bristles, Christopher read to us aloud from *The Foxfire Book,* a volume from our library detailing the many means of going primitive. Since the book merely confirmed point for point the steps we'd begun to take under Billy's tutelage, Christopher's reading had the narrative effect of a bedtime story. This enabled us, along with Norma's transfixed children, to look on in fascinated horror as Billy severed the hog's head, hugging it to his chest as he wrenched it free with a hollow crunch from its inverted carcass. Then he made the long incision that allowed the smoldering entrails to spill like gifts from a grisly piñata into the waiting washtub, where the lame black dog delved with its wallowing muzzle.

Since custom prescribed that no part of the animal be wasted, we ground and spiced the offals, scraped and rinsed the bowels and intestines for sausage casings; we even experimented with liver pudding and head cheese, items we tasted once in a show of bravado and never again. (Most drew the line at the testicles Regina had fried up for mountain oysters.) One flank of the hog, cleft in twain with a hacksaw, we rubbed with dry-curing salt and stored away on the shelves of a closet pantry; but as the slaughter had taken place only a few days before Thanksgiving, a holiday with a certain sentimental mandate, we dug a grave-deep barbecue pit for the other half. Into the open hole we poured hot coals, over which we arranged a sheet of corrugated tin, and on top of the tin we settled a side of pork the size of a batwing door. Then Finbar was inspired to concoct a sauce from a recipe he claimed to have had in his family since the time of the Druids. Insisting that the sauce tenderized the meat (useful, given its age) as it sealed in flavorful juices, and restored lost sight and potency, he basted the pig at appointed intervals for forty-eight hours.

On Thanksgiving Day, which turned out after a killing frost to be un-seasonably warm, we disinterred the slathered hog, then placed it atop a long trestle table erected for the purpose under a yew tree in front of the shack. The laden table groaned further from a variety of dishes—baked beans, deviled eggs, pasta salads, corn on the cob, freshly baked sour-dough bread, sweet-potato pie—that looked as if tumbled from a horn of plenty, though all credit was due the industrious Regina, assisted by a torpid Norma and Suzy Q. (Suzy, the farm's newest addition, was Becky Le Bon Bon's barely legal replacement, a morsel whom Muhle had intro-duced one morning as casually as the antediluvian farm implements he brought back from his freebooting excursions.) At our invitation, neigh-bors came: Farmer Benbow arrived with his wife, Jemima, a parade float of a woman, who bore her covered dish to the table like a consecrated object to an altar. Berl Booker brought his toil-worn better half, carrying a casserole whose lid still chattered from the boiling mulligan stew be-neath, and Windy and Shorty appeared with a jug of Shorty's unripe home brew. At first there was awkwardness, the guests aware of our fun-damental incompatibility, but Mrs. Benbow, devout daughter of the church, bade us join hands around the feast (pilgrims and salvages alike) to sing a chorus of "Amazing Grace." Uncomfortable with the forced inti-macy, never mind the choice of hymn, I looked around expecting sly winks from my brethren, but all (including Billy Boots, who grinned like a champion) seemed moved to the point of exaltation, to which I had no choice but to succumb as well.

Wolfish that winter, we found excuses to cull certain of the livestock we deemed expendable—hens apparently done laying, a goat withholding milk, rabbits grown too fat for their cages, a pig sulking in her sty—and slaughter them. We all tried our hands at the killing, but I, forever wanting to prove I was game, was the most frequent volunteer. With a resignation and efficiency previously beyond my imagining, I decapitated chickens with a whetted hatchet, then watched as they rushed about the yard in a headless flurry, some squawking through voice boxes still intact. I bludgeoned rabbits, breaking their necks with a lead pipe and circumscribing their throats with a penknife in order to peel off their bunny suits. I looked into the bewildered eyes of the sow Heloise, of whom I'd grown too fond to let anyone else murder, and fired a round from a borrowed Smith & Wesson handgun. "Some job for a nice Jewish boy," I quipped, vain of my heartlessness, though nobody was laughing.

But while our coffers were low that winter, our spirits were generally high. Billy Boots had come in out of the cold to sit on the hearthrug around the throbbing woodstove; he dined at our table like Marco Polo returned to tell us of his travels, which had in a sense been subsidized by our labors. But the tales were not forthcoming. Since the night he'd delivered his coup de grâce to the gate-crashing hog, he seemed chastened, even housebroken, content to stick close to Lila and the children, with whom he'd developed a special rapport. Since no one had inquired about the reasons for his self-imposed exile, so did no one question his change of heart. Having scapegoated and backstabbed him these several months, we welcomed him contritely back into the bosom of our family—a happy family who had just celebrated its first Christmas on the farm. We'd exchanged gifts that were mostly jokes: a boxing nun hand puppet, a bottle of bend-over oil, impersonal items ordered from one of Muhle's novelty catalogs. I myself had put together a little ceremony to accompany my gifts, which were meant to reprise those dispensed by the Wizard of Oz. There was a plastic replica of the Croix de Guerre from a cereal box, a jar of artichoke hearts with a ticking wristwatch inside, a certificate of third place from a fifth-grade spelling bee. I read a mock-heroic cita-tion concerning courage, compassion, and brains to the company, who grew increasingly restive throughout.

"What are you, Sauly, our mascot?" Christopher interrupted me in midsentence, while Finbar asked if it was okay to eat the artichoke hearts. They were right to interrupt me; I was trying too hard. There and then I made up my mind to stop trying so hard.

By Christmas we were performing the chores of the farm almost by rote, enjoying them most in adversity, when high winds and hailstorms lent drama to the daily round. No matter what the weather, the animals were housed and fed, the wood cut, the meals prepared. Without a thought for the incommodity, we squatted over the hole in the outhouse with our knees around our ears to keep the rats from nibbling our toes; we pricked one another with heated needles to drain festering boils, washed each other's hair in the kitchen sink, a kitchen that—with its pie safe, sausage grinder, and racks of spices, its hanging braids of garlic and orbs of cheese—had achieved an unself-conscious rusticity. Then there was the freezer purchased at auction, which we kept in the barn, stocked with chickens, rabbits, a baby kid, butchered and dressed out (it occurred to me) in what might have qualified as kosher style. Our funds depleted, we postponed the home-schooling of Norma's kids to make forays into a se-ries of odd jobs. We were "chicken catchers" at a nearby corporate chicken plant, where the hens, subjected to twenty-four-hour fluorescence, were compelled to lay eggs until they were barren. It was our task to thrust arms into their cages and drag them out, then stuff them into crates—breaking beaks and wings along the way—to be shipped to the processing factories. The other employees in the mile-long henhouse were types you seldom saw in broad daylight, who talked openly about sodomy, perceived the face of Jesus in the condensation on beer cans, and made unkind remarks about us.

For a while we relied on our talent for playful subversion to transcend the place, but after a week, beginning to identify with the defects of our colleagues, we thought it the better part of valor to quit. Thereafter we found wholesale employment in the dining room of an old hotel in Eu-reka Springs. It was a great castellated edifice at the top of the town, the kind of structure best viewed by bolts of lightning, which had once been a tuburcular hospital run by a man said to have murdered his patients for their insurance. From its vantage the hotel looked across a valley toward a truncated mountain crowned with a rough-cast Christ of the Ozarks, in whose shadow a poor relation of the Oberammergau passion play was performed each summer. As business was slack and help scarce during the winter months, we practically ran the dining room, the women waitressing while the men bussed the tables and washed the dishes in a kiln-size machine. (Billy Boots, on one of his rare tours of duty, had lain on the conveyor rack like a body en route to cremation, emerging drenched from the other side to declare, "I am born!") We had only to answer to a fractious cook recently retired from years at sea, and him we answered only at our whim. Each time he lost his temper at any one of us, the rest of us would threaten a walkout en bloc, so that the old tar, nearly reduced to tears, was forced to put up with our arrogance, our irregular hours, and our plundering of the Frigidaires. Rotating part-time shifts, we stayed on until the advent of spring, when the influx of job seekers made it possible for the cook to fire the lot of us.

In the winter, strange characters drifted about the Ozarks in search of a spiritual home, and some believed they'd found it on our farm. Most of these we made short work of, though not before accepting their tributes— music, produce, blotter acid—which we received as our due. Drugs were no longer at the center of our lives but were regarded now rather as a means than an end. When they were available, however, we never hesitated to partake, and the blowouts we held in that pulsating shack made the revels on Idlewild Street seem like mere rehearsals by comparison. We raved and stomped in a riotous intermingling, losing ourselves to reason and recordable time, somehow assured that, however far we strayed in our flings, the boundaries of the farm (whose center was everywhere) would still contain us. And in the morning we would get up, feed the animals, and take care of business again.

Of course, for all we accomplished that season, there were any number of projects that went uncompleted. There was our broken resolution to take over the schooling of Norma's kids, Simon and Bridget, who looked, as the months wore on, more and more as if they'd been reared by wolves. The original idea had been that each of us would, independently, spend time with them, imparting our own "special brand of knowledge"; though after every encounter with their near-autistic inattention, we would come away convinced that we had no special knowledge to impart. Aside from Lila, who simply read to them or attempted to groom their tangled hair, and Billy, with whom they tagged along into the woods, they seemed to have no trust in adults; they appeared with their smudged faces and covert eyes as a constant indictment of our neglect. To get even, we declared them uneducable, and even Christopher, their proxy father (whose Marxist bromides they refused to absorb), took to calling them in front of their unmindful mother "the children of the damned."

The children were not the only evidence of our short-lived interests; the land was littered with such monuments, most of them Muhle's— such as his unfinished hothouse for the cultivation of opium poppies, the sewing machine he planned to drive with methane gas, a plastic bucket spiraled in copper tubing slated for a whiskey still. There was also the tepee he'd abandoned since Suzy Q had come to the farm and the two of them had set up a domicile in the converted hayloft. That so stately a dwelling not be made redundant, and to get away from Billy and Lila (whose pleading with Billy over I knew not what was more than I could bear), I moved into the tepee myself. For a while I tried building fires, but, frustrated by the complicated maneuvering of the tent flaps for ventilation, I was nearly asphyxiated from the smoke. Unambitious with regard to developing Native American skills, I gave up the fires in exchange for wearing thermal underwear, a watch cap, and fingerless mittens to bed. Then I would slide into my quilted cocoon under a hill of blankets and the lame black dog, who slept on top of me in exchange for the warmth.

In any case, we succeeded that winter in more than we failed—that was the verdict—each of us contributing his share to the welfare of the whole. Was I happy? The question was moot: so remote was I from being anyone I still recognized that I spent little time reflecting on what I'd become. I liked that my body had acquired the stringy muscles previously the exclusive province of roustabouts and lunch-bucket laborers, and that I could work like a demon. I'd grown tough on a diet of grain and flesh, my coarse complexion dry and uninfected, my arboreal hair hanging, when wet, to the small of my back. Occasionally I would remember that I'd never actually desired such a life, that the more immersed I was in hardship and plain endurance, the more I esteemed the romance of the scholar in his study. But somehow the contrast of that image (grown abstract over time) with the audacious experiment we'd embarked on had its own poignancy.

There was no fixed place on the farm for the jester/eunuch, the role having become simply outworn; while we all still retained vestiges of our old Idlewild personalities, the specific elements were blurred. Just as we borrowed each other's clothes without asking, so did we take on one another's characteristics indiscriminately. Muhle, for instance, wearing the souvenir bell-bottoms I'd brought back from New York City, might, when the situation required, demonstrate some of Christopher's fiscal sense; while Christopher, suffering flashbacks to firefights he'd never fought, would also exhibit aspects of Finbar's voracious appetites. Finbar, mercurial at the best of times, when not refining his own machismo, might impersonate Regina's ribaldry or Norma's tropical languor, the succulent Suzy Q's studied ingenuousness. Sometimes Christopher would ape my self-pity, even more comic now as the parody of a farce; while I, feeling indispensable as drawer of water and hewer of wood, might confuse myself now and then with Billy Boots. On the farm our selves were never so clearly divided as our labor, and if you could say that we'd come into our own, then we had also come into everyone else's.

One morning we woke to the realization that we'd survived the winter. With the warmer weather, we burst out of doors, peeling our longjohns and attracting the seed ticks we burned off of one another with matches; we primed ourselves with witch hazel to combat mosquitoes and battled the swarming yellowjackets with jars of white gasoline. We gathered sprays of wildflowers to overcome the fetor of dry rot and firedamp in the shack, gathered pokeweed and lamb's-quarter for salads, furry mullein and scarlet sumac for teas, and, following Muhle's woodsy instincts, ventured into the pines by starlight to pick chanterelles—which grew in the fall. We chased blacksnakes out of the field we'd cleared for our garden and left the round granary loaves on stones to rise in the sun. In the still-icy spring, tickled by waving sedge, we bathed naked, marveling at the azure-veined firmness of our goosefleshed bodies, and once I thought I caught Regina eyeing me with unsisterly interest.

I suffered the look bravely. Old anxieties and a preposterously celibate condition still gnawed at me, of course, but these comprised only the least portion of a self defined now by industry. So what if the new definition made me something of a stranger to myself? Strangeness was itself refreshing, as I had long since grown tired of the familiar. And if, looking askance at the ladies, I continued to ache, I begrudged as well the movement afoot to terminate my virginity. For in my earshot I had heard women proposing to draw straws to see who would initiate Sauly; somebody had to—as if my innocence were a nuisance that needed to be promptly disposed of. But I had my pride, and losing one's virginity, especially one as vintage as mine, ought to have more significance than, say, hauling the compost.

Then there was the night Finbar came into the tepee, where I was reading *The Golden Bough* by lamplight. "*The Bough*, wow! bowwow!" he said, before informing me that Suzy Q, our honey-blond dreamsicle of a teenage runaway, was celebrating her eighteenth birthday by screwing all the men on the farm. It was time I lost my cherry, no? "The Revolution expects that every man will do his duty." Out of curiosity I did manage to stir myself and wander down to the barn, where the hayloft was thunderous with the sounds of galloping copulation. Apparently Suzy's initiative had inspired other women to join in the fray. But what the scene (invisible from where I stood) drove home to me was that, though desperate to relinquish it for so long, the virgin status I'd maintained in the face of impossible odds had appreciated in value. I'd had a birthday myself sometime during the winter and was getting no younger, so what, you might ask, was I saving myself for? Still, I had no wish to give it away at an orgy; the occasion must be worthy of the sacrifice. I returned to the tepee, masturbated, and wondered if I were perhaps becoming a saint.

That spring Billy Boots was again more absent than present, and we felt we'd been had. After a season of his good-natured (if reticent) company, during which he'd appeared finally to lend his blessing to our enterprise, that he should make himself scarce once again was the ultimate betrayal. Behind his back we unleashed all manner of venom, reciting the

list of his sins: his selfishness, his flouting of responsibility, the free ride
he was getting at our expense. Only Finbar, whose chance meeting with
Cap'n Billy in 1968 had rescued him from an empty round of keg parties
and fraternity pranks, made a token defense of Billy's life and hard times.
He rattled off the tired hagiography: his orphanhood and enfant terrible
high-school career, the amnesiac years that who could believe; there was
the scholarship to the university from which Billy was expelled after a
quarrel with a professor turned physical, his maniacal reading while supporting himself as a graveyard shift orderly in a VA hospital, his volatil-
ity, his joviality, the madcap mood swings that resulted in a logic that ate
its own tail.

"One time we're tripping on the river bluff," remembered Finbar,
pausing to rest his chin on the handle of his shovel, his foot on the blade,
"and Billy tells me this story about the angel who tweaks you under the
nose when you're born, so that your soul loses its memory of paradise.
Otherwise life in a fallen world would be too painful to bear. Then he
told me he thought the angel had passed him over. . . ."

We accused Finbar of hero worship and amateur psychoanalysis,
asked him what was Billy's pain compared with our arduous digging of
the long asparagus trench—an act of faith in the endurance of our project, since the asparagus would not sprout until the following year. We
were putting in a root cellar and, with reckless optimism, had laid the
foundation for a geodesic dome that would serve as both dormitory and
assembly hall. It would be none of your squat half domes but would measure an ambitious five-eighths of a sphere, with chaletlike gables to protect it from leakage, which was the most common problem with a
structure otherwise ideally suited to the Aquarian Age.

Imagining the scarcely begun edifice centuries hence, I loftily proclaimed, "Look on these works, ye mighty, and despair."

When we did catch sight of Billy, straggling down the road toward the
rear of the property trailed by Norma's waifish children (trailed in turn
by Spot the dog, who no longer needed my body heat at night), he looked
as if he'd been living on locusts, forget the honey. His sleeveless undershirt engulfed his once bulky torso like a luffing sail, his face hatchet thin
but for a briary beard. He appeared to me to be visibly shrinking in stature,
and I wondered if there were some correlation between his diminution

and our own growth in strength and confidence. Perhaps we were stealing vitality from Billy, who, if that were the case, suffered for our sake—
a stupid notion, though if there were any truth in it, I thought, so be it.

On most days, occupied as we were with the building and planting, I never even saw him, though there were occasional unavoidable
encounters—such as the afternoon when, passing the lumber pile where
Billy was dragging some lichen-starred bargeboard from under the stack,
I was ambushed by his greeting. It was a friendly enough greeting, and
when I only perfunctorily responded, he said to my back, "What's the
matter, Sauly, you don't love me no more? I thought you hippies loved
everyone?" I imagined the question mark at the end of his sentence snagging my heart like a fishhook, tearing a piece of it as I continued to walk
away. This rankled: he had no cause to make me feel petty. Wasn't I
laboring unselfishly for the good of one and all? Besides, any guilt that
accrued from our treatment of Billy was evenly distributed among the
company; there could be no particular Judas, since it was he who'd abandoned us first.

It was disturbing, however, to see Lila so lonely. I never heard her
complain, but since the children had begun again to dog Billy's heels (for
us a benefit, since it kept them blessedly out of sight), she seemed utterly
at sea. Myself, I had made a habit of avoiding her. Though I'd eaves-
dropped on her most private moans and whimpers, the noises, like pigeons set free from a cote, had always seemed separate from the woman
who released them. The noises did nothing to dispel her essential mystery. But lately, as she devoted herself to Cinderella-like chores, shoveling
out the woodstove and pottering in the garden, acquiring a certain hard-
scrabble sadness through exposure to the sun, her mystery had in large
part dissolved. Which made her look, I thought, more beautiful than
ever. And one evening, as we carried our soup bowls to chosen spots beneath the yew tree, I squatted beside her and asked (a little sardonically?)
how was Billy. She shrugged, looking pregnable, almost human, and I realized I'd been more comfortable with the idea of her as a goddess.

"He's building a house in the woods," she said, as if surely I knew. And
of course I did know, we all knew; he'd never made any attempt to conceal what he was up to, though he'd never announced it either. Meanwhile it had become a point of pride not to inquire about his project,

perhaps holding out the faint hope that he meant to surprise us. Then, making an angry tilde of her lips, Lila confided, "God's Little Wiseacre, he calls it."

That spring we were even less accommodating to visitors, running off several of the more sociopathic at gunpoint, though we allowed a few who lent a hand or had marketable skills to hang around. One such was Eli, a self-taught cobbler who removed his clothes the moment he arrived and never put them on again. He set up shop in the garage and created a cottage industry of one, his reptile boots fetching hefty prices at a consignment shop in town, income he turned over without strings to the collective. But the naked Eli's equal vote, unobtrusive as it was, altered the dynamic of our parliaments, and our tacit hostility ultimately persuaded him to leave. Others came merely to satisfy their curiosity. These included local youths, farm boys looking for the thrill of available marijuana, chasing the fable of hippie chicks as some of their fathers had done. Like their fathers they swaggered and, in their baseball caps and fresh stubble, exuded a pot-valorous air, though in truth they were shy around our self-possessed women. For their part, Regina and Suzy would flirt with and tease them, which seemed enough; for, unlike their fathers (whom Finbar had occasionally had to threaten), they took no liberties and were easily cowed into respectfulness.

So we tolerated them, although they were a bad influence on Muhle, who was drawn to their juvenile lawlessness and took to accompanying them on "ridge-running" expeditions. These involved rattling around the county in one of their corroded pickups snatching anything that wasn't nailed down—birdbaths, garden gnomes, flowering shrubbery—items taken for the sheer joy of the theft rather than their utility; for in fact there was little in that poor county worth stealing. Once Muhle and his confederates returned to the farm with five turkeys, a set of radial tires, and a bedraggled but dignified Muscovy duck, whom we named, in our passion for naming, Pete. The turkeys dispersed into the woods, the tires rotted alongside the slowly rotting VW bus, but the duck became the chief adornment of the farm. With a great deal of hyperbolic flapping, he had managed to fly up to the ridgepole of the garage, which we used as an auxiliary parlor now that the season had turned. There he perched night and day like some majestic weather vane.

Not long after we'd acquired Pete, we found a chicken on the road. She'd evidently escaped a crate toppled from a truck on its way to Campbell's Soup or Kentucky Fried and was barely alive. Her feathers had mostly fallen out, and the skin beneath them was blue crepe, her eyes glazed from the methedrine she'd been fed in the laying house to keep her producing eggs around the clock. To give her a second chance, we took the chicken home, called her Samantha, and introduced her to the henhouse, where the other hens tried to finish the job the factory had begun. We rescued her before she was pecked to death and let her range free, and in a matter of days the misbegotten creature had been adopted by Pete. Then the two of them, amid a storm of maladroit flapping, would gain the garage roof, where they perched together side by side day and night.

This genial bundling persisted until the chicken and the duck had become an emblematic fixture in the consciousness of the farm. But nothing (to coin a phrase) stays the same. Thanks to a balanced diet of organic garbage and the love of a good duck, Samantha began to regain her vigor. Her feathers grew back fleecy and white, and her blanched eye began to clear. Ultimately she was transformed into a hen of distinctive beauty and poise, who would have made a fine addition to any coop, which was precisely what our hens must have thought, because, clucking their approval, they reclaimed her—they insisted on taking her back, and Samantha seemed to accept it as her fate that she must go. Thus was Pete the duck left once again to his own devices atop the ridgepole. He'd probably never known loneliness before Samantha, and her absence was more than he could take standing still. So Pete, who'd never managed to soar higher than the twelve or so feet onto the roof, began to aspire to authentic flight.

In the days after his abandonment by Sam, heady days in which the dogwoods blossomed like fountains, he would waddle down the road quacking and flapping hysterically, puddle-jumping like an antique biplane until he gained a little more altitude with every attempt. Each day he would remain airborne a bit longer, and eventually he acquired the strength to command the breezes above the farm. At first he made small circles over our property, the circles growing ever wider with each flight, so wide in the end that he was nearly a speck and it seemed he would fly out of sight—and then one day he flew out of sight.

Had the event that broke his heart also given Pete (perhaps too late to enjoy them) wings? Feeling for the first time in months a pensive tug toward my departed Aunt Keni, I noticed that everyone else seemed to have been affected by the drama as well; they all seemed more burdened by their own specific gravity since the flight of Pete the duck. Needless to say, Billy Boots had missed the whole episode, though it was nevertheless suggested—by Christopher, who was seconded by Finbar and so on until all said aye—that Billy might be able to provide the moral to the tale. The reawakening of nature combined with the melancholy of loss had put us in a forgiving mood. It was time, by God, to bring Billy home.

We tried, by way of including them, to prevail upon the children to take us to him, but, exchanging wary glances, they refused. When we set out despite them, marching off at dusk along the dirt road toward the farm's northernmost forty, the pair of them changed their minds and, knock-kneed and barefoot, fell in at the rear. How could they resist? We were a regular parade, everyone in good spirits and pleased with our newfound generosity, looking forward to a joyful reconciliation. Not that I personally set much store in the notion that goodwill would bring Billy back—I don't know that any of us really believed that would happen. My own optimism was more free-floating, stemming from the singular achievement of having attained this fragrant season; I was awake as never before to the environment in its shameless display of abundance. Our arid dirt farm was suddenly luxuriant, the wisteria dripping from its boughs like purple ice, the willows effervescent as uncorked champagne. My awareness of it all filled me with the sense that I, too, was about to bust out; it was high time I set claim to the rightful fruition of my biological needs. This spring was somehow different from all others, not just another cruel April engendering hopes for the sake of dashing them unrealized. Who knew but I might even be ready to love someone?

Only Lila among our number looked apprehensive as we reached the pin oaks and pines that fringed our property like a tonsure, where the children, impatient with our confusion, took over the lead. It wasn't that we were unacquainted with the farm's physical landscape; despite our single-minded preoccupation with its labors, we had done some exploring, but we'd all avoided this remotest corner of the woods as the exclusive lair of Billy Boots. As we entered the trees, the world turned abruptly dark, our eyes adjusting slowly to the dappled half-light leaking through the nave of branches overhead. Then we could see that, by Arkansas standards, we were in a relatively tame and unforbidding grove. Unlike the thickety snarl that most of the encroaching forest presented, here was a gentle slope carpeted in pine needles, fretted with trumpet vines and maidenhair. There were mossy, almost parklike terraces complete with fairy rings that might have been the haunt of sylvan creatures—Bottom asleep on the bosom of Titania, that sort of thing—while ahead of us as we descended the hill, in keeping with the atmosphere of an enchanted wood, a lime white structure floated at the level of our eyes.

It was, as the setting sun (flickering through the trees like the beam from an old projector) revealed, a miniature cottage of many glinting windows. Its design was roughly that of a Steamboat Gothic cottage built to Tom Thumb scale, its shingled walls enframing a myriad of pocket-size windowpanes. The clapboard base was surrounded by a porch with a taffrailed balustrade, the turned rail (which supported an upward-gazing brass telescope) tapered at one end like a prow. There was a steep-pitched, cedar-shaked roof, a slightly tilted fieldstone chimney inlaid with coruscating bits of quartz, a dizzying array of random flourishes: scroll-worked cornice brackets, wooden jalousies, and finials redeemed from the structures we'd dismantled in town. There was a woven-wicker clothes hamper, like the gondola of a balloon, resting on the ground but attached by a system of cables and pulleys to the deck high above. The whole bravura affair glimmered in the failing light like the pale ghost of a painted lady. Wedged among a triad of tree trunks diverging from the common shaft of a single towering sycamore, it was the hybrid of a dollhouse and a boat, looking as if it had been either washed there during a flood or dropped from heaven.

"It's called . . . ," Norma's little boy started to declare, but it took his older sister, squeezing his hand, to pronounce the shibboleth of Billy's roost: "Goslilwizzaker." She pronounced it proprietarily, with more emphasis than I'd ever heard expressed by either child, who both seemed to share a sense that the tree house had been built for them: a playhouse for lost boys and girls. I supposed their attitude was understandable; Billy's ethereal creation certainly had nothing to do with the daily operation of the farm. But at the same time, such a precious, lighter-than-air confection—in itself remarkable, even breathtaking—seemed uncharacteristic of the rough-and-ready Billy Boots. Its silvery elegance was the antithesis of the rigor we'd been practicing all these months, a fierce, utilitarian rigor for which Billy himself had on occasion served as exemplar.

Preceded by the hobbled black dog, the children, in a fair impersonation of lamblikeness, skipped down into the glade, where they climbed along with Spot into the basket of Billy's ingenious lift. Clearly no strangers to the device, they began to crank a windlass resembling a two-handled eggbeater, which raised them via ropes, gears, and spooled capstans into the overhanging limbs. When they'd reached a height of some ten or fifteen feet, however, they paused in their ascent, peering across toward something hanging from an antipodal bough. The last of the sunset was mingling its rose with a deepening aquamarine sky, which canopied the clearing and backlit the branch that dipped almost indiscernibly from the weight of what we now perceived as a dangling man.

It was an effigy of course, very funny, though an artificial crow-bait ornament didn't quite square with the vision of the aerial house. But look again and the treehouse did seem to function as a kind of fulcrum for the balanced scales of the child-bearing basket and the corpse. So far no one had laughed and no one had cried out, though Suzy Q clapped hands over her stark-staring eyes, and Norma, whose tolerance for ghoulishness was slight, swooned into Christopher's arms. Meanwhile the children looked on from their aerie with a quiet reverence, as if suicide were simply the signature with which Billy Boots had chosen to autograph his handiwork. So composed were the two of them that I thought they might have already viewed the scene, and indeed the stench of decomposition which the pines had initially obscured indicated that the body must have been hanging there several days. The stench, coupled with the dolorous whimpering of the elevated black dog, argued against our ability to sustain the illusion that the thing was a practical joke. Still, I thought much time would have to pass, a thousand years of pressured observation, before the tableau could assume the diamond hardness of reality; and who was willing to wait around that long? But naturally no one could budge.

As self-elected bellwether, Muhle was the first to stir, planting a foot in Finbar's lower spine to scramble without apology aboard his shoulders, while Finbar staggered forward under his friend's awkward weight. This signaled a hopeful turn of events, an effort to exploit the situation for farce: Muhle would now attempt, with slippery fingers, to pick the pocket of the swinging manikin without jangling its bells. But Muhle was only trying to reach high enough to unfasten the rope coiled round the victim's neck, which he couldn't do. "Somebody get me a pruning hook," he pleaded, and we were impressed that he had the wherewithal to speak, though no one seemed to comprehend what he was talking about. Then Finbar, perhaps disoriented by the tears stinging his eyes, began to wobble in his Day-Glo boots, and to steady himself against sliding off the big man's shoulders, Muhle grabbed hold of Billy's legs. The body made an oddly familiar wrenching noise, like a tooth pried from a socket, as it slipped from its hempen noose. Still hugging the legs, Muhle fell along with the corpse, taking down the top-heavy Finbar in the bargain, so that all three of them—Muhle, Finbar, and four-fifths of Billy Boots—tumbled onto the marshy ground beside a trickle of stream; while miraculously (it was determined later that he must've cut his throat prior to hanging himself) Billy's hirsute head remained suspended in the noose. Lila, who like the rest of us had yet to utter a sound, stepped forward and leaped for the head like a child trying to snatch a moth out of the air.

NATHAN

If he hadn't been able to find writing materials—scrounging from rubbish bins, sneak-thieving from corner candy stores—Nathan felt he might have carved the words in his flesh with dirty fingernails. As it was, he managed to scavenge pencil stubs and retrieve the nibs of discarded fountain pens, occasionally boosting an inkpot from some Chrystie Street department store on wheels. If a slum artist, having set up to capture the motley of an outdoor market, dropped a used lump of charcoal or crayon, Nathan was there to spirit it away. As for stationery, there was never any shortage of flyers and foolscap handbills advertising the multitude of ghetto events; there were pear wrappers, unwadded invoices, dust jackets, blueprints, celluloid shirtfronts. Clutching tight his bouquet of miscellaneous pages, Nathan wrote whenever and wherever the notion seized him, and it seized him often with several tentacles. Then he would hunker scribbling on stoops and in alleyways, on benches in El station kiosks and in public privies, at tables in the talkers' cafés from which he was shooed for his unhappy smell. Sometimes he wrote as he walked, covering every available space of his mongrel document with pothooks and tottering hen tracks. Revising as he went along, he left behind him a litter of crumpled leaves, a paper trail back to where he never expected to return.

He bound the bundle with butcher's twine when he wasn't actually writing, only to unbind it moments later, like—it occurred to him—the patriarch Abraham, come to his senses with regard to his child. Because, no sooner had he emptied himself of afflatus—and knew the horror of being no one unless he was safe in the throes of composition—than

Nathan began to feel replenished again. For a time he tried to maintain his schlepper's routine, making the rounds of the neighborhood sweat-shops like a walking haymow of worsted knee pants and ladies' cloaks; but it was hard to balance the unwieldy mound of piecework against the increasing burden of his manuscript. So often did he pause to transcribe yet another nugget of inspiration that he was habitually late in making his deliveries, which very soon earned him an angry dismissal from the factory contractor. Afterward Nathan lived as best he could: "By my wits," he tried to assure himself, though, when not scattered, his wits were wholly invested in following his narrative wherever it might lead. His conviction: that it would lead him ultimately to paradise.

He wrote in the voice of Mocky Fargenish the renegade angel, which had been his original method and once more turned out to be the key to resuming his project. Mocky had come again to occupy Nathan dybbuk fashion, and his dictation made the writing a kind of gradual exorcism, during which the distinction between narrator and author was unclear. Mocky told the tale of how he'd embarked on a grueling rehabilitative campaign at his son's instigation, while Nathan Hart, the angel's ill-starred instrument, kept himself in one piece for the purpose of relating Mocky's phenomenal progress. But to survive, now that the early autumn had turned nippy, Nathan had to make certain adjustments to circumstance: there were nights when he slept under a roof, nights when he didn't, days when he never had a bite to eat.

On occasion he might lament the absence of a *bet hamidrash,* an Old Country study house where indigent Talmud scholars were welcome to stay the night, nestling in casements while the *luftmenschen* told lies around the samovar. But in America even the meanest doss-house, where a bed was a canvas strip hung between rafters and the toilet a mephitic trough—even these cost a few hard-won pennies, and in them you ran the risk of waking up minus a ring finger or a gold-filled tooth. Now and then Nathan might secure a billet in the holding cell of a local police station, the most hospitable being the jail below the Essex Market Court-house, but this was a luxury usually reserved for decent citizens down on their luck, rather than the career derelicts whose ranks the unemployed proofreader seemed to have joined. In consequence Nathan made regu-lar calls on the East Side missions. These storefront institutions, manned by zealots eager to win Jewish souls, were a constant irritant to the community; but since, in their enthusiasm, the missionaries offered inducements of clothing and ready cash, Nathan saw no reason why he should not avail himself of their charity. In a single afternoon, having submitted to two or three baptisms, taking a *goyishe* name with each one (Augustine, Luke), he could raise enough to cover his food and lodging for a week. Of course he had to take care to stagger his visits at respectable intervals, as witness the time he was recognized by a pharisaical Bowery preacher who had converted him only days before and threatened his eternal damnation as Nathan took to his heels.

He tried his hand at begging, though competition in the Tenth Ward was stiff. From choice sites such as the Delancey Street entrance to the Williamsburg Bridge, he was run off by emeritus schnorrers who miraculously found their sight (or a missing limb) long enough to drive him from their corner; or, upstaged by some grisly relic of the Spanish War, stumps protruding like liverwurst from his pant legs, Nathan would depart without waiting to be told. Nevertheless, avoiding the public showers under Rutgers Square (as cleanliness was a detriment to panhandling), he could usually count on his unsightly surface to keep him in pickles and dry bread, and sometimes to foot the bill for a flop. Then, too, as the bleak autumn promised a bleaker winter, the local charities stepped up their services; more handouts were available from the settlement houses and Hebrew aid societies. There were half-full boxes of ZuZu snaps and stale Uneeda biscuits in the trash bins; there was the rotten produce that had accumulated around the pushcarts by the end of the day. Foraging, Nathan could likely find sufficient nourishment to kindle a brain that functioned now on any fuel, while the writing seemed to maintain its own source of heat.

Less intimate sources were the grated vent holes above a subway or over a basement workshop where the rotary presses generated sirocco breezes. But for such coveted spots, Nathan had to contend with others among the legion of East Side homeless, when he preferred, for the purpose of protecting his expanding manuscript, to sleep alone. He might commandeer a scrapped piano crate or an empty stable for a night, or curl up, insulating his clothes with newspaper, among the bottles and cans beneath the East River wharves. He peed against hoardings, stole into rooftop jakes and building excavations turned cesspits, cleaning himself with his own coarse cacography. For a time he'd occupied a forsaken sukkah made of sweetly decomposing wicker and cane in a courtyard behind Forsyth Street; and once, on an especially raw night in late October, he'd come upon a nest of street arabs huddled in a synagogue niche. Shivering from exposure, and perhaps desiring the company that misery loves, Nathan tried to insinuate himself into their midst but was shunned by a flurry of insults and unfriendly elbows. The incident further confirmed him in his solitude: how, spurned by the dispossessed, he was set apart—a diaspora of one—on account of his creative enterprise.

With the first frosts, he was forced more and more to find the means to stay in the all-night dives and cheap lodging houses, the best of which provided a pest-ridden pallet on the floor near a stove. (The worst was a cellar where you were strung up by the armpits on a clothesline, which was let to fall in the morning as a signal it was time to wake up.) For all that, Nathan, still in full spate, wasted remarkably little time in self-pity. So long as he was writing, he paid scant attention to his own destitution, except on those occasions when he felt that his manuscript might be in jeopardy. Then, despite the haggard condition in which his starvation diet had left him, he thought he'd have savaged anyone who, out of malice or mere curiosity, threatened to wrest the story from his hands.

But nobody bothered. By the time of the first major snowfall, he had become something of a fixture to the citizens of the ghetto: a *shtot meshuggener* of the type who inhabits the twilight border between vagrancy and madness. No one, neither cops on the beat nor merchants who turned a blind eye to his petty thefts, made to interfere with him, as if his oddity had marked him as somehow untouchable. Some of the locals went so far as to assign him a nickname: Bintl Brief, they called him, "Bundle of Letters," after the advice-seeking column in the *Jewish Forward;* because the ragged pages he carried might have been mail. He might be a courier, as a few of the pious inferred from the faraway cast of his eye, bringing messages to the living from the dead. But while Nathan delivered no news to anyone, there were those who would pause for the mitzvah of sparing him change. This he received as if it were a gratuity for having been their personal scribe—for it was fitting that his work-in-progress should provide him with a means of sustenance as well as a kind of portable home.

He'd had to start over from the very beginning, but that proved an exhilaration rather than a hardship, Mocky's voice become as bracing to Nathan as a trade wind. He had rewritten from scratch Mocky's adventures in heaven and earth, followed by Nachman's inauspicious arrival on the Lower East Side, the arc of the greenhorn's theatrical career, his romance and ultimate fall from grace. Then, reaching the place where the story had previously hung fire, Nathan plunged ahead into the succeeding chapter—the one where Nachman, fresh from humiliation at the hands of the rabbi's daughter, bullies Mocky in the back of Mushy's Rumanian into showing his wings. Hustled from the wine cellar at closing time, father and son tramped the wet streets together, Nachman continuing (while Mocky pleaded *enough*) to outline his program for retrieving stories: "If you don't teach me to fly, then to glory I will ride on your coattails. . . ." Pausing to rest, as the dawn dissipated a gray flannel mist, they found themselves on the doorstep of the Educational Alliance, which Nachman insisted was *bashert*, it was destiny. Through persistent hounding, Nachman broke down his father's defenses and persuaded the self-confessed angel to accompany him into the building. They ascended the stairs, Nachman prodding a refractory Mocky from behind, past early-morning lectures on delousing and courtship etiquette to the fifth-floor turnverein. There, in an enormous room skewered by sunlight from high windows, pigeon-breasted candidates for the white plague were endeavoring to build up their bodies to the standards of the Golden Land. Everywhere old men were listlessly swinging Indian clubs, rolling medicine balls about like dung beetles, hanging from ratlines as if trapped in spiderwebs. Protesting that such activities were un-Jewish, especially at such an ungodly hour, the angel resisted his son's importuning; but in the end Nachman's will was the stronger, and, too weary to argue anymore, Mocky stepped into the ranks of the decrepit old *kucker*s performing military-style calisthenics in their underwear.

In this way he commenced, under his son's strict supervision, a half-hearted regimen of physical culture, ratcheting his knees and bending his creaking spine in what resembled a species of danse macabre. The more he sweated, the more he aggravated his infirmities: the gout flared, the spastic colon throbbed. It was a brand of torture whose only consolation was that, in his fatigue, Mocky thought he might actually drop dead. A not unpleasant prospect, since it would prove to the satisfaction of all that, instead of a heavenly host, he was merely a wasted scrap of a caftan. But when at length he caught his breath and got something approaching a second wind, Mocky discovered to his amazement that the aches had begun to diminish. He even started to entertain a hope he had long ago relinquished, that it might be possible to regain his lost powers, though he'd have swapped such powers in an instant for a glass of schnapps.

This he duly reported to Nachman, who led him to a watercooler and informed him that Mocky and the bottle had parted company for good. "The deuce!" cried the angel, as Nachman added that, while he was at it, he should stay away from kishkes, and rollmops in sour cream was definitely out. Mocky complained that Nachman meant to deprive him of everything that made life on earth tolerable, then marveled to find the idea strangely appealing. He was being weaned from the world with a view toward leaving it for the next. Then he asked himself what was he thinking; had he been brainwashed by his son?

Nevertheless, from that moment Mocky acceded to Nachman's agenda: he gave up strong drink with only a minimal struggle, persevered with the exercise routine, and every so often took at his son's behest a bite of some laxative fruit. Moreover, for all Nachman's needling, the old degenerate couldn't help feeling somehow grateful. He was grateful the kid didn't remind him of what was understood between them: that once a maverick angel had left his son in an alien place where the living offspring of mortal mothers were unwelcome. If only for letting him off that hook, Mocky was indebted to the boy; so he humored Nachman in the gymnasium, invited him to stay awhile in the coal cellar on Allen Street. There Nachman slept uncomplaining on a horse blanket spread over the pebbly clay floor, happily absorbed in his role as his father's trainer. He oversaw Mocky's progress according to Eugene Sandow's *Manual of Scientific Physical Development* and, when he wasn't actively involved in supervising the bodybuilding, "studied" (a questionable pursuit, since he'd never properly learned to read) texts from the Seward Park Library. These were volumes having to do with the theory of flight by pioneers of aviation such as Lilienthal and Pilcher—famous, incidentally, for their fatal experiments.

Because it mustn't be assumed that Mocky and son inhabited a vacuum, Nathan also described the prevailing atmosphere in the Jewish quarter: There was trouble in gangland, old tensions having flared between the Dopey Bennies and Jack Scipio's Five-Pointers mob, who had taken the side of management in the Greenwalt Hat Factory strike. (His loyalties always at the service of the highest bidder, Dopey nonetheless prided himself on his enduring sympathy with labor.) During one altercation the Dope's comrade-in-arms Hymie Zum, dispatched to rid the premises of scabs, was clubbed to bonemeal by the rival faction. In an act of reprisal, Dopey stationed his gunsels outside a Scipio racket at the Arlington Dancehall on St. Marks Place. During the skirmish, in which not a single gang member was injured, a civilian (a ranking city official, as it turned out) walked into the crossfire and was slain. Coming as it did in the midst of so much underworld activity, the murder led to a public outcry, as a result of which Mayor Gaynor, fresh from a freakish attempt on his own life, promised a serious crackdown on organized crime. He commenced his crusade with the blessing of Tammany Hall and Dopey's onetime patron, the ward boss Big Tim Sullivan, for whom the gangs had also become a headache.

The police made frequent raids on the hangouts of Dopey's *talmidim*, though in the absence of corroborative evidence, the mobsters were soon released from jail. Still, the Dope found it expedient to lower his flat-nosed profile, retreating from his more prominent haunts to hunker down in the back rooms of Allen Street. While there he amused himself by renewing his abiding Dutch uncle's interest in Rivka Bubitsch, who, owing to her recent reversal of fortune, had remained in the shabby apartment she'd shared with her father. Dopey had always harbored a soft spot for the rabbi's daughter dating from her slattern days, back when she'd been the domestically handicapped angel of her blind father's minyans; and now that she made no attempt to hide her charms, he'd stepped up his attentions. Nor did Rivka, always a practical girl, discourage his gallantries. Whether grateful or merely to smooth his feathers, she accepted the mob captain's largesse, enjoying under his auspices a state of semiretirement from her lapsed professional life. She countenanced Dopey's doting (even stroked the pomatumed hair that framed his brow like the tines of opposing forks) and received the chippy-style threads he favored her with—the plush capes and lingerie blouses, lace cascades and red-plumed Dolly Varden hats, items that tended to obscure her natural beauty as effectively as her cast-off habit of a drudge.

If Nachman was aware of Rivka's compromised situation, he never showed it, so consumed was he with the business of the angel's reconditioning. Though he slept beneath the very rooms in which his professed beloved entertained the notorious ganef and racketeer, he made no attempt to seek her out; in fact, he seemed altogether indifferent to her existence. Only once, to Mocky's knowledge, did their paths ever cross: one evening when Nachman was escorting his papa back from the Alliance, and Rivka, in the company of the Dope and his retinue, was on her way to the theater. (Even in the current hostile climate, Uncle Shmuel's remained a relatively safe haven for outlaws.) She was dressed to the nines in a clingy beaded tunic of cobalt blue, an opera toque sprayed with egret feathers crowning her doughnut pompadour. A head taller than her companion, himself sleepy-eyed and sartorial in a cutaway sack coat, she showed no sign of having noticed Mocky's wraithlike son—for, in his zeal for his father's reclamation, Nachman had ignored his own nutritional needs. Then Little Kishky, Dopey's first lieutentant, hulking bearishly behind his boss's sloping shoulders, made the connection:

"Rivka, give a look on what's left of your old leading man."

Rivka started at the sight, stumbling in her calfskin pumps and grabbing at Dopey's arm for support. With a solicitous air, the hoodlum helped her regain her balance and straighten her egret plume, steadying her as she summoned the dignity to walk on. While Nachman, whose dark eyes remained focused inward, lips set in a perpetual half smile, appeared to have been insensible to the whole occurrence. That was how completely he had converted the flesh-and-blood girl into pure idea.

His only concern now was in making sure Mocky practiced his daily dozens on the tumbling mat and plied the rowing machine, that he regularly cranked his dumbbells in an out-of-whack semaphore. So what if the Zionists of the Young Judean movement, chests straining the seams of their starched white singlets, had a laugh at the aged crookback's expense? This was something the angel was anyway used to. And besides, the old men, seeing one of their own grown increasingly sounder of wind and limb, had begun to pay Mocky a measure of respect, some deferring to him as to a champion.

In the meantime Mocky had become so addicted to strenuous physical exercise that he neglected the duties that had earned him his marginal attachment to Dopey's mob. As a consequence, when the senior eye gouger Ike the Plug came into the cellar to gather bomb-making combustibles, he issued an ultimatum in the name of the Dope: Mocky Fargenish should make himself useful or consider his days on Allen Street numbered. And this went as well for his bedfellow, the debased thespian Opgekumener, harmless though he might be. But Mocky couldn't help himself; he was committed to the punishing daily regime that left him aching in every fiber and joint; while at the close of day, when he was allowed to drop into oblivion (after he'd made the rounds of the settlement houses in search of handouts and foraged in the *chazzer mark* for rancid Oysterettes), he slept the sleep of the righteous and woke refreshed. Though his physique remained stringy (Mocky was not of the race of warrior angels), his muscles, once the consistency of unleavened dough, had grown taut; his belly was firm, his flexed biceps hard as the kidney stones he eventually passed. Although his face retained the hue and texture of potted meat, his wrinkles appeared to be uncreasing; there was strength, if you cared to look, in his scraggly jaw. He'd begun to feel, *kaynehorah,* like a young man in an old man's disguise, as if the years were dropping away, unreeling back to the moment when he first met Hannah and donned a garment of flesh to keep his radiance from dazzling the mortals.

Then there were the wings, which had begun to grow, their plumage billowing over his shoulders like foam over the rim of a beer. In public he tried to keep them covered, but their increased size made the hump on his back appear more pronounced. To compensate for their tumescence, he exaggerated his stoop, though in truth the added weight was no burden. Occasionally they might fidget in their itch to expand, until he was forced, despite the mild weather, to confine them to a fulvous dust coat, which he wore even in the gymnasium. But in the cellar Mocky released the wings and let them breathe. He preened and fanned them, admiring their downy growth in a shaving mirror. The contour feathers overlapped one another like ivory shingles, their shafts resilient as Torah pointers, and when in their unfolding they sometimes brimmed over his collar, he was less embarrassed than proud. He was filled with energies he hadn't experienced for centuries, and while the anticipation alone could make his nose bleed, he wanted to fly.

MOCKY

One morning in April, shortly before Passover, when we were about to leave for the Alliance, Nachman invited me to spread my wings. He made to check their span against the diagrams in his outdated books, handling them as rudely as he had on that night in the wine cellar. Rather than comment on their impressive symmetry, he jotted notes in a code of his own devising; he spoke inscrutable words, picked up from God knows where, such as *"wing warp"* and *"yaw."* Irritated with his phony science and what now seemed a clinical intrusion, I flapped by way of persuading him to let go. No longer was there a noise of rusty hinges, but instead a deep shushing like muffled thunder filled the air. A wind came up in the cellar, dispelling the mildewed closeness: bottles rattled, dust devils and egg flakes swirled about, even the vermin were airborne, and I felt I could have lifted the whole house as in a hurricane. Then my head bumped against a beam, and I realized I had risen, my feet dangling several inches above the floor. It was a moment that, in my elation, I dedicated to the failed levitations of Rabbi Mordecai the Blind.

But when Nachman declared a triumphant "If not now, when?" I confess I was chilled to the marrow of my cheese-straw bones.

Still, he was right, my son; there was nothing more for either of us to say, so we set out in hazy sunshine the color of gasoline oozing between the tracks above Allen Street. Instead of turning left on Canal in the direction of Edgies, however, we proceeded, as Nachman whistled a Goldfadn *freylakh,* southwest across the Bowery. At the tile-roofed kiosk of the Park Row station, we boarded the Sixth Avenue Elevated and took our seats in the double cane chairs. We rode north through a district of boxy cast-iron façades, past pennant-flying commercial emporia and the baroque brick follies of the theaters beyond Fourteenth Street. There were oak-shuttered brownstones with window boxes along the side streets, bishop's-crook lampposts unfurling into ramrod arc lights, purring hacks parked beneath shade trees awaiting gentlemen in chesterfields and ladies in walking skirts. Out the right-hand windows, you saw the terra-cotta towers of grand hotels, out the left railroad tenements and snatches of shantytowns. This was the farthest I'd been in an age from the Jewish East Side, and the distance made me feel that our journey to heaven, which I still couldn't quite believe in, had already begun.

At 125th Street we transferred to a suburban train, traveling beyond clusters of isolated row houses surrounded by weedy allotments to the end of the line at 177th. From a dove-warbling, barnlike structure at the point where the North River becomes the Hudson, we took a steam ferry over to Fort Lee on the Jersey shore. There we climbed the twenty-five flights of wooden steps (I had to help a puffing Nachman up the last of these) to the top of the Palisades.

It was cool along the heights, impish breezes bussing our cheeks. Turning our backs on a clutch of clapboard houses facing the commons, we followed a winding path among the gray stone outcroppings—their fissures flecked with parti-colored wildflowers for which *mameloshen*, the mother tongue, has no name. We shared some soda water on an observation deck perched like an aerie over the brow of the cliff and took in the view. It was very affecting, what with the city's shimmering reflection on the water stirred by an argosy of yachts in full sail. Having been so long in the ghetto, I was moved by the panorama, though since when did I care from panoramas? But anticipation had sharpened my senses, and for once I felt thankful to be out of doors. I liked plodding along beside my son in his laceless brogans, so proud of his reconstructed papa that he couldn't stop grinning. But when we'd departed the footpath and made our way down the terraced slope to a secluded shelf of rock beneath an overhang, I got dizzy.

Nachman helped me remove the dust coat, though I insisted on peeling the suspenders and undervest myself, after which I suffered an attack of goose pimples. This was not so much due to the blustering headwind at the edge of the precipice as to my abrupt loss of nerve. "Maybe I could use a little more practice," I suggested to Nachman, who pooh-poohed the remark and nudged me closer to the brink.

Look down and the water boiled about the boulders at the base of the cliff in whorls of angry yellow foam; look up and the sky was a fathomless azure abyss. Until then I'd been perfectly willing to admit the off chance that I was wrong: perhaps it was possible to get there from here. But it was a long way to travel, and I was a very old party whose wings drooped like branches laden with ice.

Above the skyline there buzzed a contraption that looked no larger than a flitting insect, trailing a banner advertising Platt's Chlorides. It was doubtless piloted by one of those daring young birdmen whose exploits the papers were full of. "Maybe it's only the man-made machine," I repined aloud, "that today can make a miracle." Throwbacks to another time and place such as myself were just that—outmoded; and this particular relic seemed to have developed a sudden fear of altitude.

At that point Nachman left off his grinning. "Miracle, shmiracle," he scoffed by way of inviting perspective. "We're talking here your garden-variety aviation." Then he gave me a push that, just this side of gentle, threatened to cross the line into shove.

I planted my heels to keep from tottering backward and tried to make him see reason, protesting that it was definitely too soon to test my wings. "More slower you should build up to the hop-off; almost three hundred years it's been, that you can't expect overnight I should make an angel."

He stood there appearing to consider, an elbow propped in the cup of one hand, his tilted chin resting in the other, while I marshaled more arguments. His eyes were closed in contemplation, the wind flinging his matted curls in an inky spume. But just when I thought he might be having second thoughts, Nachman opened his sloe-black eyes; he stepped forward and, without so much as a *"Shehechayanu,"* shoved me over the edge.

Stumbling backward, I dropped like a stone, hurtling toward the rocks in a river as scintillant as Leviathan's scales. My feet and head kept exchanging places, my stomach tossed like a beanbag between them, and while I clawed the air for a purchase, I knew there was no reversing my fate. I would be impaled on shards of light shot from the river's surface, shattered on the rocks and forced to drag my undead carcass about the city streets for all eternity. For my sins it was the least I deserved. But in the last instant (*Got tzu danken!*) the conditioning saved me, and my wings, owing to their rigorous education and independent of any will of my own, opened wide. They flared above an updraft so wrenching that it threatened to tear the scapulae from my shoulders; then the pain restored my volition, and, braking just short of a bloody baptism, I skidded on the wind. I flapped once, twice, beating back the flashing water, folding my-self into the loftier currents, beginning to soar.

Wheeling upward, I veered to avoid a collision with seagulls and dis-covered that I was swift; I was sure-feathered, gliding on pinions as stream-lined as fleece spinnakers, free of pain. But no sooner had I begun to adapt to the cerulean element than I entered another, a cavern—sublimely quiet—of antimony and pearl. I explored it with flutterings as much bor-rowed from fish as from fowl, getting lost in arteries as luminous as God's own innards, emerging into a theater of infinite blue. Then I was any-where, unable to gauge my bearings with a designation more precise than "beyond." The clouds below me were suds and spilled kapok ob-scuring the least glimpse of land or sea, which my eye somehow never missed, and I realized how tenuous my attachment to earth had been all along. I was on the wing again, launched like a pellet from a sling, headed irretrievably back to *Gan Eydn,* when I remembered my son.

Alighting on the ledge in a fair approximation of a two-point landing, I graciously received his applause, then invited him to "Hop on board, this is for heaven the express." But Nachman, despite looking genuinely pleased, told me no thanks, "Not today." Thinking that cold feet were only natural, as who should know better than I, I took his sleeve to try to coax him a bit, but he wrenched his arm from my grasp.

"Boychik," I reasoned, "ain't this the moment we waited?"

In a slightly chastened voice, Nachman informed me, "I got farewells yet to make . . ."

"Farewells?" He nodded to confirm I had heard him correctly. "Presi-dent Taft that his feelings are hurt you didn't say good-bye?"

". . . and I left on Allen Street my quilt."

"Tahkeh," I replied, making no attempt to hide my sarcasm. "Listen,

kiddo, how many reasons you needed to stay away from that place? One wing I got already in the hereafter, and you want to return to *Gehinnom?* Whose idea was this anyhow?"

His hair was a clump, his dirty nightshirt tucked haphazardly into his baggy pants, and I wondered what business such a misfit could still have among mortals. But Nachman's face, however sorry, was resolute, his only answer a summary shrug as he started back up the footpath.

"Sonny boy," I pleaded, stunned by my own disappointment, "do you want I should get on my knees? Didn't you know that our kind was born for flight?"

Never turning around, he gave me a dismissive wave of the hand, like "What else is new?" like I hadn't just made history. "What makes you to think I wouldn't go without you?" I shouted indignantly, as his tangled crown disappeared behind a boulder. "*Meshugah ahf toit,* may you sicken and remember! May you lie in the earth and bake bagels! Go ahead, find your own way home!"

SAUL

Back in Memphis for Billy's funeral, I visited my parents, with whom I hadn't communicated these several months. It wasn't from orneriness so much as sheer lack of motivation that I'd maintained the long silence, nor was I inclined to break it even now that I was back in town. But the continuing aftershocks of Billy Boots's suicide had rattled me to the point that I wanted to at least touch base with my family. It was not an auspicious homecoming. I had failed to phone ahead, and there was company in the house—my sister's fiancé, Milton Unger, and his mother—so the timing of the black sheep's return could not have been worse. Moreover, my sister had just come out of the hospital and was recovering from her prenuptial nose job, her two black eyes separated by a tricornered bandage like a hamantasch. So estranged had I become from the household that I almost enjoyed the vexation I caused by my entrance and everyone's transparent efforts to behave naturally.

Taking a seat after awkward introductions, I was as out of place in that antiseptic living room, with my fringes, bracelets, and hair, as an aboriginal fetish. In a nod toward sociability, I remarked to my sister, "You're a sight for sore eyes."

She gave me a look of patient forbearance, replied, "Very funny, I'm sure," and turned back to the guests, the ice yet unbroken. Slouching farther into my wing chair, I was nevertheless grateful for a reprieve from being center stage. I was a little proud of the daunting character they no doubt imagined me to be, while I wondered, what if they knew I was still a virgin? Even my mother, whose flesh beneath her corset was loose as a bloodhound's, wasn't a virgin. But the conversation was deadly, and after several minutes' discussion about caterers, floral arrangements, and bridesmaids' gowns, I was moved to inject another poor joke.

"Why don't you wait to reveal your new honker until the moment Milton lifts the veil?"

Silence, during which all eyes were upon me.

"Why did you come here?" asked my sister.

"I dunno," I answered in all honesty. "To give you my blessing?"

"We know what you think of us," she continued, proceeding to demonstrate her clairvoyance. "Well, we may be boring and ordinary," glancing at the mouth-breathing bridegroom, who nodded his courtly assent, "but I intend to be a good wife to Milton and give him fine children to make it up to our family for—"

Beating her to it: "All the grief I've brought them. I heard this one already." My cheeks hot with embarrassment for all concerned, I excused myself and rose to leave the room. I winced as I heard my mother behind me making excuses in a shrill whisper for her son.

"He's been on medication."

I was lifting the coffeepot from the kitchen counter when who should enter the room but Mrs. Unger, a full-figured woman whose Carnaby Street ensemble defied the crow's-feet of her middle years. She had ostensibly come in for another cup of coffee herself but, sighing as she took the measure of me, shook her head in solicitude.

"Saul, Saul," she crooned, as if we'd been acquainted for years, "when are you going to stop tilting with windmills?"

"Excuse me?"

"You know what you are, Saul?" she continued. "You're an idealist, and you'll never be happy."

I marveled at her presumption. "But I *am* happy," I lied.

She nodded with an even profounder sympathy, placing a gory-nailed hand on my shoulder. "That, too," she lamented, "that, too."

Returned to the living room, I shouldered my knapsack and bade the assembled a hasty good-bye: "Nature calls." I was outside and halfway up the front walk when my father shouted after me; turning, I saw him huffing down the steps, a sunburn deepening to melanoma on his bald pate, with a letter in his hand. "You got some mail while you were gone," he said. His rheumy eyes were bisected by the rims of his glasses, which perpetually slid down his nose, and he was smiling his I-too-was-young-once smile. Facing him, I very nearly relinquished my role of the injured party. I nearly reversed my judgment damning the house to bourgeois perdition and told him I could use a little time to collect my wits, that I was frightened half to death. But it would have been unfair to inflict such a burden on my father, who was already stooped from his own—and he was dead a few years hence of a heart attack before I realized that I'd once again mistaken my own cowardice for integrity.

The return address on the envelope he handed me, forwarded from my old dormitory in New York, read "Newman Shendeldecker, Pismo Beach, CA."

"Anything interesting?" asked my father.

Somehow touched by his mild curiosity, I blurted, "I'm sorry!" à propos of everything.

"Think nothing of it," he replied, and heartily shook my hand.

With hindsight it was easy to see that Lila had been mourning Billy Boots ever since we'd arrived at the farm; she had slept with the living man as if he were a phantom lover. As a consequence, his death set her free. This is not to say that she behaved with anything like normality, for she'd initially insisted on retaining the dead man's detached head. It had been confiscated from her after an ugly struggle by the local police, who'd conducted a lengthy inquest, all the while decrying our lack of cooperation and threatening us with suspicions of homicide—a routine intimidation, it seemed, since it was clear no one was losing sleep over the untimely end of one hippie more or less. Lila had even tried to prevail upon Billy's parents, stunned to passivity by the death of a son they had not even been certain was still alive, to agree to leave the head in her possession. They declined, of course, though Mrs. Boots, at the Memphis funeral home that had reunited her son's remains, nearly relented. "The girl deserves a keepsake," she said, pressing upon Lila the patchwork quilt that had doubled as a winding cloth. So fond and docile were the Bootses in their grief-stricken bafflement, their raw gothic countenances so benign, that they never even protested our making a mockery of Billy's last rites. They didn't seem to realize that Christopher's surreal eulogy at the graveside, addressed to an unexpectedly large turnout of drug cronies, professors, leathery Negroes, and a covey of fair and tender ladies, was a hostile act, designed to trivialize a solemn occasion out of anger toward the deceased. The same went for Muhle's setting fire to his guitar and Finbar's dramatic leap into the open grave. For though he had died intestate, his actions having voided all words, Billy Boots had nevertheless bequeathed us anger as his immediate legacy.

After she returned to the land, Lila was frequently seen carrying about a melon-size object she swung like a censer in the sling of Billy's old crazy quilt. Had there been any standards left by which to gauge sanity on our farm, Lila's behavior might have been judged classically insane. But Lila was in relatively good spirits, friendly, even flirtatious, sometimes bearing her article as another woman might tote the accessory of a drawstring bag. She was conventionality itself when compared to, say, Christopher, whose behavior bordered on certifiable. Attempting to rally us to our neglected tasks, he employed a rhetoric improbably cobbled from socialist tracts, Old Testament prophecies, and Lenny Bruce routines, which made him sound like an idealogue from Mars. When it was clear no one was listening, he would assume a crucified pose, shirt open to reveal a chest like a birdcage, complaining to the heavens that we knew not what we did. Asking provocatively, "Was Billy Boots the only reason we came here?" Which struck a nerve, because, yes, Billy had been the reason—though he wasn't necessarily the reason we'd stayed on. Still, nothing we'd done since coming to the farm seemed to count for much in the face of his departure.

Then there was Finbar, who had been in many respects the rock of our community, albeit a slippery rock adaptable to every contingency, who now appeared to have surrendered completely to despair. Since his return, a little later than most of us, he'd taken to moping in his lodge like Achilles and drinking cheap bourbon all day, which exasperated Regina, who did not countenance weakness in her men. So Lila's patrolling the property with her new, hip-rolling gait, her *objet* flung over her shoulder hobo fashion, did not seem especially aberrant in the scheme of things. In her Gypsy weeds and free-flowing lampblack hair, she seemed more the playful doxy than disconsolate widow, inviting the attentions of any willing men. And who would reject the overtures of Billy's de facto widow? In this way Lila had forged a fresh intimacy with an obliging Muhle, with

Finbar despite his maudlin backslide into effeminacy, and with Christopher under Norma's very nose—alliances that sowed the seeds of further dissension among the already shell-shocked ranks of our company.

Like the others, I returned to the Ozarks for lack of anywhere else to go. (We had all traveled separately, by truck, bus, and thumb, no one sparing a thought for our original convoy or convinced that anyone else would show up.) It was like coming back to the penal colony after a furlough to serve out the remainder of your term. When all the inmates were finally accounted for, we continued to go through the motions: there were animals to feed, a garden to hoe, the dozen ongoing projects that comprised our bold experiment. But having been away for a spell (our mangy livestock left in Farmer Benbow's notional care), we were disheartened to see again the desolate conditions in which we had been living for the past year. Our morale having sunk below our knees, a thing to trip over like dropped drawers, we were past caring what became of a place we now perceived as a lost cause.

The first to advertise her discontent was the ordinarily laconic Norma, who, roused by Billy's death, had decided to reintroduce her children to civilized society. She campaigned for and was given a job managing a newly opened craft shop in Eureka, where her weavings had begun to net substantial prices. The job came with a roomy apartment upstairs over the shop, and Norma was determined to take it, with or without her irresolute companion. Presented with the ultimatum, Christopher assumed his martyr's pose for a day and a night; he remained conflicted after Norma had moved to town, dividing his time between her apartment and the farm until, driven 'round the bend from vacillation, he fled both, returning to graduate school on the army's tab. He took multiple degrees and attached himself to a liberal-arts college, where, sympathetic to his radical warrior's credentials and brainy derangement, he was granted a tenured position as campus culture hero for many years— until a charge of sexual misconduct forced his early retirement.

Meanwhile Muhle, always maddeningly independent, his ties to the land grown ever more tenuous, had also shifted the focus of his activities to town. With a newly acquired pawnshop guitar, he'd begun playing music in a Main Street saloon called the Toast, where he was popular for the eclectic range of his repertoire. The Saturday-night crowds, made up

of yokels and tourists come back to the resurrected resort, appreciated
Muhle's lack of allegiance to any genre, his ability to field requests from
Hank Williams to Jimi Hendrix and Kurt Weill. He cut and oiled his
dirty-blond hair, which he combed in a duck's ass, and began to think of
himself as a cabaret entertainer—just as Suzy, the dew evaporating from
her peach-blossom cheek, had begun to style herself as his groupie, a role
she apparently didn't mind sharing with other local ingenues. (She even
nursed him when Muhle was briefly hors de combat, having been
knocked unconscious by a house key wrapped in a pair of panties a zealous admirer had flung at his head.) Muhle's only enduring contribution
to the postmortem life of the farm was the marijuana patch he cultivated
for his own uses—a habit that survived a short jail term and his subsequent years as booking agent, art auctioneer, jackleg lawyer, talent scout,
fight promoter, loan shark, and so on. . . .

Soon enough the little capital that remained to us was on its way to
gone, and no plans were afoot for any collective fund-raising endeavors;
there were no councils anymore and, aside from the gossip concerning
Lila, which diminished as she curried more favor with the men, hardly
any conversation among us at all. We tended to avoid eye contact with
one another, a detail that Christopher, to whom I'd abdicated my mantle
as figure of fun, made sport of at every opportunity. Playing the fool, he
was able to say anything, even the truth, with impunity, a faculty evidenced as well by Finbar in his cups. "Nothing is true, all is permitted!"
the big man would proclaim, reeling about in one of the paisley sarongs
he'd borrowed from Regina. He was wearing a sarong when he apologized for not being himself—or anyone else, for that matter—and eventually quit the farm to return to Memphis. There he became a cook and
a barroom fixture, an androgynous bully to the confusion of his enemies, of whom he made many. He lost his looks, and his weight bal-
looned to dirigible proportions, until, laid off from the short-order grill
to which he'd been tethered (he said) like a junkyard dog, he conveniently
perished of liver cancer. Regina, who had bade him good riddance long
before he left Arkansas, continued in her halfhearted efforts to feed
us, but she, too, was drawn to the reawakened nightlife of Eureka
Springs. Asked (after demonstrating her aptitude) to tend bar in the
very saloon where Muhle performed, she actively flirted with the mixed

clientele—wranglers, bikers, disenfranchised postgraduates—some of whom she went home with. One rangy cowpoke she accompanied all the way back to his spread in Montana, where she had his child before dumping him for another man, with whom she had another child and moved to Oregon. There she exchanged her current man for yet another, who married her, raised her daughters, and set her up in a truck-stop café that had become a local tradition by the time she ran off again.

While all of us were still officially in residence, the farm had begun to take on a deserted look, and I admit to having felt a bit thrilled by its decline. A house of cards built on sand, it was bracing to topple the whole construct ourselves before time and tide could intercede. For lack of regular milking, and because they were left to graze in a sun-blasted pasture where little but bitterroot grew, the goats dried up, becoming an unsalable skeleton flock prone to disease. Abelard, our one remaining hog, inconsolable since the slaughter of Heloise, contracted scours and keeled over after purging himself of a river of dysentery. The rabbits had vanished, presumably set free by Norma's kids in a farewell gesture, while the chickens—among whom was Pete's Samantha, indistinguishable now from the rest—were left to forage outside the broken coop. They fared best of all our livestock, though no one bothered anymore to conduct the daily treasure hunt for their scattered eggs. No one but Spot the dog, who in his malnourished condition sometimes went after the chickens as well, until a crapulent Finbar caught the mutt with feathers in his mouth and, obeying some unwritten ordinance of the hills, shot him dead. Uncompleted, the root cellar remained an open quagmire filled with malarial groundwater, its eroded corners trellised in black-widow webs. The geodesic dome, which had never progressed beyond its foundation and a few hubs radiating spokes like Tinker Toys, became, prematurely, the ruin I'd anticipated for a distant future. The weather was brutally hot ("Arkansas," complained Christopher, "is the sun's anvil"), and the unkempt garden, strangled in broom sedge, was alive with snakes.

Suicide's having darker implications in those parts than murder, no one visited us anymore. Even the pariah Leonard Beck, whom we'd heard had taken a December bride, kept his distance from our benighted farm. We had supplanted him, it seemed, in the status of the accursed. Maybe the neighbors had gotten wind of why we were compelled to hold a second funeral, wherein we persuaded Lila to finally lay her fetish to rest. It was the last ritual we performed as a community and was perhaps intended to provide a period to the sentence we were serving on the land. What prompted it was that, due to Lila's carelessness—or mischief, since in her frisky new attitude she was not above playing tricks—the unwrapped object—which turned out to be a plastic skull from a novelty shop, serving as surrogate for Billy's decollated head—had begun turning up in odd places. This was the last straw for Norma, who came upon it caught up in mosquito netting draped like Spanish moss from the lower limbs of a chinaberry tree. Regina found it in the garden among a row of moldering cabbage heads, wearing a garter-snake garland, and Muhle, releasing a shriek heard 'round the county, sat down beside it perched on a shelf in the outhouse, wreathed in flies. (Lila had stuffed it, for the sake of authenticity, with rotting meat.) Once little Bridget retrieved it from the top of a fence post and carried it in the crook of her arm back to Lila, who ruffled her waxy curls and received the thing like a naughty pet that had strayed from home. She'd glued worm grass to the crown, rubbed the vestigial cheeks with an epoxy resin that peeled to give the effect of flaking skin, inserted jujubes in the empty sockets for eyes, a lump of coal for a swollen black tongue. For a while the men, three out of four of whom she'd slept with, staunchly defended Lila's right to do as she pleased, even if it involved a mock desecration of Billy's sconce. Precedents were cited: Salomé, Judith, Sir Walter Raleigh's wife, who was never without the souvenir of her husband's execution on her person, but such arguments only increased the ill feeling toward Lila among the other women. In the end, however, everyone had to admit that the unscheduled manifestations of Billy's totem head were disturbing what little peace remained to us, and, in a final group intervention, we confronted Lila.

Expecting fierce resistance, we were surprised when she merely drew back the curtain of her midnight hair and readily agreed to a sequel to the Memphis exequies, saying prettily, "I thought you'd never ask." The ceremony itself, performed on a humid afternoon in the dim glade beneath the tree house, was lackluster by comparison to the debacle in Memphis. As no one was equal to the full ritual treatment for a plastic skull, the whole affair had the spurious formality of a goldfish funeral. Muhle didn't play his guitar, Finbar didn't leap, and Christopher's only nod toward oratory was the occasional tasteless aside: "Lila gives head to Mother Earth. . . ." Suzy tossed some wilted crocuses, and Muhle offered a "head" stone of his own slapdash manufacture, which we wedged aslant in the swampy ground above the hole where we planted the thing. Relieved of her relic, Lila seemed at last divested of every ounce of her old mystique. The gossip was quelled, and by the time I ran across the Keats poem about a girl who preserves the head of her dead lover in a pot of basil, there was no point in even mentioning it. The subject's having been laid to rest along with the skull, we seemed to have lost the single topic of conversation worth exchanging with one another anymore.

Not that I cared. For I was literally above it all, spending my days and nights in Billy's skygoing ark, which I'd appropriated from Norma's children, who tried to claim it as their own. They had had to be pried from the place when their mother, a dragon in her sudden determination to rehabilitate her offspring, rode up in the rocking basket to fetch them to their new apartment in town. Once the place was clear of urchins, I took over, satisfied that no one else (for the others tended to regard the place as a kind of airborne sepulcher) had any desire to come near. Then, having hauled up myself and a basket of picnic provisions, commencing to pee off the deck and dump in a bucket whose contents I tossed overboard, I found myself living in a tree.

It was a sunny compartment enclosed by whitewashed slats joined at eccentric angles, its ambience the happy balance of a monk's cell and an open cattle car. In contrast to the busy gingerbread surface of its external trimmings, the interior was penitentially spare, furnished with only a bookshelf, a deal table astride a dusty Persian rug, and a wooden cot reminiscent of the bed in van Gogh's room at Arles. There was an ornamental hearth whose massive weight made the boughs of the tree groan with every breath of wind. There were gaps between the unvarnished floorboards, the walls knotholed and not quite plumb, the laths beneath the roof shingles seething with termites. Visionary though he might have been, Billy was no carpenter, and despite the elegant impression it made from a distance, up close the recycled cottage was already in a state of dilapidation. With more charm than substance, it was at best a temporary habitation—or perhaps, like a shrine, it was never intended to be occupied at all. Still, inside it you felt like a giant. The many windows opened casement-wise onto the treetops, where the branches tossed like concert conductors' batons, and at night, through the spyglass, the Milky Way was as dense as swirled porridge. The whole structure swayed portentously in the long arms of the sycamore, but for me the motion seemed as gentle as the rocking of a ship on an undulant sea.

From my vantage in the tree house, life, which included Billy's death, was pure opéra bouffe; in fact, the whole experience of the farm seemed in retrospect like something out of an old Mack Sennett reel, the frames comically accelerated, the film aged and distressed by black snow. The bookshelf, opposite the freestanding fireplace that could never be used, was stuffed with books for boys, the Kipling, Stevenson, Barrie, and Conan Doyle that Billy had laid in as insulation against assailing demons. I read them on the ship-shaped deck that skirted the house, my feet propped on the rail like Mark Twain aboard the steamboat *Paul Jones,* while, down below, the farm was going to hell. When I looked up from reading, I had the distinct feeling that the tree house had been prepared especially for me. It was under the influence of this bias, shared with the abducted Simon and Bridget, that I sat down at the deal table to forge Billy Boots's last will and testament.

It occurred to me the first time I'd climbed into the tree house that the table was the perfect spot on which to find a note explaining Billy's reasons for killing himself, and perhaps a written will as well. The absence of the former left us with a riddle that would dog us to the grave, but the will I decided to manufacture myself—and through it, in an act of airy arrogation, to name myself the sole recipient of Billy's estate. In the beginning I may even have had some notion of trying to pass off the document as authentic, but as I proceeded, it became obvious that I was involved in an exercise of pure wish-fulfillment. I wrote by kerosene lamplight on yellow legal paper crawling with ladybugs, invoking the model of the legacy that François Villon, poet and thief, had composed in the shadow of the noose.

". . . In keeping with a lifelong habit of ridding myself of useless possessions," I wrote, "I, William Boots, alias Cap'n Billy, intend to give up the ghost; though in this instance you might call it a case of the ghost giving up the man. . . ."

Lapsing into a mock legalese that seemed appropriate to the spirit of the document, I began devising fanciful categories such as Disposition of Mortal and Immortal Remains, Dispensation of Properties Personal, Real, and Unreal—which was about as far as I got. But for a while, seated at the table in that precarious house, my lamp bombarded by beetles and tiger moths, I had the inflated sense of myself as reaping death's bounty: I was not only the suicide's beneficiary but my Aunt Keni Shendeldecker's as well.

Because she had in fact had the forethought to leave a notarized will bestowing on me her pixilated paintings. Newman's letter had revealed that, via a codicil to a testament that had very little else to offer, my ersatz aunt had left me the lot of her canvases, a bequest that, on the heels of Billy's death, hardly got my attention. Nevertheless I'd phoned her son, Newman, as he requested in his letter, and this time he was less high-handed than in our New York conversations. In truth he was almost ingratiating, letting me know that while, as her rightful heir, he'd received only her fondest wishes, he harbored no hard feelings toward me, which I interpreted to mean that Newman had already figured out a way to profit from the legacy himself. Still, I didn't protest when he said that, for a mutually approved commission (a lion's share, really, but I shouldn't forget he was doing me a favor), he would attempt to market the paintings on my behalf. There was a document already drawn up and awaiting my signature to legitimize the arrangement. He let it be known there were interested parties, and, while nothing was settled yet, he would be in touch as soon as the deal was final—provided I was game.

"Think it over," he said to my ensuing silence.

"Okay."

"I mean," he added impatiently, "think it over now. The potential buyer don't like to be kept waiting."

I supposed I might someday regret not having kept a single painting for memory's sake—there was the one of the skinny old man with chicken wings—but at that moment I was feeling more miserly than sentimental. "Okay," I repeated with emphasis.

"'Okay, I'm still thinking,' or 'Okay, you're a prince, Mr. Shendeldecker'?"

I told him he was a prince, gave him the address of the farm, where

I'd yet to receive a scrap of mail, and promptly forgot all about our exchange. Or rather I relegated it to a guilty secret; for, while a gift to me should by all rights have been a gift to our declining commune, I had no intention of sharing my good fortune.

Every few days I descended to replenish my larder and found that, having attained my sea legs in midair, I tended to wobble about on dry land. Nor did the remaining landlubbers seem to be faring any better, everyone's having apparently lost their footing on the planet. This was the result, as I saw it, of a collective identity crisis stemming from Billy's absence and our failure to construct a useful mythology around his death. To canonize Billy Boots would have been to elevate ourselves by association, but his disciples in their inconstancy had missed the boat. Oppressive as was the atmosphere, I never lingered long on the ground but beat it back up the sycamore tree. There human voices were drowned by the noise of rustling leaves, a rustling that sounded like surf during summer showers. So what if the roof leaked, the joists splintered, and the birds built their nests in the rafters, pelting the floor with their gentian blue shit; let the windowpanes crack, the shingles fall, the snails leave their silver graffiti all over the boards. At peace with my environment, I never lifted a finger toward its maintenance. Instead I read boys' adventures, dabbled at Billy's will, and pressed a weather eye to the brass spyglass, thinking I might keep this up indefinitely without ever touching earth again. From where I sat, life could be deferred until I died.

Then, one evening around dusk, a time of day that lived in infamy since the late afternoon we'd discovered Billy's dangling body, I heard a voice below making an echo as she called my name. "Go away," I whispered, secure in the knowledge that no one could reach me unless I lowered the elevator basket. She called again, and I lowered the basket, because, frightened as I was, hadn't I been waiting for her all along?

When the round wicker hamper reached the level of the deck, I saw that she was holding a large pot containing a flowering plant with crimson blossoms. Despite the muggy air, she was wearing the crazy quilt draped over her shoulders like a shawl.

In my nervousness I inquired, "That wouldn't be a basil, would it?"

"Don't be silly," she replied, handing me the plant as she nipped her skirt over a shapely leg to climb out of the basket, "it's a Judas." Though she'd uttered it lightly, the word momentarily froze my insides. "I brought it as a peace offering."

"Are we at war?" I asked, trying hard to swallow as I placed the terra-cotta pot on the table.

"I don't know," said Lila, pouting, "seems like you've been avoiding me."

"No . . . I mean, well, I've been sort of avoiding everybody."

"Everybody includes me," she replied, but her tone was distracted, suggesting that the subject was already exhausted. With her hands on her hips, her elbows making wings of the quilt, she was looking about the tree house, which to my knowledge she'd never set foot in before. "Interesting place you got here," she observed, and again I felt the frost forming on my vitals: was she insinuating that I was an interloper and the place wasn't mine at all? "So, Saul," she asked, "what do you do up here all day?"

I appreciated that she hadn't used the diminutive of my name. Except for the times when her cries of passion had disrupted my sleep, she'd always been respectful and considerate. "This and that," I answered evasively, and asked if she would like to sit. I offered her the single cane chair, but instead she traipsed across the buckling floor and, pinching her nose with the fingers of one hand, removed the sleeping bag from the narrow bed with the other. She drew the quilt from her shoulders, snapped it in the air, and allowed it to settle over the bare mattress ticking. Then, flouncing herself atop the quilt, she folded her legs up under her blue print skirt, the bed slats creaking plaintively beneath her. Winsome and easy in her movements, she was a different Lila altogether from the enigmatic creature she'd been prior to Billy's death. Would time, I wondered, have to be reckoned from now on as before or after Billy's death?

"Don't you get lonely in your tree?" she asked suggestively, still casting her eyes about. She noticed the tiny etched portrait of William Blake, Billy's patron saint, which, in one of his few gestures toward interior decoration, he'd clipped from a book and tacked to the planks above the bed. Without a word Lila tore the picture from the tack, wadded it up, and tossed it on the floor. Then she smiled, grasping her bent knees with her hands, rocking as if in time to the swaying of the aerial cottage, revealing with each backward-leaning motion the tender undersides of her thighs. She leaned back and shook out her hair, enjoying the cat's-paw breezes that precede a summer storm, her full breasts straining the thin batik of her halter top.

Swallowing again to fight the dryness in my throat, I emitted a squeak. "I've been busy," I said, hoping to disguise my uneasiness with mystery. "How 'bout something to drink?" Turning to the tea crate I used for a cupboard, I removed a plastic jug containing the dregs from a quart of Regina's homemade elderberry wine. I poured us each a Dixie cup–ful and made to steady my trembling hand as I gave one to Lila, saying inanely, "Château Wiseacre, a very good year."

Instantly she raised her cup in a toast. "*La chayim!*" she said, which reinforced my sense that she was needling me. Still awkwardly standing, I bent to clink cups, then took a seat at the deal table adjacent to the bed. She quaffed the wine like a Tartar and hurled the empty cup at the floor as if to smash it, while I tried to ignore the trash collecting at the foot of the bed and the hostility it implied. Meanwhile she'd withdrawn from somewhere in her halter a stick of marijuana and a book of matches. She struck a match, which a prankish breeze immediately blew out, then struck another, which she shielded with her hand as she lit the joint. So intensely did she inhale that half an inch of cigarette paper was burned away, leaving a red ash to drop onto the quilt. I leaned anxiously forward from my chair to brush away the ash lest it be fanned into flame and was offered the joint. Then, with eyes closed, she was rocking again, fingers locked around her knees, the long skirt riding halfway up her mahogany thighs. Watching her face in its transports, I felt my own body playing host to a reunion of every ache that desire could levy, the weed as always stimulating my appetites.

By way of making nervous conversation, I mentioned that I'd been doing a little writing, and Lila's lids flew open as if I'd alluded to something salacious.

"Hmmm," she sighed, fluttering her eyes coquettishly, "is it about love?"

"Not exactly."

Disregarding my answer: "Are there scenes of ecstatic abandon, men and women surrendering to their most secret fantasies?"

"No," I replied, growing more uncomfortable by the moment.

"Do they squeal and go at it like rats in heat . . . ?"

"Lila"—I finally found the temerity to interrupt—"what are you doing?" Because I was onto her; I knew that this whole sex-kitten routine
was just a plea for help, her aggression an effort to conceal the extent of
her pain. Where others might take advantage of her vulnerability, I remembered that she was Billy's relict and should be treated accordingly.
With me she could drop the mask and take comfort; she could unburden
herself of confidences and tears. Toward making myself available for that
end, I rose and crossed the distance between us to sit gingerly beside her
on the bed. "You should respect yourself more," I said, stressing my concern by placing a tentative arm around her bare shoulders. She heaved a
reposeful sigh and cocked her head so that it rested at the base of my neck;
she laid a hand upon my thigh. My nose was in her hyacinth-fragrant
hair, its ebony sheen spectral in the lamplight, whereupon my trembling
appoached apoplectic proportions. Hastily I stood up, leaving the girl to
fall sideways, and asked,

"Can I read you something?"

Recovering herself, she answered drowsily, "Can I initiate you into the
mysteries of the flesh?"

I pretended to ignore her, reaching for the forgery that lay beneath a
book on the table. Maybe I thought the reading would serve as a spur to
the writing I'd forsaken, but no sooner had I begun ("I, Cap'n Billy, being
of unsound mind and ruined body . . .") than I trailed off in embarrassment. Who did I think I was to try to usurp Billy's voice in the presence
of his own grieving lady? Stealing a peek over the top of the page, I saw
that Lila had knitted her brow in consternation. "It was a not-so-funny
joke," I lamely explained, grateful that she seemed to let it go. She leaned
back again on her elbows, legs carelessly splayed, a gumdrop-size nipple
poking out of the halter she'd untied from around her neck.

"C'mon, Sauly,"—there was the diminutive—"let me be your nympho
love slut. Isn't it time you got lucky?"

"Stop it, Lila." I was feeling nauseous.

"What's the matter? You afraid you can't follow Billy's act?"

And Muhle's and Finbar's and Christopher's, I thought, and God
knows who else she'd dragged home from the taverns in town.

"You know, Billy wasn't really so hot in the sack," she continued, her prurience acquiring a sharper edge. "Fact is, he didn't know a clitoris from a genital wart. Hell, he could hardly find the business end of a woman. Like you, he never grew up. I mean, look at this place—a little boy builds a big birdhouse, then ties a rope around his neck and tries to fly . . ." Having put down the fake will, I was bankrupt of defenses. "So, Sauly, are you soldiering on in Billy's place? It's not so hard to take Billy's place, is it? Is it hard?" Her gaze had dropped to below my waist. Then, kicking off her sandals, she lifted her legs and planted her heels wide apart on the mattress.

"Billy's dead," I said, as if she needed reminding.

"That's exactly what I mean."

"Eh?"

"Aren't you kind of a proxy dead man yourself?" At that moment I could have believed she was a witch. "C'mon, Sauly, don't be scared," she taunted, "I need some consolation. Can't you show me you're alive?"

Short of surrendering to my first impulse, which was to fall at her feet, I shouted, "Shut up already!" It was the first time I had ever raised my voice to a woman. Then, to my relief, she did shut up, though her goading smile remained, a challenge she left me no choice but to try to meet. Inspirited by my outburst, I took a step forward and knelt on the mattress between her spread thighs. I, who in my whole life had kissed one solitary old lady, gripped her shoulders and kissed Billy's widow fiercely on the mouth. If she returned the kiss, I couldn't tell; her lips never parted, but so enflamed was I by the heat of her skin and the lathe-turned suppleness of her spine, her spun-silk hair, so fixed on the various parts of her was I that I was scarcely aware of the integrated woman at all. She was nothing to me but a means to the end of a grotesquely overextended condition, an item I'd left myself in Billy's name that I might now take possession of.

I shoved the skirt over her syrup-smooth hips and ran my fingers between her legs, finding no fabric there to impede me, only crisp curls and soft flesh as dry as a turkey's throat. Though (having after all invited me) she didn't struggle, I pinned her wrists to the bed with a single tenacious hand to show my strength. With the other I urgently fumbled to unfasten my jeans, releasing my organ like an animal that had crawled into my pants and engorged itself on my blood. An animal that, once liberated, lunged forward in a blind attempt to nose its way into the nearest burrow. Some portion of my brain was conscious of the wind picking up, rattling the window sashes and shaking books from the shelves; there was the crackle of thunder (or was it the breaking bed slats?) auguring a serious storm. Bring it on, I thought, daring either fire or hurricane to foil my intentions this time. I was anyway beyond the reach of calamity, home free inside a woman I was fucking, and nothing could touch me now.

Not even when I happened to look at Lila's face and saw her jaw clenched in resignation, her body suffering me less as a violation than an annoyance, was I disheartened. Though I had to wonder where were her trills and mourning-dove moans; why didn't my plugging away at her elicit the traditional music? But while her submissiveness provoked and incensed me, and her parched womb painfully chafed, I remained single-minded. Then my hips seemed to be laboring independently of any will of my own, as if all their thrusting had been in the service of cranking an engine in my loins, but the engine was no sooner started than it began to run down. My seed escaped me like a hemorrhage, so that I asked myself where was the grand deliverance, the explosion to rival the thunderclaps and reverse the congestion of so many frustrated years? Where the discharge like lava? Instantly I felt cheated, robbed of some essential part of myself that could never be retrieved. Was this what everyone felt the first time? I had in any case done my duty, having given the needy woman what she'd asked for, so why was I sick with the enormity of my loss, to say nothing of my crime?

Witless with shame, I rolled off of Lila and sank into a furrow left by the ruptured bed slats. The storm, in contrast to my fizzling, had graduated to a biblical fury. Rain was lashing the roof and threatening to tear the shutters from their hinges; a stone tumbled out of the hearth and gashed a jagged crevice in the floorboards where it lodged. The thick trunks that upheld the whole structure shifted and lurched as if trying to part company, which—if they succeeded—would leave the fretful house to plunge or float on air. I turned toward Lila, who lay on her side with her back to me, convinced that the only way I could vindicate myself was to have her again, this time with feeling. I tugged at my member, trying to restore some of its former rigidity, while with my free hand I reached out to the girl, caressing the hip over which she had pulled her skirt. At my touch she abruptly sat up, saying over the drone of the wind,

"This place is going to collapse."

"No, it isn't," I insisted, though any imbecile could see that the elements were conspiring to shake us out of Billy's tree. I was still kneading myself toward a possible resurrection as Lila got to her feet, addressing me without rancor, without emotion of any kind, saying as if to a stranger, "I'd get out of here if I was you."

Leaning against the torrents, she edged her way onto the deck, climbed back into the tossing basket, and began rapidly working the egg-beater windlass to lower herself to the ground. I trampled on the pants at my ankles in order to escape them, snatched up the quilt and was at the place where the wooden taffrail formed a prow, shouting into the downpour to tell Lila what she'd left behind. "Keep it for a memento," she shouted back at me, an indistinct shape moving away from the basket and the sycamore's tentacular roots. Groping for some parting sentiment, I called out after her, "A captain always stays with his ship," then could have sworn I heard her mocking me with a bar of "Rockabye Baby" as she climbed the hill in the driving rain. She, too, left the farm soon after and when last heard from was on the coast, living north of San Francisco in a remote mountain fastness that many men tried to penetrate, though none were able. Later, it was rumored that she married a rich man who gave her beautiful children and that she took to wearing tennis skirts. . . .

Left standing on the rain-pummeled deck, while the house heaved and pitched, the windows shattered, and the shingles (along with the fake will and testament and the Judas plant on the traveling table) blew away, I continued to tug at my limp dick. Drenched but encouraged at having achieved a minimal erection, I mounted the rail and straddled a broad bough, one of the inverted tripod of spiring trunks growing from their common base. I wrapped the quilt around myself and the bough, making the type of sling a stork might have held in its beak, then tied a fat knot at the level of my gut. Breaking off an overhead branch, I inserted the stick through the knot and wound it tight, until I was lashed hard to the stout, upward-thrusting limb. The storm raged about me, whipping my hair and multiplying my tears; the chimney toppled, its spangled stones crashing through the roof, leaving the breached walls to tilt at weird angles. Lightning struck and sizzled, intermittently minting the night in platinum, while the wind smashed the lamp globe, spilling kerosene onto the table, which burst into flames. The trees shrugged, the floor beams brayed, and as the once skyworthy structure was torn from its moorings, reduced to flying debris (some of which was on fire), despite my constraints, I jerked myself off to a fare-thee-well.

Though I managed to retain the soggy quilt, I never made any effort to salvage the pages of the phony will that were scattered far and wide. A few days after the storm, I was notified by mail that Newman Shendeldecker had sold his mother's paintings to the Museum of American Folk Art in Manhattan. Enclosed was a check for twenty-five hundred dollars made out to me. While not a king's ransom, neither was it a sum to sniff at, and, on the strength of my windfall, I left the farm confident that, should I lack the resources to attract love free of charge, I could probably buy it.

NATHAN

On the charity ward of the Gouverneur Street Infirmary, Nathan Hart, in and out of delirium, divided his time between heaven and earth. All around him lay creatures that might have been washed ashore from a shipwreck, coughing and rattling, groaning and expiring without fanfare, while Nathan, as oblivious to their suffering as to his own, hugged the pillow he mistook in his fever for the buoy of his unfinished manuscript. He slept the sleep that had eluded him during his days in the streets, his vigilant nights in the dead houses and seven-cent stews, and waked to more troubled dreaming. There were periods when he was dimly aware of his surroundings: his iron cot among a regiment of others in a large room appointed with steel-mesh windows and cracked tile floors. There was the stink of carbolic acid, must, slops, and suppurating wounds, the stink of the slaughterhouse in the lane beyond the smirched stucco walls. Patients tossed in rigors, drowsed in stupors, some comatose, some animated enough to swat marauding rats. They lifted unlaundered gowns with no backsides to squat over enamel chamber pots, spit a yellow bile into the hot-air flues, wept, and cursed God.

The nurses, incongruously crisp in gingham uniforms, their organdy caps like scallop shells, administered here a laxative, there an enema or an infusion of brandy and calomel. Abetted by full-buttocked orderlies, they force-fed recalcitrant patients through dented funnels and garden hose; they sponge-bathed the putrescent, whose silhouettes resembled thrashing eels behind the thin folding screens. Once in a while, a doctor with a beard like a mitten would appear at a bedside, rousing some wretch in his final throes to inquire, "So how is Number Seven today?"

The patient would moan, and the doctor, mumbling token encouragement, would scribble indecipherable glyphs on a chart he left hanging from the narrow bed.

But for Nathan the ward existed only during sporadic bouts of consciousness, between which he spent his days in the yarn-spinning minyans of the Celestial Academy or listened, wide-eyed alongside his sisters atop the smoky tile stove, to his mama's table talk in their hovel off the market *platz*. With her wig askew, her putty face as mobile as her gesticulating fingers, Froika the Troika would regale her captive audience with another of her dead husband's tales: the one, for instance, about the bridegroom who comes upon a finger poking out of the earth and for a lark places a wedding band over the protruding digit. Straightaway a demoness erupts from the ground to claim the groom for her own. Vivid as a flicker reel behind Nathan's quivering lids, the event unfolds: as does the one about the underground forest, the crown of shoes, the legend of Nathan's father, Reb Jakob Hart, who, only twelve and not yet bar mitzvahed, is kidnapped from his home and sold into the army of the czar. Decades later, a veteran of untold abominations (some for which he was personally responsible), he returns to find his family deceased or scattered, himself a stranger to his native soil. In an effort to try to reclaim a lost heritage, he takes up with the local Hasidim, who have untethered themselves from its inflexible letter to cleave to the spirit of the Law. He becomes a *frumeh,* a pious radical, studying Kabbalah and participating in ritual ecstasies. With his pension Reb Jakob purchases a matchbox general-merchandise and seeks a capable helpmate to manage the business while he prays. He sets his sights on the spinster Froika Sara, whom he woos with the fables he's had from his mystical confederates.

The story continues: how, after Reb Jakob's murder at the hands of rampaging Cossacks (which resulted in the premature birth of her boy), Froika Sara tried to pass on to his children her husband's legacy. But the youngest, the nervous *ben yochid,* her only son, clapped his hands over his ears rather than hear those sick fancies. From the confections with which his father had shored up an unutterable past, Nathan took shelter in the *bet hamidrash.* He cleared his head with the logical conundrums of *halakhah,* the legal texts, whose formal language insulated him from the dangerous allure of Froika the Troika's tales.

And if the study house weren't far enough away, Nathan (writhing in the brine of his affliction) fled aloft to an unpruned bower of the Lower Upper Eden, where he listened to nostalgic dead men rehearsing episodes from the fallen world. Seated on gem-studded shivah boxes, they made a show of mourning the living, saving their special regrets for the more volatile of the mortal passions. These they liked describing at length and in graphic detail. But such debauched recollections were as unsettling to the prostrate ex-proofreader as were his mother's hand-me-down tales. Take for example the one about the timid ghetto youth who becomes a what you might call Schehera-*tzadik* in order to seduce a redheaded girl. Soon, however, the youth finds himself as enchanted by his own fabrications as by the girl, carried away by the evolving fluency of his own voice. But, lacking stamina, he grows weary and, unable to hang on to his galloping narrative, loses his grip on the story just as it begins to take flight. Letting go, he hobbles along in the shadow of "The Angel"'s wings, attempting to chronicle the story's progress from below; but in his fatigue the young man writes with a limp, his fingers knotted with cold, and when the shadow has so far outdistanced him that he despairs of ever catching it up, he stops writing altogether.

He huddles in the doorways of blighted buildings, wrapped in a fetid blanket lifted from some nickel flop, or in the ice-bearded ruins of tenements torched for their insurance, whose smoldering embers still rendered some warmth. The cruel places he squatted in at night spit him out in the mornings, and Nathan drifted through the streets dodging the roving burial societies lest they take him for a restless corpse. The quarter was strewn with the manifold casualties of winter: evicted families along Pitt Street and Broome shivering beside ice-glazed washtubs piled with their bedclothes and crockery; horses frozen upright in their traces, become the monstrous playthings of urchins who set astride them equestrian golems made of snow. Golems that Nathan, if he remained stationary long enough in his foot rags and haircloth shawl, might have been mistaken for.

At odd moments in his wanderings, the ex-proofreader had still heard the voice of the dissolute angel, but so faintly that it was nearly out of range, while other voices vied for his attention. Among them was the girl Keni Freischutz's spicy rasp, though Nathan never thought to look for its source. He took solace instead in the conviction that, should she see him in his current state, she wouldn't recognize him. It was better that way, though hadn't she once (in a time beyond redeeming) looked on him with a face gone soft with desire?

No longer driven to composition, neither did Nathan crave the little food he had occasion to eat. He waived handouts, ignored the open doors of fraternal halls where before he might have crashed a wedding feast. Instead he breathed with difficulty, his lungs wheezing like an accordion, rustling like a clutch of dry leaves. The sweat congealed on his flesh in the glacial winds, and he hacked a convulsive cough that left him light-headed and made him want to lie down, which he did at every opportunity. Overcome with exhaustion, he might curl up in a coil of hawser under the prow of an oyster wherry docked beneath the Brooklyn Bridge, or facedown in a snowbank behind a chestnut vendor's cart on Henry Street. It was there that a covey of raglan-cloaked sob sisters from the nearby settlement house had found him frostbitten and out of his head. Identifying him by his ravaged parcel as the neighborhood character Bintl Brief, they consulted hastily with one another; then together they packed him into a cab and took him to the old infirmary in Gouverneur Street, a stone's throw from the East River wharves.

Lifted bodily and carried through eroded portals, Nathan was confused by the overheard negotiations: wasn't everyone a charity case in the sweet hereafter? He listened hard to catch the still-chattering voice of Mocky Fargenish, no more than a whisper now, telling him of the angel's return to the world. How, having flown off in a huff, he'd had a change of heart; he had turned around and relocated the shrouded planet via the signpost of a verdigris hand thrusting a giant torch through a lake of clouds. Then he'd ducked beneath the clouds above the harbor to give his son one more chance.

On the drafty ward, the patients fouled themselves and spoke, if they could speak at all, to absent relations and notables of the day. They clawed their chests as if to open new apertures, heaved and turned up their toes, while Nathan oscillated between the precincts of his fatherless family and kingdom come. His deep-tolling cough wrenched his frame like a rifle report, and he shuddered from his fever like a trestle under a passing train; fighting for breath, he often felt he was drowning in flames. He spit up the mealy broth they attempted to feed him, spit a rusty sputum when his stomach was empty, and grew spare as a crucifixion. The salve-slathered areas of frostbite on his cheeks and hands were shrill with pain. More and more he thought he was kibitzing in the humbler reaches of paradise, where he seldom bothered opening his eyes; already dead, he was sentenced to a station much lower than that of the angels, where he was eternally flayed with improbable tales. Until the morning (or was it late afternoon?), when the sun, shining through the window grate above some sinking figure across the aisle, struck his face, and Nathan squinted through fluttering eyelids at the drooping boughs of a lone tree of heaven outside.

A nurse with a bloody towel over her shoulder, her bosom in repose upon her considerable girth, was patrolling the rows of beds when Nathan asked her what day it was.

"Bless us, it speaks!" She was genuinely shocked. "Lie back down," she cautioned in a husky brogue. "You been tagged already for the potter's field."

Nathan said, though no one had asked, that he felt better, and re-peated his question.

"It's Friday, if you must know, the fifteenth of April, the Year of Our Lord Nineteen and Twelve," he was told. "The Honorable William Howard Taft is in the White House, Mayor Gaynor is in his mansion, Police Chief Becker is in jail waiting trial for the murder of the jew gambler Rosental, and Big Tim Sullivan, God keep him, is in the Ward's Island Asylum piss-ing out a dozen holes." Walking away, she informed the patient that he was incidentally on the contagious wing of the Gouverneur Street Infir-mary, where recovery was frankly not in the prospectus.

Having hauled himself to a seated position, Nathan, sapped and de-pleted, was ready to slide back into recumbency and continue his decline. On the white metal nightstand jammed between his and the neighboring cot, there was an untended bowl of a gummy gray substance garnished with a cockroach. Observing it, Nathan was revolted, while at the same time discovering that he had an appetite. It took a tremendous effort on his part just to flick the roach and lift the bowl (sans spoon) to his dust-dry lips. The taste and tepid texture—there was a rubbery skim on the surface like a lily pad—made him gag, but he told himself that with each sip he was gaining strength. Since when did he care about gaining strength? Still, shutting his eyes (whose inner lids retained diamonds of light from the caged window across the room), he choked down the vile repast.

He reflected, trying to descry landmarks that might signal his location in time, that it was Shabbos eve, nearly Passover.

In a week or so, he was sitting up more than sleeping. While his chest (he could feel it scored with internal scars) was still irritated by the mere act of breathing, his fruity cough had subsided to no more than a parched tickle in his throat. The plum patches on his face and fingers had given way to tender pink flesh, and he'd become a virtuoso in the use of the chamber pot. During her erratic passes the sack-bosomed nurse spoke fleeringly of Lazarus, "who the heathen hebrew know nothing about." If he didn't fully appreciate her gift of gab, Nathan was thankful— though why should it matter?—that she had stopped insisting on his inevitable demise. On the contrary, she behaved as if he had already returned from the grave, and feigned a superstitious alarm at the sight of him. She hinted that his discharge was imminent—"And I don't mean, hee-hee, the phlegamy kind." Nathan wondered if her duties in this infernal place had driven her mad.

She gave him to understand that his pretense to minimal health would ultimately disqualify him from further occupancy of a hospital bed. "We don't allow no convalescent Lazaroosians round here."

Instead of heartened at the prospect of release, however, Nathan was seized with panic. Perdition-like as it was, by comparison to the streets that he'd seen more than enough of, *dayenu*, the ward was a relative sanctuary. It was in his best interests, he decided, to prolong his illness. He began to deliberately revive his sonorous cough in the hope of gaining more time, but such energetic malingering only increased his appetite, which in turn fueled the nascent vitality that made him restless. Unready to rejoin the living, Nathan knew that neither did he belong among the dying anymore.

When next the nurse (whom he thought of as *his* nurse, for better or worse) made her insouciant rounds, he asked her in his abraded voice, "With my clothes, please, what did you do?" He felt vulnerable in the flimsy *shmatte* of a linen gown.

"We burnt the nasty things," said the nurse, holding her gin-blossom nose for effect. "Besides, you weren't supposed to need them again." Her tone was fraught with blame. "Anyways, where do you think you're going?"

"I thought you were soon to outkick me," replied Nathan.

This was true, but first a doctor must sanction his official dismissal; then there was no end of paperwork to attend to. "And I repeat," said the nurse, color suffusing the ruddy capillaries of her cheeks, "where do you think you're going?"

Nathan conceded he hadn't a clue, and, having once more fulfilled her function as gadfly, the nurse moved on with a satisfied nod of her treble-chinned head.

Nathan sighed, profoundly tired but grateful for the temporary reprieve. Days could pass before a doctor appeared on the ward, and meanwhile he might drift in his lassitude, his mind blessedly barren of material concerns. But the knowledge that he was soon to be turned out of doors with noplace to go continued to vex him, and in his uneasiness, rather than becoming further enfeebled, Nathan found himself endeavoring to rise. The effort was intended as no more than an experiment, which initially failed, a wooziness having suddenly come over him, but when the vertigo passed, Nathan tried again. This time he got to his feet, remembering despite his spinning head that there was something he had yet to do, wasn't there? Wasn't there something he'd returned from death's threshold (if he hadn't in fact crossed over) to do? Inching along the cold, hexagonal tiles in his stocking feet, Nathan began to make his way between opposing rows of cots.

The charity ward was a gallery of piteous tableaux—a designated orderly plucked from among the handful of able patients made to scrub the floor on her knees; a soon-to-be-widow weeping over a figure in the process of falling where he lay—among which Nathan moved with perfect insensibility. He was a phantom, or rather its opposite number (as the nurse had suggested): a flesh-and-blood creature purged of its soul. It was an oddly refreshing idea. Then, as the vapor began to unravel like a gauze from about his brain, Nathan presently conceived a purpose. Whenever he arrived at an unconscious patient whose family had (optimistically) folded fresh garments over the bedstead, he paused to appropriate an article or two. When in the course of his travels, he wondered, had he acquired such sticky fingers? He was lifting a well-trodden pair of rubber galoshes from under a cot when he spied, through a rent in a nearby muslin partition, a desiccated old man. This one was distinguished from the others by virtue of his sitting up, an outsize rug coat draped over his shoulders, his stick legs dangling off the edge of his flock-stuffed mattress. Having secured his measure of privacy, he was unconcernedly coughing up blood, spraying the clump of pages, dense as cabbage leaves, that lay in his diapered lap.

Nathan slapped his own forehead with one of the boots and asked himself, "Did I truly forget?" though his next thought was that he ought to leave the reader in peace. There was no telling by what cunning the old *fortz* had managed to rescue the jacket from incineration, and as for the manuscript, which, if he weren't mistaken, had been resurrected from its ashes once before: how many lives did the thing have? *"Shoyn genug,"* said Nathan to himself—"Enough"—thinking what a shame it would be to disturb one so rapt in his reading. Then it was pleasing, almost liberating, in fact, to feel so detached from "The Angel" and the bedeviled events that had brought him to this juncture. To think of the discord the story had wrought in his life! But when the moment passed, Nathan was overwhelmed by a prodigal impulse that began in his entrails and invaded his extremities. He dropped the borrowed garb, pushed aside the screen, and flung himself with a whoop upon the old man. Clambering over him, Nathan wrestled his victim out of the coat and relieved him of the document in a complicated assault that the geezer was powerless to oppose.

Shaken to his bones, the sick old man wheezed a bubble that burst in a shower of red rain over his beard. "But I didn't yet know how it ends!" he complained, his toothless lower lip engulfing the upper in an attempt at defiance.

Nathan noted with some small disappointment that the poor *momzer*'s uncovered shoulders, the color of soap laved by dirty hands, revealed no outstanding appendages. He replied apologetically, "If I myself would know it what happens," pulling the sheet over the old man's nakedness, "I would tell you."

Gathering up his plunder, Nathan turned to see if anyone had observed his impulsive behavior, but there was only the crowd of marrowless sufferers worrying their bedclothes, clutching them as if to keep from tumbling off into the void. After such exertion Nathan's heart pummeled his aching chest like a speed bag and his breath eluded him, but his desire to find out what came next—in his life or his narrative?—overruled any inclination to return to his bed. Unnoticed, or simply ignored, he shambled through the swinging doors into a dismal, gaslit corridor. There were gurneys on which patients awaiting surgery were indistinguishable from napping orderlies, wheelchairs containing human bundles bound with lint dressings, trussed like scarecrows with splints.

Nathan ducked into a cluttered pantry, where he caught sight of himself in the dark amber glass of a specimen jar. His face, sere and distorted, partially obscured by shadows, by a sparse beard and fringe of greasy curls, gave him the sinister look of a ghoul. It was a face that, in the melancholy knowledge it seemed to possess, Nathan both feared and aspired to. Then, exchanging his hospital gown for the pilfered apparel (a turtleneck sweater in a bumblebee stripe, corduroy trousers whose crotch hung to the knee), hugging the bloodstained pages to his chest like a nursing infant, he felt less cowed by the face in the glass.

There was a racket in the corridor, the doors having burst open to admit some litter-borne victim of plague or calamity. Startled by the noise, a rodent-size terrier leapt from beneath the coattails of a little boy who'd smuggled it in for a visit. The frightened animal ran yelping in random directions, causing one nurse to lose control of her trolley (which spilled its cargo of mustard paste and cod liver oil), another to topple from a stepladder she'd mounted to wind a clock. Under cover of the disturbance, Nathan stole out of the building, though there was no particular need for stealth. No one remarked his leaving the pesthouse—galoshes squeaking as he descended the steps into the incarnadine onset of dusk—any more than they would have noticed his departure from earth.

He went where you went when there was nowhere else to go. Real life, Nathan reasoned, was best reentered gradually, via a preliminary passage through make-believe. Ambling up Delancey to Forsyth, heading north to Second Avenue, Nathan panted as if he were trudging uphill, but it was invigorating to be abroad once again. Along the way, pausing to catch his breath, he snitched a burlap sack from a block of ice on a distracted fishmonger's stall; he pulled the sack over his manuscript like a mantle over a scroll, then slung it across his shoulder peddler style. From a saloon opposite the Essex Market courthouse, Nathan procured, while the barkeep was otherwise occupied, some links of cold garlic wurst left over from the free lunch buffet. One piece he ate on the spot and was relieved to find that his stomach, fed on glutinous hospital pabulum for weeks, received it with minimal complaint. The other he slipped (along with a vermicide cordial he'd filched from the infirmary for just such an occasion) to the uniformed usher in the third balcony of the National Theater, in exchange for admission to the shnorrers' heaven.

Pleasantly fatigued from the long walk, Nathan settled into a rickety folding chair among the quarter's human offscourings and leaned over the dimpled brass rail. The play was already in progress, and Nathan recognized it instantly: his memory for books and plays was less clouded, it seemed, than his memory of recent events. It was *Der Vilder Mensch*— The Wild Man—by the late, lamented Jacob Gordin, which had become since his death a standard of the Yiddish repertoire. In the present scene, Lemech, the idiot son of an oppressive family, played by the aging but still sprightly Zygmund Mogulesco, was involved in some stage business with his shadow. In ragtag attire, his snarled pumpkin hair upstanding, his tiny eyes glinting like gas points, he capered with a shadow elongated under a lime-filtered calcium light. One moment he was fascinated, the next frightened, alternately projecting a childlike innocence and the overwrought sensitivity of a lunatic. His loose-limbed movements seemed at once capricious and choreographed, his elastic shadow appearing almost to detach itself and dance to its own peculiar tune. Watching the comic through increasingly heavy lids, Nathan yielded to a deep sympathy: for hadn't he himself been similarly enchanted and tormented by a shadow life that mocked his own? In pursuing it, in chasing the story whose stillbirth (so to speak) he held in his lap, Nathan had traveled beyond the limits of what it was possible for him to imagine. Now, on the verge of nodding off, he felt inclined to reject the faith he'd formerly placed in dreaming; there were more possibilities, he decided with a yawn (then wondered where such an out-of-step notion came from): there were more possibilities in life than in art.

His drowsy brain had begun to confuse the breast-beating melodrama onstage with his own checkered past. Not that the idiot's circumstances—

his whippings at the hands of a brutish father, his uncomprehending passion for a two-faced stepmother—had much in common with Nathan's experience. Yet, watching the comic's simultaneously pathetic and hilarious antics, Nathan couldn't help but discern an affinity. He imagined that Mogulesco, flinching and posturing like a marionette with tangled strings, performed in an entirely different drama, an original *shpiel* depicting the very rich hours of the vagabond Nathan Hart. It wasn't a bad entertainment, as interesting in its way as the annals of Nachman Hannah Hinde Mindl's, the thief of stories, and his reconstructed supernatural father, Mocky Fargenish; though with that tale Nathan felt he had made his peace. So much of his energy had he invested in "The Angel" that he thought the thing might now proceed on its own. Though he still held its pages securely on his knees, Nathan pictured himself dumping the sack that contained them in a paper blizzard from the third balcony. Meanwhile he was curious to discover where the tale of the nearly dozing ex-proofreader emptied of obsession (its absence a space in his scoured chest) might lead next.

MOCKY

When Manhattan Island came again into view, an alligator in a puddle of mercury, I swooped toward it by slow, circling stages. Taking a scenic route back to the East Side, I dipped low enough to hedge-hop the white-caps in the harbor; I hovered above a garbage scow and an excursion boat from whose afterdeck the passengers craned their necks—but who believed? Though you might have made a case that the packet *Fürst Bismarck* headed for Ellis Island, its steerage crammed with human fodder for the sweatshops, may have carried on board a credulous few. Afterward, having returned from the firmament to the rubbish-choked streets, I went where you went when there was no place else to go.

To the coal cellar (from which they had anyway evicted me for being a parasite), to the pawnshops, the outdoor bazaars, the various seats of depravity I used to frequent, I'd already said so long. I'd done the same with regard to Uncle Sam's Burlesque, but a lingering sentimental attachment—not to mention a strong paternal hunch that my son might be similarly drawn—took me back. I swapped a pinch of snuff for a seat among the sullied citizens of the third balcony, then plunked myself down with a terrible case of the *shpilkes*. I had strengths I couldn't wait to deploy, folded wings that could scarcely stand their confinement another minute. Having tried them and found them quite frankly magnificent, nothing would do until I felt them spanking the wind again, carrying me and my boy, Nachman, beyond the upper atmosphere. The boy, however, was nowhere in evidence, though everyone else seemed to be.

The orchestra, the parquet, the dress circle and stalls in their tacky elegance were aswarm with fine-feathered mobsters and cadets. With eyes grown lately hawkish in their acuity, I made out a few familiar faces among them: Ike the Plug with his working jaw and alderman's belly, Yoshke Nigger, Little Kishky, the canine-faced Pinchy Paul—and, from the prominence of a gilded box where he nodded to his minions as if he were counting heads, Dopey Fein himself in his Shabbos best. Seated beside him was his chief ornament and number-one girl, Rivka Bubitsch, recently retired from the Yiddish stage. This was also (I had to remind myself) the same Rivka who was the primary impetus behind our plot to leave the world, if not the reason for its temporary postponement; because I suspected that Nachman, if he hadn't already, intended to tell her good-bye.

She, too, was dressed to the nines, in a high-waisted, bottle green evening frock of lace-trimmed taffeta, a heliotrope corsage at the bodice, though the effect was typically paradoxical: the callow *maidele* aspiring to the role of adventuress, the adventuress still nostalgic for the maid. Survivor that she was, I felt sorry for the girl, who'd made her pact with the devil too late—now that Dopey's dominion was in serious jeopardy.

Indeed, there was little left of it that hadn't already suffered incursions. What with the teamsters resolved to break his horse-poisoning trust and all the intrusive municipal meddling in his extortions, with the legitimization of the Garment Workers Union, the days of Dopey's sovereignty were numbered. Commissioner McAdoo, architect of the anticrime crusade, had been quoted in the press as pledging to personally deliver the coup de grâce to the syndicate of Boss Benjamin Fein. Which perhaps explained the preponderant mob presence in Shmuel's tonight: it was an act of defiance. Hiding in plain sight, the Dopey Bennies must have decided that the "stood for" raids would not be stood for anymore, and the outlaw playhouse, likely target though it was for police persecution, was as good a venue as any for making a stand.

Before the houselights dimmed, I noted among the regulars a number of irregular faces as well. There were of course the usual uptown slummers, called "elephant hunters," to whose silk-lined coattails clung an assortment of pickpockets, panders, and whores, but there was also a disproportionate representation of the sons of Esau—swarthy types sweating pomatum and speaking a decidedly un-Yiddish jargon, whom I suspected of belonging to Jack Scipio's Five-Pointers Mob. Their presence was further evidence of the Dope's vulnerability: his wounded condition had attracted the vultures, and while the other gangs were themselves under fire, few (as I saw it) could resist being on hand for Dopey's possible waterloo. I'd picked a night when it seemed the potential for mayhem was never riper, though some might have said it was mayhem already, given the cries of the cold-borsht vendors, the screeching laughter of the harridans.

The act curtain parted, and Lazar Waxman, wearing pants with a barrel-hoop waist held up by suspenders, stepped onto the apron to warm up the crowd. After a few droll stories *mit viskers* ("So agrees the rabbi to marry Irish Rose to Abie, but only if there's 'a little Jew in her'; 'Oh, there is,' says Rose. 'Abie couldn't wait!'"), he announced the evening's feature presentation: "This is from Leon Kobrin his delightfully indecent operetta *Yankev Doodle*—but first will compete for prizes our Amateur Night talent. Tonight was donated by Schatzoff the Apothecary a case Fletcher's Castoria, which you take it like this. . . ." He took a long pull from a liver-brown bottle and, accompanied by a strident trumpeting from the orchestra, began to grimace and quake. Then silence, upon which he stepped out of the baggy trousers, holding his nose.

"Which it brings us to prize number two," he went on, composed despite wearing only his shorts. He did some more funny business with a string of salamis and a perpetual *yahrzeit* bulb, items handed him by a scantily attired chorine, before announcing the first contestant.

This was a moldy magician who billed himself as Motl the Litvak Mahatma. Dressed in swallowtails and a chimney-pot hat with an open lid, he worked exclusively with what he termed "domestic properties," releasing rats in place of doves from his elbowless sleeves. After he was yanked from the boards and the havoc among the ladies assuaged, a plump infant prodigy was introduced. He commenced playing a humoresque on the violin as accompaniment to the Dancing Margolis Sisters, a pair of Siamese twins joined at the spine. Partnered by boutonniered mobsters (one of whom was a twinkle-toed Pinchy Paul), they were heartily applauded, until a misstep by one of the sisters spoiled the other's timing and sparked a quarrel—as a result of which each stomped off with a rending of fabric into opposite wings.

The next act on the roster was a troupe of newsboys known as the Jewtown Ensemble, whose human pyramid was always a shoo-in for top prizes. The boys were announced to raucous applause, but before they were given their entrance cue by Waxman, a rope fell from the overhead grid.

SAUL

The lost years of Saul Bozoff: there was really only one, which began, I guess, under a sycamore tree on a soft spring night in Arkansas and ended in the attic of an ancient synagogue in the old Bohemian capital of Prague. When I came to Prague in the raw spring of 1972, the city, under the cloud of a humorless regime, looked like antique furniture over which a gray dust cover had been thrown. I'd traveled there on the flimsiest of excuses, something to do with a reverence for the works of the writer Franz Kafka that I shared with my dead friend Billy Boots. It was a pilgrimage, I told myself, though since jumping bail on a drug charge in London, I'd felt compelled for reasons that came clear only much later to travel east. Only later would I presume to apply to my haphazard journey the myth of the Wandering Jew, though maybe the prophet Jonah in flight from a reckoning with himself would have been more to the point.

I'd returned to New York City, where, without the excuse of school or dying relations, I had no particular reason to be. With money in the bank, I sprang for a room in the fabled Chelsea Hotel, the rococo address fretted in lace balconies on Twenty-third Street, which was a haven for artists, writers, and reclusive émigrés, some of whom went there to die. I was given a narrow room with a molting geranium and a gaudy light fixture from which it was easy to picture some misunderstood genius swinging by the neck. In New York, against the backdrop of riots and never-ending war, young people claimed they were dancing in the ruins of the Republic, but I'd had enough of the apocalyptic frame of mind. I figured that, thanks to my Arkansas interlude, my dues as a member of tragic America were paid in full. Convinced that to change my place was to change my luck, I decided that New York was simply not far enough away. Away from what? you might ask, though I pointedly did not. I told myself I was moved by the spririt of adventure, that Billy Boots had died to take away our fears, a notion that alternated with the conviction that Billy died to scare us out of our wits. Eventually I hit on the idea of putting an ocean between myself and what had gone before, and bought a ticket on a luxury liner bound for the English port of Southampton.

I decided that, having survived the scuttling of Billy's ship-shaped house, I should set sail as soon as possible in order not to lose my sea legs, or something like that. A little embarrassed by my nouveau prosperity, I had the restraint to purchase a ticket in tourist class rather than first—which I imagined as a running soirée complete with white ducks and rolled stockings in uninterrupted progress since F. Scott Fitzgerald. Three days after my visit to the Park Avenue booking office, I stood on the afterdeck of the *Queen Mary,* hoariest vessel in the Cunard fleet, watching the towers of lower Manhattan recede in the morning haze like a family of cyclopes blinking at a human quarry who'd managed to get away.

During that late-summer crossing, I spent much time on the afterdeck looking backward. Even during foul weather and choppy seas, I would hang on to the taffrail eating pills and smoking the kef I'd smuggled on board in an eviscerated copy of *Decline of the West.* I would stand there watching storybook monsters slapping their tails in the green ocean trenches, and eavesdropping on a cabal of Irish retirees in their nautical caps. Blanketed in deck chairs, they passed pocket flasks and blathered so incessantly that you'd have thought they'd had carnal knowledge of the Blarney Stone. One moment they might be comparing the character of the rainfall in their home counties ("In Cork the rain passes through like a tired army . . ."), the next competing as eyewitnesses to history ("I was in O'Connell Street when the patriots took the Post Office. I hid behind the curtain in Maude Gonne's dressing room. I came upon a Firbolg in a bog . . ."), conversations that contributed to my sense of being definitively elsewhere. Between the muddle I'd escaped and the uncertainty toward which I was headed, the waste of the North Atlantic presented me with an opportunity to review my life thus far. Problem was, I could no longer be bothered to recall much about myself prior to meeting Billy Boots and his crew. My subsequent experience, underwritten by pharmaceuticals, had created a gulf between me and my own past, a gulf that yawned ever wider with every churning knot the ship traversed.

I flattered myself that my abnormal presence caused the other passengers some discomfort, though the company at the table to which I'd been assigned in the semicircular dining room tended largely to ignore me. For the most part, they commiserated with one another over their tourist-class accommodations, which one of them, a British export merchant specializing in fine wines, characterized as a not-so-glorified version of steerage.

"Let's face it," he said, a bachelor who liked to call himself a professional gadabout, "the party on board the *Queen Mary* ended decades ago, and the ship sails now on the fuel of its own nostalgia."

These witty observations were made, as I saw it, principally for the purpose of impressing the bleached blonde at our table, and occasionally, when the bachelor's conversational well had gone dry, he might stoop to a remark at my expense. He might turn to me and say blithely, "Pass the chutney, Dr. Zhivago," or some such inscrutable dig, which never failed to prompt titters from the dapple-gray schoolmistress or the mother and daughter from *Dallas* in their identical sweaters. The blonde, however, seldom joined in their merriment, but whether it was out of sympathy for the weirdo or due to her efforts to maintain an air of mystery (at odds with her revealing décolletage) was hard to say. Eventually it came out that she was from New Jersey.

"Lily, is it?" the wine merchant had asked. "Are you the original Jersey Lily?"

She told him repeatedly, rolling her eyes to eclipse their matte blue irises, that her name was Lolly, not Lily. I allowed myself to believe that her impatience with the merchant implied some solidarity with me—for hadn't I detected that, the counterfeit courtesan routine aside, she, too, shared my bewilderment over such items on the menu as aubergines, courgettes, sago puddings, and saveloys? Lolly Fewter by name, the girl was the subject of much malicious shipboard gossip, though I suspected that the talk was in large part undeserved. A provincial girl perhaps unused to so much attention, she looked from my vantage—nursing a beer at a far banquette in the garrulous lounge—as if her only crime were her bogus pose as Mata Hari.

The most outspoken in his disapproval of what he perceived as her deliberately provocative behavior was my cabinmate, Klaus. Lard-bottomed and baby-faced, Klaus was the son of a member of the Luxembourg parliament, as he liked frequently to remind me, returning home after a bus tour of the States. Convinced that only the salubrious waters of his ancestral château were worthy of receiving his gross anatomy, he had refrained throughout the tour—ninety-nine days for ninety-nine dollars—from bathing. Of his abstinence he was almost boastful, as if the meaty odor that filled our portholeless compartment were not advertisement enough. Late at night after the bar closed, he would stumble into our "stateroom," wedging himself sidewise between the bunk beds in order to fold himself into a lower berth; then, gruntingly indifferent to my slumber, he would begin his indictment of a certain kind of woman. Speaking a slurred English for my benefit, his native bouquet (further soured by gin) corrupting the air, he complained that the ladies of the lounge were nothing but "shluts und hoors, mit painted fazes und de boozum shpillink out from de drezzz. . . ." Of course I knew that all his vixens were in fact only one bleached blonde, who, in dispensing her nearly universal flirtations, had quite understandably neglected the stinky Luxembourghese.

When Klaus had subsided into snoring and posterior reports, I sniped at him, "Is that a virgin berth you're sleeping in?" I imagined plunging a dagger into his heaving belly, whose fulminations would propel the *Queen Mary* all the way to the shores of Ithaca.

Klaus doubtless regarded me, as did anyone else who cared to notice, as a harmless degenerate, not to be taken seriously, but I was full of desires that would no longer abide their quarantine. True, I couldn't yet make the leap from wanting women to believing they might want me in return, but when I looked in the mirror above the washstand in the closet-size cabin, I saw, rather than just an ill-featured postadolescent, a species of satyr. I had the cratered face, the thicket of hair, the caprine limbs of a creature formed for venery, and Lolly Fewter, dish that she was with her jiggling cleavage, had never known the likes of me. This was what I told myself, though I couldn't have anticipated the night when, weary of blandishments, the girl herself came onto the afterdeck for a breath of air and reinforced my delusions.

She was leaning against the rail with her broad face jutting into the phosphorescent spray, a reverse figurehead. Her shoulders beneath her sequined shell were bare but for the strap of a heavy leather purse slung over the left one, which caused her clavicle to tilt like a pair of scales.

"What have you got in that thing," I asked, edging close enough so that I didn't have to shout, "the Great Books series?"

Only just become aware of me, she turned. "If it isn't Mr. Smartypants," using the affectionate term of address she'd employed once or twice at dinner. And while I'd done nothing I could think of to earn the honorific, which seemed as off the mark as "Dr. Zhivago," it emboldened me. "What are you up to, Mr. Smartypants?"

"I'm counting sea monsters," I told her. "So far I've seen five krakens, two behemoths, six leviathans, Frankenstein stranded on an iceberg—"

"And a partridge in a pear tree. What are you, stoned?" she said, obviously a little squiffy herself. She had entirely dropped her vampire act.

"As a matter of fact . . ."

She followed my downcast eyes to the lit joint I was shielding from the wind with cupped hands. "Don't mind if I do," she said, snatching the joint, which she brought to her lips, filling her lungs with a practiced inhalation. This before I could warn her that she was smoking a mixture of shag tobacco laced with Moroccan hashish, not your everyday dope. Exhaling, she began to cough violently until I slapped her back. Then she heaved a contented sigh and grinned, as she handed over the joint.

"You probably think I'm a bimbo," she said, gazing in pie-eyed wistfulness back out to sea. I could scarcely believe she cared what I thought.

"No," I lied, daring to presume, "I think you're bored."

"Me, the belle of the ball, in whose pants every lech on this ship wants to . . . ?" She snickered. "Damn right I'm bored!"

It was here that I summoned the nerve to place myself in harm's way. "What you need," I prescribed, "is to be mounted by a Jewish faun."

Then I braced myself for the inevitable slap in the face, but instead she only snorted, as if, however unconventional, I had handed her just another line. "You're Jewish?"

"Well, orthodox hippie."

Another snort. "I'm the kinda gal, you say 'hippy,' I'm thinking love handles. So what planet do you hail from?"

"No planet. I fell from the North Star."

"And blah blah blah," she cut me off. "I'm from Passaic, where I'm a . . . what am I? Oh, yeah, secretary to the commissioner of sanitation. A thrill a minute, if you take my meaning. I saved up years to make this trip. Okay, so I'm not above a little gold digging, but I thought I'd meet a . . . y'know, more sophisticated class of guy on a ocean liner, not just another flock of horny goats."

"Baa-aa," I bleated.

"That was a sheep."

"That's right. I'm trying to separate myself from the goats."

She looked hard at me, crinkling her brow, then snickered again and broke into a whinnying laugh. When the laughter seemed as if it might disintegrate into hysteria, I resolved to parlay it to my advantage; I leaned over and kissed her on the mouth. Astonishingly, though she staggered a step, she did not resist. I pulled back to find her quiet, even contemplative, eyes blinking like signal lamps.

"What was that?"

"A kiss?"

"Was it supposed to be friendly?"

I nodded to reassure her that she shouldn't take it personally.

She thought it over. "Could you make it a little less friendly next time?" Then she shrugged, dropping the shoulder bag with a clunk that shuddered the deck. The surging vibration of the ship's turbines was outmatched by the throbbing of my pulse in my ears. I saw how the wind on her freckled bosom had raised goose bumps, so I excused myself a moment to fetch Billy's quilt from the foot of a deck chair where I'd left it. In the process I suffered the scrutiny of a shadow gallery of reclining Irishmen, who were themselves comparing notes on long-ago trysts. ("I dallied one time with Oonagh of the western fairies. . . .") I donned the quilt like a cape, which, returning to Lolly, I folded about the both of us, leaning in to kiss her again. Then I did a mad thing. I lifted her onto the rail, marveling that the woozy girl seemed to trust me not to release her into the vasty depths. The quilt flapped around us as I made to hold both it and the girl in place with one arm, while with my free hand I parted her legs; I brushed my fingers from the calf of her plastic boot up along her thigh to the place where her stocking (think of washing onto a beach from a silken sea) gave way to warm flesh. I felt the garters and fantasy trappings that the girls I'd known had all forsworn. When we were fused together, her bottom drumming the wooden rail, she cried out with a mewing sound, like a seabird might make when speared by a sailor.

Hanging on to her, I let go of Billy's quilt, which flew away into the dark and settled on the waves before being claimed for a mantle by Neptune himself, who'd fallen on hard times. When we were finished, Lolly Fewter slid back onto the deck, tugged down her brief skirt, and reshouldered her bag like a soldier slinging on a carbine. "I needed that," she said with a simpering smile. "Now I think I'll go back inside and be flattered some more."

That was the beginning of what you might call my out-of-character experience, during which I was convinced that my true vocation had all along been that of libertine. I was the one with whom you could satisfy your pure animal lust without consequences, without making believe the act had any significance beyond sport. With me it somehow didn't count, and the women I met seemed quick to recognize this fundamental truth. Also, I had in my favor the element of surprise, for the ladies seemed tickled that one such as I, body like an ithyphallic hat rack, should presume to believe that success with them could be possible.

In London, when not putting myself in the way of women, I visited spots where the guidebooks advised that the past had been liveliest. These also tended to be places paradoxically consecrated to death. For instance, just behind the Marble Arch at Speakers Corner, felons had once been strapped to a hurdle and drawn to the triangular gallows at Tyburn Hill. A stone's throw from Spitalsfield Market was the site of the Finsbury plague pits, where citizens had been tossed by the score (some of them not quite dead) into a common grave. There was the Brick Lane bazaar, from whose chimneys, in Victorian times, the child sweeps were pried out daily, charred and stiff as jerky, and of course Tower Hill, where the head of the Welsh king Bran had been buried as a charm against invaders (it hadn't worked) and Japanese shutterbugs swarmed about a yeoman warder quoting Sir Thomas More: "How should I fear the shadow of the ax when I fear not the ax itself?" There were battlements atop which the heads of traitors were displayed on pikes above the river where pirates were chained to the bank for the space of three tides. I imagined them debating with one another until they drowned, the pirates, over who had seen more monsters during his respective term at sea, but mostly I tried to make up for lost time.

I stayed awhile in a tiny bed-sitting room above the Portobello Market in Notting Hill and spent my evenings in the Dog in Clover, a pub that moonlighted as a clearinghouse for every sort of illegal substance. There I remained until an afternoon when, exploring the very streets of Whitechapel that had witnessed the butchering of whores named Annie or Liz, I chanced across a curious parade. To the delight of an assembly of neighborhood schoolkids, a single file of spherical blue creatures with wavy antennae and multiple segmented arms was marching jauntily along the pavement, singing a song that boasted their provenance as the moon. Since I'd taken no chemical supplements that day, I thought this was a most unusual spectacle and, with no pressing business at hand, decided to investigate. I discovered, when the creatures announced an original production to be staged that very afternoon in a nearby park, that they were a street-theater troupe called Professor Fogg's Fun Consortium. Though I would not have gone out of my way to seek out such companions, I was intrigued by their Pied Piper–ing appeal, and once I'd seen their artistry in action (in a skit unaccountably entitled "Dancing Shoes"), I began to wonder how I might sign on.

It was, after all, almost autumn and premonitory winds, freshly arrived from across the North Sea, were beginning to whip around the London streets with stinging tails. Of course, having just done time with a surrogate family, I wasn't especially eager to find another; I had sufficient funds to keep me sheltered and fed. But by then I'd grown a little bored with my own company, and I'd also noticed, when after the performance they removed their igloo-size headgear, that the Moon Men included among their ranks several comely young ladies. So, falling in behind, I followed them back to their squatted headquarters in an abandoned button factory in the Mile End Road. There I unshouldered my rucksack and proceeded to offer my services to the Fun Consortium. I told them I was a draft dodger and assured them, when they'd gathered about to assess me, that I could overcome the handicap of being a Yank; I auditioned a pratfall or two. Only mildy amused, they nevertheless agreed to take me on at least provisionally as an intern.

At first I was a mere dogsbody, a humper of stage properties, which were minimal since most performances took place on street corners and in municipal courts and arcades, where the show might be conveniently terminated at a moment's notice. This was frequently the case, since many of the angry young playwrights whose works the Consortium performed specialized in a theater of provocation, a guerrilla theater that involved offending the audience—through insults and attacks on shared values—to the point of inciting violence. But the violence, while a measure of the play's success, had still to be kept relatively in check, as the company, like almost every creative undertaking in those days, was dependent on Arts Council grants. Consequently the offerings of the Fun Consortium (called the Fog Machine in its guerrilla guise) must have some relation, however slender, to the public good in order for the group to retain its funding, and this was where the children's theater came in. Though the players maintained an attitude of official cynicism toward the youth component of their mission, it was the participatory presentations for slum kids that absorbed their purest energies. By the time I arrived on the scene, their experimental productions were no longer the main focus of the arts cooperative, the agitprop stuff having diminished to heartless exercises, whereas the children's theater remained a labor of love.

Dressed in outlandish costumes, the troupe would parade into rundown districts where they were greeted like conquerors by spontaneous gatherings of dirty-faced tykes. Then they would stage a skit, performed either on the spot or later in the "Fog Factory," which included previously scripted parts for their juvenile audiences. The current offering, "Dancing Shoes," involved an emigrant colony of Moon Men living surreptitiously under the city, until a new branch of the London underground forces them to emerge from their subterranean kingdom and take jobs in the public sector. In the course of the skit, there were songs the kids were invited to sing, roles they were encouraged to play, issues of conscience they had, somewhat prematurely, to resolve. That was the objective of the Fun Consortium, to combine confidence-building, hands-on entertainments with a vital social message, or so the grant writers proclaimed. To say nothing of the fact that the kids' plays gave the troupe more license for making chaos than even the most avant-garde vehicles could provide. And when my own modest antic bent was eventually noticed, I was allowed to don the blue Moon Man (or the Red Devil or the Green Monkey) costume and march through the streets of London in step with the players.

Under their auspices, as gravity seemed less burdensome in the British Isles, I learned to walk on my hands. But despite all my mugging and prancing, I never graduated from the ranks, my limited repertoire a poor substitute for the fine-tuned talents of the regular performers, talents with which my sad jester shtick couldn't compete. These were men and women groomed for the footlights, some of them alumni of the Royal Academy, who might have been luminaries of the West End theater had not their careers taken unforeseen detours into radical aesthetics and drug abuse. To be sure, they were a tattered bunch, given to extreme fits of temperament, but for all their high-strung unpredictability, they remained professionals. Take Cyril, with his princely profile and Artful Dodger's greatcoat: but for his Sorbonne education during the riots of '68 that left him committed to *"épater-ing le bourgeoisie,"* Cyril's histrionic range might have earned him (as he often asserted) a place in the pantheon of English players. There was no situation in or outside the Consortium that didn't have for him its analogue in Gilbert and Sullivan, and it was owing to Cyril's archness that activities in the Mile End Road turned to light opera even as they unfolded. It was an atmosphere reaffirmed by Geoffrey, his body wound tight as a whippet's, flaxen head shaped like an onion bulb. Circus-trained, Geoffrey was an accomplished mimic, a shape-shifter whose own personality, if he had one, was subsumed by his tireless diddling of the other members of the cooperative. To be skewered by Geoffrey was a mark of distinction, though it also meant having your identity bent, folded, and spindled, then handed back to you in a form you might no longer recognize.

There was the high-flown, pudding-faced Milo, who called himself the Countess Verisoft and enjoyed wearing sensible women's clothing; and Roland, severe as a Russian icon, his lank hair half concealing his delft blue eyes, his slight body (encased in a sheepskin duffel) as stooped as Richard III's. Both author and performer, Roland was famous for his moods, which the rest of the company read like a weather report, though in fact his manner of a classic tragedian was so out of place in those shabby environs that it resulted in the broadest comedy, an effect of which he was perfectly aware. They were large characters, the members of Professor Fogg's Fun Consortium, and by contrast all life outside their sphere of influence, including the undisciplined one I'd been leading, was in danger of seeming amateurish.

But as prepossessing as were the men of the Consortium, it was the ladies that held my fascination. Take Lucy with her pollen-dusted hair and double-barreled surname, which sounded when pronounced like an opening cash register: Somethington-Thring. For all her comedic skills and willingness to strip to the skin in the adult productions (her skin like a peeled hazel wand), Lucy was cool and aristocratic in her private life, or as private as life ever got in the Mile End Road. Because we all resided behind the abandoned factory in a collection of derelict row houses, which trembled from the wrecking ball pounding the flats at the far end of the block. Each day the demolition advanced a little farther toward our end of the street. As a consequence we occupied our rooms like transients, furnishing them, as in my case, with a scrounged mattress (rat-nibbled and urine-stained) and a one-coil electric fire. At night, risking incineration, I had fairly to hug the fire to my chest in order to gain sufficient warmth for sleeping. As the toilet was down three flights of stairs and over a wall in a neighboring back lot, I generally peed out the window, for which I was often roundly cursed by passersby. But for all the precariousness of our habitation, from which we were prepared to retreat at the next blow of the wrecking ball, Lucy kept her "garden flat" as bright with bric-a-brac and cut flowers as a still life by Matisse.

She always gave the impression she was slumming, ticking off transgressive experiences like items on a caterer's list. Prone to a kind of *nostalgie de la boue,* she must at some point have concluded that no one could smear her with more *boue* than myself. It was known that she was in love with Roland—what woman in the arts co-op wasn't in love with Roland, who dallied with them as it suited him and cast them aside when his mood turned introvert? He had recently discarded Lucy, whose humiliated state became her, and I felt that it was in some part to show off her serene devastation that she'd invited me to tea. We sat drinking some chlorotic concoction from Wedgwood cups and smoking the fluted joints of Lucy's own making on the steps outside her defunct kitchen, where she posed in a dusty rose ballgown borrowed from the Consortium wardrobe racks. On her it was a definite statement, the sort of frock Marie Antoinette might have chosen to be executed in, and while the back garden was a jungle of mallow grass and purple willow herb, Lucy gazed into it pensively, as if at a bower.

At first she made superficial small talk, avoiding my eyes, referring to actors on the conventional stage as if they were intimates, as if all theatricals moved in the same society. I sat in relative silence, waiting for an opportunity to inject some personal note, maybe make my Marie Antoinette observation, when suddenly she interrupted her own train of thought to inquire, "What's it like to make love on acid?" as one might ask, What's it like to die in battle? I thereupon produced two tabs of orange sunshine, muttered an old saw about their being guaranteed to open your third eye, and dropped one in each of our teacups. Lucy drank determinedly, as if she were taking hemlock, then set aside the cup and clasped her hands over her knees, which she began to rub together like kindling, the hem of her gown working toward her lap. When the drug started to take hold, her movements became more solitary: she stretched and preened like an alley cat, threw back her head to expose her slender throat to the sun, which offered little warmth on that late-October afternoon. In truth it was a gloomy day, and Lucy's seated dance, really just a stylized version of her normally stagy body language, was making me mental. After what seemed like eons, she at last remembered me. Then she abruptly turned her back, flounced up the gown behind her, and, kneeling bare-kneed on the hard bricks of the garden, insisted that I take her like an animal. Those were her words, and even in my own simmering condition, they sounded ridiculous. But there was no defying the mandate of those pale twin hemispheres, like a cloven apple whose core, once penetrated, led to the land of infernal light.

After Lucy there was Glenda, the sharp-tongued Welsh seamstress with her gouged cheeks and cloud of copper hair, the long russet coat from which her gas-green eyes borrowed fire. On first impression (and perhaps ever after) she came across as a petulant scold, full of complaints about being underappreciated and a blanket disapproval of the flightiness of her fellow Consortium members; but if you risked a prolonged look, you might detect behind her brittle exterior a hint of mischief. Naturally, when I teased her for being an insufferable harridan, she flared, excoriating me in her native Welsh, but if I persisted, I might be awarded a sybilline smile. Eventually I became her confidant, the repository of her jealousies regarding the women who dared compete with her for the affection of the man of the moment. Sometimes she threatened to cast spells on them, Celtic cantrips imported from her home in the Prescelly Hills. This was the lunar landscape from which the blue stones had been quarried and dragged across the Salisbury Plain to be erected at Stonehenge, and all who hailed from those hills, Glenda assured me, were endowed with chthonic powers. In our one-sided conversations among the scraps of lamé and chiffon heaped about her rooms, she would sometimes agitatedly touch my arm or knee. Then I would reciprocate quid pro quo, until we had established between us a kind of sibling intimacy. When we finally fell to petting, our contact surprised us, or at least we pretended that it did: for it seemed both fitting and perverse that we should find ourselves tumbling about the wardrobe free of our clothing, our lovemaking possessing an incestuous dimension that Glenda found hilarious.

After Glenda, Rosalind, the dark Jewess with whom it gained me nothing to recall that, coincidentally, I was also a Jew. She was formidable, Rosalind, with a bone-deep beauty augmented by the dusky weeds she affected—the long black skirts, the black velvet cloak with its mauve silk lining and tasseled hood. The combination of her supple, night-clad frame, her burnt-umber tresses, and her tantalizing elusiveness was a potent mix that frustrated and ultimately frightened away would-be suitors—with the exception of Roland, who was rumored to have used and abused her as if she were anyone else. I was convinced that it was, in fact, the "anyone elseness" she craved, though all signals argued to the contrary. Even as the soubrette in "Dancing Shoes" with whom the Moon Man (who is not actually a moon man but a human child stolen by the alien invaders and raised in their colony beneath the streets) falls in love, she preserved a formal distance and mystery. It was a quality for

which I, the proverbial pal she would never mistake for a hopeful, twitted her whenever I got the chance. That was my strategy, to ingratiate
myself the way a dwarf might curry favor with a queen; and it worked.
Whenever Rosalind's turn came up on the cooking rotation, it was I she
chose to assist her. Then, side by side in the reclaimed kitchen on the bottom floor of the button factory, we split the brussels sprouts, scraped the
parsnips, braised the chops, and sliced the rhubarb for the crumble that
was Rosalind's specialty. (As the cooking was highly competitive and the
Arts Council subsidies generous, we ate well in that deserted factory,
with its glass-brick walls and obsolete signs prohibiting frequent toilet
breaks.) And all the while we steamed and broiled, scalloped and seared
at Rosalind's instruction, I made fun of her vintage getup.

"Why do you always dress like the French Lieutenant's Woman?" I
had asked her more than once. "Don't you have, maybe, a nice party
frock, something in, say, a modest floral print?"

The question was especially pertinent on an evening when the cooperative had chosen to follow dinner with a party to celebrate a favorable
notice in the press. (An unfavorable notice, or no notice at all, would
have made just as good an occasion for those revels.) It was also on the
evening of the party, around the picnic tables in the onetime sweatshop
we used as a dining room, that Geoffrey chose to target me for his
nightly impersonation. Thus far I'd been spared or overlooked as perhaps unworthy of parody, or had he only been storing up material to nail
me with? At any event, once he began to walk on his hands behind the
backs of the seated diners, who swiveled their heads to watch him, I knew
as did everyone else that I had been singled out for a rare privilege. Remarkably, he remained upside down throughout his performance, a tottering red onion with a kicking stalk, pausing behind the chairs of
various ladies of whom it was known I had had the pleasure.

"Hello, guess my name and I'll roger you. Give up? Never mind, I'll
roger you anyway. For I am Coyote and Eulenspiegel and Robin Good-
fellowstein, demon lover of the sensitive tribe." His accent was ludicrous,
but more comic for its crude approximation. "I am the creaking of your
frozen knickers hung outside your window on Hanukkah Eve; I'm the
American acid eater, five hundred mikes of blue cheer I can consume on
an empty stomach without losing my skin. It's the Night of the Long

Schwantz, and I got one the size of Cleopatra's Needle. But I ain't just another ugly face—I'm the lad who can see you for who you really are. Arse *longa, vita brevis,* sweetheart: what I lack in a résumé I make up for in hot air. I'm a shtupping machine, baby, batteries included, and you can use me with impunity, because I'm not quite a real human being. . . ." Hopping like a chicken in a skillet from hand to hand.

The tables were convulsed with laughter, everyone delighted at how handily I'd been exposed, and I laughed loudest to prove that I was a good sport who understood the transparency of his means. Besides, it was an honor, wasn't it, to be roasted by such a pro, who had, after all, only advertised my prowess. On balance, I'd gotten off pretty lightly, though I couldn't say I had actually enjoyed the send-up; with respect to accuracy, I thought Geoffrey had been kind of hit-or-miss. While, on the other hand, there were those who would contend he'd done a better job of being me than I'd done myself. That was the trouble with the Consortium: all available roles were executed by the players more masterfully than we lay folk—we humpers and schleppers—could hope to perform them; the players were more effective in their contrivances than were the rest of us in our routine authenticity, and when all was said and done, there were really no roles left over for anyone else to assume.

As a consequence, when Rosalind showed up later that evening looking almost demure in a floral-print dress donned for my sake only, her availability presented an occasion I was incapable of rising to. The long tables had been shoved back to the walls against a rack of rusted augers and gimlets, while over the PA a rock band was attempting to subdue its tomcat screeching for the length of a ballad. Couples swayed and groped one another in a lavender cloud of cannabis. Of course I knew what I was supposed to do; I was supposed to take the girl in my arms and waltz her across the floor, not as some sad fey creature but as a man. Instead, having been revealed as neither one thing nor the other, I lost heart and fled the factory.

It would be too simple to say that the events of that night put an end to my career as Priapus Junior. The ladies still continued to pass me around like a recipe or a cunning toy, and the desire I felt for them was as fervid as ever, but the problem was, having renewed its acquaintance with fear, my body sometimes refused to cooperate. This had never happened before, and the increasing incidence of such lapses made me an object of pity, a condition that admitted certain advantages of its own. Because then it became a game to try to restore my manhood, a jocular operation for those who had the patience. Among the more persistent was Glenda, who, having goaded me to a degree of rigidity, exclaimed in a kind of left-handed awe, "Behold the miracle of the eunuch's horn!"

It seemed that I was still a sort of mascot.

I tried to compensate for my failings by outworking everyone else, and, thanks to a constant supply of the methedrine that had become my drug of choice, I seldom slept. In this way I earned the reputation for being an iron man, or a reasonable facsimile thereof. Though I never succeeded in rising above supernumerary status in the Consortium productions, the technical skills I'd acquired on the farm qualified me as a perennial assistant, aiding carpenters and stage managers, riding shotgun in the delivery van that I insisted (as a nameless penance) on unloading single-handedly. It was the dead of the English winter, and I was living abroad in a theatrical community; I had entered the culture, shagged the ladies, caught the clap and been cured by the National Health, purchased an overcoat. On the debit side, I was a craven drug fiend. My virtues counterbalancing my sins, I was even with myself, neutralized; I was nobody in particular. But while I tried to suppress the impulse, I kept wanting to make a more significant contribution—though what did I have to offer? Well, for one thing, I had ideas. Why not, I suggested, do a play about a kid who, for a science project, rigs up his mother's Hoover to extract the souls of dead people impacted in objects? No? Then why not a play about a mute who breathes the smoke from the stories a dying storyteller orders his daughter to burn, after which the mute falls under a spell that makes him a storyteller as well for one night? He wins the love of the dead man's beautiful daughter, though only for as long as he can keep talking. . . .

Not that my ideas were dismissed out of hand—there were assurances from those who indulged me that they had merit; I should write them up as treatments, which a duly appointed committee could then peruse. But I should also keep in mind that Roland could be very territorial about his scripts and might not appreciate my trespass, so perhaps it was best to leave well enough alone. Further, I was advised that my ideas were a little too metaphysical in nature for kids, a little lacking in the kind of social relevance exemplified by the gold standard of "Dancing Shoes." Meanwhile I should take solace in the knowledge that I was providing a more important service than the mere perpetuation of theater.

For it had fallen to me to secure the drugs that fueled the inspiration of the players and their entourage. This was my primary function and perhaps the reason I was tolerated so well. Once every couple of weeks, I was endowed with precious hard currency, a scarce commodity in Bethnal Green, and dispatched to Notting Hill, where I still had connections. There I purchased the hashish cured in goat's-urine brine for Cyril, amphetamines for Geoffrey and myself, custom barbiturates for Rosalind and Milo, laudanum for the moody Roland with his petit mal delusions, hallucinogens and dope all around. I would return with my rucksack stuffed like a portable pharmacy. I was proud of the service I rendered through repeated trips to the Dog in Clover, where I was reasonably successful in negotiating wholesale transactions. In these dealings I was enjoined by my colleagues to be discreet, since the arts cooperative was, after all, funded by the state, and it wouldn't do to be caught biting the hand that fed us. Stealth was of the essence, which who understood better than I? Or so—swelled by a combination of crystal meth and Guinness stout—I told myself, though in reality I couldn't have been an easier target.

This was how, after the new stop-and-search laws were implemented to deter those of my medicated persuasion, I was collared in Westbourne Grove while on the way to the Bayswater underground. I was accosted by a uniformed cop with muttonchops and a chin strap cradling his lower lip, frisked, and found to be in possession of at least three categories of illegal substances. But by the time the officer, unarmed as only British constabulary are, had read me my rights and detached the cuffs from his belt, I'd cut and run. Thanks to the chemical mix in my system, I believed myself capable of speeds that no copper, let alone one so thick about the middle, could hope to attain.

Somewhere between lumbering and flying, I crossed the Portobello Road in the direction of Shepherds Bush, where the terrace houses, turf accountants, and fish shops were overshadowed by what looked like a mammoth crown roast. If I squinted, I could see that the roast, with its ring of bones studded in lights, was in fact a gasometer, but squint again and the gas tank became a looming castle keep—which, having acquired a head of steam, I decided to storm. The police whistle had faded in the distance, and, without bothering to turn around, I was certain I had lost my pursuer; but I'd gained so much momentum that I continued to sprint, slowing only to navigate the space between semidetached villas and climb a wire fence into the gasworks. I crossed the gravel yard, sprang onto the metal stairs, and began the long, clanging, circular climb. Along my way a thousand frightened pigeons flew from beneath the steps, which exhilarated me as much as if I'd released them from my sleeves. At the top of the tank, the curving steel girders, which continued to soar above the broad convexity of the dome, supported a halo of lights that upstaged the stars. The dome itself, when I tested it with my heel, had a springy quality, so that my footfalls resounded like a kettledrum as I bounded across it, bouncing like an astronaut on the moon. I loped from one edge of the gasometer to another, remarking how every compass point revealed a new vista of the city, spread out like a nest of glowworms below. There, beyond a scattered deployment of chimneys, stood the towers of Westminster, the broody hen of St. Paul's, and, on the horizon, beneath a madder-stained indigo sky, Hampstead Heath, where John Keats had lived. Having kept my nose so close to the ground for so long in drab quarters, it was thrilling to survey London from a Peter Pan's–eye view. The February wind yanked my shirttails and threatened to knock me over, my woolly hair caught in my chattering teeth, but I felt triumphant, my soul as if cleansed of its slimy afterbirth. When the blinding lights were beamed in my face and an amplified voice announced that CID (Cops in Disguise?) had arrived, that I should descend or face unspecified consequences, I declared, after Jimmy Cagney in *White Heat,*

"Top of the world, Ma!"

After which, having added resisting arrest and creating a public nuisance to the counts already leveled against me, I had the wit to climb down.

I was placed in a solitary cell in the Wormwood Scrubs holding facility, my belt and shoelaces confiscated lest I hang myself. Outside the bars a spit-shined cop, manicured hands clasped behind his stiff spine, paced slowly up and down the aisle, pausing each time he passed my cell to make some menacing remark. "You're killing yourself, mite," he might say, continuing on clicking heels to the far end of the row of cells, turning around to stroll back. "Why don't you frow yourself in front uv a trine?" Strolling to the end of the row and back again: "It's faster." In the morning I was arraigned and, my trial's having been set for a few weeks hence, released on a bond of 150 pounds, which the Consortium, whom I'd contacted with my single phone call, scratched together somewhat grudgingly. I paid them back from the funds I'd only dented since my arrival in England, but for this gesture I was not thanked. First, there was bitterness on the part of my fellows that I had been in silent possession of such a sum. Secondly, there was suspicion as to where, if not from the surreptitious sale of drugs, the money had come from. And thirdly, although arrest was a risk I'd always run, the very fact of my having been nicked seemed to revoke all prior successes on behalf of my colleagues. Overnight I was persona non grata, unwelcome in the Mile End Road. Roland himself, exchanging Lord Byron for Pontius Pilate, took me aside to admit this was indeed a nasty business, that the least I could expect was deportation, and there was of course the threat of a possible jail term. "In any case, you're on your own, lad." Then, delivering a line whose campiness embarrassed us both: "You'll understand that the Consortium can no longer have anything to do with you."

I made no appeal, though, God help me, I wanted to beg them to let me stay. Divested of stimulants, I went to a nearby pub and steeped my guts in a sauce of one part whiskey to three parts stout. At one point I looked around and saw that it was a workingman's local, not a freak in sight. The bloke standing next to me at the bar, five o'clock cheeks and potato nose, noticed me canvassing the place and seemed to read my mind. "You're all alone 'ere, mite," he said, to which I fatalistically replied, "Aren't we all?" Staggering out, I stepped off the curb without looking and was struck by a passing Humber, its chrome grille tossing me into the air like a gored matador. I was thrown shoulders foremost over the louvered bonnet into the windscreen, off of which I rebounded, landing somehow on my feet in front of the car that had skidded to a halt. But rather than congratulated for this acrobatic marvel, I was chastised by the tweedy driver, who'd leaped from his car to upbraid me for my carelessness. Claiming to be a doctor, he made no move to examine me, which was clearly beneath his dignity, but instead sent his fur-swaddled female passenger into the pub to call an ambulance—this despite my protests that I felt fine. In fact I felt grand, my sloshing insides awash with alcohol and adrenaline, though my legs had turned to rubber.

Before the ambulance arrived, a squad car pulled up at the scene, and from the passenger side emerged none other than the same poker-stiff cop that had tormented me in my jail cell the night before. "Mistah Bo-zoff," he sang out upon seeing me, seated now on the curb with a swim-ming head, "you must be the unluckiest man in London!" Half a wince was by this time all I could afford him. At the hospital I was cursorily examined by a not unattractive lady doctor, who was impressed neither by my injury-free survival nor by the way I overcame nausea to make an indecent comment as she palpated my lower limbs. I thought I even de-tected contempt when she denied my request for painkillers, dismissed my impaired vision, and sent me empty-handed into the frosty night. I took a taxi back to Bethnal Green and asked the driver to wait while, as close to tiptoing as I could manage in my queasy condition, I retrieved my handful of belongings from the half-demolished house. From there I had the driver take me to Kings Cross Station under its roof like a vaulted glass aviary, where I boarded a train to the coast. I hugged the toilet in the rattling lavatory during most of the trip, while passengers beat on the door to be let in, and at dawn, feeling tapped out in every fiber of my be-ing, tottered up the windy gangplank onto a ferry headed across the North Sea.

"*Žid?*" asked the spidery fellow in the transparent plastic rain slicker on Maiselova Street in the Old Town section of Prague. He was probably no older than I, though the pulled taffy of his weathered face and the haunted eyes so at odds with his forced grin bespoke a witness to cen-turies. It was a face I'd seen many variations of (minus the eagle beak) in this somber city, which, although it was already April, seemed far from the outset of spring. On first hearing the charged syllable on the man's lips, I stiffened, assuming an insult, but the interrogative lift he gave the word diminished its sting. So I paused, not so much out of curiosity as that I was in dire need of human contact, albeit unsure that this one qual-ified. However, I had never been so lonesome. During my four or five days in the Soviet Bloc, I'd had personal exchanges with only a dour concierge and a waiter at a proletarian café that featured lard cutlets and boiled bread "dumplings." Then there was the starched and officious iron maiden at the Ministry of Fear, or whatever they called the government agency I reported to every day to have my visa renewed, and the shadow bands of black-marketeers, one of whom I suspected this rumpled joker might be.

In the moment I hesitated, he asked again, this time in a heavily accented English, "You Jewish?"

The question would have been less loaded in the streets of New York, where he might have been hawking discount matzos or scalping tickets to Yom Kippur services, but here in a city where being Jewish had once been a capital offense (reduced now to only a felony?), to answer seemed a complex affair. Still, I was grateful to hear English spoken in a land whose native tongue was composed of gnarled and tasseled consonants closing ranks about a few lonely vowels.

"Who wants to know?" I replied, which I suppose was in itself a give-away, since who answers a question with a question but another Jew?

He immediately withdrew from the pocket of his slicker a card as soiled and limp as a piece of rag and handed it to me:

Jewish Heritage Society
Present
Magical Mysery Tour
Svatopluk Lifshin, Professional Guide
11 Široká, Praha 4.

No sooner had I read the inscription with its unfortunate typo than he snatched it back again. Evidently it was his only card.

"I show to you," he said in a terse near whisper, "Jewish Prague," as if he were peddling stolen merchandise. "Seven hundred fimfty crown the individual, but for you special off-season rate—five hundred, no problem, take or leave. Also special group discount if you got group. . . ."

Relieved as I was to hear words I could comprehend, I was nevertheless inclined to tell him that what I hadn't already seen of his dreary city, I would just as soon not see at all. Moreover, after nearly a week of knocking about a place where most of the attractions were suspiciously closed for repairs, I had another agenda. As discreetly as he'd questioned me, I inquired of him, "Do you know where I can cop . . . y'know, find, um, purchase some . . . amphetamines? Some speed?"

Then right away I regretted having asked; it was foolish, the risk too great. But since leaving London I'd been strung out and insomniac, confused, depressed, aching in every joint from my accident. In Amsterdam I'd managed to score a little Dexedrine, enough to give that waterlogged town, chiming like a plague of cicadas with bicycle bells, a temporary glow. A light came on, illuminating the tableaux vivants of naked ladies seated in windows along the canals; then the light went off, the city again pitched into darkness, and, afraid of the dark, I beat a hasty retreat. Technically a fugitive from justice, I had disposed of the drugs before leaving the Netherlands, and, since arriving in Prague, the mother country of paranoia, I was reluctant to approach its wintry citizens for illicit purposes. But now I was desperate.

In response to my query, the stranger had risen to his full gangling height and dropped the phony grin. "Do I look to you like enemy of state?" But before I could offer my humble apologies, I hadn't meant to offend, he relaxed into his former slump and replaced the grin. "No problem," he said, sotto voce again. Downwind from him on that cobbled thoroughfare, I caught his scent of slivovitz and pickled cabbage, spiced (if I weren't mistaken) with a hint of gefilte fish. "What you want I can get you, bargain basement," he said, his voice never quite overcoming its sad timbre, "whites, reds, finest Iraqi, Owsley Blue Cheer LSD, heroin, mescaline, grass. . . . But first we make walking tour of Jewish Prague, six hundred crown, yes?"

"Uh-hnh—" Unbalanced by his variability, I didn't know how to respond. All I knew was that I didn't care to waste time on some pointless sightseeing junket whose rates were increasing by the minute. If he was going to fleece me, let it be purely for the sake of illegal substances. I was attempting to get my tongue around the preposterous moniker I'd read on his card, when, apparently seeing my difficulty, he offered,

"Lifshin, Svatopluk," his given name sounding as if dropped from a leaky faucet, "but am called by associates [what associates?] Svat, which is pronounced like Safed in Holy Land, magical city where Jewish wizards are traveling house to house on flying prayer shawls."

I don't know what the guy took me for that he felt compelled to lay it on so thick. What was left of my instincts told me he wasn't worth the trouble, but, having found an English-speaking contact in those unfriendly streets, I was loath to let him go. "Svat—" I started, immediately uncomfortable with the intimacy the diminutive implied, "—opluk, I'm not a tourist. I'm an American abuser of drugs in urgent need of a little of what he fancies." Also, I was thinking, I did the Jews already.

"And I," he replied, swelling again, sweeping the greasy hair from his forehead as if to lift the shade on his baleful eyes, "am experienced . . . what you call? . . . cicerone? with mission to introduce visitors of our sublime and martyred city to rich ethnic history. First make tour," he insisted, "then abuse substance. No problem."

I sighed: there was no room left for negotiation. "Okay," I conceded, handing over a five-hundred-crown note, "you win." He reminded me of the extra hundred, which he explained as VAT or some such, plus another 150 in advance of the promised additional service. I watched his brows rise and fall beneath a crest of stringy hair, half expecting his hooded eyes to roll like cylinders in a slot machine, as I tendered the cash; then, clearly vivified by the transaction, he plunged into motion.

It hadn't been easy to get there; in Amsterdam they'd sent me from consulate to embassy back to consulate again to secure a visa. I'd ridden dingy trains that, as if literally turning back time, changed from diesel engines to steam as they traveled farther east. I crossed border checkpoints where submachine-gun-toting police entered my sleeping compartment in the middle of the night to inspect my papers and solicit bribes. Whenever, during the journey, I recalled that I was a wanted man, a suitably straitened expression would lay hold of my features, but I knew perfectly well I was small fry; there was no Inspector Javert obsessed with my capture. Nobody was in pursuit—so why was I traveling so unthinkably far afield? *Far from what?* Still I continued heading east, trying to will an unpremeditated impulse into a necessary quest.

Billy Boots had sometimes spoken of Prague in that way he had of sounding familiar with places he'd never been. He pictured himself strolling arm in arm through crooked streets with Franz Kafka, whom he portrayed as a Charlie Chaplin figure oppressed by a city that traded in things for which he (Kafka) had no tolerance, such as magic and

beauty. Billy imagined cajoling his buddy Franz into a degree of tolerance. But this was the same paradoxical Billy who had courted death
throughout his brief life and declared that the Prague he'd never seen was
death's capital. There, in the words of Billy quoting Kafka, "with our eyes
open we walk through a dream, ourselves only the ghosts of a vanished
age." Very ooga-booga and all that, but by the time I arrived, the ghosts,
too, seemed to be sound asleep.

They were unlikely boosters, Billy and Kafka: death and dusty burea-
cratic corridors made for poor Chamber of Commerce copy and did not
advertise the city to its best advantage. But at the same time, I'd heard
that Prague was beautiful, virtually untouched by the war, its storied architectural treasures left perfectly intact. Beauty might be just the thing
to soothe my desolation; it was anyway the straw I clutched at. So I suffered the indignities of the journey, passed through whorls of barbed
wire and red tape to reach a city where everyone looked as scared as I
felt. It did not give me a sense of belonging. A condition of my being in
Prague was that my already limited visa might be revoked at any moment, and without ceremony I would be sent packing back to the West. I
half hoped the time would come soon. But in breathing the city's toxic
air, I had compounded my own private malaise; I'd reached an outpost
in the middle of Europe that was neither East nor West but stood at a
threshold, or on a cusp if you like, of two worlds, and, wandering about
it, I couldn't tell if I were coming or going.

I'd taken a room with a sloping floor off a loggia-like courtyard on a
steep street crisscrossed with clotheslines in the Mala Strana, the Little
Quarter below the fenestrated walls of Prague Castle; I registered with
the designated bureau and reported daily, bringing in the receipts that
proved I was spending a sufficient per diem to justify my stay. Imperial-
ist running dog that they no doubt thought I was, the authorities would
nonetheless have been content to let me stay until my money ran out, but
it was hard to find ways to spend even the minimal specified sum. Most
museums, galleries, and churches were closed to the public, undergoing
endless repairs—or so said the regime, who made certain that the great-
est sources of national pride were obscured by superstructures of steel
scaffolding. Even some of the sculpted saints along the historic Charles
Bridge, in the name of protecting them from decay, had been shrouded

in burlap like kidnap victims, and most of the elegant old marble-and-brass cafés had been closed to discourage gatherings of dissidents. There were a few decent-looking restaurants in vaulted cellars and faded palaces, amazingly cheap by Western standards, but they were full of apparatchik types in library-frame glasses, never mind the Gypsy musicians playing polkas. So I ate when I ate at stand-up cafeterias, leaving schnitzels like wood pulp in cloying sauces mostly untouched, circulating the bulk of my currency in beer halls among men as stolid as the cast of Fritz Lang's *Metropolis*. I left generous tips that the good Marxist barkeeps pretended to be insulted by.

There were dark passages hung with crimson placards around Wenceslaus Square, where hard-bitten prostitutes wobbled on stiletto heels, and I supposed I could have exhausted my funds on them, but desire was no longer active in me. All my appetites seemed, like the city's main attractions, to be shut down until further notice. I was too weary even to attempt the forbidding language, indifferent to the suspicion that I was watched by men in shiny, box-back suits. At some point, having checked my background and determined that I was on the run from the law, they would pick me up and attach electrodes to my privates to exact a confession; then my screams would merge with those I thought I heard from the caged windows of baroque buildings, their lintels upheld by granite giants. But my enervated senses were proving themselves unreliable, and, besides the bruises I'd sustained from my collision with a moving vehicle, I suffered lapses of memory; or rather past events seemed flat and foreshortened like stacked scenery gathering dust in the wings. Prague itself was already a memory that refused to come alive.

"The streets of Prague—please to notice—" said Svatopluk, his tongue seemingly on automatic pilot; he was walking slightly ahead of me, his torso canted backward, arms drooping, as if he were the passenger of his own scrawny legs. "The streets of Prague, as you may know, correspond to configurations of human brain. Think brain of Franze Kafky, eighteen and eighty-two to nineteen and twenty-four, Czech author of Jewish extraction whose works are proscribed for decadent modernism in current political climate. To negotiate thoroughfares of Prague is, in manner of speaking, to explore brain of Franz Kafka, though many other strenuous

Jewish brains also repeat map of city. But Kafka, assimilated and godless writer in German language, is representative Jew of Prague and is logical starting point of tour. Following convolutions of Kafka's brain, we make circuitous journey into Jewish past. . . ." All of this delivered in a matter-of-fact, though richly resonant voice, reciting a script he apparently had by heart.

I wondered what I had gotten myself into. Not that there was much danger of his arousing my interest, since any interest on my part depended on the aid of stimulants, but I nevertheless wanted to nip his efforts in the bud. He needn't waste his breath on me concerning Kafka; I did Kafka already. "It's all right, Svatopluk"—pronouncing his name seemed somehow a joke on me—"save it for your real customers. Just show me the goods."

He turned and shushed me with a finger to his polypy lips, then became reassuring—"No problem"—after which he promptly cranked up his shpiel again. Once in a while, his nonstop monotone seemed about to break into some ardent expression, which he instantly choked down. In this way he led me on a wild-goose route through the Old Town streets, conducting me despite the hazy brightness of the late afternoon farther into shadows. Was this some tactic to evade the surveillance of the box-back suits, or was he, like a pilgrim retracing a labyrinth on a cathedral floor, simply being true to his theory of the "convoluted brain"? I told myself that, notwithstanding my reasons for coming to Prague in the first place, I couldn't care less.

"Please to remark building on left side of square," he was saying, pointing with his wispy chin toward an undistinguished socialist heap. "This is site where Kafka is born, though all that is original is doorpost, upon which you will notice no mezuzah hangs. When Kafka is child in knee pants with center-parted hair like jackdaw wings, he is dragged by sadistic nursemaid out of door to school. Tearfully he looks over his shoulder, and what does he see?"

I looked down Kaprova Street toward the river beyond which loomed Petřín Hill and the spires of St. Vitus like masts above the Hrad, its eggshell prow riding a swell of red roofs. "The Castle," I said, irked with myself for playing his stupid game but more disturbed by the pride I felt when he commended my answer.

"Kafka,"continued Svat, pedagogically, "was inventor of twentieth century, sounding theme which reverberates more loud with every year. The theme, as you"—swiveling his head as if to imply especially me—"are aware, is fear, and Kafka, because he is afraid of everything, is fear's prophet. Fear is concept he is getting from Jews, who are cultivating it for ages: fear of capricious tyrants, of blood libel and mob that makes of ghetto a charnel house, fear of own *pipik,* of love, fear of horrors that often preview in Prague before they are exported to rest of Europe. World bequeaths to Jews raw material for manufacture of fear, which Jews are refining over centuries, until fear is rectified to perfection in person of Kafka." Then, without altering his teacherly cadence, he got personal. "Dissolute individual such as yourself brings to Prague his own trifling fears the way human target returns to knife thrower his knives. Every Jew comes to Prague is *baal tshuveh,* master of return. This is corollary to mystical notion of *tikkun,* repairing of universe, in which scattered sparks of righteousness are restored to celestial source. In century of Kafka, who shares Jewish legacy of fear with world, best one can do is carry fears back to place they are broadcast from."

What the hell was he talking about? As if I didn't know. It was a discourse worthy of Billy Boots's own mumbo jumbo, the sort of half-baked erudition that might play well to the gallery, but I for one lacked the patience to pay heed. As far as I was concerned, the city of Prague was fast asleep—a sleeping beauty I had no wish to wake up. I was, after all, no prince, nor was I in a kissing mood. The only interesting thing about what my eccentric guide had to say was how he said it, so I asked, as much to change the subject as out of curiosity, "Where did you learn your English, Svat?"

He replied without skipping a beat in his practiced tone, "I am gifted with language, have English in which I am excellently fluent, dispensing with articles not from ignorance but because they are unnecessary, employing occasional malapropism for humility's sake. I have Czech, Deutsch, Russian, a *bisl* Yiddish, some Hebrew—air of Prague is full of tongues, as is my home. My father is polyglottal professor of German literature at Charles University until 1954, when falsely accused of being Trotskyite traitor, he is tried, convicted, and sentenced to salt mine, from which he never returns. This is long ago when I am boy but is sorrow upon which one's life is predicated. Being spoiled bourgeois parasite yourself, you can know nothing of such sorrow. If what I say to you is repeated, I, too, may be arrested, but as I am confident that all I tell you falls on deaf ears, it is no matter. For paraphrase of this sentiment, I refer you to famous epigraph to 'Prufrock' by T. S. Eliot which he is taking from Dante. . . ."

If berating me was included in the price of the tour, it was another feature I could have done without. How dare he make such snap judgments about me, even if they might be more or less accurate? Had I any pride, I'd have told the voluble crackpot where to get off, but I badly required the service he claimed to offer, and so I kept mum. Meanwhile, all about us, the streets of the old capital did their best to illustrate the idea of hopelessness: A squad of soldiers in brown tunics were scrubbing some presumably anti-Russian graffiti from the wall of an arcade, just as I supposed they would rub out the perpetrator in time. A drunk, stumbling out of a doorway, was expedited in his headlong fall into the gutter by the truncheons of a pair of passing police. A lit cigarette was tossed from the window of a sputtering Tatra, the headlight in the center of its hood like a luminous snout, while, single-minded as the Ancient Mariner, Svatopluk persisted in his narrative.

"City is also, you will observe, preoccupied with mortality. This you see in Town Hall astrological clock, where Death, like master beckoning servant, tugs bell to chime hour. Memento mori greet one at every turn: Chapel of Dead in Church of St. Nicholas, Street of Dead in Mala Strana, crypts, tombs, cenotaphs, monuments to Black Death, which Jews are said to cause by poisoning wells. City leads one always into subterranean element: dungeons, catacombs, sewers, which one may think of as clogged cloaca of Franze Kafky, for whom irregularity was lifelong complaint. Sewer under Café Arco, where Prague circle of Kafka, which includes Max Brod, Egon Kisch, and Oskar Baum, convenes to discuss Zionist ideology—this sewer, they say, leads straight to Jerusalem. . . ."

Now I was trying actively to ignore him. The more his references took an underground turn, the more I was compelled to look up, admiring architraves and heraldic devices, turrets tossed upon a tidal wave of terracotta roofs. But as if to scold me for my wandering attention, Svatopluk asserted,

"Is not quaint spookiness served up for titillation of tourist. This is genuine existential article. You are perhaps familiar with words of poet: 'Death is mother of beauty'? Should be inscribed on city coat of arms. Did not Kafka refer to Prague as 'little mother with claws'?"

Preceded by his large feet in their floppy brogans, the plastic mac bellying about him like water wings, Svat lurched through the city at a pace I had fairly to trot to keep up with. No sooner had he noted some singular point of interest than he was dragging me through one more vaulted passage to draw my regard to yet another. Utterly disoriented, I remembered a ride at the county fair my father had taken me on when I was a boy: the Old Mill, in which you floated in a rowboat through a tunnel periodically illumined by macabre dioramas. Only instead of dioramas we had Kafka's houses—the one whose exterior was ornamented like a music box with cameo-like sgraffito images, the one with the bedroom window that gave onto the interior of the Tyn Church. There was the café where Kafka first encountered Yiddish theater and the actor Itzhak Loewy, about whom his father warned, "Lie down with dogs and you get up with fleas;" the tenement where the outcast Jiří Langer, in his *ostjuden* outfit, introduced the fastidious Franz to the Belzer rebbe, who blew his nose into his fingers while taking food; the Jewish Town Hall where, in his single public speech, the young author told the assembly, "Jews of Prague, you know more Yiddish than you think." Which applied as well to the disenfranchised Herr Doktor Kafka himself, who had caught, so to speak, the Jewish bug.

Then we seemed to have come full circle back to Maiselova Street, one of the few remaining original arteries of the old ghetto, whose typhus-infested warrens were razed at the turn of the century, a place about which (according to Svat) Kafka had famously remarked, "'In us all it still lives—the dark corners, secret alleys, shuttered windows, squalid courtyards, rowdy pubs, and sinister inns. Our heart knows nothing of slum clearance; unhealthy old Jewish Town within us is far more real than hygienic town around us. . . . '" Pausing a beat to allow the point to sink in, Svat then briskly resumed, "Is called Josefov, old Jewish quarter, named in honor Emperor Joseph Two, who opens ghetto gates in seventeen and eighty-four. He also outlaws Hebrew and forbids all but eldest son of Jewish family to wed. It is Josefov that archfiend Hitler, ordering Jewish artifacts be brought here from all over Europe, designates site for Museum of Extinct Race, which is precisely"—he swept a bony hand to indicate buildings girded in scaffolding, streets denuded of Jews—"what ghetto has become. This is fresh insight, which tomorrow is already cliché."

Who was this guy? I asked myself, wondering what Aunt Keni (whom this Jewish ghost town had put me in mind of) might have made of him. Doubtless, in her glib credulity, she'd have pegged him as one of her hidden saints, or perhaps a visitation of the protean Elijah himself, who conducted the dead via devious routes to paradise, rather than an educated lunatic out to extort a buck. Well, he might turn the head of a less informed traveler with all this hokum, but he should know better than to try to bluff a bluffer. Having worked myself up into a minor rebellion, I grabbed his elbow to ask, respectfully,

"Svatopluk, just who is it you think you are?"

At that he stopped dead on the cobbles, his fake grin a touch diabolical, and seemed to take stock of me head to toe. Then he shook off my arm and declaimed with his fishy breath in my face, "If you take silver goblet fresh from smithy, fill with pomegranate seeds, circle with roses, and set between sun and shade, eh? you got only approximation of my beauty."

"Whoa," said I, stepping backward, "is that supposed to scare me or what?" But he could see that I was quaking in my boots. At that moment the chemical fix I so desperately yearned for seemed negligible, and all I wanted was for this character to release me from what I apparently lacked the will to release myself from, to lift the spell of his palaver so that I could go home. Wherever that might be.

The sun was setting as he directed me (in the manner of Scrooge's third spirit) to look through the iron fence into the old cemetery. There the jagged, moss-grown monuments leaned against one another like a congregation turned to stone by a Vesuvius of molten centuries. As we peered between the bars, he explained to me, his attitude softened now almost to paternal, how, given only this postage-stamp parcel, the Jews had had to bury the generations on top of one another, twelve layers deep. He recited the iconography of the headstones: blessing hands for the *ko-hanim,* an *etrog* for a greengrocer, a rose for a lady named Rose, a female head framed by chicken beaks to identify an adulteress whose eyes were pecked out. Indifferent to chronology, he read me the riot act of local

Jewish history, reciting the thousand-year cycle of expulsions, pogroms, accusations of ritual murder. It was in an effort to protect his people from the endless cycle of violence that the sixteenth-century rabbi Yehudah Loew, called the Maharal, had formed his creature, the golem, from the mud of the Vltava embankment. This was during the reign of the mildly insane Emperor Rudolph, who collected rhinoceros horns and cyclops heads.

I was ready to plead "Uncle! Enough already, *shoyn genug!*" when Svat abruptly announced, "For conclusion of story and finale of tour, we proceed now to Old New Synagogue, famous Altneushul."

My ears pricked up. Was the end of this ill-advised expedition at last in sight? Eagerly I followed my guide around the corner to the tent-shaped Gothic synagogue, the oldest in Northern Europe, he had me to know, "that it replaces even older, which is reason for undignified name." From inside it you could hear a poor remnant of antediluvian daveners gathered for evening prayers. Until recently the interior of the steep-pitched structure with its crennelated gables had been stained with the blood of the *kiddish ha shem*, the martyrs slain in the massacre of 1389— "but current government, which otherwise ignores ghetto, sees fit to scrub walls clean, as blood is viewed as embarrassing anti–*realní socialismus* graffiti. . . ."

It was the reedy, beehive murmur of the old men within—or so my foggy mind perceived it—that generated the honey-colored light that leaked from the dormers and grilles of that nearly hermetic shul. As we passed through the alley separating the synagogue from the Jewish Town Hall, my guide enjoined me to "please note famous clock with Hebrew numerals in Town Hall tower, whose hands run backward, encouraging return to yesteryear." Then we'd come into Pařížská Street, lined with once opulent art nouveau mansions, their balconies festooned in drying underwear. From this vantage I was asked by Svat, stepping onto the margin of grass surrounding the building, to regard an iron ladder that climbed the eastern wall of the sanctuary to a small door high in the gable. "Which recalls ladder of Jacob, or *sullam*, whose letters have numerical equivalent to 'Sinai,' where Torah is received. This I have calculated myself, though you are unworthy receptacle for such illustrious pedantry. . . ." Here he bent his knobby knees and entwined the fingers of both hands to make a sling. "For pièce de résistance we will proceed now to viewing of golem remains."

My jaw dropped open like an unhinged visor.

"Synagogue loft," he related as a matter of course, "is where Rabbi Loew stores for safekeeping deactivated corpus of monster when monster has its usefulness outworn. Is still there today, though much putrefied, as you will see. Alley oops."

I stared at him. "What can you be thinking?"

He stood erect again and explained as if to a child, "Viewing remains of golem is traditional last stop on tour; is quintessential feature attraction, no problem. Image of golem, you should know, is buried in deepest recess Kafka's brain, which he never manages to exhume, though in diary reference to clay monster he makes effort." The consistency of his tutorial tone, I finally realized, was the deceptive counterpoint to sheer madness. Again he bent his knees and cupped his hands.

"Thanks all the same," I told him. "It was a very educational experience, I'm sure, but now I think I'll be getting along."

"But what of substance I promise to abuse you with?" As if I'd hurt his feelings. "I am man of word." His supplicant's stance was a little subverted, however, by his plastic slicker, which the wind had inflated behind him like a cobra's hood.

"Forget it, you abused me enough," I assured him. "And you can keep the money," which he'd made no offer to return.

Retaining his bent-kneed posture, hands clasped like an unfolded prayer, he allowed a gentleness to suffuse his voice. "You must not be afraid, Jews do not exist here. We are in zone of invisibility. Nobody care what we do. Also, drug with which you will yourself revitalize is stashed away in synagogue loft."

"You really expect me to believe that?"

His shoulders gave a slight shrug.

An odd thought crossed my mind, which my lips let slip. "What if I'd been a group?"

Svat readmitted the hint of his original grin, assuring me, "This tour is especial for you."

That's when I wanted to break free of him and run, but, having already fled past some undetected point of no return, I had no more energy left for flight. Besides, while the lunatic's woeful eyes were still pleading, the set of his unshaven jaw issued a challenge, and, condemned to disprove my cowardice at every opportunity, I was a sucker for a dare. After all, I had come this far. So I stepped onto the grass, placed my foot in the catapult of his hands, my own hands atop his oily head, and was instantly flung into the air. I caught the bottom rung of the ladder, maybe nine or ten feet from the ground, and felt myself pushed farther upward by the soles of my shoes. When I was securely attached to the rungs, I looked behind to see that Svat, who seemed to count human fly among his attributes, was already clambering at my heels. Impatient with my progress—having lost something of my former agility, I kept pausing to examine the rust that oranged my palms—my guide somehow managed to scramble over me. He reached the top of the ladder in seconds, where he removed from its hasp an already sprung padlock the size of an alarm clock; then, wrenching open the reinforced metal door, he crawled in. With my heart in my teeth, I followed.

There was darkness and an earthy fug more redolent of subterranean musk, I thought, than of a moldy attic—though if you sniffed, you could also catch the scent of mildewed parchment and rotting leather; you could hear the skittering of mice, the ancient timbers groaning like the ribs of a ship at anchor, the muffled chanting of the old men in the chapel below. Having switched on a penlight, Svat let its beam play will-o'-the-wisp over a small avalanche of ruined siddurs spilling pages from their unstitched spines. There were stacked Torah scrolls looking beat up and leached of holiness, and here and there the glint from a ritual object, a menorah or kiddush cup, that may have been only the bare outcroppings of a large hill of relics. There was an uncoiling mother-of-pearl serpent guarding the hill, but look again as the beam darted across it, and it was only a ram's horn. While I could not cease my shuddering, I was thankful: a ram's horn was not a golem, which, in my low-grade hysteria, I'd half expected to discover dangling by a single leg from the rafters overhead.

Having settled himself cross-legged on the creaking plank floor, Svatopluk invited me to do the same. "Now we may to relax."

"No problem," I managed thickly, and took a seat.

From a deep pocket of his baggy trousers, Svat had removed a smooth clay meerschaum with a gracile stem, which he clenched between his carious teeth; then, laying aside the penlight, he began to creep forward on all fours, as if stalking the *genizah*—a word I remembered as the Hebrew for a place where old books and Torah scrolls too precious to be discarded are stored indefinitely. The memory was involuntary, a knowledge that seemed to belong to someone else, and I was uncomfortable with having appropriated it for myself. After crawling a few feet, Svatopluk paused at a heap of dust swept into a low-lying barrow, from which he scooped up a small mound with his hand. Then, sitting back on his haunches, he poured the dust in an hourglass trickle from his fist into the bowl of the pipe, tamping it down with his thumb, whose dirty nail he then used to strike a match. As he inhaled, the glowing pipe bowl made a momentary gargoyle of his features.

"Is righteous shit," he ventriloquized from the depths of his diaphragm, his face strained with the effort of holding in the smoke. "Dust of golem is premium righteous shit." Exhaling an ectoplasmic plume as he handed the pipe to me.

Unnerved as I was, I felt that the situation had taken such a ludicrous turn that I had to laugh out loud. Okay, so now we were smoking dirt, it had come to this—and the cream of the jest was that the act somehow seemed an appropriate end to this whole fruitless escapade. I was giggling manically when Svat, to shut me up, lifted the hand that held the pipe to my mouth, then rekindled the bowl. Having emptied my chest of air in my hilarity, I saw the pipe stem (through the warped logic of the moment) as a convenient means of attaining more oxygen, and so I sucked. The taste was surprisingly undusty, tart to the palate like an essence of sugar beet tinged with chicory; and, having taken in a deep draft, I felt at once that my lungs and lights—all, in fact, that my rib cage contained—had been replaced by a gaping cavity filled with pure dread. It was a sensation further intensified by the fact that the cast-off penlight had extinguished itself, plunging us, but for the red glow of the pipe bowl, into pitch-darkness.

"There is famous passage in Kafka's diary," my guide was saying, his resinous voice my only connection to a familiar world, "which is unfinished description of wonder rabbi making golem. In it amorphous hunk of river clay sits in wooden washtub in foul courtyard amid garbage and starveling dogs. When rabbi is not present, curious neighbors prod lump of clay; they smell and taste, then spit: '*Feh!*' Maharal, who is genius but slovenly in his toilette, his underwear visible beneath sagging breeches, descends stairs with docile son-in-law and mystic volume Sefer Yetzirah. With sleeves rolled like washerwoman, he begins to knead clay like bread dough in trough, which is as far as sketch for story goes. You may perhaps want to complete yourself?"

Close to tears, I complained, "Is this a quiz? The tour's over, and now there's . . ." A brief eternity elapsed before I could speak again, during which the image of the rabbi molding his creature scalded my brain like a brand. ". . . a test?" But even as I helplessly shared with my guide the vision of the rabbi punching mud into human form, Svat presented an alternate notion: "The golem is for Franz Kafka big headache." The ache, he confided, grew in Kafka's head, spreading throughout his bones, his joints swelling until there was no longer room in the writer's skin for both himself and the golem; then his skin split at the seams, and the creature burst forth like the Incredible Hulk, thereby expelling Kafka from his own body.

" 'What do you have in common with Jews?' " Svatopluk was whispering in my ear. "This, Kafka is asked at crucial point in life, and replies, 'I have nothing in common with myself, and should sit quietly in corner content that I can breathe.' "

Highly suggestive, I saw the monster born from Kafka's brain not as a magical or supernatural creation but a *behaimeh* member of a community that trafficked in the impossible. I saw the mute creature lumbering Gumby-like behind his plodding master just as I had followed Svat, or poor dead Billy or Aunt Keni Shendeldecker, the only woman I'd ever loved; I saw the citizens of the rabbi's courtyard gossiping, making lame jokes about the golem's marriageability and his alleged prowess in bed.

"In beginning," continued Svat's disembodied voice, again shifting gears, "Adam, too, is golem of formless clay, until God breathes into him life, and with first breath of consciousness, Adam knows everything. . . ."

In a last-ditch effort to reclaim some vestige of normative reality before I was lost forever to the known world, I accused my guide with a muzzy non sequitur: "You put hashish in the pipe!" upon which it was Svat's turn to snicker, "What is expression you have in English? 'Butter would not in his mouth melt'?" Then he went on with his lecture, giving me no choice but to surrender to his words in the dark.

"It is only split second, time it takes camera shutter to snap, before God sends angel to snuff out wisdom of Adam stillborn, but in split second Adam can see by holy light, which is light God is making on first day before He makes sun on fourth, he can see to end of universe."

He witnesses his own *gilgul,* which is the journey his awestruck soul makes from host to host until the cycle of reincarnation is closed. It passes through an assortment of patriarchs, prophets, and fools, Adam's soul, entering and exiting bodies with the frequency of Kafka changing rental units, bodies that perish from fire, water, hunger, heartbreak, and fright. It escapes through the teeth of a captured Zealot as the Romans flay his skin with iron combs, only to inhabit a bride snatched by crusaders from under her marriage canopy and violated unspeakably. It dwells a while in the mortal frame (with its hideous skin condition) of the medieval kabbalist ibn Gabirol, who in his loneliness manufactures a female companion out of acacia wood, splinters notwithstanding, and entertains her with tales of the Book of Raziel. This is the tell-all book the Angel Raziel gave to Adam, who sealed it in a stone whose whereabouts he promptly forgot. The soul of Adam resides eventually in Isaac Luria, the Ari, magician of sixteenth-century Safed, who reads the characters of his students by the Hebrew letters he sees emblazoned on their foreheads; it occupies as well the earthly vessel of Rabbi Nachman of Bratslav, who hides the secret of summoning the Messiah in his beautiful stories. Distilled through the rabbi's piety into beatitude, Adam's soul nevertheless elects to remain in the world rather than assume its heavenly reward, whereas the rabbi's stories, unlike those of Kafka that his disobedient friend Max Brod refused to destroy, are dutifully burned by a faithful disciple—while the less faithful sniff the flames in the hope of recovering the gist of the cremated narratives. For a time Adam's soul resides in the slippery instrument of Hershel Ostropolier, jester to the court of the Medzibozer rebbe, who explains on his deathbed, "Not dying, dieting—I'm trying to get back to my original weight of seven pounds." And when his relations, thinking he'd expired, praise his wit and irrepressible spirit, he opens his mouth one last time to ask reproachfully,

"About my modesty you say nothing?" Then Adam's soul, with diminishing returns, is inherited by a bar mitzvah boy, so aware of the world of spirits he takes a lamb with him into the privy, and a young mother, who tells her daughter, en route to the gas chamber, the story of Serah bat Asher, one of the holy nine who were taken to heaven alive. But here Adam's bone-weary soul, choosing not to depart the young woman, becomes ashes along with her and her little girl, thus terminating its *gilgul* and the possibility of ever visiting earth again. All this and much more Adam sees in the instant before the angel comes to blot out his vision, breaking his connection to wisdom as neatly as an umbilical is severed or a foreskin snipped.

"In same manner that you will no doubt forget famous heritage tour of Prague," said Svat, "so Adam in Garden forgets everything." The floorboards creaked as his voice grew simultaneously more distant and harsh. "*Na shledanou,* good-bye and good luck, *zolstu krenkn un gedenken.*"

May you sicken and remember.

And that was how the tour guide and tutelary spirit Svatopluk Lifshin—you see, I remembered his name, though he never even asked for mine—that was how he abandoned me to reconstitute myself out of the lump left behind in the synagogue attic, while the ghost minyan cried up hosannas for the living from below.

NATHAN

Shaken back into consciousness by the wild man's noisy murder of his stepmother and subsequent bout of epilepsy, Nathan found himself wide awake in a compelling drama of his own. As principal character (what you might call the "star") of that drama, he rose refreshed; he stumbled over grumbling spectators to exit the gallery, then made his way back down into the avenue. With a hastily improvised resolution, he headed straight for the editorial offices of the *Jewish Daily Forward,* which percolated by night as they did by day. He had never really been out of sight of its tower, whose electric sign with its giant Hebrew characters could be seen from three river bridges, but since he'd received his pink slip, the building itself had seemed inaccessible, a lighthouse glimpsed from a stormy sea. He could scarcely believe that nothing now prevented him from walking down East Broadway and entering its neoclassical portals. Once he was inside, his nerves were soothed almost instantly by the rataplan of the rotary presses throbbing their counterpoint to the hornet drone of the neighborhood sewing machines. Then he was mounting a creaky staircase into a dusty hive of Workmen's Circle lectures, *landsmanschaft* meetings, conspiracies, rivalries, trysts; as well as the round-the-clock labors of the Yiddish daily and ongoing *pilpul*-like disputations among the ink slingers—such as the one brewing now about the city desk as Nathan drew near.

"Since the Triangle Fire," a mutton-faced man was complaining, his bulbous nose pinched by a beribboned pince-nez, "even the uptown *yehudim,* they get in the act. Where's the fun to be anymore a Bolshie when the rabbis are on your side?" He was perched somewhat precariously for one of his bulk on the edge of a captain's desk, surrounded by colleagues slouched against filing cabinets, seated on a cast-iron stove. Copyboys and harried slot men breezed in and out, a voice cried some impending catastrophe from the teleprinter bay, but the scribes were as insensible to it all as they were to the prodigal's diffident approach.

A florid gent with a kaiser mustache, leaning against the wooden rail that separated the city editor's office from the newsroom, was quick to challenge: "That's just like you, Krantz," poking the air with a cigar whose ash spilled onto his pants, "to jump ship just when everyone else is coming on board."

"Ah, Mistah Winchevsky," replied Krantz, a little smugly, "at least for me free thinking ain't to parrot what Moe Hillquit said at Cooper Union the night before."

Winchevsky winced from an apparently struck nerve. "Morris Hillquit delivers the goods; he's the only Yid that's got Tammany's ear, which it's more than I can say for your man Barondess, that walrus, that he *farkokht* himself at his sentencing and shamed forever the name United Hebrew Trades."

Now Krantz was the offended party. He was about to make a reply when another—a natty fellow with crow-black hair anointed in beeswax, an arm draped languidly over the top of a cabinet—took his turn. "It wasn't Hillquit was at Cooper Union last night," he informed them, looking up from examining his nails. "Where you world eaters been, you didn't hear we got now our own Joan of Arc?" He began rehearsing the events of the previous evening, when Feigenbaum the labor leader had come to the Union to mediate the Diamond Shirtwaist deadlock, "and this little operator, a *pisherkeh*, what was her name . . . ?"

"Lemlich," offered the lath-thin chap sitting cross-legged on the flat-topped stove, a comma of sandy hair half concealing a melancholy eye. "Clara Lemlich," taking up the narrative in a dreamy voice that nevertheless commanded the floor. "Feigenbaum, he's *fonfening* after his folksy fashion, when this empty slip of a thing pipes up"—his voice ascending to a sweet contralto—" 'I'm a working girl, and I'm tired. I don't listen no more to generalities. I move should be declared a strike!' So Feigenbaum

asks will she take the Jewish oath, and on the spot she raises her hand."
The slender young man raised his own. " 'May this hand wither on the
arm I now raise . . .' "

The others joined in, lifting their right hands and reciting in varying
degrees of earnestness, ". . . if I forget thee, O Jerusalem."

"Then the cops break up the meeting, and everyone they can get their
hands on, they drag off to jail."

"*Undzere farbrente meydlekh,*" scoffed Krantz. "Our hot-blooded virgins. So now she can remember Jerusalem from the jug."

"Where she wears the black-and-blue badges of her valor," added the
thin man elegiacally.

"Give a listen to Liessin," said Krantz, "the bard of Mintz's Cafeteria.
The lumpen take their lumps on the head while the bosses take theirs in
their tea." He chuckled over his own bon mot.

Then the natty fellow shot his cuff-linked sleeves to pose a question.
"So, Philip, whose side are *you* on? Maybe you agree with the judge that
the girl is on strike against God, whose law is 'By the sweat of his brow
man earns his bread'?"

"Is it my fault, Rogoff," replied Krantz, "that it thinks itself, this medieval America, in the intimate personal confidence of Ha-Shem?"

"Bernard Shaw said that," submitted the gentle Liessen almost to
himself, which gave Winchevsky ammunition for another barb.

"Originality was never the fortay of Philip Krantz."

"Better Shaw than that *trombenik* Trotsky you *patshken* around with
in Schreiber's . . . ," returned Krantz.

Eavesdropping on the backchat of the lords of the Yiddish press, whose
names and reputations he'd known since his proofreader days, Nathan had
found himself lulled into a passive contentment—which he must force
himself to snap out of if he hoped to get an audience. Sidling through the
open gate into the city editor's domain, he tendered a soft, "Excuse me,"
and was ignored.

"Look to yourself, Krantz." Winchevsky was fuming. "A little less kre-
plach and a little more dialectic might do you in your diet some good.
That's a regulation bourgeois behind you're sitting on."

Krantz slid heavily from his desk to confront his accuser. "You would
question my credentials?" he said, abandoning mordancy to mount his

high horse. "On the streets of Kiev, I handed out leaflets before your bris!"

Nathan attempted another, more emphatic, "Excuse me," tugging at Hillel Rogoff's sleeve. The columnist turned toward the intruder and started: "What's this?" though it was unclear whether he meant Nathan himself or the item Nathan was in the process of removing from a gunnysack.

"It's"—Nathan's sore heart was racing—"a book?"

"Looks to me like from Horn & Hardart its three-day-old kugel," observed Rogoff.

Then Winchevsky, grown bored with Krantz's ad hominem sniping, also turned to inspect the quaintly attired newcomer. This left the city editor, deprived of his audience, with no choice but to to join his colleagues in ogling Nathan.

"What has it brought us, this restless spirit from *di yenne velt?*" he twitted.

Suggested Winchevsky, evidently not above consorting with his adversary when it came to poking fun, "Maybe it's the lost book the angel gave Father Adam."

Nathan understood that their raillery was in keeping with tradition; it was the kind of reception a *yold* might expect from a theatrical company on delivering an unsolicited script. He wouldn't have had it any other way.

Hooking thumbs in magenta suspenders, Rogoff added thoughtfully, "Maybe it's for the 'Bintl Brief' column a long lament?"

Upon which the meditative Liessin was moved to exclaim, "Bintl Brief!"

"You maybe heard of it?" chided Krantz. "That you edited it over a year."

Liessin paid no attention. "I know this one," he declared, uncrossing his legs to straddle the stove. "It's Bintl Brief."

"What's he talking?" asked Krantz.

"He's a character," Liessin persisted, not without a hint of admiration.

"We can see that."

"A local character they call Bintl Brief on account of he carries a bundle of pages that nobody knows what they are."

"They're a book," Nathan offered again with a measure of pride. Nor did he object to the nickname, since it was more politic for the present to be Bintl than recalled as the delinquent employee Nathan Hart. What he neglected to add, however, was that the book was still unfinished, though its serial publication in the *Forward* might serve as the needed spur to its completion. He realized, of course, that this was optimism gone amok, but Nathan was curiously sanguine, feeling that his uninvited presence in these offices somehow signified a homecoming.

Hillel Rogoff was squinting at the draggled manuscript that Nathan had insisted on placing in his hands. Turning over the leaves that seemed to offend his nostrils, he nevertheless tried to make sense of their hen scratches and stains; he browsed until he arrived at a passage that he was able to make some headway in deciphering.

" 'In the beginning I could negotiate the journey almost . . . effort-lessly,' " he read aloud, falteringly at first, then began a little to get the hang of it. " 'Like the other hosts, I traveled from branch to branch of the Tree of Life with a leisurely hand-over-hand brack-y-a-shun—' *vos ist?*"

"Like *krykhn,* 'to climb,' " said Liessin, the dictionary, while Nathan blushed at his fetish for arcane words.

" '. . . saving my wings,' " Rogoff continued, " 'for the final stage of descent.' "

The circle of journalists had left off making sport of the author in favor of trying to catch the thread of his narrative. Interested despite himself, Philip Krantz lumbered forward to peer myopically over Rogoff's shoulder—until, impatient, he took hold of the text to wrest it from his colleague's clutches. There was a momentary tug-of-war, at the end of which the dapper Rogoff, recollecting his dignity, surrendered the pages to Krantz. Then the stout man began reading almost greedily under his breath, while the others strained to hear him.

" 'You know, of course, that the Tree is shaped like an hourglass . . .' " His voice acquired volume as the words—for such was the impression he gave—began to make themselves more legible. " '. . . or rather, like twins conjoined at the crowns of their heads, their feet planted in either world. Thus, in climbing up the Tree from its serpentine roots in the Garden, you found yourself, at its apex, climbing back down. . . .' "

As if suddenly coming to his senses, Krantz broke off his reading and removed the pince-nez to complain, "This is drek!" And, glaring at

Nathan, "Didn't you hear already from social realism?" He began a speech perhaps intended to reassert his authority in the eyes of his peers. "It only feeds the superstition of the masses, such self-indulgence, when what they want is an honest picture of the proletarian condition—"

"Has spoken the voice of the people," jeered Winchevsky. "Leon Trotsky couldn't have put it better." But also addressing the author, he was forced to concede that his colleague had a point. Liessin, too, contributed to the general consensus. "Your prose is what we call *der reiner,* the pure," he explained, "when what today we need is *der pleiner,* the plain. We need Gorky, his unimpeachable fidelity to the workers' struggle, with a *shtikl* the passion of Nikolai Chernyshevski—have you read his *What Is to Be Done?*"

Rogoff nodded his sage approval of Liessin's recipe, while Krantz proffered a flagrant omission: "To say nothing of the divine genius of Ivan Turgenev."

At which point another voice was heard from. "You know what you can do with your Turgenev, Philip." Everyone turned toward the tall man with his escarpment of bushy bronze hair, standing just outside the office enclosure. His eyes, behind their circular lenses, were magnified like sable fish in twin bowls; his watch chain spanned his cheviot vest like a military cordon. Having thus announced himself, he stepped imperiously through the gate.

Clearly chastened, Krantz made a token effort to rise to his own defense. "We all know your prejudice against Turgenev, Abe," he chuckled amiably. "Everyone is entitled to their blind spots."

"Turgenev's got no spleen," pronounced the tall man as if that settled the question; though a slight, disparaging sputter from Krantz triggered additional indictments to the effect that the Russian writer was a reactionary and a pantywaist. Having silenced his city editor, Abraham Cahan—for Nathan recognized the godfather of the ghetto, who had stooped to take a chance on him an age ago—turned his attention to the ex-proofreader.

"What happened to you?"

It was a question that might have been asked of anyone with Nathan's anemic pallor, never mind his clownish attire, his rubber galoshes. But Nathan chose to believe he'd left at least some impression in the mind of this personage, a notion that reinforced the growing sense of his own validity. Not only was Nathan Hart *not* a figment, but he'd come back to where he truly belonged. Of course, he knew he looked like a perfect idiot, a wild man, but standing there before the managing editor and his staff, Nathan felt he was already, de facto, a member of their fraternity. As Cahan's query still hung in the air, he looked back over his recent history for a concise explanation of his current straits.

"I fell in love," he confided at length to the assembled newsmen.

There was a flurry of ambivalent laughter, which fell off as Abe Cahan appropriated the ragged manuscript from a deferring Philip Krantz. He slid his spectacles up and down the slope of his nose until the writing came into focus—it seemed to have the property of coming eventually into focus. " 'When you reached the bottom branches,' " he read, " 'which were still too far above the sublunar world for most mortals to grab hold of, you had to fly the rest of the way.' " He paused a moment to look askance at Nathan, then continued. " 'It's written that it takes the angel Gabriel six flaps of the wings to get to earth, Simon four, and the Angel of Death only one, but I did well to manage the distance with a couple of dozen. . . .' "

He skipped some pages but continued reading random snatches, his lips still moving though his gruff voice had fallen silent. Nathan was thankful, having himself heard enough: his own words had started to grate on him, beginning to sound as callow to his ears as they must certainly have sounded to the scribes. Already he could anticipate the editor's judgment, though when it came, it was unreservedly severe.

"You're right, Philip," said Cahan with a casual shrug, "pure *narishkeit*. Exotic to be sure, but drivel all the same. Still, Bintl . . ."

"Nathan," Nathan humbly submitted, the name apparently ringing no bells.

". . . there's nothing wrong with your writing"—absently handing back "The Angel"—"that a stiff dose reality wouldn't cure."

Nathan waited for the disappointment to set in, curdling his stomach and rocking his fledgling faith to the core, but instead he felt only profound relief. Further, he was actually grateful for the attention that had been paid him, which more than compensated for the adverse judgment he'd received.

Having turned his back on distraction, Cahan was informing his staff of a recent news flash concerning a fire in a *bordel* on Allen Street— "Number Ninety-six to be exact, which, as you know, was also from the Jewish Black Hand its headquarters."

Philip Krantz, whose position as city editor made such events his special province, said he'd get Shimon Goldfogle on the job posthaste.

"Oy, Goldfogle," groaned Cahan, "I sent him already, the deficit. That one could make Masada sound as dull as a sermon in an uptown temple."

Krantz made a halfhearted attempt to defend his leg man, while Liessin, whose calm intensity lent him a certain cachet, motioned toward Nathan, who had started to tremble. Seized with an excitement that surpassed his understanding, the ex-proofreader was trying to clear his throat with near-volcanic crepitations. It's the fever returning, he thought, though was it likely that illness should feel so much like illumination? When the editor in chief swiveled his leonine head again in his direction, Nathan braced himself to contest the dismissal he knew was forthcoming. "So what you waiting?" said Cahan, and the sable fish leaped in their bowls. "Go already and get yourself bar mitzvahed by fire."

Nathan struggled to grasp the meaning of the injunction, as Liessin smiled and Philip Krantz feebly protested, "But the red lights was always Goldfogle's beat."

Snapped Cahan, "Will it kill him, a little competition?" And back to Nathan, who, not at all sure that he hadn't become the butt of renewed ridicule, was nonetheless flooded with audacity and resolve:

"You heard me, *lekh lekho*—get thee gone and write something real for a change."

MOCKY

"Ladies and gentlemen," a familiar voice rang out, "I, Nachman Hannah Hinde Mindl's, formerly known as the Opgekumener, will perform for you my original fable that it's titled 'Escape from the World-to-Come.' Maestro, if you please . . ."

So this was my son's reason for postponing our flight, I asked myself, that he wanted first to hang himself in public? But such a display would be consistent with neither his nature nor our purpose; and besides, instead of a single cable ending in a noose, the rope he had lowered was the tinseled Jacob's Ladder from the play *Dancing Shoes*—which Nachman now proceeded to descend.

"From heaven," he clamored, with a notable absence of the musical assistance he'd called for, "the journey, I can tell you, was pure hell."

First you saw his feet in their toeless topboots, then the quilt like a Harlequin's ritual garment through which he'd poked his shock of sooty curls. I waited for the audience to give vent to their outrage, for those in charge to deal summarily with the intruder and get on with the program. But amazingly the show-stopping hush that had followed the release of the rope ladder endured.

"I wasn't but just a kid when I left there," he continued in his now fecund Yinglish, "so how should I know that in meters you didn't measure the distance, but in years . . . ?" He paused on each rung of his descent to offer another portion of the story. "In the beginning like a monkey I scrambled up the balm-dripping branches of the *Etz-Chayim,* the Tree of Life. Lickety-split I climbed, until I reached the point I couldn't see no more the Garden . . ." Which was where, he explained, the dizziness set in; and feeling *"mit kop arop,"* topsy-turvy, it came to him that his head belonged where his feet had been. After this adjustment his clambering upward became a clambering down, the downward journey tenfold more arduous than the ascent. The place he was leaving, at that stage of his progress, had a much more potent attraction than the place he was going to.

I thought I understood, God help me, something of his motive in telling his tale: Where so many before him had aspired to ascend the Tree of Life, no living man (save special cases such as Elijah and a handful of screwball saints) had ever climbed all the way down from on high—Nachman alone, though himself only halfbred to humanity, had survived such a descent, and clearly he did not mean to leave the world until the story of his impossible arrival was known. I wondered if he was aware that Rivka was in the audience.

Nachman was halfway down the ladder, and the spell he'd cast from the moment his voice had been heard was still in effect. But there were rumblings from downstage, a few actors doubtless resenting the exile's unbidden return; plus, the phalanx of the preempted Jewtown Ensemble had stepped from behind the tormentor curtain to mill about forebodingly. I sucked my single incisor, fearing the worst: What would happen when everyone realized that, whatever this was, it wasn't vaudeville?

"From one branch to another," asserted my son, who seemed blindly confident of his audience, "it took you to travel many months. Sometimes you would slip; you would tumble in the dark (this was by me my first experience of darkness) and bang your head. In a fog you would wake, and you didn't know where you was—*tahkeh,* you didn't even know it who you was. And sometimes"—Nachman's roguish grin was discernible, even from the third balcony—"you was somebody else. . . ." He lowered himself another rung.

"The souls, you would pass them, and some that they got stuck on the way down—like caterpillars in spun-glass cocoons they looked. And you would see also the unhappy mortals that wasn't neither dead or alive, so who knew if from the earth they climbed up or from heaven down. But didn't none of them have the zizz to go back where they came. . . ."

He described how one by one you shed the qualities that had been second nature in the Upper Eden, such as wisdom, courage, joy; how the stale manna in your pockets tasted like sawdust and bad salmon in the lower altitudes. Then there were the times when there didn't seem to be any reason to continue a descent that probably had no bottom. But now and again, like the sod-fragrant breeze that signals dry land to sailors, a new sensation would greet you. "In place what you lost would come by you desire and fear," and you would know that the world must be close at hand.

The displeasure in front of the tormentor had grown more vocal. I could see Lazar Waxman in consultation with his surly stage manager Yonah Poupko, around whom were gathered a few grips awaiting a cue. Meanwhile, from the opposite wing, some of Dopey's ranking gorillas had shambled forward, Little Kishky and the cud-chewing Ike the Plug among them. They were looking over their shoulders for prompting, toward the box where their boss sat grumbling something confidential in Rivka's ear. Something like, "For Mrs. Klein's milk bath I had a heart, but this is strictly from hunger," I'd have bet.

While I myself had come around to the view that, as theater, one could do worse. Nachman's narrative of climbing down was after all a fitting complement to the last time I climbed up—when I struggled under molting feathers to haul the burden of myself and my child aloft. When the kid described how, exhausted, he had tumbled from the bottommost branches through a dormitory skylight on Ellis Island, I remembered falling into the Garden from the lower branches of the Tree; and there in the shnorrers' gallery of Uncle Sam's Burlesque, which some called "the gods," I felt again the apprehensive weight of my wings.

"By the time I arrived," declared Nachman over the hubbub erupting in scattered pockets among the crowd, "I wasn't no more a *shayne kind,* I wasn't beautiful. . . ." He dropped from the last rung of the ladder some ten feet to the stage, landing with a dust-raising thud, startling any still-rapt members of the audience out of their trance. "But," he added, "I remembered what it was, beautiful. . . ."

The houselights had come up, and the hooligan newsboys, along with Yonah Poupko and his stagehands, were advancing in a body from the edge of the curtain, as from their side Ike and Kishky, backed by a spiffed-up Pinchy Paul, came forward to meet them. Some carried props they'd acquired in the wings, jointed walking sticks and spiked shillelaghs. In his box below the first balcony, sleepy-eyed beneath center-parted hair like a lacquered black clamshell, Dopey Benny made a scimitar of his forefinger under his chin.

It was the signal for the chaos to commence. As one, the strongarms made for Nachman, still in the process of taking his bow. "Now you got out from your system the story," I said to him under my breath, ending aloud, "so *ver farblondjet!* Scram!" But with the hooligans and sceneshifters pressing from stage right, the angry Shmuelers from the left, where would he run? Having sized up the situation himself, however, the kid was a study in acrobatic dexterity. With the nimbleness he seemed to possess only in the spotlight, Nachman flung his arms as if tossing a nosegay to throw himself into the air. He jumped straight up, catching hold of the rope ladder's bottom rung, and began to climb with grappling hands.

"I forgot to tell you," he called out above the increasing din, his tone betraying the fact that he was having fun, "when I was on the bottom branch of the Tree, I got cold feet . . ." Stripped to his waistcoat, Kishky and one of the stagehands had succeeded in grabbing either of Nachman's dangling legs. ". . . but it's too late already," he continued despite their tugging, "since to resist the pull from the world, they don't help by you cold feet." His boots came off in the hands of his assailants, who fell backward onto the boards as Nachman hoisted himself to a higher rung.

The spectators were out of their seats, cheering the *shtarkers* and heckling my son—or was it vice versa? I couldn't tell—while Maestro Fruchter, in an effort to soothe the crowd or taunt the interloper, struck up the lullabye "Did you think you live forever, *kleine menschele?*" Beneath the ladder the gorillas had rallied, their ranks swelled by grips and shpielers and the scrappy Jewtown Ensemble—who proceeded to scramble over each other on all fours to erect a pyramid. Egged on by Little Kishky, Ike the Plug, spitting a jet of tobacco, began to scale the hill of newsboys, nearly crushing their heads and shoulders in his heedless ascent. Attaining the ladder, which he clumsily mounted, he stretched his fubsy length to grab hold of Nachman's ankle once again. Above the commotion one voice rang especially shrill:

"*Shmendrik!*" I yelled, on my feet to protest Nachman's antics that were selling our stratagem down the river. "What am I supposed to do now?"

What else, I realized, but leave him to his fate? His murder, however

brutal, would nevertheless be a tidy solution to the interdict against bringing the quick into the realm of the dead. His soul, following a routine
purging—it shouldn't take long, he wasn't such a bad kid—would eventually ascend to *Olam Ha-Ba,* where I would welcome him to a happy reunion. Of course, the dead were not free to come and go, which would
preclude his returning to earth with more stories, but had he ever truly
believed in that harebrained scheme? So my path was clear: I would beat
a retreat from the theater, leaving my son to the justice of the mob, then
meet up with him later on in kingdom come. There was a problem, however, in that my folded wings, atwitch under a shopworn dust coat,
seemed to have a mind of their own—and, despite all, their wish was my
command.

After a much-practiced shrug, I shed the coat; I tore off the celluloid
shirtfront, dropped my suspenders, and peeled the *gatkes* to my waist.
Then, preparatory to rescuing my boy from the mounting bedlam, I spread
my wings. Several old parties in the gallery, displaced by my sudden ex-
pansion, complained I was taking up too much room.

"Pardon me," I said a little testily, stepping onto the balustrade, from
which, after flexing my knees, I launched myself over the unsettled crowd.

SAUL

Rabbi Nachman of Bratslav said, *Every story has something that is concealed. What is concealed is the hidden light. The Book of Genesis says that God created light on the first day, the sun on the fourth. What light existed before the sun? The tradition says this was spiritual light, and God hid it for future use. Where is it hidden? In the stories of the Torah.*

Saul Bozoff of the Mermelman College of Arts and Sciences in Old Binstock, Massachusetts, midway between the mountains and the sea, said, *Sometimes, when I couldn't afford to pay the utility bill at the end of the month, I was forced to read by the light of the stories themselves.*

Given my poor academic record and aborted university career, I was reduced to an undignified pleading before I was finally admitted to the groves of Mermelman College. I convinced the entrance committee, through a series of antsy interviews, of my fervent commitment to Jewish studies, a special program for which the otherwise backwater institution had gained some renown. It was this program that had drawn me to Mermelman as the terminus of my *wanderjahr*. Of course, by the time I'd reached the autumnal New England village of Old Binstock, I had exhausted the last of Aunt Keni's bequest. I had also, just after arriving back in the States, made a flying visit to Memphis to register my existence with my estranged family, but I had at least enough pride not to ask them for money. My father was anyway ailing, my sister pregnant, and the prodigal's unheralded return passed without fanfare. Back in school, I did, however, succeed in securing a small student loan. For a while I supplemented the loan with the pittance I made from part-time copyediting at the *Binstock*

Docket, a free-press weekly that combined puff pieces on local events with real-estate listings. In this way I was able to defray the cost of tuition for an inaugural semester, during which I survived on cans of Dinty Moore Irish stew eaten out of a saucepan with crumbled saltines. By the second term, my fanatical devotion to my courses had earned me the skeptical looks of my professors and a work-study scholarship. I was given the job of filing and cataloging books in the college library, where I pushed my cart along aisles between stacks that presented themselves like soldiers for my personal inspection. It was an environment fragrant with an attar of intellectual rigor and worn leather bindings, and I lingered among those books, browsing and fondling, for long hours after my tasks were done.

Upon my arrival in Old Binstock, I had rented a furnished room on the second floor of a large frame house on a shady street a leisurely half mile from the campus. The room, three out of five of whose walls were windows, had also an inoperative fireplace and heavy oaken furniture of the type moved about in heaven when it thunders. The place had the feel of an old-fashioned boardinghouse (though no board was provided), complete with a shrewd old matron named Mrs. Rudelhuber in hairnet and faded housedress, beneath which her slip always showed. She was a banjo-eyed, slack-bosomed tavern keeper's widow smelling of depilatories, whose maternal concern for her tenants was contradicted by her scrupulous rules concerning rent payment, kitchen usage, garbage disposal, and access to household appliances. Each rental unit—there were four—had its own separate electrical meter, so that utilities could be monitored and billed accordingly. It was a fastidiousness reflected in the regimental behavior of the other boarders, all male scholars like myself, who fussily labeled the items in our shared refrigerator and marked the levels of unemptied beverages. They were a civil enough lot, my fellow boarders, though (like myself) a little distant and self-involved. Still, we never failed to extend a courteous nod as we passed one another, bathrobe-clad, on our way to and from the single shower. Sometimes we made small talk in the common kitchen amid odors of instant coffee and frying eggs, though our conversations never seemed to advance beyond polite inquiries into respective fields of study. It was a formal atmosphere into which, uneager to form close attachments, I felt myself perfectly assimilated. Meanwhile my library salary covered my tuition, with enough left over to support a spartan diet and the luxury of an occasional movie. If I was strapped for rent at the end of the month, during which time I might suffer a temporary loss of gas and electrical power, I forwent the movie.

I was scarcely aware of the passage of time. As for the years that had elapsed since my first brush with Yiddishkeit in the company of Aunt Keni, they seemed, if I turned around, foreshortened almost to imperceptibility—folded up like an accordion I'd left in a pawnshop without remembering to save the ticket. I was alone again and celibate, the satyr of London havng become an extinct pagan species that, in my mania for things Jewish, I'd lost interest in. You might say I had reverted back to what I was before I met Billy Boots, though there were differences. For one thing, I wasn't scared of the ladies anymore but simply regarded them as too expensive and complicated a diversion. At some point I cut my hair and traded my hippie threads for more conservative thrift-shop chinos and broadcloth shirts. I had become the thing that, in Kafka's book, was the most pathetic creature of all: a bachelor; but it was a condition to which I was happily reconciled.

I learned to savor mundane details: the lichen-chased inscriptions on marble slabs in an old church burial ground, moss on the eaves of the red-brick college buildings sunk in drifts of particolored leaves, the snow-bound *goyishe* landscape with its tobogganers like scrimshaw figures etched in ivory. I liked the brisk, sober, Puritan air that slapped my cheeks on my safe return from excursions into the Jewish past. I exulted in routine, adhered to a schedule that guaranteed that tomorrow would be a carbon copy of today. In two years' time, I had attained my baccalaureate with honors, then went on to pursue a graduate degree; in two more years, I'd earned a master's, and while there was no doctoral program at Mermelman, neither was there any question of my going elsewhere. I had accumulated too much inertia during my years in Old Binstock, my student digs become a cave of books in which I was cozily immured. The walk from my room to the campus, along a street whose overarching lindens dropped and renewed their leaves with dependable regularity, was all I needed of the natural world. After all, what does it say in *Pirke Avot*? "He who is walking along and studying, but breaks off to remark, 'How lovely is that tree!'—Scripture regards such a one as having hurt his own being."

Still, it was a pretty town, Old Binstock, the kind of place for whose preservation young men go off to die in foreign wars. Its architecture was celebrated: the slate-roofed Federal-style cottages, the Victorian houses with captain's walks and wrought-iron weather vanes, the stone walls and wishing wells. The town itself was nestled in a valley where the western winds blew in mists from the Berkshires, winds from the east importing gulls and the scent of salt. Tourist destinations were strewn about the surrounding hills, outdoor amphitheaters for concerts and operas, hamlets with curiosity shops stuffed with rare books and antiques. There was the bay city of Boston just up the road, and Cape Cod, Nantucket, and Martha's Vineyard, their maritime names a tonic to my sluggish southern blood. Sometimes I took bus rides into Boston to scour the bookstores of the Brookline district, just as the bibliomane Gershom Scholem had haunted the back alleys of Jerusalem in search of mystical arcana. I made forays into the countryside to inspect used-book shops in the lofts of old barns, but I was mostly content to stay put and plug away at my studies. Untempted by the charms of the region, I was nevertheless cheered by their proximity.

When it became clear to my former professors—ex-urbanites all, who'd shed their punchy, City College personae for more mandarin affects—that, despite their recommendations, I had no intention of leaving the security of Old Binstock, they pulled strings to keep me on at Mermelman as an adjunct instructor. I suppose they realized that, like themselves, I'd been spoiled by the rarefied atmosphere of the place, and so made unfit for any other. My instructorship enabled me to continue the hand-to-mouth existence that was my custom, and I couldn't have been more satisfied on all counts. In time a position opened up in the Jewish Studies department, the field having begun in recent years to enjoy a resurgence; and though I was underqualified with no area of specialization, lacking a Ph.D. and the ambition to seek one, I was nevertheless encouraged by my colleagues to apply for the job. It was not that I was especially cherished by the department; though complaisant enough toward others to stave off hostilities, I had always kept largely to myself. But I'd proven myself reasonably capable, and, feverish investigations aside, I was an unthreatening presence who posed no serious competition. Moreover, I had become a fixture. So, after a national search failed to turn up a candidate of star caliber, or even a mediocre one that fit the collegial bill, the hiring committee fell back on the known quantity that was myself. I was given the title of assistant

professor and received an appreciable raise in salary that caused me to alter my habits not one jot, although I may have become a little more liberal
in the purchase of books. But on the whole I stepped into my new role
without a crimp in my plodding stride.

While I assiduously guarded my solitude, I was never an actual *nozir,*
a hermit. Over the years I had become a frequent guest at the tables of my
married colleagues, who regarded me more or less as an object of charity. In their tasteful homes, often restored in period fashion, I received a
vicarious dose of domesticity, more than which would have disagreed
with me. I was a reasonably housebroken dinner companion, able to hold
up my end of a conversation while steering away from controversial top-
ics, to engage in light departmental gossip without descending to malice.
I even managed to be a venerable uncle to their children, bringing them
the slightly inappropriate gifts—farting cushions, boxing nuns—that gar-
nered eye-rolling disapproval from parents but made me popular with
their young. I staggered my appearances in their homes as insurance
against becoming a nuisance but visited often enough that my subsistence
diet (I joked that for me every day was Yom Kippur) was periodically for-
tified by essential vitamins. Still, their elaborate meals were largely wasted
on me, since these days I had small interest in gratifying my senses; eating for me was strictly a means of staying alive long enough to engage in
the next day's scholarly pursuits.

Once in a while, the families would attempt a "fix-up," inviting to
dinner some women's-studies professor with a bone to pick, or a recently
divorced faculty wife attempting unsuccessfully to conceal her distrust of
men. Then there would be tension and a squeamish discomfort on my
part, with which I eventually infected the unattached lady. Embarrassed
by their obviously failed effort at matchmaking, our host and hostess
would try to deflect the conversation into neutral areas, while the woman
and I tacitly acknowledged the total lack of chemistry between us. Afterward I would feel doubly protective of my independence.

Because anything that threatened to interfere with my studies unbalanced me. Since entering Mermelman College, I had seldom looked back,
or forth, but always in *that* direction—the one I'd accused the *gekept* (be-
headed) Billy Boots of looking in exclusively. The thesis on which I based
my researches (a thesis I'd first heard put forward in a synagogue attic in

Prague) went like this: Adam saw eternity by the light God conceived on the First Day. That light, after the invention of the sun on the Fourth Day, was then revoked by God and hidden in the books of the Torah, the mother of stories. It was thereafter dispersed in increasingly diluted versions throughout the generations of stories the Torah spawned. Nevertheless, one could still read these stories with the hope of recovering something of the original holy light, reclaiming a flash of eternity by which you could see briefly forever. So I began at the beginning with the Five Books of Moses, whose stories gave off the most brilliant light, like the marriage of a hurricane lantern and a crimson *tsoyer,* which is the gem that brightens the Ark. After them the light, disseminated throughout the sophistical riffs of the rabbis in their ocean of commentary, was less glaring, a limelight though still suffused with rose. A milder amber light, call it moonlight, pervaded the medieval legends and fables, becoming softer and paler the further the stories strayed from their biblical archetypes—though it flared again in the magical tales from The Zohar. The didactic *Haskalah* or Enlightenment stories burned with a guttering wick, but the Hasidic tales had the glow of the *ma'or katan,* the small lamp of Kabbalah. The Yiddish classics were illuminated by a language in the process of shaking off the luster of holiness; then came the generations whose work, written in darkness, nevertheless emanated a black light through which all subsequent stories are filtered prismatically.

I made it my business to gauge the volume and intensity of the light generated by the stories I read. For this project it was necessary to try to make of myself a sensitive instrument capable of registering Judaic photons broadcast over millennia—no mean task. Fetching tales from the time of the primordial Adam, I followed the metamorphoses of Noah's olive-branch-bearing dove, transformed in *The Alphabet of Ben Sira* (a lewd apocrypha unearthed in a Cairo *genizah*) into the crow that Noah accuses of having relations with his wife. The bird turns up again as a beleaguered immigrant leaning on a crutch in Moishe Leib Halpern's poem "Der Foigl"and in an even more compromised state in Bernard Malamud's short story "The Jewbird." I followed the transformations of the concept of death by divine kiss, *b'nshikah,* which was God's gift to Moses, and its diabolical variations in the kiss with which the avatars of Lilith steal the life from their unsuspecting bridegrooms. There were the tales of the deathless, such as Enoch the cobbler, translated for his virtues to the Celestial Yeshiva, where he becomes the recording archangel Metatron; and Elijah, who ascended in a flaming chariot but returns in humbler guises to attend weddings, seders, and *brises*. There was the patriarch Isaac, who, while bound beneath his father's upraised knife, believes himself to be studying Torah in Gan Eydn. It was the kind of secret miracle that recurs in the works of authors like Ambrose Bierce and Jorge Luis Borges; for as Rabbi Nachman says, "God's glory is proclaimed even from tales told by the gentiles."

Of course, by the time I'd stuffed the essentially empty vessel of Saul Bozoff with stories, years had passed, and the walls of the room I called home were buttressed with books. Books were piled atop the talon-footed chiffonier, heaped in the recessed seat of the Sleepy Hollow chair; they covered the horizontal hardwood door on sawhorses that served as my desk and spilled from the shelves made out of fruit crates. In the unmade sleigh bed, where I slept as if in a giant's sabot, lay an open volume of the Sefer Haggadah with friable pages, ordered from an antiquarian bookseller in Haifa; and on the floor beside the bed, also open, a facsimile edition of the En Ya'aqov omnibus. A fat black Bible sat on the crowded desk, roofed over by an open Mimekor Yisroel, full of *oshshpekherin* exorcising demons, *klogmuters* lamenting the dead, and *brivn shreibers* writing letters for the illiterate to deceased ancestors. Next to them lay a well-thumbed *Shulchan Arukh,* in which the God who conquered Canaan in a storm wind was bound by the legal code as if with the straps of His own phylacteries. The seven volumes of Ginzberg's *Legends of the Jews* anchored the woven rug, along with *The Book of Jubilees,* the *Pirke de Rabbi Eliezer,* and Martin Buber's *Tales of the Hasidim.*

Buber's German I could read only in translation, but after innumerable midnights I was able to comprehend the original Hebrew and Yiddish texts myself. To accomplish this I'd had first to learn the Hebrew alphabet like a schoolboy, relying on mnemonic verses:

> *Zayin—a zelner, a zelner shist*
> *Khes—a khazer, a khazer nis*
> *Tes—a toyter, a toyter mest*
> *Yud—a yid, a yid fargest*

(A soldier shoots / a pig sneezes / a dead man dies / a Jew forgets.) Having gained a gradual proficiency in Hebrew, I learned Yiddish with the

aid of the Weinreich grammar, limp as an old phone directory from frequent reference. Though I read both languages haltingly, I was pleased
with my inchmeal progress, tasting each word as if its pages were slathered
with honey. This was how I made my hobbled way through Judah Halevi's
moresque account of the eighth-century Khazar king converted to Ju-
daism. I conned the medieval Yiddish *Bovo Bukh*, advancing to *Fishke
der Krumer* and *Tevye der Milchiger*, which reeked of pumpkin seeds and
the sand-strewn floors of study houses. I memorized poems by Itzhik
Manger (*"Oyfn veg shteyt a boym"*) and Mani Leib (*"Shtiller, shtiller, redt
nicht hoich"*), and the sentimental folksongs of Goldfadn (*"Unter Yidele's
ziegele/shteyt a klor veiss ziegele"*), whose tunes I listened to in archive
recordings that crackled like cellophane.

Since it was expected of me, I wrote occasional articles—prooftexts, if
you will—for scholarly journals that existed for their own vanity's sake. In
these I merely reported the routes I had taken in tracing themes through
various permutations to their present form. My chronicles of the journey,
the *gilgul,* were objective and analytical, never disclosing the rush of emotion that flooded me in the process of my investigations. Like Muhle's
roach, which had incubated so long in the front-porch sofa before engulfing the house in flames—that's how I thought of the passions that had
reemerged to overtake me, though I deliberately suppressed the excitement
rather than betray it to an audience that did not in any case exist. They
were similar, these articles, to the perfunctory autoeroticism I indulged in
on alternate calendar days. (Though on Jewish fast days and High Holidays—which I observed alone, faithful to my own brand of lenten zeal—I
refrained from touching myself altogether.) Regarding my academic career, I was proud of my reputation as a dryasdust teacher. It was crucial to
me that I kept hidden from my students my private excesses, which were
none of their business. The stories were my sovereign abode, and while I
might invite students in for a time if they behaved themselves, they should
not by any stretch make themselves at home. Never did I allow a speck of
personality to vitiate the classroom, and I especially enjoyed the sense of
having a secret identity, a double life—the bloodless professor in the lecture hall, the besotted scholar in his moldering library.

In short, I was never so content. Myth and history were indistinguishable, nature a rumor. I was the contemporary of Hershel Ostropolier

manufacturing a new coat for Destitution; the Ba'al Shem Tov traveling to Chernobyl via Kfitsat ha-Derekh, seven-league boots; Avrom Sutzkever lying in a Warsaw flophouse listening through the floorboards to the jargon of the underworld. He arrives in the Vilna ghetto, Sutzkever, just in time for the murder of his mother and firstborn child, then joins a gang of warrior/dreamers melting down the leaden plates from a famous Hebrew press to make bullets. These were the bedtime stories with which I cured my insomnia.

As my internal kingdom expanded, so did the external world shrink proportionately, my body reduced to a garment I put on to meet my classes and dine with acquaintances. I hardly blinked when I observed in a mirror how that body was in need of repair, the hair thinning, the spine drooping like a stem under a heavy blossom, the once defined musculature become soft and pasty. After all, didn't it say in Talmud, "It is good to destroy oneself in study"? I had the look of an authentic inkhorn academic, which is what I was—a moth-eaten scholar with half lenses and a patch-sleeved jacket, a fusty character with only the remotest relation to primary experience. Political scandals, presidential resignations, hijackings and assassinations, my father's death—they came and went as I looked briefly askance. In truth, it was a long time after I'd stopped taking drugs before the so-called real world had again acquired any color or depth, but I looked no further for edification than the page under my nose. A glutton for stories, I still remained thin, though my skin was a little crepey around the neck and jowls, and I'd developed an incipient paunch. I suffered from shortness of breath, frequent constipation, and lower-back pain, though such physical complaints (insults to a body I could almost have done without) seemed scarcely worth noting. I was at peace with my reinvented self, never moved to behavior that might suggest I had an interior anyone would care to penetrate.

NATHAN

Nathan's articles on the Allen Street fire and its aftermath struck a fine balance between sound investigative reportage and lurid sensationalism. Beginning with rumors, which he tricked out as objective fact, and facts, which he distorted to serve his needs, Nathan pieced together a story beside which the account by the veteran Shimon Goldfogle seemed tepid. (The haphazard Goldfogle was subsequently demoted to writing obituaries, then banished to stringing in some far outpost of Brooklyn.) Because his reports made good copy, whatever license Nathan had taken with accuracy was overlooked; their excesses set the standard for his future contributions and advanced the yellow-journalistic leanings of the press.

In his maiden effort, Nathan had revealed, based on only the flimsiest evidence, that the fire was caused by an explosion of combustible liquids. These liquids, he maintained, had been stored in close proximity to a newly installed hot-air furnace in the cellar of the disorderly house. On the evening of the conflagration the Jewish Black Hand—the surviving incendiary arm of the syndicate once headed by the labor racketeer Dopey Fein—had been called on to toss a bomb; and a talented young arsonist, Bockso Weiss by name, was sent into the cellar of Number 96 to fetch the ingredients. Looking for a lamp in the dark, Bockso had struck a match, then opened a bottle to savor the pent-up vapors—phosphorus vapors being pure ambrosia to your arson mechanic—and released a furious genie. The explosion that followed rocked the neighborhood and reduced to rubble the tenement's six floors.

The wreckage, according to Nathan, was the subject of much gloating in certain circles, the Kehillah bunch predictably declaring the disaster an act of God. When their ambassadors—who included both local and uptown rabbis, reformers, philanthropists' wives, and a zealous new crime commissioner—arrived to sniff the damage, they uttered no end of pieties. They poked about in the charred bricks and timbers, clucking their tongues over here a burst bottle, there a scorched ace of diamonds, a blistered condom tin, a lace cascade. In language that veered between professional detachment and mawkish sentimentality, extreme even for the *Forward,* Nathan called the roll of the lost. Among the *shtuss* addicts and mobsters (a legacy from the days of the Dope) were the versatile Joseph Toblonsky, alias Yoshke Nigger, horse poisoner, thief, and corrupter of children; the gunsels Billy Lustig, Joe the Greaser, and Felix Rothkopf, called Cutcher-Head-Off, once a creature of the holy terror Monk Eastman. There was Little Yutch the cat burglar; Candy Kid Phil the flesh peddler; Freddy Bialy, who, true to his sobriquet "Lighthouse," flung himself from a third-floor window in a fair impersonation of a fire beacon; there was Bockso Weiss, whose mother (Nathan reasoned he must have had a mother) said he might have been a surgeon or a financier, had he not fallen into bad company. While there was no hard proof of their passing (or in some cases their prior existence), Nathan was confident that most would be grateful for the cover of an untimely demise and so would not come forward to dispute his facts.

Naturally the heaviest toll was taken among the ladies and their clients. Several of the latter, as Nathan determined, were on the *Forward*'s roster of vanished men, whom few would mourn in any case; but Big-Nosed Malkeh and Sadie the Chink, Ida the Goose with her honking catarrh, and the brawler Bessie-in-the-Barrel Schneour, all were incinerated, as were the promising novices Princess Shprintze and the satin-skinned Lotte Tobach. The fledgling journalist listed the casualties with an odd combination of reverence and a righteous contempt for their degeneracy. It was a tone he deemed appropriate for chronicling the end of an era. In his follow-ups Nathan informed a growing circle of readers that some who survived wished they hadn't, having been so disfigured that their remaining years would be a curse. Though efforts were made to defray their hospital expenses (notably by the Hochstim Benevolent Association, known for its extensive sporting-house holdings), the community chest was soon dried up. As a result, the girls languished in charity wards or were released maimed and sometimes raving into the streets.

Gutted as they were, the complex of buildings that comprised Number 96 doggedly refused to topple, at least not until several days later, when the wrecking crew finished them off. Three of the surrounding four walls had remained erect, a monument (as one apocryphal rabbi put it) to the durability of the evil intention; but the street façade had collapsed over the Elevated trestle, damaging the tracks so that downtown traffic was tied up for days. On-the-spot witnesses (surely there'd been on-the-spot witnesses) had reported that when the smoke cleared, the relatively unimpaired top floors exposed an active cross-section of every vice known to man and some hitherto unknown or forgotten. These Nathan felt duty-bound to describe in a voyeuristic detail that skirted the very limits of good taste.

The series of articles on the fire spawned the sort of controversy that would follow Nathan (often at his own invitation) throughout his career. For it wasn't lost on the scribblers and balladeers of the quarter that his version begged comparisons with the Triangle cataclysm. As a result, published broadsides began to appear asserting that the victims of Allen Street, like their sisters in the factory, were martyrs to an unjust system. This proposition raised the hackles of respectable citizens: it was an insult to the memory of the Triangle dead to draw parallels between their fate and that of whores, who'd gotten essentially what they deserved. The succeeding debate came to eclipse the incident itself, but by then Nathan had already moved on.

On the night of his first assignment, having swiftly sized up the situation, the cub reporter had hurried back to the press, where—on the stooped back of an obliging printer's devil at the door to the typographer's shop—he dashed off his article. The piece was approved over Goldfogle's summary submission, and Nathan, having expended his available fund of energy, collapsed on the spot. He spent the night curled in the undercarriage of a web press, and in the morning, at the advice of a coworker, found temporary refuge in the parlor of an apartment on Henry Street. There, despite the cottage industry in ladies' vests and bloomers racketing about him, Nathan slept on a rented campaign cot for two days straight. He woke to discover that he had launched a new vocation in which he'd already attained the status of a minor celebrity. With the promise of financial security, he was able, in due course, to take a flat of his own on Essex Street, catty-corner from the paper and overlooking Seward Park. Modest enough, the two-room apartment had a sink with a gooseneck pump, a coal-burning range, cheesecloth curtains that strained the impurities from jaundiced sunlight, and a water closet on the landing outside the door. There was a tin mezuzah on the doorpost that Nathan, renewing an immemorial habit, touched upon going out and coming in.

He bought an iron bedstead on credit from Wanamaker's, along with a cassimere suit, a butterfly necktie, a pair of oxfords, and a roll-brimmed derby hat, but continued wearing the nappy rug coat out of a sentimental attachment. With boards purchased cheap from a local casketmaker, Nathan threw together some shelves and slowly began to reconstitute his lost library. He dutifully replaced a few Yiddish classics, even included a weather-warped Haggadah and some volumes of commentary, though they were soon edged out by books in English on diverse subjects: practical philosophy, American history, the political theories of Karl Marx and Theodore Herzl. Harriet Martineau's *Auguste Comte,* G. P. MacGreavey's *Social Darwinism,* Plekhanov's *Materialism and Synthetic Monism,* Horatio Alger's *Luck and Pluck* brashly elbowed aside Israel Aksenfeld and the *Pirke Avot.* Nathan meantime began amassing an impressive archive of play programs, court records, civic brochures, union minutes, and any random tidbits of local interest, which he tucked away, magpielike, in an overstuffed cabinet at the *Forward.*

In the beginning he was paid by the word like the feuilletonists; then he graduated to a regular salary and a desk of his own, though he was seldom there. Philip Krantz, at first a bullying taskmaster, was soon persuaded of the rookie reporter's natural instincts and ended by granting him virtual carte blanche. Dispatched to cover crime and industrial relations, Nathan roamed the ghetto looking for trouble. He early on commenced a routine that included spending a portion of every workday in the pressroom of the Mulberry Street police headquarters. There he learned to play pinochle with seasoned newshounds from the various dailies and to take his turn at the peephole that gave onto the stationhouse. He kept a lookout for Jewish faces among the miscreants hustled into the station from a motorized Black Maria outside. He bribed cops to give him details he might later discard for livelier constructions of his own, pestered felons for disclosures he could revise to suit his whim—though in truth most stories resisted Nathan's embellishments. Ultimately he had to allow that his imaginative powers were no match for the East Side's raffish affairs, and it was sufficient that he meet reality halfway.

In that spirit he wrote a disquieting portrait of the Yid thug known as Chaim the Mummy. An echt American, as he styled himself, Chaim prided himself on maintaining certain ties to tradition, such as keeping a special *fleishik* knife for the times he might have to cut a throat on Shabbos. Then there was the case of the gangster Spanish Louie, who had gut-shot his hapless girlfriend Hodel the Mattress for carrying another man's child. (The child, surviving its mother, was subsequently born missing an ear.) Louie, whose trademark accessories included an embroidered sombrero and chaps, a brace of revolvers and an eight-inch dirk in a hand-tooled scabbard, let slip to an all-ears Nathan that his father was a Division Street patch tailor of Sephardic descent. Covering high-profile executions, Nathan filed an unflinching report of the hanging of Big Jack Zelig's one-time button man Tiny Levine. Tiny was a gorilla so gross that when his gargantuan body dropped through the scaffold, his head remained in the noose above. Then there was the death by electric chair of handsome Harry Horowitz, called Gyp the Blood, a glad-handing fiend who liked to crack the spines of his victims over his knee; whose last words, if you could believe Nathan's version, were, "Tell my ma I'm still circumcised. . . ."

Nathan also haunted the emergency room at Bellevue Hospital, where he was often rewarded with stories of specific Jewish interest. He was there when the stunning corpse of Mrs. Ezra Seidenschnier of 44 Hester was carried in with her broken husband sobbing on her breast. She had killed herself after failing the test her fanatical spouse, following the example of the esteemed Rabbi Meir of old, had devised for her. It seemed that Reb Seidenschnier, aging and insecure, had placed temptation in his young wife's path in the form of a comely yeshiva student. The old fool had practically orchestrated her seduction, and when she succumbed—as had Rabbi Meir's bride in ancient times—Mrs. Seidenschnier, stricken with conscience, hanged herself from a gasolier. Nathan lamented her death in the doleful rhetoric he later refined when eulogizing the actress Emma Finkel, Tomashevsky's little sister, whose bullet-riddled body he'd also had occasion to observe firsthand. She'd been brought in to Bellevue along with the remains of her jealous husband, Maurice Finkel, who'd shot himself in the head after blasting his inconstant wife. Shamelessly exploiting this Second Avenue tragedy, Nathan punctuated his account of the fallen actress with the refrain from Joseph Rumshinsky's lugubrious ditty: "Little birds, don't forget me!"

Owing to the popularity of his talebearing, a guilty pleasure for even those who faulted it, Nathan was ultimately given the authority to write what he pleased. He began, after a scant few months, to expand his orbit beyond the familiar coordinates of hospital, police headquarters, and labor rally, broadening the parameters of Jewish New York. One day he might detail the fate of an East Side girl held in thrall to the head of a Mott Street tong lodge, on another recount the wedding of a daughter of the Jewish Four Hundred in the ballroom of the Santos-Dumont airship moored to Coney Island's steel pier. He described the making of a Pathé picture in which the denizens of Tischler's Tea House and Blattberg's Saloon had been engaged to play their sordid selves; and a performance of Zisha Breitbart, the modern Bar Kochba, a Jewish strongman who drove nails with his fists and raised brewery wagons with a heave of his chest, proclaiming, "I break like matchsticks the bones of anti-Semites." Suicides having become something of a specialty, Nathan wrote of the poet Moishe Varshe's heartbroken plunge from a Pike Street rooftop. He wrote about the girl whose cinnamon hair was torn from her scalp like deracinated turf by a rampant sewing machine, about a burial with full honors in a Brooklyn cemetery of the script of a flopped Yiddish play. He reported the story of an infant thread picker who burrowed under a pile of scraps to elude discovery by a factory inspector and was never seen again.

Once, journeying into the Catskills to investigate a utopian community founded on the principles of Herzl and Fourier (which the skeptical had dubbed Wise Acres), he discovered a squalid settlement where the Jews had virtually reverted to savages.

Sometimes Nathan toyed with the idea of adopting a nom de plume. Bintl Brief was of course taken, but there was a fine old tradition of dashing pseudonyms among the Yiddish bylines: Tashrak, Der Tunkeler, Der Nister, Mendele Mocher Seforim; or, like B. Kovner and Z. Libin, he might use only the first initial of his given name. But finally he decided that these days it was distinction enough to be Nathan Hart. Besides, so many masks did he wear in his writings—accidental observer, concerned citizen, champion of the oppressed—that to disguise his name as well would be a redundancy. But one thing that remained consistent in Nathan's articles—his signature if you will—was his knack for creating something akin to an authentic narrative. And if he was guilty of manipulating his readers, if he exaggerated certain particulars and manufactured others, at least they couldn't accuse him of inventing from whole cloth. However far Nathan might stretch a story's attachment to actual happenstance, the connecting tissue between fact and fantasy still held.

He dined regularly now at Mintz's Cafeteria on roast *bulbes*, stuffed cabbage, and sugared fish, the rich diet beginning to fill out his starveling frame. After a meal he might repair to Schreiber's, where the musicians played unheeded before an altarlike credenza and gentlemen of the press came in from the cold to shmooze. In Schreiber's, Nathan rubbed shoulders not only with his own tribe from the *Forward* but with representatives from the rival papers. At one table you might see the ramrod-stiff John Paley, sanctimonious and (some said) unprincipled editor of the *Tageblatt*, holding court; while at another Abe Cahan's rabbity nemesis Louie Miller of *Der Varheit* inveighed against his enemies. Also on hand were the unscrubbed contributors to the Labor Zionist and anarchist gazettes, the jokers of the satirical rag *Der Groyser Kundes* (The Big Stick), sporting opera cloaks like the wings of bats. Nathan was grateful for the cordiality with which he'd been welcomed into their company, though not so humbled that he shied away from their leg pulling and stentorian arguments.

Naturally he kept closest to his brethren from the *Forward*, some of whom used the café as a second office. Among them was usually Abraham Liessin, called by his colleagues a "silken youth" and by the unsalaried literati—the poseurs and hangers-on who occupied the outer circle of tables—a *zoineh*, a prostitute. Despite what he liked to think of as his own earthier temperament, Nathan had conceived a fellow feeling for the moonstruck idealist, which didn't prevent him from making fun of his romantic affections. "How is it, Abie," he might ask, having acquired the hang of professional banter, "that the rest of us are still on Canal Street while you're in the Promised Land?" (After considering, Liessin had offered, "Imagination?" citing what Nathan had begun to regard as a highly overrated faculty.) Like the others, however, the young journalist had also to take his turn as the target of friendly derision. Bernard Kovner, for instance, the elfin-eared cartoonist of "Yente Telebende" fame, was fond of calling a teasing attention to Nathan's penchant for hyperbole: "A few heads get broke on the picket line, and Nate here, he tells us it's a regular *khurbn* instigated by Cossacks under imperial ukase." Hillel Rogoff, the ladies' man, at times with a girl on each knee, liked to hector Nathan concerning his apparent disinterest in women: "Eva wants to know are you a *faigele*?"—because Schreiber's on Canal was full of free-spirited maidens adoring of the fourth estate.

But Nathan had no intention of complicating his life just when things had fallen so neatly into place. Lately he had begun receiving letters at the press, sometimes from solicitous fathers and matchmakers asking if he were a bachelor, sometimes from the daughters themselves. Coyly they inquired, in a Moorish script on perfumed pages, as to his taste in literature and women. But Nathan, untempted, never answered their letters, since what did he need that he didn't already have? Wasn't he at the very center of events in the immigrant world?—events that occasionally overlapped a larger world he would not hesitate to enter for the sake of a story. Where couldn't you go and what couldn't you do if you were merely unafraid? Nathan was running on an energy he had not known he possessed, never pausing to look back, enjoying the crackling forward propulsion of his days. They were full and fruitful, his days, and at night, heroically weary and a little flushed from schnapps, he would return to his flat to fall into an untroubled sleep. Not that it was an especially quiet apartment, having in common with his Cherry Street loft the unending clangor of bedsprings, the all-night squabblings in several tongues, the pungent odors that seemed to have volume and weight. But unlike on Cherry Street, where he would lie apprehensively awake for hours, now the noises assumed something in the nature of a lullabye, soothing Nathan in his awareness of the proximity to his own kind.

Once or twice, before bed, he had placed a brief note, along with some newspaper clippings, in an envelope and posted it to his estranged mother and sisters. Having recently opened an account at Jarmulovsky's Bank, he might also enclose a little cash. It was a nominal gesture, made with half a heart, and Nathan hardly noticed when months passed with no response. Eventually he received a communication from his sister Beilke—the name conjured only pink ears jutting through tight strands of dishwater hair—informing him that his letters had been forwarded to her in Vilna. It seemed that their beloved mother, Froika Sara, and sister, Shoshana, had both perished during a smallpox outbreak the previous winter in Zitsk. Beilke had escaped along with her husband, Fishl (who was writing the letter) to Vilna, where Fishl had found work as a stoker in an anvil foundry. But life was not easy for them there: Beilke was expecting a child and Fishl making barely enough to feed the two of them, never mind an extra mouth. Further, the political climate was perilous, the blood-libel trial of Mendel Beilis having sparked a fresh round of pogroms. They much appreciated the money Nathan had mailed them and would kiss his footprints when next they met—which, please God, would be soon if he could perhaps see his way clear to sending them a *shifscarte* passage to America. . . .

Recalling the words of Sholem Aleichem's Motl Peysi: *"Mir iz gut, ikh bin a yosem"*—"I'm lucky, I'm an orphan"—Nathan tasted again the thrill of his own independence, then felt profoundly ashamed of himself. Had they become so unreal to him, his mother and sister, that he was incapable of properly grieving their loss? Or was he simply too selfish to interrupt his ongoing complacence to entertain a filial sorrow? He tried picturing the warmth of the family circle, himself and his sisters in their leaky hovel being force-fed their mother's steady diet of humbug— which he found he resented more than ever, just as he resented the absurdly murdered father who'd bequeathed them such an intangible legacy. Indeed, the very notion of "family" seemed foreign to Nathan's current idea of himself, but this attitude did not mitigate his shame. Determining to make his surviving sister, Beilke, the beneficiary of his guilty conscience, Nathan wrote to condole with her over their shared tragedy; he repined that life on earth would be diminished by the absence of Froika the Troika and her extravagant tales. He also congratulated Beilke belatedly

on the end of what he'd assumed was a confirmed spinsterhood, wished
her an easy pregnancy, and promised to send whatever assistance he
could afford.

Hypocrisy notwithstanding, Nathan was bolstered by his resolution,
feeling that he was becoming an ever more solid member of society. No
longer a sui generis "character," he was a mensch, tethered again—after a
period spent as good as outside of history—to the passage of time. He
had begun to mark his days (including Jewish holidays, during which he
attended a conservative Norfolk Street synagogue) on a calendar provided by the Grand Street Theater, each page displaying a tintype of Jacob Adler in a role he'd made famous. The advance of days seemed to
consolidate the time he had spent as a reporter (since graduated to features writer) and to reinforce the distance that separated him from the
time when he'd been no one at all.

It was already late March, and while the gutters were still clogged
with a salt-and-pepper slush, the newly released stench of ripe garbage
and horse manure proclaimed the advent of spring. This was the case
one mild Friday morning as Nathan passed through Seward Park on his
way to the daily. The lifting mist revealed the old men slouching toward
morning prayers, the job seekers laden with hammers and trowels falling
in line for the sunrise shape-up, women pushing prams their babies
shared with sheaves of cut flannelette. Snow was still banked along the
gravel paths, but on a certain leafless box elder tree, if you looked closely,
you could see buds like fingertips poking through leather gloves. The tree
in question, surrounded by a dwarf wire fence, had a dark, diamond-
shaped rift in its bunchy trunk, and Nathan, taking note of it, was struck
by a remembrance: this was it, the very tree in which he'd stashed the
needless burden of his manuscript on the night of the Allen Street fire.

He recalled how he had first peered into the fissure to make certain it
didn't serve as a conduit for fugitive angels, then shoved the burlap-
wrapped package inside for safekeeping. In the heady days that followed,
while forging his new identity, Nathan had neglected to retrieve the
abandoned pages; they had remained as forgotten as they'd been during
his long amnesiac fever in Gouverneur Street. Now, pushing back his
coat sleeve, he reached into the hollow bole of the tree. It gave him a jolt

to find the package still undisturbed, as if (though he'd hidden it there himself) the thing had been left for him by some other agency. But once he'd recovered it, rather than inspect its contents on the spot, Nathan pinioned the gunnysack under his arm and hurried back to his flat. Entering, he withdrew the manuscript from its grubby sheath to find it remarkably little the worse for wear. There were a few wormholes, a speckling of versicolored mildew, but on balance it was no more dog-eared and flyblown than when he'd forsaken it months before. The butcher's twine that crisscrossed its pages like window struts, though gnawed at, was still knotted tight. Handling it with care, Nathan placed the manuscript bookwise on a shelf, nestled between Alexander Harkavy's Yiddish-English dictionary and a copy of *How the Other Half Lives*. Then, satisfied at seeing his trussed but unbound volume so cozily situated, he proceeded to forget about *The Angel* all over again.

That morning Nathan completed a human-interest piece about a boy orator who, overcoming a harelip, had electrified an audience at a United Garment Workers conclave in the New Irving Hall. After lunch he rode the El train up to Second Avenue and Seventh Street to visit the candy store where a recent ghetto craze had been inaugurated. The craze involved a carbonated drink called the egg cream, containing neither egg nor cream but said to have mysterious healing properties. It was claimed that the drink could, among other things, cure rheumatism and gout and increase one's amorous potential. Nathan stood among a bunch of idlers taking notes as one of the regulars downed eight or nine glasses of the sparkling tonic on a dare. Despite his age the man achieved a sort of horizontal pavilion in his trousers, but his feet swelled as well, his shoes expanding with every glass he drank, until the laces snapped.

Afterward, confident of an amusing and cautionary article and in no hurry to return to the office, Nathan wandered the world below Houston Street. It was a clear and crisp late afternoon, the sun already descending, the noise of the hucksters and hagglers somewhat muffled by proliferating shadows. The walls of the tenements, barely holding back the flood of laundry and children that threatened to pour from their windows, nevertheless appeared as tranquil as so many spice boxes on a shelf. Strolling south, Nathan was acutely conscious of belonging to this place, and vice versa; graduated from "character" to personality, he was a young man of promise and independent means, complete with profession, cronies, and even (however attenuated) family ties. Counting his blessings, the features writer enjoyed a sensation as sweet in its awareness of something missing as any associated with fulfillment, though he was much too pleased with himself to bother giving the feeling a name.

MOCKY

In flight I might have been a rococo detail escaped from the ceiling fresco, sweeping cobwebs from ceramic pendants and rattling the chandeliers. "Look out, you grubbers," I wanted to advise them, "Mocky's in his element again!" But for discretion's sake I held my tongue. From on high I surveyed the house, still unsure as to whether the pandemonium below me was pro- or contra-Nachman, though my guess was neither and both: it was a simple case of theatergoers grown emotional over stirring dramatic fare. Some of the more excited had resorted to brawling in the aisles, their scuffling probably instigated by members of the Five-Pointers Gang—if not the Gas Housers or the Dock Rats, whose ambassadors were also in attendance. They were taking advantage of the general confusion to settle old scores.

Above the stage my harried son was still clinging stubbornly to his perch. Meanwhile the journeyman ganef Yoshke Nigger, having doffed his coat and climbed onto the catwalk, was at that moment lowering himself from the rigging into the rope ladder's upper reaches; then, dangling spectacularly by his feet, he seized Nachman about the shoulders to block his ascent.

Swooping toward them, I was struck with the thought, half elated and half forlorn, that I was revealed at last for what I was—though the unveiling was doubtless lost on these habitual witnesses, who would've mistaken an actual angel for just another theatrical effect. Once I'd ducked under the proscenium, I back-flapped to maintain a hovering position over Nachman's ladder, calling to the kid to hurry up and grab hold. I anticipated his resistance and was surprised when he obeyed me without

hesitation, clutching my neck in a choke hold that left me gasping, asking, "Tateh, how did I do?" It didn't help that to his own was added the
weight of two hoodlums hanging on to his shoulders and feet. But once
Nachman was at least tentatively on board, I beat my sturdy wings for all
I was worth, creating a tempest that forced his would-be captors to drop
with evil oaths to the stage.

When he'd relaxed his hold of my windpipe, I exclaimed in a rush of
optimism, "Now we're in business!" Nachman himself let out a yip that I
at first interpreted as fear, though its persistence convinced me I was mistaken: he was enjoying himself. Then I couldn't tell where his jubilation
left off and mine began; we were two parts of a single creature: he was
half an angel, and I was the angel he was half of.

We were above the orchestra, on the point of mounting aloft, when a
disturbing new development sent me flittering back under the booms: for
below us the doors to the lobby had swung wide, admitting down all four
aisles a company of nightstick-wielding constabulary. At the back of the
house, an officer in a custom uniform—gold braid festooning his yachting
cap, gold-buttoned his swagger coat—was announcing himself over a
bullhorn.

"This is Police Commissioner Thomas McAdoo," he fairly crooned.
"All present are under arrest on account of you're a public disgrace. These
premises are hereby closed till further notice!"

In the wholesale disorder, the rowdies who weren't busy battling each
other began battling the cops. There were canisters drawn, shots fired.
Leaving behind their hired escorts, the swells made for the exits, fleeced
by a gauntlet of pickpockets stationed along the way. In their box I saw
Dopey Benny trying to take Rivka's arm and lead her from the ruckus,
but, apparently transfixed by the airborne spectacle of myself and my
son, she wouldn't budge.

With Nachman hugging my torso in a taut embrace, I renewed my resolve; I intended spiraling upward under cover of the fray to the third balcony, then out a fire door into the soft evening air. In my mind we were
almost there: I could smell already the aromatic herbs of the Garden, feel
underfoot the squish of overripe fruit dropped from the Tree of Knowledge; I could hear Hannaleh's laughter like trolley bells.

But dipping again beneath the arch to begin my climb, I happened to pass over the box where the Dope was still coaxing an obstinate Rivka. I wheeled sharply to give them a wider berth, about to soar in the direction of the high-wrought ceiling, when I felt a snag that brought us to a sudden standstill. I twisted my neck to find that my son, on some mad impulse, had let go of me with his left hand in order to snatch the Bubitsch girl by the wrist. Beside her Rivka's companion took his heavy-lidded measure of the situation. First Dopey looked about for his lieutenants, most of whom were engaged in the knock-down-drag-out with the bulls; then he looked from Rivka's hand, the one that remained in Nachman's possession, to the one yet in his own, which he tugged gingerly like the string of a kite. He gave another, harder pull, as if to crank an engine that wouldn't start. Frowning, Dopey addressed Nachman with an authority that suggested he was accustomed to dealing with the offspring of renegade angels:

"You, *shtik drek,* turn her loose or you are already history."

"Give a listen who's talking," Nachman shouted back at the gangster, his pluckiness sounding oddly rehearsed. "You're history, I'm . . . a myth!"

"What are you doing?" I cried to my son, whose talonlike grip on the girl I couldn't dislodge for all the agitation of my wings. "Show for Mr. Fein some respect."

"But, Papa," he blared, "I want that Rivka should come with us."

This was too much. "What if she don't want?" I had it in mind to say, when the girl herself, coming out of her momentary torpor, stole the words from my mouth. "What if Rivka don't want?" she shouted, trying to take back her arm. With her ostrich plume drooping over her face along with the unraveled skein of her pompadour, she was the rabbi's bedraggled daughter again: a rare bird, if not exactly built for flight.

Again I admonished Nachman, "Stay the course, boychikl!"—demanding to know was he or wasn't he committed to visiting the upper yeshivas again.

"I didn't change my mind," he assured me, "but I want now that Rivka should come, too."

That this would defeat the purpose, I didn't bother to mention, since we both knew that the purpose was defeated from its conception. Stalled in midair, I was unable to gain altitude so long as Nachman and Dopey kept up their tug-of-war over the girl. "Please excuse my son, Mr. Fein,"

I entreated, conditioned by years of deference. "He's a *bisl* headstrong. . . ."

But Rivka demonstrated no such reserve. "Let go from me, the both of you!" she cried, and when neither gave an inch, she struggled to break the impasse herself. Making no headway with Nachman, she turned to Dopey Benny and, with a high kick that had seen good service in the chorus line, planted the toe of her patent slipper in Dopey's groin. He doubled over with a grunt, leaving exposed his receding chin, which Rivka cracked with an abruptly upflung knee. His head snapped back with a velocity that lifted his feet from the ground before he collapsed into the folding chair behind him, which collapsed beneath him. And that was it: that handily did the girl give the lie to Dopey's fabled omnipotence.

As if awaiting their cue, the police burst into the proscenium box and, exclaiming over their good luck, laid hands on the incapacitated mob boss. In no shape to struggle, the Dope allowed himself to be hauled to his feet and hustled out of the box. On the way, shaking his head as if in wonder that a mere skirt should have been the instrument of his downfall, he seemed oddly resigned—which didn't prevent him from groggily proclaiming his imminent return. (He would indeed return, though not before he'd read the writing on the wall and sung like a canary, divulging the secrets of his operations and fingering his cronies for a reduced sentence; after which—try to keep a good man down—he would resurface to initiate a new career in legalized crime.) In departing the box, one of Dopey's escorts, remarking our situation, turned to ask of his partner, "Ain't that a angel the poor lad is riding piggyback?" To which the other, speaking as if from some expertise, assured him that "The t'ing's too plug ugly for a angel."

Meanwhile I'd tried to take advantage of one less hanger-on to claw my way skyward, but Rivka was still ungovernable. She persisted in attempting to unfetter herself from Nachman, dispelling any suggestion that Dopey's elimination had favored his rival. "Let me go already!" she hollered, yanking at the kid with such force that I was nearly capsized in the air. I echoed her sentiment: Nachman should release the girl, whom it made no sense to hold on to in the first place. I couldn't carry the pair of them anyway; we should stick to our original plan. But, ignoring my protests, my son hung on tenaciously to the rabbi's daughter.

"I want to take you with me to paradise!" he pleaded with Rivka, the tendons strained like fiddle strings in his outstretched arm.

"Paradise you wouldn't know it if it sat down in your lap," she bawled back at him. "You already had your chance—now let me go," and when he refused: "I'm gonna have a baby!" she proclaimed. The violence of her effort to jerk free of his clutches cost Nachman his one-armed bear hug about my trunk. To compensate for lost leverage, he again made a grab for my throat, constricting it so that I could hardly breathe.

"Lnghnghgrrrshhh," I gasped, which was the best I could do toward exhorting him to give her up, we were getting nowhere. Again I punished the air with my wings to no avail. Still insisting that Nachman unhand her, Rivka's voice was losing its force, while my son, apparently indifferent to whose child she might be carrying, kept up his unrelenting suit.

"In heaven they got midwives there can take care of you. . . ."

"I don't want to go to heaven!" she cried, rallying her strength to give another tug that tipped me to starboard. "I ain't dead yet!"

Despite his difficulties Nachman acknowledged that she had a point.

"Nghoonghlsh," I choked, meaning that the kid should make his choice: which was it, the girl or the stories? Somehow he must have understood, because, desperate to try to buy time, he reminded me it was Shabbos, when a Jew has a *neshoma yeseyreh*, an extra soul: in theory one soul might rise to glory while the other stayed behind. Unimpressed, I repeated the ultimatum as best I could.

"Both, I want both!" declared Nachman. "Tateh, I didn't have yet a wife." "Rivka, my life," he told the girl, "I need you! You are the jewel from the universe its *pupik*—"

"You need me!" Rivka mocked his ardor, though her voice was cracked, the tears coming in rills. "You didn't even know me. Let go, you're hurting my arm!" Then she sank to her knees, dangling from Nachman's hand like a leaden rag doll.

I could feel my son's sweaty hold of my windpipe starting to slip, just as I assumed he must be losing his grip on Rivka's wrist at the other end. Perhaps I might have kept him secure, reaching behind with my arms to boost him higher on my back; I might have used my new powers to help him make up his mind—but who remembers arms when you have wings? Again I put it to him, making a mighty effort to speak words that resembled words, that he must choose between above and below. Then Nachman said something that to my way of thinking had small relevance to the situation at hand.

"Papa," he said confidentially, "in heaven they wouldn't believe it what goes on down here. . . ."

SAUL

I was thirty-five years old when the world caught my attention again. I suppose I'd reached a point of critical mass with regard to my studies, my brain overloaded with the lore that had begun to clog my arteries and stiffen my joints. Feeling claustrophobic in my own skin, it was only natural that I should look outside myself for a change, and that was when I saw Miranda Pratt. Better her than, say, some carnival oddity with a ribbon-twined beard whom I might as easily have been smitten with, so ready was I (apparently) for love. But, thankfully, Miranda, who was just this side of beautiful, entered my field of vision instead. She had an oval face with a pale pink complexion like a backlit abalone shell, a tapered aristocratic nose, and large, beryl-blue eyes that looked somehow sub-aqueous, as if gazing at you languidly from the inside of an aquarium. Her breasts joggled like fruit under her loose-knit sweater, and her legs in their gray woolen tights were strong and spare. Long ago, when I'd thought about such things, I had imagined that my ideal woman would resemble a youthful Keni Shendeldecker, with intense emerald eyes behind tiny spectacles, a pinched Slavic face in a nimbus of candescent hair. But Miranda's hair was a nest of light brown curls tinged with only the faintest of strawberry highlights, her countenance the very essence of WASP. Nevertheless, seated at the table in Gerald and Hildegarde Winegarden's copper-hung kitchen, watching their twin daughters playing with the troll dolls I'd brought them, she wore an amused expression that struck a primal chord in my chest.

After a couple of bootless attempts, the Winegardens had given up trying to play matchmaker for me. Rather than question the nature of my undeclared sexuality, however, they had concluded along with everyone else that I had none at all, that I was a member of a species indigenous to academe: namely, the confirmed bachelor. An energetic man who wore a variety of hats at Mermelman College (no doubt in order to cover—my dig—a spreading bald spot), Gerald Winegarden was forever threatening to bring me into his Gender as Metaphor class as Exhibit A: the self-impregnating androgyne. Gerald's wife, Hildy, was a generous but sometimes abrasive public defender, her top-heavy presence discouraging all and sundry from making the poor joke of calling her "Hildegarden" a second time. With her attitude of patient exasperation, she had pronounced me during my introduction to their visitor "a lost cause, though we continue to feed him pro bono, if only to keep him alive. Is he worth keeping alive? You tell me."

At that, Miranda Pratt had allowed a sly, dimple-making smile to quicken her features, as if she suspected there might be more to me than met the eye. But the smile had flickered out by the time she extended her fine-boned hand, which, when I took it, gave me a frisson that tickled my scrotum and constricted my tongue. This was a good thing, since my standard MO on such occasions was to proceed by alienating the guest with a combination of condescension and self-abasement. It was a type of behavior that had become habitual: present me to a woman, any woman, and I straightaway offered her unsolicited reasons she shouldn't look to me for a suitable companion. Not that the ladies were beating a path to my door, but in case one showed up, she should know that the door was locked. There was, of course, the real possibility that I was in fact the undesirable thing I advertised myself to be, but did I care? Suddenly, yes, it seemed that I did.

Which didn't mean I was able to curb my tongue for long. Once I'd absorbed the initial shock of feeling attracted to the guest, I tried my best (which was more than sufficient) to be a boor. I learned over dinner that Miranda, an old school chum of Hildy's from their salad days at Smith College, was an artist—who wasn't? She was currently illustrating a children's book while in residence at the nearby artist's colony of Hiram's Rock, affectionately called "The Rock" by its fortunate inmates. I knew of the place, though I'd never been there, and imagined it full of pampered types preening themselves as they strolled among topiary hedges wearing togas and laurel wreaths. It was a vision I felt compelled to share with the table, though, rather than offended, Miranda picked up the thread of my satire without dropping a stitch.

"That's right," she assured me, at once entering into the mischief and shooting me down for my bad attitude. "We sit around sipping aperitifs on the piazza, recalling the banquet years in Montmartre before the Americans arrived to spoil the fun. . . ." I resented her all the more for inciting my admiration.

Thereafter, as Miranda gave an animated account of an outing to a village antique shop or a performance by a local opera company, I made to deflate her exuberance with some uninvited comment. "I've always found fun to be highly overrated," I might offer, or, "For me a stuffy, closeted existence puts your rich, full experience in the shade." During one of my sallies, Miranda turned toward me, chin perched fetchingly in the palm of her hand, to say, "I *so* wanted to know this about you." At that point Hildy, just returned from upstairs with the twins—washed, paja-maed, and ready to say good night—threatened me with a restraining order. As the two little girls were still carrying their grotesque tchotchkes, I fell to explaining how the dolls were really Uziel and Azazel, a pair of fallen angels that God had turned ugly for pitching woo with mortal ladies.

"What's pigeonwoo?" asked the less sullen of the little girls, rubbing an eye already drooping with sleep. Their redoubtable mother warned me to stop corrupting her children, while Gerald amiably threatened to throw me out by the scruff of my neck. Then Hildy excused herself again to "put down" the twins, which prompted from me an unwelcome refer-ence to Medea. By the time she'd come back to rejoin the grown-up conversation—consisting largely of comparing notes on regional points of interest that Miranda was more familiar with than I—I had with-drawn into a peevish silence. After a while I said it was time I ought to be going and waited to hear protests regarding my premature departure, though none were forthcoming. In fact, they scarcely paused in what I now perceived as an exclusive confab to acknowledge my leaving.

I returned to my rooming house in an agony of regret. Hoping to di-vert my mind from thoughts of the illustrator, I tried dipping into the books that lay facedown around my bed—Solomon ibn Verga's *Shevet*

Yehuda, Itsik Kipnis's zesty *Khadoshim un teg.* But the books cold-shouldered me, the words refusing to yield up their essence, as if, by desiring a woman, I'd forfeited my right to comprehend them. I'd betrayed, if for only one evening, my ruling passion, an act punishable by guilt and fear, and in the small hours, I began deeply to dislike the woman who'd awakened in me such mixed sensations. This will pass, I told myself; by morning Miranda Pratt will have faded into a mild distraction. But in the morning, which I thought would never come, I felt like an exile in my own room, the room a lonely satellite circling the earth.

Miranda Pratt: with a slap, her surname revoked whatever dreamy promise her "Christian" name might hold out. My ears were offended by such an unbiblical name. Yet I wanted the fresh-faced woman in some way that bypassed the libidinal, wanting not so much to sleep with her (though her lean-limbed body incidentally made me ache) as to possess her like a dybbuk. But wanting Miranda Pratt was tantamount to wanting something other than the equipoise I'd enjoyed for a decade or more, wanting to upset that contentment and wreak havoc with the predictable life I had so painstakingly put in place. My only consolation was that, given my performance of the previous night, I hadn't a prayer of satisfying my craving.

All the same, when a decent hour had arrived, my heart tolling like a bell buoy in a swell, I dialed Hiram's Rock. Since the colony was known for protecting its own from intruders, I was not surprised when a curt receptionist confirmed my sense of trespass by informing me that there were no telephones in the artists' studios, but I could leave a message if I wanted. *Dear Miranda, my life is bubkes without you,* I thought of saying, but settled for *Please call if you get the chance.* I left the request along with my name and number halfheartedly, wondering why, after the impression I'd made, Miranda Pratt would ever bother to get back in touch. I'd been told she had only two weeks left in her residency, and couldn't imagine she would want to spend any part of that precious time with a *nudzh* such as myself. So when a day and a night passed without my hearing from her, convinced she would never call, I wrote the whole thing off. Or at least I told myself that was that, while my stomach turned over like a barrel churn.

She phoned the next evening, curious to know what I wanted, saying, "By the way, I thought you were a total jackass the other night."

"I'm glad you feel you can be honest with me," I replied.

"What do you want?"

"Maybe we could get together."

"For what? So you can tell me how spoiled and bogus I am again?"

"Did I say that?"

"More or less. You were really dreadful company."

Even then I had an urge to assure her that she hadn't seen anything yet, but I stifled the impulse. "Look, I'm sorry," I said at length. "I didn't mean to be so disagreeable; it's an old tic I'm having a hard time kicking. I've kind of lost the knack of being social."

"A tic." She was still weighing the word.

Once more I asked if we could meet.

"You mean, like a date?" She was incredulous.

The word was as loaded for me as it apparently was for her but, unable to think of a handy euphemism, I let it stand.

"A date with you?" Still wanting to get it straight.

"Why not?"

"Just let me check my calendar. Oh, sorry, I'm booked till the millennium."

I sighed. "You're right, it was a stupid idea. You'd be wasting your time with the likes of me."

Silence.

"Anyway, my apologies for having disturbed you . . ."

Still nothing.

". . . in your peace and tranquility . . . ," I was saying as she simultaneously submitted, "Okay, I guess I could meet you sometime tomorrow after work."

"What's that?" I asked.

"I said I guess I could see you after work tomorrow."

"Work?"

"Work," she repeated. "Despite your picture of coddled decadence, I am here to work. How about three o'clock?"

"You sure you're not just doing this because you feel sorry for me?"

"Don't press your luck," she snapped, and, discomposed as I was, I managed to suggest the bar at the Peregrine Inn.

We met amid the pewter and varnished spruce of the restored

eighteenth-century coach house on Broadway, which, in all my years in Old Binstock, I had never entered. There were a few middle-aged tourists in cardigans with designer insignias sipping mulled cider, and in my conservative professor's outfit (tweed jacket, tan chinos), I went virtually unnoticed, though I felt like a sore thumb all the same. But for my room, the campus, and a few safe houses, I felt out of place everywhere; moreover, I was intensely aware of the imprudence of this particular appointment. In my youth I'd known women, I reminded myself, though they had all been fly-by-night affairs that dissolved almost immediately upon consummation. But this was something else: a date, forgodsakes. It occurred to me that, checkered history aside, I had never been on an official date. I hadn't a clue how to conduct myself.

Still, the bar at the Peregrine in its understated pretension seemed a neutral enough spot for our meeting. But as I sat gazing through the mullioned windows, which refracted the lemony light of the early-April afternoon, I realized that, since meeting Miranda, I'd spun such a web of sentiments around her that I could scarcely even recall what she looked like. So it was with a mixture of relief and terror that I saw, when she sauntered into the bar in her hiking boots and tight jeans, a purple scarf holding back the floodtide of her butterscotch hair, that she was lovely.

She seemed completely at ease as she stepped up to the table and told me, as I stood, not to stand. Removing her parka, she squeezed into the opposite side of the booth and asked in her manner of simultaneously teasing and being in earnest, "Do you come here often?"

"Used to," I lied, trying to conceal the tremor in my voice, "until the Americans arrived to spoil the fun."

She made a puzzled face, not catching the reference, and, seeing her confusion, I wanted to set the record straight. "I don't get out much."

"So you implied."

We ordered drinks—wine for her, beer for me—from a white-haired waiter whose exaggerated deference seemed almost a taunt. I wanted to hurry up and find common ground between us, establish at least that we shared the mortal condition of our race, but I was uncertain how to begin. Meanwhile I was convinced that nothing I said could undo the damage I'd done at dinner the other night. Then there was my instinct to compound that damage, to call attention to my purulent cheeks (dormant now for years) and my terminal retreat into the Jewish past. The Saul you got in the here and now was no better than a dissembler, the mere eidolon of a human being who wasn't quite there.

Attempting a gambit, I discovered that I was really and truly tongue-tied. "I . . . um . . . that is to say . . ."

She anticipated me. "You want to apologize for being such a jerk the other night?"

I nodded, and she seemed satisfied, not so much with the nod as at having correctly guessed the answer to a riddle.

"Forget it," she assured me, awarding me a sardonic grin. "I'd decided pretty early in the evening to dismiss everything you said. Anything else?"

"No . . . well, yes, I mean, it's just that I . . . um . . ."

"You're a scholar and a recluse who's lost what few social skills he ever had but still can't resist the urge to come out and play? You said as much already—though I added the part about coming out."

I made a feeble attempt to smile; there was nothing left to impart.

"Saul," she continued, wrinkling her satiny brow, "can I call you Saul?" I gaped: what else would she call me? "All this trapped-in-an-ivory-tower stuff—isn't it a bit of a cliché? After all, you're not Rapunzel. So why don't you just drop it and find a less hackneyed script?"

"This from a woman who asks if I come here often," I apostrophized to the rafters, thinking on the one hand, What a presumptuous minx, while on the other that she was remarkable: only just arrived, and already she'd left me without a leg to stand on. Floundering for purchase, I found myself suddenly asking her, "Can I tell you a story?"

The question caught us both off guard, but, taking advantage of her momentary silence, I did in fact launch into a tale. It could have been any tale—my brain was a regular grab bag of them—though it happened to be the fable of "The Four Who Entered Paradise," which I told hurriedly, without stopping for details, as if only to get to the end before I was interrupted. This I managed to do in fairly short order, concluding on a pithy note, ". . . Of the four rabbis, Ben Azzai died, Ben Zoma went mad, Aher lost his faith, and only Rabbi Akiva descended in peace."

Miranda's expression was a total blank.

"I didn't say it was a very good story," I was quick to assert; nor, I realized, did it have the least bearing on our present situation. "But you

should know that the four rabbis correspond to the four levels of understanding implied by the acronym PaRDeS, which itself corresponds to
the four things one is forbidden by divine law to ponder. To wit: what is
above, what is below, what came before time, and what will come after.
'For he who contemplates these things,' it says in Talmud, 'it would be
better for him not to have been born. . . .' "

With her eyes closed, Miranda alternated between showing me the
ink-smudged palm of her hand and placing a forefinger to her lips. When
at last I shut up, she opened her nacreous eyes. "All right," she said, as if attempting to get something straight in her mind, "so this is . . . what? To
try and wow me with your erudition? Like you're not really one of us but
live in some ethereal realm of mystical stories?"

I considered. "That's about the size of it." But when I began to explain
how I was practically made of stories, that they'd come to replace my very
internal organs, Miranda held up her hand to shush me again, evidently
still weighing my case. Then, having apparently arrived at a decision, she
gave a nod and announced, "What you need is to climb a mountain."

It took a minute to realize she was serious, by which time she'd stood
up and come around to hustle me to my feet. Even as I took one last swig
of beer and handed some money to the groveling waiter, she was shoving
me toward the door, then out into the chilly afternoon. She had a rusty
Volkswagen the color of split-pea soup parked beside the curb, and once
we'd settled ourselves (still without speaking) into its crumb-dusted
seats, she started the engine and bucked off in the direction of the Berkshires.

I remembered that she'd been to school in the area and was acquainted
with the lay of the land; so, after stating my nominal protests (it was late in
the day, I was improperly dressed, the mountains were beyond the gravita-
tional pull of my desk), I relaxed and began to enjoy the scenery. The vertical meadows were divoted in new crocuses, maculate with blotches of
creeping green; dandelions wafted like spindrift; leafless trees sprouted
buds like droplets wagged from a wet dog's tail. Everything was poised
to explode into fecundity, and I, willing abductee, felt close to bursting
myself.

We left the car in a roadside lot near a trailhead, then began—as I followed Miranda—to make the ascent up a rocky footpath that hugged the

gusty north side of Garnet Hill. There were tall trees through which the cold sunlight slanted in luminous chutes and ladders that we seemed to be clambering up as we ascended the steep slope. There were clumps of early wildflowers that I recognized (along with the trees) from my pastoral days in Arkansas, though I couldn't remember their names, but this posed no problem, since Miranda made a point of identifying for my information whatever flora and fauna we encountered along the way. Hickory, silver beech, burning bush, wintergreen, maidenhair, lady's slipper, larkspur, trillium, Star of Bethlehem—she named them as if introducing me to friends. She held out a hand to still me when she spotted a baby deer and its mother, a milk snake striped like a barber pole just emerged from hibernation, a fox beside a sudsy cascade. So conversant was she with the wilderness that I imagined that, like Solomon or Rima from *Green Mansions,* Miranda Pratt might also speak the language of birds. Yet she lived in Manhattan and was an artist, which was the sum total of what I knew about her so far. I should draw her out, I thought, but I was much too busy complaining on principle about my inappropriate attire, how the wind pierced my jacket and the torn scabs of my blistered feet were filling my oxfords with blood. It was how I concealed the pleasure I took in my long-latent body's exertion, at entering with an athletic woman as surefooted as a mountain goat the unexplored landscape that was the umbral backdrop of my scholarly years. Light-headed at being so far from my desk, I was in danger of experiencing joy.

What's more, I was having too much fun inventing her story from scratch to want to taint my fantasies with the truth. An orphan, she had been left on the doorstep of a strict Lutheran minister and his stolid wife in Kansas, and, rebellious from the first, had grown up a tomboy running loose on the prairie with the children of red Indians, et cetera. But when I began to grow a little weary of listening to her christening everything in nature, I started to quiz her a bit and learned that her background was closer to Edith Wharton than Willa Cather. She hailed from a downwardly mobile family of old-moneyed Boston brahmins, who disapproved of her lifestyle and considered her an unregenerate "spinster"—a word that, barely thirty, she clearly savored. For all that, she seemed to enjoy being her family's chief source of gossip and appreciated them for the retrograde eccentrics they were.

This was altogether too sanitized a picture, and, instinctively distrustful of her hardihood, I wondered what was missing. What, for instance, was her history with men? For all I knew, she could have been married. "Are you married?" I asked, and received a withering look over her shoulder; then, turning again to watch me trip over a rotten log, she warned me of the obstacle after the fact. So she was single; that was a start, but more than that I wasn't anxious to know. For the time being, I had enough of the subject before me for study: the shifting lobes of her blue-jeaned buttocks, the elongated S of her spine beneath a tea rose parka, the apricot-scented farrago of her breeze-riffled curls. All these features warranted scrupulous examination, and, following Miranda Pratt up the mountain, I became an ardent student of her parts. I learned also that she had the well-traveled worldliness of her class, an intimacy with art and culture that was her birthright, a fluency in several (living) languages. Her résumé included a wide range of part-time jobs in the service industry and years of penny-ante freelance commissions, but these days she'd struck it relatively rich. She was supported by a publisher's advance divided between herself and the author of the children's book for which she was currently making illustrations.

The climb up Garnet Hill—too tall for a hill, really, and too short for a mountain—took us just over an hour. Sharing with Miranda the view from the top, which included three darkling states and a vermilion sunset, I thought I could also see the sad entirety of my life so far. By the time we'd congratulated each other on our conquest of the summit and begun our twilight descent, I was convinced that all my experience to date had been merely a protracted prelude to meeting Miranda Pratt. Almost jaunty, I came close to telling her another irrelevant story or two; I seemed to have found my footing at last. But the near dark had a quieting effect, and her face, clearly lit from within, seemed to elicit an echo in the hollow of my breast that left me speechless. "I guess I miscalculated the time," she admitted, as we were overtaken by shadows, and her apology touched me: she was fallible, no longer a Natalie Bumpo. The trail back down was at times nearly perpendicular, a giant's staircase of treacherous stones, and both of us, occasionally stumbling, had to steady each other. This necessitated some reciprocal touching, and, while grabbing an arm through layers of clothing hardly constituted a tender contact, I nevertheless felt that our bodies were in cautious dialogue. When the craggy incline finally gave way to a gently sloping pine-needle floor, I declared myself suffering from exhaustion, inflamed joints, hypothermia, and rapture at having been aired out by such a vital woman.

"Oh, stop it," Miranda scolded me, but I knew I'd gained stature in her eyes through my willingness to tag along with her into the clouds. This was especially evident when, dropping me off at my Hawthorne Street residence, she invited me to come see her studio the following afternoon.

Back in my room I collapsed on the sleigh bed, home free, relieved to have returned in one piece to my scholar's grotto. I had an impulse, but not the energy, to pull books off their shelves and heap them on top of me, then pictured myself crawling out from under them as from a bomb site. I thought of the unborn infant in the legend who pleads with the presiding angel that he's not yet ready to leave the womb. "You were formed against your will," says the angel, "and must go forth into the world against your will." Still, there were a number of things that, according to the books, were worth entering the world for—such as love? But love stories had never figured prominently in the Jewish canon, which tended to favor tales about heroes, saints, and knaves. Then I had to remind myself that Miranda Pratt was not a story; she was a flesh-and-blood woman for whom, if I wanted her, I would have to leave my pentagonal room. I would have to marry her, of course, and adhere to the commandment to be fruitful and multiply—but wasn't I getting a little ahead of myself? After all, just days before, my life had been perfectly complete, so how was it that all of a sudden something so crucial seemed to be missing? It was a question that kept me bedridden until the alarm rang for my morning survey class in the Culture of the East European Jews.

But I was on the porch swing waiting for her when she pulled up that afternoon in her split-pea Beetle. I was a little ashamed at not having asked to see her work in the first place, and that she'd had to volunteer to show me of her own accord. Also, I worried I might lack the vocabulary to judge it. And what if I didn't like it? What if I found her art shallow and insipid, revealing a humdrum soul unworthy of my blind infatuation? Then I would be thankfully let off the hook. But when she took me by the hand and led me into the snug stone studio she'd been assigned at the Rock, I was duly captivated; she was a dreamer, too. The images pinned to the plasterboard walls were conceived in various media—the "spot" illustrations executed in woodcuts in the style of the German expressionists, the full-page plates done in a medley of rich acrylics and gouache. The woodcuts consisted entirely of animals, real and imaginary, a bestiary designed for the book by the children's author Leticia Teasel (née Blaustein), with whom Miranda was collaborating. While the monochromatic woodcuts of individual animals were necessarily spare of detail, the painted scenes involving the exploits of a little girl in search of her lost tabby cat were shot through with color and intricately wrought. Heath Robinson, Sidney Sime, Arthur Rackham, and Edmund Dulac were some of the names Miranda conjured with, artists (she lectured me) who combined a certain graphic formality with bold invention and playfulness. Then she apologized for having lectured me.

The book itself was called *The Animals' Lost and Found* and told the story of Amelia, who loses her kitten and sets out to find her by following the string from an unraveled ball of yarn. The string leads her through forests and over mountains to a place at the edge of the sea, where lost pets have turned up since the beginning of time. There are cats and dogs, but also barnyard animals, wombats, lemurs, cockatoos, woolly mammoths, hippogriffs, manticores, and dragons—all of them living in a peaceable harmony, bonded by their abandoned condition. Reunited with her kitten, Amelia sets out, with the animals' help, to build an ark to bring them back home with her. I suggested that certain other fabulous beasts, such as the ziz, the shamir, and the Messiah ox, were conspicuously absent from the catalog, then took the liberty of mentioning further paradigms of the quest theme in Jewish folklore. But when I saw how I was stupefying the illustrator with my pedantics, I changed course and assured her, ingratiatingly, "You're a wizard."

Miranda searched my face for sincerity, then seemed indifferent at having discovered it. "You think so?" she said flatly, turning to observe her own work. "I think I'm too derivative by half, kind of a skillful faker without an original bone in my body."

Her verdict alarmed me. Where was yesterday's intrepid trailblazer? This one was vulnerable, with holes in her confidence I wanted to rush to shore up: "Your work occupies its own unique dimension. . . ." But it was clear she wasn't fishing for compliments, that she had in fact not a trace of self-pity. She let me gabble on a moment before abruptly changing the topic, allowing as she did a mote of devilment to enter her eye.

"What about you? Do you write anything or do you just . . . teach?" Her voice dropping a baleful octave on the last word.

"Do I detect a swipe at my noble profession?"

"Not at all," Miranda was quick to insist, but, having heard what I'd heard, I admitted that my job was merely an expedient. "Sometimes I write articles," I muttered contritely, "which I publish in places like *Prooftexts* and *Hebrew Hermeneutics,* all your standard beach-reading mags. . . ." Then I confessed that I used to write poems.

Mercifully, she let the subject go.

I turned again to appreciate the fruits of Miranda's labors, which seemed in part the product of the environment that was nurturing them. The art colony's setting, among avenues of pines radiating from the hub of a Tudor mansion (the mansion itself overshadowed by the preglacial sugarloaf from which the place took its name), invited fanciful creations. Her live-in studio, with its inglenook and snowy owl perched on a limb outside the leaded window, was a page from an album of architectural genres—half-timbered cottages, log hunter's lodges, stone chapels tucked about the grounds behind spinneys and under boulders, so that no single retreat was in sight of another. Cynical as I'd been about the Rock, I now saw Miranda Pratt as a naturalized citizen of her surroundings, inhabiting her sanctum along with her mythical menagerie like a lady St. Jerome. Or maybe Prospero's daughter. When we climbed back into her Bug, I felt, as I had the day before, that an age had elapsed since I'd last seen Hawthorne Street. At the curb in front of the rooming house, I asked her if she would like to come up and breathed a sigh when, touching my sleeve, she said another time; she wanted to get back to the colony for dinner.

"Tonight is roast-basilisk night."

I wish I could say that Miranda and I became inseparable during her last week and a half at the Rock, but she continued to stick to her routine throughout most of the day, and I had my teaching duties, though they were by now fairly rote and required only minimal preparation. For all her ironclad work ethic, however, Miranda still had a taste for afternoon outings; further, she seemed keen to have me along as an escort, and, while the terms of our association remained undefined, I was more than eager to put myself at her disposal. Together we attended an open-air concert of Prokofiev in a locust glade with paper lanterns hung overhead; we saw a performance of *The Red Shoes* in which, when the woodsman lopped off the dancer's feet, the bloody stumps unfurled scarlet ribbons into the audience; we saw a traveling exhibition of Fauves in Williamstown, whose colors put the natural world to shame. Thus expanding my horizons, as Miranda assured me, into uncharted latitudes. We took a hike through an orchard and a bog, stopped at a colonial tavern above a millrace for coffee and pastries, where I listened like a disciple to Miranda's throwaway judgments on art and life and me—about whom she fancied she was becoming an expert.

"So what you're telling me," she tersely observed, after I'd given a brief account of my conversion from wanderer to scholar, "is that you've degenerated from a Puck to a shmuck." And on another occasion, when I allowed that the sequestered life might have had some adverse effects, "You're like the George Burns character who feels bad when he feels good for fear he'll feel worse when he feels better." Concerning my Jewish mania, about which she could be critical to the point of anti-Semitic, she once suggested, "Maybe you should have your heart circumcised as well?" And when I told her that was very cute, she begged my pardon and asked if I would teach her some secret Jewish stuff, "like how to dance the kaddish?"

Her conversation ranged in tone from Dorothy Parker to Mahatma Gandhi. If she had a headache, it was, "I think my brain is trying to make a pearl." Or, tired from overwork: "I've been in my studio so long I'm starting to feel like Anne Frank." On the subject of a chronically dejected friend: "She suffers from an inoperable sorrow." And yoga, which she had practiced for years: "I bagged it when they told me to breathe through my vagina." On God, with whom she maintained an affectionately adversarial relationship: "The rumors of His death have been greatly exaggerated." Her allusions to sex were equally casual, though I suspected her of calculating their unsettling impact on me. As when, removing her sweater to reveal a sleeveless jersey through which her nipples poked like pushpins, she waxed grandiloquent, "In the best orgasms, the soul sneezes and the heart says gesundheit." And with respect to an ineffectual lover: "He was about as adaptable as a herm."

"You be the Hunger Artist," she might exclaim upon the arrival of food at our table, "and I'll be the hungry artist," for she did indeed have an appetite like a horse. Little was lost on her; she was continually calling my attention to some passing phenomenon I would have otherwise missed, such as a kite tangled in telephone wires like a clef in a musical score, a root system raising a slate paving stone like a skeleton pushing up the lid of a tomb. I would have missed these things because I am unobservant and because, whenever she looked elsewhere, I stole a peek at Miranda Pratt and felt the galvanic hum of her aura in my gut. She was full of political and cultural opinions that sounded marvelously sophisticated to my ears; but then, since immersing myself in the Jewish corpus, I'd managed to stay largely ignorant of world affairs. With Ben Azzai, I had declared, "What shall I do? My soul desires Torah. Let the world continue by the efforts of others." Hostages and meltdowns, détente and intifada, perestroika and glasnost, all occurred while I was otherwise disposed. And though Miranda's pronouncements sometimes inspired me to want to stay abreast of current events, I was seldom moved to look beyond the erotic stimulus her intelligence evoked.

There was an afternoon when we were accompanied on one of our country excursions by another artist from the colony, an older woman named Candida, who got on my nerves. By virtue of her age, in addition to the caparison of an inverness cape and tam-o'-shanter (and the near-rhymed affinity of her name with the illustrator's, with which she set such store), Candida came on like Mother Courage; she made me cringe by repeatedly bestowing her blessing in whispered asides on my relationship with Miranda Pratt. Of course, I would have resented sharing Miranda's company with anyone, but more than that I resented that there was really no relationship for Candida to give her blessing to. During my time with the illustrator, I'd been determined to comport myself as a model suitor, though I had no hint as to how such a person behaved. Add to my inexperience a conflicted nature and a fear of transgressing unwritten laws, and you can see why I trod so softly, so gingerly in fact that it was easy for Miranda to regard me as no kind of a suitor at all. Apart from her palsy squeezings of my forearm or knee, and my quasi-accidental brushings against her in doorways, we scarcely touched. She would announce to me and anyone else we ran into—my Mermelman colleagues, for instance, or her fellow colonists, even my students, who shared (I was aware) bizarre theories about my sex life—that I was her project. Like my colleagues she viewed me as a charity case, though rather than merely feed me, it was her self-appointed task to reintroduce me to firsthand experience.

I could hardly hide the fact that I was panting after her, though I was careful not to demonstrate any manifest symptoms, which made it all the easier for Miranda to pretend my desire didn't exist. If I allowed so much as a sigh to escape my larynx—the most salient eruption of yearning I'd yet expressed—she treated me like an ill-bred pet passing gas. Once, however, after a second cocktail (my tolerance for alcohol having diminished with the years), I succumbed to an urge to assert myself as a sexual being; I recalled aloud my heyday as the rogue *schwantz* of London's East End, "my penis legendary as the Ripper's knife." "Of course it was," said Miranda, patting the back of my hand; and, had I seen fit to present my privy member, I'm confident she'd have patted its bald pink head with the same condoling delicacy. She seemed not to acknowledge the least scintilla of physical tension between us, an attitude that was its own unspoken caveat; and if I were honest, I had to admit that, mythical bestiaries notwithstanding, we had very little in common. Still, I told myself it was enough just to be with her; more than that I wasn't ready for.

Then, before the dynamic of our friendly relations could drive me mad, Miranda was gone, though there'd first been a parting scene in my apartment, which she stopped by on her way out of town. Shown to my door by Mrs. Rudelhuber, who seemed to teeter between disapproval and outright pandering, she entered my room for the first time and surveyed it with a wry regard. "How will you ever bust out of this place?" she wondered sadly.

Standing before the ramparts of books, I sniffed her apricot fragrance, admired the viper's nest of her hair, her beryllium eyes, and felt that, materialized here in my stronghold, she was somehow more unattainable than ever. "What do you mean?" I asked, playing along with her joke. "I can always tie sheets together and lower myself from the window." Then, perceiving that perhaps she wasn't joking: "Or I can walk out the door." This said with some determination, as if I hadn't already done it for her sake a dozen times.

But if she heard me, she made no sign. "Well, if you ever make a clean getaway, I've been known to harbor fugitives."

She gave me a hug that I complained was painful, shattering as it had the plaster cast around my newly circumcised heart; she offered her satin cheek to be kissed but neglected to give me her number in Manhattan. I assumed it was an oversight rather than a deliberate omission but reserved the right to entertain a suspicion or two. In any case, the absence of her phone number (and address) made her departure seem so final that I relaxed into an anodyne resignation: it had been a close call. Having ventured nothing, I'd gained nothing, but neither had I lost anything in the process of adoring Miranda Pratt. I settled back with a raggedy first edition of Mendele's *Dos kleyne mentshele* and marveled at the degree to which I'd tempted fate. Now I could carry on with my program; I could look forward to growing older and wiser while looking back with a bittersweet pang on unrequited longing—it was the best of all worlds. But the restlessness Miranda had engendered in me had taken root. The words in my books had begun to aspire to flesh, and while my very bones resisted the idea, I knew that I would soon have to quit my room for the wide world again. The illustrator was a clarion call I could never have forgiven myself for failing to answer, but, rhetoric aside (rhetoric be damned!), I wanted desperately to be near her.

I called the Winegardens for her number and braced myself for the inevitable ragging from Gerald, who relayed the information to Hildy that I was in pursuit of her former schoolmate. I could hear her shrill disbelief in the background ("Not our Sauly, the epicene!"), while I wondered why I hadn't merely dialed Information. Perhaps I'd wanted to announce the beginning of a nervy new chapter of my life, a departure for which brass bands should play and ladies wave hankies from windows. Gerald rang off with an acerbic, "Good luck, old man."

Before dialing Miranda's number, I had rehearsed what I would say several times over. *I have some research to do at the Forty-second Street*

Library, pitching my tone between business and pleasure, *so if you're free . . .* When she answered, her voice on the line sounded so chillingly distant that I started over again: "Saul Bozoff here; maybe you don't remember me, we met at the home of Gerald and Hildegarde—" "Please, Saul, I'm awfully busy," she interrupted. "What is it you want?" And at once it was clear we were strangers again. My brain was already framing the words: *Sorry, my mistake, another time . . .* , which I managed to override in order to speak my piece: "I've got some research . . ." Magnanimously she agreed to have dinner with me on Friday night.

"Don't do me any favors," I groused, when I'd hung up the phone.

I took the train to New York and got a room in a cheap hotel full of retired merchant seamen near Union Square. It had been more than a decade since I'd been in the city, and its filth and ferocious energy were a jolt to my system. In the streets, armies of the upright dodged the strewn bodies of the homeless stuffed into bags or camped in refrigerator crates like makeshift mangers. Preposthumous cadavers afflicted with AIDS, jostled by tides of pedestrians, wandered as dismally as images out of a plague year. I imagined the morning garbage brigades shouting, "Throw out your dead!" and longed for the old black-and-white New York of the movies, in which liveried doormen tipped their caps to Nick and Nora Charles. In the brutal face of things, I had to remind myself repeatedly that it was springtime and I was a man in love.

Miranda's apartment, where I'd been told to meet her, was in a battle-scarred warren on East Third Street just above Houston: two rooms in a narrow L with a closet-size kitchen, its peeling plaster showing the laths beneath like a gaping wound. One of the rooms, in its cramped conversion to a studio, was chaotic with the tools of her trade—a drawing table covered with disposable palettes dolloped as if from a leaky rainbow, aluminum paint tubes like dead sardines, wooden plaques gouged in animal shapes, and brushes left soaking in jars on a bowlegged sideboard. The woodcuts and scenes of the heroine's travels from *The Animals' Lost and Found* were pinned about the walls, but rather than transforming the space as they'd done at Hiram's Rock, the illustrations were themselves overwhelmed by postcards and photos torn from magazines, train schedules, phone numbers, and quotations like items caught up in a maelstrom.

"Behold the digs of an East Village hipster artist," said Miranda, who, in a paint-smeared T-shirt and jeans, looked a little stranded amid the clutter. Her hair, gathered carelessly from her forehead by an elastic head-band, resembled corkscrew noodles on the boil, while her eyes, slightly narrowed and raw about their edges, seemed to challenge me to make a disparaging remark.

A sulfurous odor of kitty litter permeated the atmosphere, but when I asked where was the cat, she told me it had died sometime ago. Then it seemed to me that her departure from the Rock had involved an actual fall from grace, and I was as moved by her circumstances as I was disap-pointed that she had taken no pains to prepare for my visit. She was Cin-derella after the ball, and I couldn't help comparing the scruffy Miranda Pratt to women I'd seen on my walk from the subway—sylphlike women free of Miranda's edge and attitude (I surmised), beside whom the illus-trator would have appeared almost plain. That's when I decided that my obsession with Miranda was arbitrary; any of her tribe who had crossed my path would have served as well. It was all wrong, my coming to see her. I was an interloper, a dim figure from her Hiram's Rock retreat, who should have had the decency to remain a memory rather than show up here in her life. The scales dropped from my eyes as disillusion prevailed; though why, I wondered, was I still unable to stop ogling her paint-flecked face?

At dinner in a neighborhood dive, where we were served some weird fusion of Neapolitan and Cajun cuisine, the conversation was at first a little awkward; she had, after all, left Old Binstock on a somewhat sour note—sour because I had sulked at her farewell: the chaste buss on the cheek she'd offered me had seemed such small change. But eventually, af-ter a glass or two of wine, she began to relax and confide in me as she had done during our several jaunts. The advance for the kids' book was all but spent, and, taking on one too many projects to compensate for her losses, she had spread herself too thin. Meanwhile she'd attempted to re-cycle an old wastrel boyfriend, which had turned out to be a definite mis-take. It was the kind of disclosure usually reserved for parsing with close women friends.

After dinner we strolled the neighborhood, which was undergoing a radical transition. The dark streets and decaying tenements that had formerly been the haunts of junkies were strung now in garlands of lights. Storefront art galleries were replacing the nefarious shooting galleries; cafés, bookstores, and boutiques cropped up in once abandoned shops. Proud of having been a pioneer in this former urban wilderness—was there no wilderness in which she did not feel at home?—Miranda was skeptical of the creeping gentrification. Her egalitarian sympathies were offended by the young careerists that followed on the heels of bohemian homesteaders, inflating the rents and hounding squatters out of the parks. But to my mind the neighborhood, awash with so much showy youth, was reminiscent of the late sixties and early seventies, a time when, for better or worse, I, too, had been at large in the world. Still reeling from the information about the boyfriend, I made an effort to overpower my mood; I told her in a burst of sham exuberance that this visit was something of a homecoming for me. But Miranda was quick to provide perspective.

"You're a greenhorn, Bozoff, and you'll be a greenhorn till your dying day."

"Bozoff " was new, and I wondered if the shift to my surname was a deliberate distancing device. When we'd rearrived at her stoop, she apologized for not inviting me in, but she was operating on a deadline and had work to do for a commissioned piece that very night. "I'm not at the Rock anymore," she sighed, giving me the same soft cheek she'd offered on that afternoon in my apartment a scant week before. She wished me luck with my research, whatever it was, and told me it was nice to see me; I should call the next time I was in town. I'd had some vague notion we might get together again the following day, but now that the entire weekend stretched before me minus Miranda's company, I felt I had no further business in New York. I took the train back to Massachusetts early the next morning.

She feels nothing for me, I told myself on my return, and, after all, why should she? I knew enough of her history to have a sense of her taste in men—hunky international types with Levantine pedigrees, some of them dangerous, one in fact a Cypriot terrorist in exile. The kind of men who took love on the run, which was in some way a convenience for an artist committed to her own independence. What made me think she would ever view my sedentary self as a serious candidate for her affection? Once again I waited for the great relief of having been set free. I had narrowly escaped a messy situation with a complicated woman—I complimented myself on seeing through my infatuation to the difficulties of her character. But a sense of easement never came, and when all was said and done, I was still determined beyond reason to see Miranda again.

Forbearingly patient, as I saw it, I allowed a respectable couple of weeks to elapse before informing her that I was returning to New York. She had agreed rather hesitantly—did she see through my ruse?—to have dinner with me again, and I'd decided that, come what may, the trip wouldn't be a total loss. This time I really would seek out some material for a projected essay: a piece I'd been contemplating about the sixteenth-century *Bovo Buch*, whose Danish sources were said to be the same that Shakespeare had drawn upon for his *Hamlet*. It was an enterprise that once would have given me a charge. There were no end of resources in the city; there were the archives at the YIVO Institute and the Arbeiter Ring, the out-of-print Yiddish books in dusty shops on the Lower East Side, where I hadn't set foot since the days of Aunt Keni. Funny that in all my years of reading the texts, I had never once been tempted to visit the dead culture's most thriving repositories. But after another dinner with Miranda, during which I could scarcely believe that my feelings for her (which showed no signs of being reciprocated) had not abated, after another stroll and perfunctory invitation to a peck on the cheek, I had little heart left for mucking about in outdated lore. Miranda had displaced my abiding passion, and this was the sad fact I took home with me on my otherwise empty-handed train ride back to New England.

There I stewed in a broth of self-pity for another week before rallying to phone her again. Call me a glutton for punishment, but this time I resolved to bring matters to a head: I would press her to either recognize me as an official suitor or dismiss me forever. After some negotiation, during which she gave me the distinct impression I was being a pest, she conceded to see me that Saturday afternoon. Though I called myself every kind of a fool for continuing to run after her, the assignation made me hopeful: we would at least be keeping company in broad daylight as we had in Old Binstock, and perhaps our initial rapport would return.

When we met, Miranda asked (somewhat hopefully?) if I wouldn't rather continue my research, but I assured her that the morning had been sufficient for my needs. She said she wanted to see an exhibition of

American vernacular paintings at an uptown gallery, and I was welcome to tag along. Afterward we could maybe grab a bite before she returned to work. It was by now the middle of May, and she looked like a down-at-heel Persephone in her sandals and dimity dress. Seeing her so entirely unself-conscious, I struggled with the melancholy conviction that this was a futile exercise; it was merely an opportunity to prove once and for all that I was meant to die alone. Whatever it was I felt for her was simply a function of this sweet and savory season, to say nothing of my own loneliness—you couldn't call it love, could you?—though no other label seemed to apply.

The gallery was in temporary quarters on the second floor of an aseptic glass-and-steel tower near Lincoln Center. Until it could be moved to its permanent facility, which was under construction, the Museum of American Folk Art would have to make do in a converted complex of modular antechambers and conference rooms. This seemed altogether too corporate a setting for the array of hanging crazy quilts and wooden pitchforks, the porcelain pottery and Pennsylvania Dutch samplers, the handmade furniture, cornhusk dolls, tin weather vanes, and cypress carvings wrought by slaves. Single-minded, Miranda led me through the maze of permanent exhibits to the current show, which consisted of domestic paintings mostly on loan from private donors, though some belonged to the museum's own standing collection. The majority of the paintings had been executed on found materials (plywood, masonry, horsehide, brass) by untrained artists of various ethnic backgrounds, most from poor urban and rural communities. Outsider art, they called it. Even without Miranda's running commentary—which told me frankly more than I cared to know about this artist's technique or that one's unspoiled lack thereof—I would have been charmed. Depicting farm hamlets and cityscapes, their compositions crowded with quotidian activities (panoramas of Main Street, cross sections of apartment buildings exposing the tenants at love and work), the paintings were indifferent to perspective, ordinary color schemes, or the generally agreed-upon bounds of reality. They were a visual complement to the kinds of stories I'd been searching out these several years, and seeing them along with the illustrator made me feel like a Hansel to her Gretel, both of us having stumbled into a sacred grove.

In one painting there was a cardinal-red barn to the side of which the flayed hide of a jaundiced Christ had been nailed, a litter of hogs kneeling at his bloody feet in apparent prayer. Another composition depicted a Harlem church with an ecstatic swaying choir and a reverend with cotton-boll hair, his split coattails tugged at by angels and devils respectively. There was an Indian warrior with a breastplate and feathered bonnet dancing on a high steel girder, and a tree resembling a carousel of lynched men whose shadows ran away like slouching cats. There was an evocation of the *chazzer mark,* the Hester Street marketplace of the old Lower East Side, in which an untidy, bearded patriarch with chicken wings hovered above the pushcarts, carrying in his arms what looked like an idiot child. Before the latter, Miranda paused awhile, expressing a measure of admiration but claiming that the graphic virtuosity of the piece disqualified it as naïf and put it in the realm of the deliberately primitive— like Gauguin, say, or Dubuffet. The image itself seemed to reference Goethe's "Erl-King." Then she moved on but returned after a minute to ask what was I thinking, because I had not budged from in front of the painting. She was reprising her explanation, in a clinical language which irked me, that it was indeed an accomplished work but mislabeled as folk art, when I interrupted.

"This is my Aunt Keni's signature piece."

"What?"

"My Aunt Keni Shendeldecker who I must have told you about— that's her piece. She wasn't really my aunt, but she was as good as, and she left me her paintings in her will, which I gave her son permission to auction off. . . ." I was trying to sound matter-of-fact, as if I'd anticipated the revelation of *Der Chazzer Mark* and had perhaps been saving it expressly for Miranda, when in fact its presence was a total surprise to me—so thoroughly had the bequest of the paintings slipped my mind. In the face of Miranda's astonishment, however, I gave up any pretense to composure and was keen to tell all. Because it wouldn't do to stand in the middle of the gallery listening to a narrative of such waxing urgency, Miranda conducted me to the garden café in the building's atrium, where I continued talking without a break. Somehow, in rehearsing my past in snatches to the illustrator, I had barely touched on this chapter, concentrating instead on my overseas peregrinations. But today Aunt Keni figured larger than any experience subsequent to her demise; she was the episode out of which all others had proceeded.

I told Miranda how I'd nursed the old woman and sat vigil at her deathbed, confident that the story was lending me honor in her estimation, just as it was in my own. Maybe I should have been less profligate in the telling, but once I'd let loose my tongue, there was no stopping me; I couldn't help connecting the rediscovery of my aunt's quirky art to my adoration of Miranda Pratt. The sudden apprehension that I had come full circle made me bold, and I was convinced that with my tale I was weaving a spell.

"So you see," I concluded with more avidity than good sense, "you're the catalyst, Miranda. You lured me away from living with ghosts and brought me back to where I belong—"

"And where's that?" she asked, propping her tilted chin in her hand.

"To"—I sought the right word—"possibility!"

She simulated a smile. "Do you mean, like, today is the first day of the rest of your life?"

But no remarks, however caustic, could dampen my ardor, and I launched without preface into a description of Aunt Keni's raconteur husband, who may or may not have been blown to bits. I had begun to tell her about his campaign to seduce my aunt with a story when Miranda, annoyance fishtailing the corners of her eyes, called attention to the fact that I was talking too much.

"Excuse me, Saul," she said gently, so that I missed the familiar sharpness of her tongue, "but I don't really want the responsibility of—what's that phrase from *A Tale of Two Cities*? 'Recalled to life'?—I don't want to be responsible for recalling you to life. This is your myth, not mine."

"What do you mean?" I protested. "In Old Binstock recalling me to life was exactly what you claimed you were doing."

"Listen, bucko," she continued with a quiet finality, "if it's romance you're looking for, I have to tell you that between you and me romance is not in the cards."

"Bucko?"

I rode the train back to New England in a thunderstorm that was the all-too-obvious analogue to my own battling emotions. I was angry, primarily at myself, for having been so quick to take no for an answer. Wasn't my easy acquiescence to her rejection evidence that I hadn't wanted her enough? On the other hand, how persistent did I have to be? After all, it was she who had been the deceiver: for when you looked at the facts, hadn't Miranda led me on? Hadn't she given me grounds for hope, only to squash it at the moment of its ripening? It was she that had broken faith with our unuttered contract—Miranda Pratt, child of divorce, survivor of endless short-lived relationships, who simply distrusted men in her heart. All right, so given the mutual baggage we carried, I supposed we'd never stood much of a chance, though I still couldn't help taking it personally, thinking it was *me* she'd rejected rather than the hazards of an amorous attachment.

By the time the taxi dropped me off at my rooming house, the storm had subsided, leaving downed power lines, torn branches, and a soul-heavy sadness in its wake; it was a sadness that settled in my lower abdomen, seeping into my testicles, which ached as if they might drop like bad fruit from the bottom of a wet paper bag. I was inconsolable, and it didn't help that outdoors the immodest spring was tossing its posies with a liberality that made me feel like a luckless bridesmaid. Having lost interest in my studies, I could find no comfortable place to rest my mind; the books that once fueled me were as flat as old soda. Spiritless, I sleepwalked through my classes, teaching only through force of habit, my lips moving exclusive of the brain's engagement. The term was nearly over, but I dreaded the summer holiday. Though teaching was never a calling, it was at least a distraction, and the summer would leave me with nothing to shift the focus from my forlorn condition. It occurred to me that, having lived so long on such slender means, I'd socked away a sizable sum over the years. Even though Mrs. Rudelhuber (apologizing profusely while citing increased expenses) had raised my rent whenever it suited her, the cost of my single room had scarcely eaten into my professor's salary. I had options: I could travel if I wanted. But while the thought of pursuing tedious literary projects held no further appeal, neither could I find the motivation for leaving my room. I'd tried that already.

Came the afternoon of my lecture on the metempsychosis of the soul of Rabbi Nachman of Bratslav, a talk I had once been proud of, since it involved describing the transmutation of some of my favorite classical motifs over time. It was the talk I saved as a kind of dessert for the end of the semester. Of course, I had long since lost hold of this particular class through my phlegmatic semipresence, and on the day in question, with the sun saturating the lecture hall in its buttery light, the bees drunk on nectar stumbling in through the open windows, the students were especially indifferent—some looking out into the leafy quadrangle, others nodding over their notched and scored desks. Not that I cared; I was only going through motions. But as I scanned the room, I noticed a face in the last row of desks even less recognizable than those of the usual alien assembly. Or rather the face had a familiarity that constituted an aberration among the standard-issue strangers that populated my class. It belonged, that face (when it came into focus), to the illustrator Miranda Pratt, looking uncharacteristically glamorous in scarlet lip gloss and mascara, her curls fanning out from behind an amber headband like Clara Bow's.

I was in the middle of recounting for the nth time the death of Rabbi Nachman and his wish that the manuscripts of his stories be destroyed— "His scribe Nathan, like the knight that King Arthur commanded to throw his sword back into the lake, lied to him twice before submitting to his master's will . . ."—when, convinced that Miranda was not an apparition, I lost the thread of my lecture. My vocal chords seized in mid-sentence, and all I could manage was a quavery, "I seem to have drawn a blank," before I was forced to dismiss the class.

There was a buzz of bewilderment as the room emptied of students, some of whom, accustomed as they were to my public woolgathering, collided with one another in their haste to depart their petrified professor. In the end only Miranda remained in the hall. When she rose to approach me, looking both apologetic and pleased, the sun outlined her form through the diaphanous material of her cornflower dress. The closer she came, her ankle-high boots clumping up the hardwood aisle, the more she seemed to abandon herself to her amusement at having had such a paralyzing effect on me. She paused in front of the lectern where I stood, slid it aside with her foot, leaned forward, and gave me a hug with (I thought) a difference.

"Poor baby," said Miranda, "have I teased you unmercifully?"

"As a matter of fact . . ." I wanted to say more, but my throat was still choked with suppressed emotion. She took my hand and began to lead me out of the classroom, while I, still incapable of speech, felt like Kaspar Hauser blinking in the harsh light of day. In the quad, sunbeams fell through the canopy of oaks in columns resembling a celestial pipe organ, its music apparently audible to dallying students sprawled in the grass.

"What you need," proposed Miranda, a loose ringlet blown like a streamer across her forehead, "is to climb a mountain."

All the way up Garnet Hill, the wind fluttered her sundress, lifting the hem to expose her strong legs, which gave me to understand that she was in cahoots with the aromatic breezes to bewitch me. I followed her up the mountain in a trance, smelling colors and tasting smells: her scent was amethyst, the shade in the valley below us cinnamon and port wine. Growing warm as I slogged behind her over green stones and fallen trees that crumbled to powder underfoot, I shed my professor's carapace, only to find there was nothing beneath it but the exposed nerve of desire. At the summit of Garnet Hill, I made to hold her, but she slipped from my arms and scampered over to sit yogi fashion on a slab of dolomite that jutted above the checkerboard pastures. I mounted the rock, afraid she might jump up and spring nymphlike from the ledge, but she remained still and expectant as I seated myself opposite her. Then, straightening her arms to push herself closer, Miranda Pratt uncrossed her legs and calipered my hips with her open thighs, pulling me forward into an embrace and a kiss. A moist kiss that left my brain and vitals lit and humming like the chassis of an old radio. Overcome by her pregnable attitude and the painterly view from the mountaintop, the sudden relinquishing of the tensions of the previous weeks, of the celibate years, I lost control, and, shuddering, I released my seed into my khaki pants.

"Pathetic," I moaned, but Miranda, placing a forefinger hard against my lips, said, "No!" It was an emphatic *no* that brooked no compromise, the *no* that precedes the threat to wash your mouth out with soap. Then she laughed away my shame; it was only an accident, flattering really; there was no disgrace. And once we'd returned to my apartment, passing up the stairs beneath the watchful eye of Mrs. Rudelhuber—who, despite her own rigid rule against parietal visits, placed her hands on her battleship hips but said not a word—Miranda unbuttoned her dress. She shucked off her scant white underwear like clinging spume and, naked but for her hiking boots, knelt in front of me to undo my pants. Shoving them to my ankles, she urged me to step out of them, then removed my sticky shorts as if peeling a plaster and began to cleanse me with her lips and tongue. When I'd begun to show signs of restored virility, she rose and turned her back, walking over to perch on the edge of the sleigh bed. She studied me with a limpid but unblinking gaze as, one at a time, she lifted her legs to untie her boots and kick them off. Her body, but for its pendulous breasts, was sinewy and lithe, boyish hips in fine contrast to the coy fur of her sex and the vampiness of her beckoning forefinger. I hesitated, thinking how far had been the journey from clothing to nakedness, farther than which was to venture into the bodeful unknown.

"Have you forgotten what to do next?" she asked me.

I told her I felt like I should take off something else.

"Well, you can shuffle off your mortal coil if you want, but then you won't be much good to me."

Going to her, I did feel, once she'd enfolded me in her stripling skin, that I was somehow vacating my own; that, as we turned together on a lathe of light, my old self continued unspooling, shivarees of tiny *klezmers* and *badkonim* spilling from its folds.

Afterward, in the drowsy glow of satiety, I asked her, "What made you change your mind?"

"Who says I changed my mind?"

So I let it go: there was that in her voice that warned against further probing. Her actions may have been unexplainable to herself, and further interrogation might prove a tactical error. There was a woman—of my dreams, no less—stretched beside me in sweet lassitude, a contraband woman whose presence was in violation of all the rules. So happy a violation that the rules no longer seemed to apply. I had succeeded in bringing animate nature into my lair without so much as disturbing the order of my books, which remained serenely standing on their shelves and in their scattered archipelagoes about the floor.

The next morning, over coffee and bagels at the Broadway Café, Miranda, her face scrubbed clean of yesterday's makeup, offered out of the blue, "Because you made me feel alive."

"Eh?"

"I'm not going to say it again."

"*I* made you feel alive?" This was incredible, and I tried to quiz her as to how I might have effected such a thing.

"You got a compliment, Saul," she replied, stirring a yolky glob of honey into her tea. "Don't push it."

End of conversation.

Naturally I didn't believe her; there was of course no logic in her having come to me, no earthly reason for our being together, but I thought I knew why she'd said what she had. It was a statement of faith in who I might become. From that moment I pledged to myself that I would strive to be the man who made Miranda Pratt feel alive; I would devote myself to being worthy of her declaration.

And so began our summer idyll, which seemed from the first an unimaginable circumstance I was nonetheless determined to grow into. I muddled through to the end of the semester without further embarrassment, and suddenly the notion of a holiday had real meaning. Having no itinerary of my own to promote, I let Miranda steer the course; as far as I was concerned, it was her world and I was the inductee—though that notion could admittedly get a little tiresome. For a while we kept to a routine of seeing each other only on weekends, alternating our visits between New York and Massachusetts, but since neither of us had to abide by a strict schedule, during the breaks Miranda allowed herself between projects, we took trips. We rented a camp in the Adirondacks, a musty cabin on stilts with cane furniture and a cedar-shake roof that leaked into a carillon of strategically placed tin cans. We took a bungalow in a Catskills colony with a screened-in porch and a frog-infested cistern, where our neighbors wandered bleary-eyed in their bathrobes talking recipes and dividends. We hiked, we climbed, we swam naked in a spring-fed millpond that turned our extremities blue: on the bank we rubbed our bodies against one another until the friction made sparks, then reimmersed ourselves, causing the water to seethe as from an iron brand. We made love al fresco, at the edge of a stone quarry and in the fork of a tree, and I marveled at the easy transition from conversation to touching, how we would grow suddenly shy at discovering that we weren't talking anymore. Acquainting myself with the illustrator's anatomy, I became reacquainted with my own, my aches and pains diminishing through vigorous activity, and while Miranda was always stingy with her compliments, she sometimes praised my increasing strength.

Our country junkets—during which we ventured into deep woods by day, discovered new constellations (such as Rabbi Yedvab's Bladder or van Gogh's Ear) at night—were eminently wholesome, but in the city we were decadent. We groped each other while passing a joint beneath the table of an East Village bistro, danced a slow drag in a downtown night-club where we had first to pass muster before a doorman as forbidding as Kafka's gatekeeper. (This after I'd been previously inspected by Miranda, who dressed me in silk shirts with thin neckties until I looked like Nathan Detroit.) Having met standards, I was introduced to some of Miranda's friends, mostly impecunious artists with underground credentials, with whom my own counterculture memories seemed more a hindrance than an aid to communication. There was a gay cartoonist who had turned his hairless body into a kind of illustrated color supplement, who cut me dead when I compared his facial piercings (favorably, I believed) to a fish that had escaped many lures; and a bustier'd photographer whose gallery opening in SoHo we attended. She was exhibiting a series of photographs of little folk in daedal suits and curled slippers assembled under toadstools in community allotments, and when I congratulated her on the credibility of her hoax, she assured me with umbrage that her subjects were "taken from life." Standing back, Miranda seemed to enjoy watching me put my foot in my mouth. Indeed, those aspects of my personality that had previously set her teeth on edge—my Rip van Winkle cluelessness, my social ineptitude—now appeared to tickle her; and for my part I was more than willing to be an object of amusement so long as it afforded me another night with the illustrator and a morning after in bed eating buttered toast with fingers still rank from her scent.

Sometimes it was hard to remember what I would have been doing had she not appeared on the scene; what had I ever done without Miranda Pratt? Still, it troubled me that, but for the fact that I was coming to love her unconditionally, there seemed no obvious explanation for our involvement; a part of me was always waiting for the other shoe to fall. There were, for instance, whole areas of Miranda's nature that remained inaccessible to me, untapped mysteries more a source of discomfiture than allure. She could be selfish, short-tempered, unforgiving in ways that kept me feeling I had yet to prove myself. But while she never told me in so many words that she loved me, she would sometimes dote on me and was frequently lavish in her displays of affection. Often her teasing erupted into spontaneous parodies ("I'm the voice of your ancestor Rabbi Gefilteh from Fishstok, and I know that, from your shiksa which you're having with her relations, you are unclean!") that left me laughing till I gagged.

By the end of the summer, tired of commuting back and forth between New York and New England, Miranda and I had begun to talk about co-habitation. Or rather, I, to my amazement, had begun to suggest our living together, while she didn't rule out the possibility. Just how we would manage such an arrangement was anyone's guess, since she needed to be in Manhattan for her work, close to the places she peddled her wares, and I in Massachusetts for mine. Or did I? Because there were any number of institutions in New York City where my specialized area of learning would be marketable; New York was a Mecca, so to speak, for Jewish studies. Leaving Mermelman and my furnished room was a sobering prospect, but Miranda had already shown me that change, however daunting, could be for the best. And while I wasn't yet accustomed to the emerging mensch I now conceived myself to be, while I lacked an absolute faith in his stamina, I felt bracingly confident a change of place would consolidate my change of character.

Meanwhile the summer vacation had ended and the fall semester commenced, so we were back for the time being to what was for me the acute frustration of visiting on alternate weekends. Still, there was much to look forward to, and I remained astonished at my own freshly minted optimism, my growing conviction that books should take a backseat to experience. Weren't there, after all, more possibilities in life than in stories? Speaking of which, *The Animals' Lost and Found*, fast-tracked for publication thanks to its author's ready audience, was due out in October. A date had already been set for a combination release party and exhibition of Miranda's work at a downtown gallery, a gala occasion that would mark a turning point in her career. The weekend had assumed a certain prominence in my own mind as well, especially now that I'd begun to anticipate the eventuality of moving to the city. I'd made some discreet inquiries into job alternatives, going so far as to wangle an interview at

the Jewish Theological Seminary. Lacking a Ph.D., I would naturally be
ineligible for all but the humblest entry-level positions, but I was willing
to make sacrifices; and if this job didn't pan out, I could risk living on my
savings until something else turned up. I was convinced that something
would turn up.

On the weekend of the party, I met Miranda in her apartment, which
I gave a critical once-over: we would have to find a larger place, of course,
and even with our combined incomes, the increased rent would be a hardship; though for my part I was prepared to absorb it. I kept these thoughts
to myself, however, not wanting to burden the illustrator with such knotty
considerations on her banner night. Leaving Third Street, we headed south
across Houston, walking down Clinton Street below Delancey to where
the little storefront gallery was located. I hadn't been on the Lower East
Side proper since my time with Aunt Keni, but I was too full of enjoying
my girlfriend—dolled up for the evening in a tartan kilt that showed her
knees like russet potatoes, her snaky hair lifting the lid of her red beret—
to take much notice of my surroundings. I was congratulating myself, as
I frequently did, that so sightly and talented a woman had chosen me. I'd
long since stopped looking for the flaws in her character (what flaws?)
that might undo our solid connection, and even though I continued to
feel that I myself was on trial, that the trial might never end, I had ceased
taking the blame for every wrong chord that was struck. Together we
seemed to have reached a stage wherein we were cozy with the proposition that neither of us was perfect; and while Miranda was more cautious
than I in her affirmations, it was she who had suggested we might manage, between the two of us, to pull off a happy ending.

The book launching was, by the common yardstick for such events, a
success. Leticia Teasel, author of *The Animals' Lost and Found,* a woman
in a wimple affecting the look of an ursine Mother Goose, was present to
sign copies of the elegantly printed book. She was a hale and good-natured
charlatan, Dame Teasel, clearly accustomed to being fawned over and returning saccharine compliments in kind, but the real glory of the evening
went to Miranda. The high-colored whimsicality of the illustrations and
etchings mounted around the walls of the crowded gallery lent the balmi-
ness of a drunken boat to little Amelia's floating zoo. Miranda's friends
and admirers—turned out en masse in their regulation black attire: the

women dressed like merry widows, the men like Lash LaRue—expressed their universal approval, though their remarks seldom rose above the fatuous. The work was "fraught with a surface sunlight that can blind you to its depth . . ."; it was, "in the words of Marianne Moore, 'an imaginary garden with real toads,' not to say monsters and unicorns. . . ." There was an effusive character in an Eton jacket laying claim to the higher sensitivity who declared that, despite being found, the animals remained lost, as witness their grieving eyes. There was even a contingent of the target audience on hand, for some of the attendees had brought their children, whose greedy fascination with the book, which they dragged to solitary corners and pored over on the floor, was a more accurate index of its appeal.

Miranda had attempted to introduce me to her guests as they trickled in, but eventually their numbers overwhelmed her good intentions. Then I was left alone to appreciate how the New York art world endeavored to outdo its caricatures in legend and film. At first I tried my best to represent myself to them as vital and engaged, a discerning fellow and worthy foil for the likes of Miranda Pratt, but as nobody seemed especially interested, I gave it up; I kept to myself, pretending to study the illustrations I knew so well while savoring the secret knowledge that, though the art was spoken for, the artist belonged to me. But as the evening wore on and the cheap wine began to give me a headache, I started to grow out of sorts. Perhaps all the attention the illustrator was getting (and I wasn't) had begun to make me a little jealous, which, if so, I was ashamed of.

When all but a few stalwarts had departed, Dame Teasel, employing her cane like a shepherdess's crook, hustled us from the gallery to a restaurant in nearby Chinatown, where I had the impression we were eating in the kitchen. It was a noisy gathering, what with the clattering dishes and piping waiters, the oceanic sound of sizzling rice, the rapid-fire conversation in which Miranda deferred (a bit obsequiously, I thought) to the author, while the others (fairy photographer included) deferred to Miranda. The diners at our table were all women but for the tattooed cartoonist, without whom I would have been left again to my own devices, but he kindly deigned to talk to me. He told me that *The Animals' Lost and Found* was the inspiration for his own next project, a fable in verse about where socks go when they're lost in the dryer. It was

an idea he related at some length, and since no response beyond the occasional *hmph* was required of me, I was free to sit nursing a beer as he
chattered on. But later, after we'd said our good-byes in the street and I
was once more alone with Miranda, after I'd suffered her laundry list of
the evening's triumphs—the art director for *Vanity Fair* had requested
her portfolio, a celebrated illustrator had invited her to visit his loft—I
decided it was my turn to talk.

Given our whereabouts, I began on a proprietary note, feeling called
upon to cite certain points of interest—here was a onetime Yiddish newspaper office, there a long-vanished East Broadway café—though I was by
no means certain of these designations. The sad old quarter was dead, all
right, and I for one was glad that the ghosts had been laid to rest, though
gone didn't necessarily mean forgotten. Thanks to Miranda's updates
(she had assumed some of my interests now that she'd replaced them as
my chief concern), I was aware that the neighborhood had become, in
the absence of Jews, the locus of a nostalgia industry. There was a tenement museum that preserved a few cramped turn-of-the-century flats
and sponsored regularly scheduled walking tours with guides in period
costume. There were surviving businesses like Shapiro's Winery, Streit's
Matzoh, Ratner's Dairy Restaurant, and Yonah Shimmel's Knishery,
which had become veritable shrines. The turreted pile of the Eldridge
Street Synagogue, with its broken rose window, whose ongoing restora-
tion was funded by private donations, stood as yet another monument to
heritage fever. That so many others had taken up the cause came as a relief to me: my debt to the Jewish past was met; I could let it go, move on,
expand my interests, explore other avenues, wherever they might lead. I
could get out of the resurrection racket, which was what they used to call
robbing graves.

All this I reported to Miranda, who didn't seem to be listening, no
doubt still basking in the swirl surrounding what amounted to, let's face
it, the publication of another soon-to-be-remaindered kiddie book. Feeling myself starting to sulk, I shut up. Around us the autumn wind fanned
the strata of local scents as if turning pages: hot and sour soup, salsa,
puttanesca and marinara, garbage and human waste; but if underneath
these there still lurked some vestige of chicken schmaltz, I couldn't detect
it. The old Garden Cafeteria, where Emma Goldman once binged on

cheese blintzes, was now a chop suey house, the *Forward* building an enormous joss temple. The few shops that still advertised *talisim* and *seforim* on their creaking signboards were not quaint; they were merely the crumbs of a past that, despite a few nods toward revitalization, had been otherwise swallowed whole.

As we turned off Canal into Essex, walking past Seward Park, whose leaves seemed to be falling all at once like departing birds, I overcame my sullenness to speak again. "You know the book that Aunt Keni gave me?" I said, invoking a wistful memory aloud.

Miranda shook her head absently. I knew in fact I was talking to myself, that in regaling her about my days with Aunt Keni, I'd omitted this particular detail, which I had managed to disrecollect myself until now.

"The unfinished manuscript I told you about?" I continued, though I hadn't told her, so why did I persist almost badgeringly? "The one she suggested I might want to complete?"

Again she shook her head.

"Well, I stuck it in the trunk of a tree over there in the park."

"You what?"

It was the first time all night I had her undivided attention. "After Aunt Keni passed, I was distraught," I explained. "I didn't want any keepsakes; I wanted her alive again. So while I couldn't quite bring myself to destroy the thing, I stuffed it in a hollow tree."

"Hold on, what thing?" asked Miranda, coming to a full stop. "Which tree? What are you talking about?" There and then she made me repeat the story of how I'd received and disposed of Nathan's book. She stood an instant digesting the information, then snatched up my hand and began to lead me across the street into the park, insisting that I show her the tree. I appreciated that she wanted to make it up to me for having neglected me most of the evening (though it was, after all, *her* night), but now I felt that my tactic had backfired. All I'd meant was to grab a little of the limelight myself, but suddenly she seemed more concerned with my story than I was.

The trees in the unkempt park looked so similar—mostly gnarled plane trees of the type that grew as rampantly in the city as mimosas in the South. Realizing that I had no special desire to rediscover Nathan Hart's folly, I was at the point of digging in my heels. There were thousands of untranslated Yiddish books by praiseworthy authors, writers deserving of a readership they would never receive, so who needed a frivolous narrative composed by a penny-a-liner who hadn't even been able to finish the tale? Then I spotted, near the fence on the library side of the park, a tree with a nodular base like a dripping candle, its mottled trunk riven as if by a lightning bolt.

"That's the one," I said with a certainty that surprised me, instantly regretting that I had spoken. It was anyway a relief to see that the cleft in the tree, which I felt I had somehow betrayed, had been surgically sealed with bricks and mortar.

"The book's in there, in the box elder? Are you sure?" asked Miranda.

"Box elder?" Impressed as ever by her nature lore.

She made a face, oddly impatient with me, and I told her, "It was just an empty cavity when I hid it there."

"Well," she stated unequivocally, "we have to get it out."

"Why?"

"Because it's your legacy," she declared, "and besides, I'm curious."

Now it was my turn to be impatient with her. "You can see for yourself the thing's sealed up for all eternity. Just how would you suggest we get it out?"

"With a pickax?"

I sighed. "It's not worth it," beginning to feel genuinely uneasy. The whole business of a book sealed in a tree: it smacked of Bluebeard's closet or Merlin ensorcelled by Morgan le Fey—a spooky phenomenon that shouldn't be tampered with. "Best to let sleeping stories lie," I said, wishing I'd never put the bee in her bonnet. "What are you, Nancy Drew?"

But on my behalf Miranda had become resolute.

"Look, it's late," I argued in vain. "I'm tired. We can come back another day, when we're both better prepared to be arrested for destroying public property."

She maintained, however, that the book's recovery could not be postponed.

I told her that I knew she was just trying to compensate for having hogged the stage all night. "But I'm over being jealous," I assured her.

She raised an eyebrow at this admission and shook her head, as if unable to fathom the magnitude of my childishness. Beneath the streetlight the curls escaping from under her beret appeared as if in the process of being spun into gold; her eyes contained a fullness that could have attracted tides. I think I had never wanted her so much as at that moment, never been so convinced that she was all I needed and the rest of life was gravy. But she had already set off in search of an implement.

"Where do you think . . . ?" I called after her, jogging to catch her up. "Where do you think you'll find a pickax at this time of night?" I wouldn't have put it past her to take drastic measures, maybe break into a hardware store, but Miranda was cleverer than that. We had earlier passed a street crew on Division doing repairs on the sewer system; they would have, she confidently informed me, all manner of tools. And sure enough, rounding the corner, we saw a tent like an ice-fishing pavilion above an excavation in the pavement. Inside were a pair of laborers hunkered over a Coleman lamp, swag-bellied fellows caked in grime and wearing hard hats, showing buttock cleavage as they squatted to have a smoke. Greeting them, Miranda concocted an emergency out of Edgar Allan Poe: her cat had been accidentally immured in the basement of her building by a careless super who was nowhere to be found, and we desperately needed a tool to tear down the wall. The story was wholly implausible, but, perhaps due to her distressed demeanor and naked knees, the laborers actually offered to do the job themselves. When Miranda assured them her boyfriend could handle it, they looked at me doubtfully, while I grinned to suggest it was my unenviable lot to perform such tasks. I don't know that they accepted the complicity, but they nevertheless handed over a mud-encrusted pickax like an unstrung crossbow, with the proviso that it was city property and we should return it as soon as we were done.

Back in the barren park, Miranda hid the tool behind her, whistling until a bag lady pushing a bundle-laden baby carriage decorated with whirligigs had passed by. Then, with a motion like a pendulum in full rotation, she raised the ax over her head. But before she could swing it, I grabbed the rough hickory handle and, possessed of a sudden need to do the honors myself, wrenched it out of her hands. Recalling my woodcutting days on the farm, I told her, "Stand back!" and, wondering if this was the ax I'd been waiting to fall, swung the blade toward the bull's-eye of the reinforced tree trunk. The mortar and bricks, which I'd assumed would have to be chipped away at gradually, caved in like a crust of old snow from the impact; they tumbled at the first blow from the pick, leaving me with the eerie sense of having broken into a tomb. In the dim chartreuse light from the streetlamps, it was difficult to see into the open fissure, but once I'd stretched my arm through the hanging mist of blasted mortar, clearing out a few large chunks, I found with my fingers the hidden gunnysack. Then I didn't know whether it was joy or fear that gripped me, as I hauled from its yawning bolt-hole the coarse, ragged package of *The Angel of Forgetfulness.*

Miranda was for examining its contents on the spot, but I put her off, saying we could better peruse the thing in the sanctity of her apartment. Returning the ax to the tent, from which the laborers had disappeared below the surface of the street, we about-faced and headed back toward the neighborhood north of Houston. We entered her studio, where, unable to prolong the suspense, I immediately let the manuscript out of its bag, so that it lay on the sideboard with its irregular pages scalloped like lasagna left over from the Pleistocene. When I started to untie the knot from the twine I myself had long ago fastened about the book, it snapped like dried ligaments. I thought the pages might crumble, too, but their several textures, besmirched and bloated as they were, remained intact. Then I shuddered as if in the presence of some miracle akin to the lamp of the Maccabees that had burned with only a spritz of oil for eight days.

Where my feelings were hopelessly mixed, Miranda continued to evince an unalloyed excitement over the disinterred manuscript, which she entreated me to read to her. The fact was, I was no great shakes at deciphering the Yiddish cursive, and Nathan's hand, smeared in places to illegibility, had not been the steadiest or the most exact. But with the text in front of me, I recalled how my aunt had read aloud from it in her final days; and that memory plus my own dogged commitment to conning a defunct language moved me to attempt the opening passage, written in the voice of the angel:

"My son, Nachman, as you know, was reared in paradise. . . ."

And that was all it took. No sooner had I begun to read than the long years since my first encounter with the manuscript retracted like a collapsed telescope: it was as if no time had intervened from the moment Aunt Keni bade me take down the book from the wardrobe, suggesting circumspectly that I might like to complete it—as if to complete Nathan's book were somehow to complete myself. Miranda was still demonstrating a heated interest in the document and its outré contents; she even teased me, beginning to unbutton her cardigan, that the story turned her on, exclaiming at certain of the angel's gnomic locutions, "Oh, Mocky, I'm yours!" But I knew that, for all her melting enthusiasm, she could never match my own, which I didn't wish to share. The book, like the heavenly portion of Torah intended only for the eyes of the beholder, belonged exclusively to me.

Later on, though she was especially desirous, I was unable to make love to Miranda Pratt, nor could I sleep. Lying beside her melodically snoring body, I began to resent all the hoops she'd had me jump through before deeming me worth her while. No matter that for some time now she had been tender and attentive, seeming finally to trust that I wasn't going away, referring to herself as my girlfriend and to me as her man; I was nonetheless exasperated by the insecurities she refused to admit, the standards she held me to, so that I was forever pretending to be other than I was. I thought about how fundamentally incompatible we were. Then I rose from the lumpy mattress we shared on the floor beneath a latticed window to wander into her studio, switch on a lamp, and take another peek at the unbound pages of Nathan's book. I sat and traced the words with the stylus of my forefinger and felt ticklish, as if I were inscribing the frenetic script on my own skin. Morning found me still on a stool at the sideboard, my head cradled in my folded arms, which rested in turn on the worm-eaten manuscript. I was vaguely aware of Miranda passing to and fro behind me, pottering about the kitchen with a banging of cabinets and clash of utensils, indicating her continued vexation with my impotence from the night before. I tried to ignore her like some poltergeist that had lingered into daylight past the nocturnal moment to which it belonged. Lifting my thick head, I rubbed the shards of sleep from my eyes, which I opened hungrily upon a banquet of Yiddish characters. Then all I wanted was to stuff that un-fair copy into its sack and hightail it with my prize back to the refuge of Old Binstock.

Entering the room in her tatty silk dressing gown, blowing curls from her forehead that dropped instantly back over her brow, Miranda plunked down a cup of coffee beside the manuscript, splashing it in the process.

The coffee stain on the page having mingled with the patina of others, I transferred *The Angel,* without regarding the illustrator, from the surface of the sideboard to the drawing table, which was tilted like a monk's escritoire. When I swiveled to resume my reading, Miranda exploded.

"Maybe you'd be more comfortable reading that somewhere else."

"I was thinking the same thing," I replied, still without looking up.

"Somewhere more private," in case I hadn't gotten the point, and again I concurred. Then she was at my shoulder, modulating her tone to a needling taunt. "What's the matter, Sauly, you don't want to share your spoils with the goyim?"

I looked up. "You must have read my mind."

"Would it help if I changed my name to Shifra?" she asked, in earnest for all I knew. "Should I get maybe a nose extension, use a tanning booth, learn to cook flanken—"

"No," I cut her off, "it wouldn't help." Then, feeling immediately remorseful, I apologized. I told her I was sorry to be such a grouch, but the truth was that I was distracted; I had a big class preparation for Monday, and while I wouldn't have missed her book release for the world, I really needed to get back to Massachusetts. What I didn't say—what I maliciously hoped went without saying—was that it was all her fault; she should never have pressed me to salvage Nathan's indelible manuscript. As she stood openmouthed in the doorway, I brushed her cheek with my lips and hurried to the train.

Back in my room on Hawthorne Street, I pored over *The Angel* by the relentless light of my gooseneck lamp. There was no explaining the hold it had taken on me. As stories went, I knew many more compelling by far, better crafted and broader in scope, though to none of the others was I connected (in a sense) by blood. All that week my teaching duties, of secondary importance at the best of times, were supplanted by my fixation on the text in which I was mired. On the weekend, after an exchange of mutually conciliatory phone calls, Miranda showed up as scheduled: it was her turn to visit, and I welcomed her as best I could, though inwardly I chafed at the interruption. For her part the illustrator seemed to have forgiven me my rude departure of the previous Sunday. Very tentatively she suggested that, since it was foliage season and the weather glorious, we might take a hike. The invitation made me ill. Further, it was humiliating to us both that she should have to tiptoe around my feelings, so I tried to keep the irony out of my voice as I recommended she go alone, I had work to do.

I was aware that Miranda had taken extra pains to make herself appealing. The whorled accents of her hair reverberated the rose madder season; her cheeks were cherry pink, her round breasts unrestrained beneath a pullover brief enough to reveal a finger's breadth of flesh between its rib stitch and the waist of her skirt. She was wearing the hiking boots for which I had acquired an almost fetishistic affection. A vibrant woman, Miranda Pratt, she was eloquent in her contradictions, her watery eyes reflecting places I would never see. Only once before had I allowed myself to care so much for a woman, but that one was dead and this one on her way to becoming a stranger. Even as I nearly swooned from her fragrance, I could no longer imagine our having been together, but if she could read the distance in my expression (and I'm sure she could), Miranda registered no surprise. Perhaps she'd known all along it would come to this.

Gently she chided me, "Have you found a new muse, Sauly?" There was the diminutive again. "Are you afraid you might be two-timing her with me?" Her lips so close that her warm breath funneled augerlike into my ear. "Did you forget that life is the muse?" Then she backed off, changed her tack, and, despite having been ambivalent about the issue thus far, made a halfhearted stab at raising the subject of our living together ("What about your job interview?"), only to drop it upon receiving an evasive answer from me. I hated her for so readily letting the subject go. Though she was gazing coolly enough at the stack of moldy pages on my desk, I rested my arms defensively on top of them, my stomach tight. She sighed and shifted into the past tense, stating how much she had liked the way I cherished her, how she would miss it. Then she called me a bastard.

"You fuck, you disappointing fuck, you!" she was suddenly shouting, assaulting my head and shoulders with her clenched fists. Trying to protect myself, I rose from my chair only to be knocked backward onto the carpet by her flailing arms. She was on top of me like a tigress, straddling

my chest and cursing me through her tears as she roughly fumbled to unfasten my pants. She reached into my fly and yanked out my prick, gripping it like a throat she intended to strangle, pulling it the way a bird tugs
at a worm. She jerked it and kneaded it and, having twisted her face into a
savage mask, even bent to give it suck, but as the thing remained inverte-
brate, a wilted wand, she tossed it disgustedly aside. She cursed me once
more for a useless piece of gristle as she got to her feet, grabbed her
knapsack, and flung herself out the door. Zipping up, I crawled back to
my desk and climbed into the sheriff's chair, ignoring the pain between
my legs; I ignored Mrs. Rudelhuber, who'd claimed to have taken a shine
to the illustrator over the months and appeared frowning in my doorway
to ask what all the ruckus was about.

When Miranda was gone, I realized that she must have actually loved
me, and if she had been withholding of herself, it was only because she
suspected I would revoke what I had given her in time. But even as I felt
my heart starting to rupture, I turned back to Nathan's narrative, whose
translation was what I'd been working toward all these years; I'd been
preparing for it my whole life in fact, though I hadn't known it till now.
The manuscript was, simply put, my homeland; Nathan Hart's story, *c'est
moi*. The time that had elapsed since Aunt Keni's death had been necessary, a kind of apprenticeship, but now that the composition was restored
to me, it was as though the years had never intruded. Of course, I wasn't
entirely without objectivity; I realized I was embarked on a dubious enterprise. It wasn't as if I'd stumbled upon some lost treasure by Dovid
Bergelson or Yankev Kreplak; this one may not even have been publish-
able, but I continued to swot away at it with a will. The text itself was in
such a sorry state, however, that it was often unreadable, and in the absence of Aunt Keni as interpreter, I had to bridge the narrative's many la-
cunae with my own conjectures. I took liberties in this, thinking that the
story's unfinished status justified my emendations. I polished the rough
stones of Nathan's Yiddish in its conversion to English and, where the
latter language lacked the sparkle of the former, added baubles hatched
from my own imaginings. Assured that I had my deceased aunt's blessing, I began to feel that my task amounted to an authorized collabora-
tion between myself and the vaporized journalist. I was engaged in

writing a kind of pseudepigraphon, already picturing the title page, which would read:

T H E   A N G E L   O F   F O R G E T F U L N E S S
by Nathan Hart,
with Saul Bozoff

I was in the tradition, wasn't I? Like Moses de Leon, who had plundered the apocryphal texts of Shimon bar Yohai and embroidered them beyond recognition for his *Book of Splendor*.

A scribe, I was also a fabulator, because in tracing Nachman's adventures on earth, I imagined Nathan's parallel progress in composing the story. It was an exercise I performed in the margins of *The Angel* itself, so that its often immoderate lexicon was hedged about by my own raveled notations. In this way the manuscript took on the appearance of a secular Talmud. Still, you couldn't have accused me of inventing Nathan's labors from whole cloth; I had the considerable information that Aunt Keni had imparted to me, but, expanding on that, I could not curb my habit of manufacturing circumstances, some of them dire, surrounding the genesis (and exodus) of *The Angel*. I worked toward completing the tale of Nachman, emigrant from kingdom come, but, failing that, I might at least complete the driven story of Nathan Hart and his ink-slinging ordeal in tracking Nachman's destiny. At least I knew, more or less, how that ordeal was resolved, though I was as anxious to reach its conclusion as I was to realize the mystery of Nachman's own end, which I had yet to conceive. But ignorance of the story's outcome was never an obstacle to its continuation. Sometimes, as I worked, my brain seemed to soar clear out of my skull—as if, riding a galloping horse that occasionally balked, rather than come a cropper, I was launched into flight. Also, there were self-aware moments when it occurred to me that some member of a future generation, struck by my efforts, might be moved to record the story of Saul Bozoff writing the story of Nathan Hart writing the story of Nachman who called himself Opgekumener. The prospect made me dizzy, and somewhat euphoric.

By the end of the semester, my thoughtless neglect of my classes had become notorious. It was the middle of the academic year, and it would have been out of the question to request a sabbatical, though I had yet to take one in all my years at the school. But the chair of the department himself—a sympathetic chap from whose mouth depended a briar pipe like a deflated speech bubble—independently recommended I take a paid leave of absence. An emergency replacement could be found for me before January. Then, very diplomatically, he suggested that I would have time to consider whether teaching was my real vocation. Feeling at once out of place in such collegiate surroundings, I decided to decamp, saying an abrupt good-bye to Mrs. Rudelhuber, whose scalp shone through her hennaed hair like a gosling's. She apologized that, due to my having given her such short notice, she would have to retain my deposit, then wept crocodile tears at our parting. Emancipated, I took up *The Angel of Forgetfulness* and returned to the Lower East Side, where I rented a seedy flat in a dumbbell tenement on Ludlow Street, call it a pied-à-terre. I had a table and chair, an army cot, a dish, a glass, a battered wardrobe, and a handful of books salvaged from the library I'd sold for peanuts to the secondhand shops. There was an ancient tin mezuzah fixed to the doorjamb, which I thumped like a stuck thermometer upon entering and leaving. For a time I worried I might run into Miranda, but after a while my hair and beard had grown (and my general appearance declined) so much that I doubted she would even recognize me.

It was the year 5748 by the Jewish calendar, and I took a peculiar pleasure in the picturesque squalor of the old ghetto. The gutters were clogged with smashed fruit crates and wriggling fish like the detritus at the bottom of a drained swamp. The walls of the buildings wore Joseph's coats of graffiti, Chinese toughs patrolled the sweatshops and brothels, and the thieves' market in Seward Park was rumored to peddle children. The pullers in front of the haberdasheries along Orchard Street were as aggressive as recruiters for the HMS *Bounty,* and the carved driftwood totem in the wagon at the corner of Shtibl Row turned out to be, on closer inspection, a limbless beggar of astronomical years. I liked the Russian steam baths on Pitt Street, where naked elders flogged themselves with sassafras switches, and the earthen odor in the cellar of the ruined Rivington Street shul. There I joined a fossilized congregation to say kaddish for Aunt Keni Shendeldecker, Billy Boots, and on occasion (*olev hasholem*) my father. Sometimes I wondered idly who would say kaddish for me. As I labored over my "translation" beside a babbling radiator, I barely acknowledged the fact of the bitter winter: the ice hanging in walrus tusks from the clotheslines and fire escapes, from the ceilings of basements in which the pipes had burst. Then a brief efflorescence of spring was followed hard upon by an infernal summer, the clammy air thick with bluebottles whose hum rivaled the drone of the sewing machines in their lofts. Colicky babies wailed, meat spoiled before you could carry it home from the market, rats surfaced from the sewers to gnaw the kishkes of fallen truck horses. . . .

NATHAN

He told himself he only wanted to replace the antique pair of longjohns he'd worn to shreds; though why should he want new longjohns at the outset of spring, and from a store he knew from personal experience to traffic in inferior goods? Waiving these questions and others, Nathan opened the jangling door and stepped down into the sunken shop, stuffy as a humidor and not much larger. He parted the curtain of hanging Prince Albert coats and saw, behind the gilt register, a lady clerk no longer (he thought) in her first flush of youth. She was dowdier than he remembered, seated on a stool in a washed-out eggshell shirtwaist, the skirt billowing to accommodate her ample hips. Her head remained bent as she continued making annotations in an open ledger propped on her knees, a Russian cigarette dangling from thin lapis lips.

Having missed her in the cafés and theaters, he'd relied on his legman's instincts to tell him where she might have gone to ground. And there she was—shoulders a little rounded and sagging, eyeglasses slipped to the tip of her nose like a schoolmistress or (*l'havdil*) a salesclerk. Her yarn-thick hair was twisted and pinned into a ball at the nape of her neck, but even by the lambent light of the gas mantle, he could see how her crimson tresses had faded at the roots, the color in retreat like an ebbing tide. It was reassuring to Nathan, his ability to regard her with so dispassionate an eye—not as a stranger exactly, but rather an acquaintance with whom he shared memories best left undisturbed. He was also relieved that she hadn't bothered to return his scrutiny, though he judged himself—with his rakish derby and freshly sprouted mustache, his self-possessed air—as good as disguised.

He was satisfied that his desire for the girl (though "girl" seemed a misnomer now) was as extinct as his desire for completing his cockeyed story about the seraph-and-a-half. If the drudge in front of him had once inspired intractable passions, they were as well consigned to the past, along with his unfinished book. Content that she no longer held him in thrall, nor ever could again, Nathan was on the point of turning to exit the shop, when she asked him without looking up,

"Can I help you?" Then she raised her head, emerald eyes blinking over the rims of her spectacles. Nathan imagined he felt a mild breeze from her eyelids' fluttering.

"I don't need no help, thanks all the same," he said, with an emphasis that might have given him away. Did he want to give himself away?

Keni placed the ledger on the beveled-glass countertop, removed the cigarette from her mouth, and shoved the spectacles back onto the narrow bridge of her nose. Though her expression remained relatively neutral, Nathan chose to avoid it, his eyes shifting left and right. He took in a rack of fusty overcoats and chinchilla ulsters, a tree of felt fedoras, a display case heaped with band bow ties and rime-gray scarves. Atop the display case, leaning against the wall whose cracks fanned out like a river delta, was an unframed painting of a ghetto street scene—the same one Keni had been daubing at the night he'd spied on her from the fire escape. In its unrefined rendering of people and conveyances, its spendthrift use of brilliant reds and golds, the thing looked giddily anomalous in that somber atmosphere. It looked to Nathan almost dangerous, as if its undisciplined whimsy threatened to leak out of the canvas and contaminate the whole neighborhood. Then the solid East Side would be converted into precious unreality.

Why couldn't she leave well enough alone? Nathan wondered; why, for instance, saddle a tired old man with an incongruous bundle and a pair of chicken wings? It should have been hidden away in an attic or a cellar, her handiwork, left to gather dust like the white elephant it was.

When he allowed his glance to shift back to the lady clerk, their eyes locked. "I said *nu*," she repeated in her cross-grained voice what he apparently had not heard the first time, "then for what you came in here?" Nathan was taken off his guard. "You are maybe the bank examiner, that a potential buyer sent you to look over our quaint *gesheft* which it's not for sale? Or you're a firebug that we are definitely not interested should for a nice piece indemnity torch the building?" And when the intruder, raising his hands, pleaded guilty to neither of these, "Or maybe a scribbler who wants to write about our glamorous business a story?"

So she hadn't been deceived by his refurbished self after all. In that case, removing the stiff-brimmed hat to expose his oiled but still unruly hair, he would show her he had nothing to hide. She arched a brow as if to punctuate the anticlimax, and, feeling foolish, Nathan rifled his mind in search of a defensible reason for being there.

"I got something belongs to you," he said at last, his hand dredging the pocket of his mangy rug coat. He was himself a little astonished to find them still there where he'd enshrined them: Keni's pair of cast-off cambric drawers. Fishing them from his pocket, he had the sense of plucking a material item out of a dream. He dangled them in front of the clerk, who, stubbing out her cigarette in a saucer, rose from her stool to snatch them from his hand. She stuffed the telltale garment into the pouch of her apron and remained determinedly unamused, though Nathan thought he detected a slight twitch at the corner of her mouth.

For an instant he imagined she might say, teasingly, *You want a refund or an exchange?* But instead, recovering her gravity, she offered this short admission: "I'm sorry what I done you."

Fighting down the rising thickness in his throat, Nathan decided that her apology referred to their history in general rather than any specific offense. He tried his best not to be moved by it, nor reminded that his own regret was not so much for having been her victim as for having made her his. When he replied, it was more to prove his equilibrium (and his command of the American idiom) than to express his shame.

"Likewise, I'm sure.

They looked at each other a long moment, Nathan finding it hard to keep Keni's features in focus. Did he need glasses, or had a puffy quality come to blur the unconventional beauty that once had turned his head? Had she ever really been beautiful? Realizing that he was staring and that she was stoically suffering his gaze, Nathan lowered his eyes. They lit upon—affixed by a sticking plaster to the back of the register next to the photo of the absconded Mr. Pishkin—another picture clipped from the *Forward*'s "Gallery of Disappeared Men." This one was the face of a bald man grinning ruefully through a grainy Vandyke.

Keni volunteered an explanation. "To Paris, France, he ran away, Yanobsky, with a gang of painters that they call themselves the Eight. Yanobsky is the ninth. You see him"—now she allowed herself the luxury of a wan smile—"say to him business is good. Don't come back."

Fleeting as it was, the smile had triggered a palpitation in Nathan's chest, which he took as his signal to depart the shop without further ado. Having formally closed a troubling chapter of his otherwise brave new life, he was free to begin another episode. The options were limitless.

But just as he prepared to excuse himself, the dust-heavy drapery at the rear of the premises was parted and out stepped Keni's Aunt Pesha Pishkin, goitered chin asway like an udder. "I'll take over from you now the shop," she announced, bustling behind Keni to tug at her apron strings. Keni lifted her arms to ease the process, and Tante Pesha, having removed the apron, touched her niece's waist to turn her partly around. She pointed to the extinguished cigarette in the saucer and grumbled, eliciting only a vague shrug from the shopgirl; then she leaned forward, cupping an ear to listen stethoscope fashion to Keni's dilated belly, which revealed what the shadow of the register had obscured: that she was with child.

"I can hear him, *di benkart oyfn pripechuk,*" declared Aunt Pesha. "The little bastard in the oven, he's saying his eighteen benedictions."

"Tante, stop!" scolded Keni, though her displeasure was clearly tinctured with pride. Then, observing how the journalist had gone pale, his jaw hanging loose as an empty bucket, she assured him, "Don't worry, it doesn't belong to you."

He chose to believe her avowal without calculating its accuracy (he was a flop at calculations), then welcomed the warm relief that flushed his system, rolling what felt like a stone from his gut—only to release a party of other emotions. Guilt, anger, and jealousy were among them, though they were pushed to the margins by a weltering disappointment, which frightened Nathan, his disappointment, by the way it socked his heart like a kicking steed.

Having read the fluctuations of his face, Keni again saw fit to let Nathan off the hook, though not before giving the hook a twist. "Don't think for a second, Nathan Hart," speaking his name for the first time since he'd entered the shop, "that around here you are needed. We manage fine." Her hands were planted gamely on her hips.

Swallowing, Nathan wanted to protest that it hadn't even occurred to him he might be needed, but somehow he thought better of saying as much. He tried hard to suppress the mental picture of a knob-headed baby with a miniature Vandyke.

Meanwhile Tante Pesha, having discovered the undergarment in the pocket of the apron, was examining it as if to determine its kosherness. Then, evidently sensing something fishy, she threw down the garment and closed ranks with her niece, folding her adipose arms like a bailiff so that the two women comprised a wall of defiance. Nathan noted the milk-swollen breasts under Keni's blouse and muttered something about being able to take the hint. Again he made to turn and exit the shop, tail between legs, when he stumbled over the memory of a story his mother once told him. She'd had it from his dead father, who'd had it from the Hasids, who lifted it with God only knew what variations from the ancient texts. In the tale the primordial Adam is given at birth the gift of seeing his life (as well as the history of his race) from beginning to end; but no sooner is he granted the vision than an angel comes to nip him under the nose. Then the amnesia sets in, and afterward Adam, along with his randy wife, is expelled from the Garden by the selfsame vindictive angel.

Nathan shuddered, wanting suddenly what he did not want, admiring the exquisite ordinariness of all he perceived. He was struck with the overriding desire to shoulder the burden of his past like a bale of piecework, to spirit it like a stolen book or a rescued infant into the future. Without remembering where you'd been, how could you know for certain who you were?

He wanted to court the expectant shopgirl with promises of home and fidelity, with laborsaving devices such as household mangles and self-wringing mops to enhance her days. But before he could object to his exclusion from the destinies of Keni Freischutz and her unborn child, Tante Pesha, never taking her eyes off the journalist, not even when the door chimes jangled behind him like shattering glass, inquired of her niece,

"This is him, that Nathan Hart who writes in *Der Forvarts* those stories which who can believe?"

MOCKY

So, my esteemed fellow members of the Zitsker Landsmanshaft, Tenth Ward Chapter of the Upper Lower East Side, that's how I abandoned my son on earth as I had in heaven. If the story sounds familiar, it's because I've been sentenced to repeat it until Nachman's soul comes home again. It's the penance the archons have exacted for my delinquency, and it looks to be a long atonement, since the boy, like his father before him, has become addicted to the world. His soul, rather than detach itself and fly back to where it belongs, prefers to wander from host to host, infecting each one it inhabits with impossible desires. In the meantime apocalypses come and go, and, unable to compete with so much evil, the demons have packed it in; Gehinnom has closed up shop, forcing the damned (mobsters and shpielers not excluded) to take up residence in an already overcrowded Abraham's Bosom. All this while Nachman or Norman or Sheldon or Shloyme, or whatever his present incarnation, keeps on chasing the ladies, trying to woo them with tales that increasingly fall on deaf ears. Why this is so, I'll explain to the kid if he ever returns. First, along with his mama and the others—the formerly blind rabbi and his daughter, who died of complications in childbirth, and so on—I'll welcome the greenhorn; then I'll remind him that on earth everybody's a skeptic, whereas here in heaven they'll believe anything.

Acknowledgments

The author wishes to thank his agent Liz Darhansoff and his editor Paul Slovak for their generosity and support, Eliezer Hyman for giving him shelter, and Debra Spark for her unerring advice.